TEN NORTH FREDERICK

TEN NORTH FREDERICK

John O'Hara

RANDOM HOUSE · NEW YORK

To K. B. O'H.

This, of course, is a work of fiction, but I also have taken liberties with those facts that sometimes help to give truth to fiction. To name one: the office of Lieutenant Governor was created by the 1873 Constitution, so it would have been impossible for Joe Chapin's grandfather to have been Lieutenant Governor at the time I state. There are one or two other deliberate errors of that kind, but I hope they will be pardoned by the alert attorneys who are sure to spot them. If this were straight history, and not fiction, I would not ask to be pardoned.

J. O'H.

Pacific Palisades, California
August, 1955

PART ONE

Edith Chapin was alone in her sewing room on the third floor of the house at Number 10 in Frederick Street. The room was warm, the day was cold and unbrightened by the sun. The shutters in the bay-window were closed, but the slats in the shutters were open, and Edith Chapin could, when it pleased her, go to the bay-window and look down on her yard and the two-story garage that had been a stable, and above and beyond the gilded figure of a trotting horse on the weather vane she could see roof upon roof upon third story upon third story of the houses on the rising hill. She would know the names of nearly all of the people who lived in them, she knew the names of the owners. She had spent her lifetime in the town, and it was easy to know who everyone was and where everyone lived. It was especially easy for Edith because she had always had a reputation for shyness, and it was not expected of her to make a fuss over people. She could notice them and study them, if it pleased her, without any further social effort on her part than simple politeness called for. It had always been that way.

At a gentle knock on her sewing-room door—two knocks, not an unnecessary third—Edith Chapin cleared her throat and said, gently, "Who is it?" Her enunciation was slow and precise.

"It's me, ma'am. Mary."

"Come in," said Edith Chapin.

Mary was an Irishwoman from Glasgow with a clear skin and brown eyes full of self-respect behind her tortoise-shell spectacles. Her bust was abundant and her waist not thick.

"What is it, Mary?"

"It's Mr. Hooker, the newspaper editor, wants to see you, ma'am."

"To see me? Is he here?"

"Yes, ma'am. I put him in the sitting room."

"Alone, or is Mrs. Hooker with him?"

"Nobody with him, just himself," said Mary.

"Are there a lot of other people down there?"

"There's quite a crush, ma'am, sitting and talking. There isn't chairs for all."

3

"I know. Did anyone offer Mr. Hooker a chair?" said Edith Chapin.

"Not by the time I left. I come right up. Maybe somebody did offer him one since."

"Mm-hmm." Edith Chapin nodded. "This is what I'd like you to do, Mary."

"Yes, ma'am."

"Go downstairs, and if Mr. Hooker isn't sitting with someone, if he's just standing with the others, you go up to him and ask him if you can speak to him for a moment. Then when you get him out in the hall, tell him I'll see him. But if he's sitting down with some people— You see, I don't want to make an exception for anybody. I haven't seen anybody, as you know. But I think I ought to see Mr. Hooker. Such a good friend of Mr. Chapin's."

"A great admirer of Mr. Chapin's. Great. The article yesterday, it made you realize if you didn't already."

"Yes, that's why I would like to make an exception in his case."

"Will I bring you a cup of tea, ma'am?"

"No, no thanks. I don't want him to stay that long. Remember now, if he's sitting down with the others, don't single him out. But if he's standing, it'll look as though he had an appointment with me."

"I understand perfectly, ma'am," said Mary.

"You can bring me a cup of tea after he's gone. I'd like a cup of tea and two soft-boiled eggs. Some toast and some of that grape jelly, if there's any left."

"There's a whole new jar I opened."

"Oh, then there was some more. I was sure we had some left. Where did you find it?"

"It was in with the currant, on that shelf. It didn't have the label on it."

"Oh, that's where it was. And some cigarettes when you bring the tea. It might be a good idea if you put the cigarettes under a napkin. Some of the older ladies . . ."

"Yes, ma'am," said Mary, and left.

Edith Chapin composed herself in the ladderback rocking chair, and was so arranged a few minutes later when Mary's knock came again. She knocked twice, and waited, then knocked twice again.

"Yes?" Edith Chapin called out.

"It's me, ma'am, with Mr. Hooker," said Mary.

"Come in, please," said Edith Chapin.

Mary swung the door open, making way for the man. "Mr. Hooker, ma'am."

4

"Good morning, Robert," said Edith Chapin.

"Good morning, Edith."

Mary closed the door behind her.

Robert Hooker went to Edith Chapin and took her extended hand in his two. "Edith, I call myself a dealer in words, but today I have none to offer."

"Today, but not yesterday."

"Oh, you saw my editorial?"

"If I hadn't seen it on my own—you have no idea how many people called up about it. Joe would have been—well, pleased is hardly the word. I consider it one of the finest pieces of writing I've ever read, and not only because it was about Joe."

"It was from the heart, Edith."

"Oh, yes. Yes," said Edith Chapin.

"The Bar Association is having it reprinted, I thought you'd like to know. Henry Laubach called up this morning and ordered a thousand cards, about the size of a postcard, with my small tribute to Joe printed on them. I feel signally honored, but it's a pretty empty honor, when I think of—well, I wish the occasion hadn't arose. Arisen."

"Joe was very fond of you, Robert."

"Well, I always hoped so. We didn't see nearly enough of each other. In this crazy old newspaper business, I work in my shirt-sleeves, you know. Joe, the soul of dignity. Not what they call a stuffed shirt, by any means. But as I said in my editorial, the very presence of Joseph B. Chapin in a courtroom provided the room with the dignity one associates with the court of law, but so often lacking in these days of spectacular circus tactics."

"Joe would have liked that, every word of it. The dignity of the law was precious to him," said Edith Chapin.

"How are *you*, Edith? That's a foolish question, of course. What must be going on inside, but I don't think there's a man or woman in town that expected you to behave any differently than you are. It's a rare sight to see such courage in these days."

"Courage?" said Edith Chapin. "I have no courage, Robert. I am so used to living the kind of life I've led that now, at a time like this, it's one advantage of having a naturally retiring disposition. I've always lived for my husband and my family, nothing else. No outside interests, no hobbies, really. So that now, if I were to make some display of how I am feeling, it wouldn't be at all typical of me, would it?"

"No, it wouldn't."

"Even my friendships, they had to come through my husband. If they were friends of his, they could be friends of mine, but I was think-

5

ing this very morning how few women friends I have. Oh, I like women, I have nice relationships with the members of my sex. I suppose I'm as womanly a woman as the word could mean. But when you have reached my age—and you know how old I am, Robert. But as I was saying, if you've lived in a town all your life, except for boarding school, you would think I might have formed some close friendships with women of my age and so on. But the truth is, so many men came to this house, clients and friends and associates and men in the political world, that I neglected my contacts with my women friends. Do you know that outside the family, I haven't received a single woman acquaintance in the past three days?"

"A great symbol of your devotion to your husband, Edith."

"Well, I hope it will be taken for that, and not as an indication that I don't like the members of my own sex, and don't interest myself in their problems, because I do. When things settle down here I'm going to have to find something to do with my time. I have no idea what *sort* of thing I'll do, but I imagine anything I do will involve working with other women, and I don't want to start with any more handicaps than I have already."

"You have no handicap in whatever you do," said Hooker. "Whatever you decide to do."

"Oh, that's nice of you, but you forget my—shyness," said Edith Chapin. "Whenever I had to go to any public function with Joe, oh, it was sheer torture. I was always afraid. Not afraid I'd do the wrong thing, or say the wrong thing. I think one's natural instincts or upbringing carry one through. But my—*reserve*—that's what I was afraid might be misunderstood. Has it been, Robert?"

"Not one bit. Not one bit. I know the people of this town. I know what they think. I know how they feel. It's my business to know. And I can reassure you on that point. Your what you call shyness and reserve, that's one of the things that has endeared you to them."

"Joe was so good with people. He could mix with them and be friendly, to the exact degree that he wanted to be. He really could handle people, couldn't he?"

"One of his greatest gifts."

"It was hard for him, too, you know," said Edith Chapin.

"It was, Edith?"

"Yes. Joe was not naturally gregarious. When we were first married, I think it was before you moved here, Joe confined himself to the people he grew up with. Two or three friends that we saw a great deal of, and as a matter of fact, Joe actually used to seem to prefer the

6

company of older men. Judge Larkin. Old Mr. English, Doctor English's father, that is. And they seemed to enjoy his company, too. It was a great change when he decided to enter public life. He had to force himself to be patient and tolerant of other people. But I remember his saying to me later on, how he'd been missing a lot of fun out of life by not getting about more in his young manhood."

"I never knew that, Edith. I never knew that. I would have said that Joe Chapin was one of the greatest mixers I ever saw."

"And he was, but he had to learn it. It wasn't the natural thing for him to do, the way it is with some men. He practically made a study of it. But of course Joe had one thing I never have had. Confidence. Complete confidence in himself."

"The aristocrat, in the better sense," said Hooker.

"Well, of course he didn't like that word, but I'm inclined to agree with you."

"You have it too, Edith."

"Oh, no. Not a bit."

"I think so. I think you have. You may be shy, but I've watched you, I've studied you. You may not be the outgoing type, the extrovert, but people know that underneath that shyness is a woman of great courage and principle. Look at you now. If they could see you now they'd know they were right. It's a great honor for me, you letting me have these few moments to pay my respects."

"I wonder why I let myself prattle on this way. I've talked with you more than any other person. In fact, I haven't really talked to anyone else at all."

"It's a great honor for me. I suppose we newspaper men, we're told so many things in confidence, there must be something about us that makes people trust us."

Edith Chapin hesitated. "It must be more than that, too," she said. "Thank you for coming to see me. It was very kind of you. And later, when things—settle down—I'm going to ask you for some advice."

"I am at your service."

"And remember me to Kitty."

"She wanted to come with me, but I was sure there'd be too many people. By the way, I had a very pleasant visit with Joe Junior downstairs. Amazing, how much like his father."

"Yes, at least in appearance. They're really quite different."

"That's what I meant. This is a grand old house, isn't it?"

"Full of memories, happy ones and sad ones."

"The way a house should be," said Hooker.

"Frederick Street isn't fashionable any more, but it's much more convenient than Lantenengo Street. We've always had the noise and the smoke from the trains, and some of the neighbors on William Street leave a lot to be desired, but we're used to it."

"A speaking tube. I guess there aren't many houses left with a speaking tube."

"Oh, it has all those things. I suppose you noticed the dumbwaiter. And on the second floor, the busybody."

"I had a story about busybodies last year. I sent one of my reporters out and he counted I think eighty-seven left in the whole town."

"When I was a girl I don't suppose there were eighty-seven houses that *didn't* have one," said Edith Chapin. She smiled her sad smile and Robert Hooker went to her and shook her hand in both of his.

"You are very brave, Edith Chapin."

"Thank you," she said.

"And call me for anything, anything at all."

"Thank you again, Robert," she said.

He braced his shoulders like the National Guard lieutenant he once had been, and marched out of the sewing room. She waited until she heard his step on the second-floor landing, then went to the speaking tube and blew the whistle.

"Yes, ma'am," said Mary.

"I'm ready, Mary," said Edith Chapin.

The will of Joseph B. Chapin contained no surprises. It was an orderly document, meant to be read in public. Certain sums were to be paid to servants and charities, and those sums were specified in dollars, but the bulk of the estate was in stocks, bonds, and mortgages, identified by name or location.

The sum of $100,000 was to be paid to the son, Joseph Benjamin Chapin Junior, and a like sum to the daughter, Ann Chapin. The remainder was to be used to create a trust fund for the widow, Edith Chapin. Upon her death the fund was to be divided equally between the son and the daughter. Personal items such as cuff links, cigarette cases, pearl studs, watches, watch chains were to be the property of the widow, but it was suggested that they might be distributed among friends: Chapin's law partner, his physician, the steward of the Gibbsville Club and the first, as yet unborn, grandson.

Edith Chapin, as she always had been, was a woman in comfortable circumstances. Now, in fact, in 1945, she was in more than comfortable circumstances. She was rich. But it would not be known that she was rich. The details of her wealth were known to only a few persons, who were not likely to discuss those details with others not privileged to have the information. The directors of her bank would know, her husband's law partner would know, the county Register of Wills would know. But there was no gossip value in the size of Joe Chapin's estate or the terms of his will. He had left more money than anyone had expected him to leave, but not so much more that the amount was sensational. If he had died poor, or enormously wealthy, the public, the public curiosity would have had to be satisfied. He had not died poor, and only a little richer (and that was to be expected of a man like Joe Chapin); consequently there would be no dislocation of the Chapin family status, and the status had always been described as in comfortable circumstances. There was a butcher on the West Side of town who had less money than Edith Chapin, who lived on the East Side of town. The butcher had a Cadillac, and so had Edith Chapin, but the butcher's was newer. The butcher's son was studying for the priesthood and was no great drain on his father's income; but Joe Chapin Junior was not studying for the priesthood, and he would be no great drain on his mother's income. The 18th Street butcher was said to be getting rich; the Frederick Street widow was said to be in comfortable circumstances.

The butcher was not in attendance at the funeral of Joseph Benjamin Chapin, which took place in Trinity Church. The butcher and Joe Chapin never had spoken a word to each other in all their lives, and yet the butcher would have been surprised to discover how much Joe Chapin knew about him. A clever man who is a lawyer and bank director, and whose family have lived in a town through three generations, acquires and usually retains a great deal of information on his fellow citizens. And it was too bad, in some ways, that the butcher and the lawyer had not been friends, or at least closer acquaintances. There was only a small difference in their ages, an inconsiderable difference; and the two men had several matters in common. Each man had a son and a daughter, disappointing children. Both men had remote wives, from whom they never had been separated. And now, with most of life gone in the one case and all of it gone in the other, it was too late for either man to realize his great ambition. The butcher had wanted to be heavyweight prize-fight champion of the world. Joe Chapin had always wanted to be President of the United States, and thought he ought to be.

One man among the imposing company of honorary pallbearers in Trinity Church knew how deep and serious Joe Chapin's ambition had been. One man knew, and another suspected. The man who knew was Arthur McHenry, Joe's law partner. The man who suspected was Mike Slattery, state senator and chairman of the Republican county committee. Arthur McHenry always thought Joe Chapin would have made a good President, and Mike Slattery hardly thought of it at all. Arthur McHenry knew more of the thoughts and deeds of Joseph Benjamin Chapin than any other man had known, and through all phases of Joe Chapin's life; his boyhood, his young manhood, his middle and declining years. He knew how much Joe Chapin depended upon him, and he knew that Joe Chapin believed he depended on no one. Joe Chapin never required a pledge of secrecy before revealing a matter to Arthur McHenry. And there were few matters he did not reveal. Indeed, it was not so much that he revealed a secret as bestowed it. In the reporting of an intimate detail, the pledge of secrecy was taken for granted, as Arthur McHenry himself was taken for granted. From another man the details that Joe Chapin felt free to discuss with Arthur McHenry would have been distasteful, but there was a kind of arrogant and trusting innocence in Joe Chapin's revelations to Arthur McHenry, and Arthur McHenry respected the innocence. Somewhere along the way he realized that Joe Chapin's dependence on him gave him strength. Seemingly his status was secondary to Joe's; Joe was a handsomer man, possessed of immediately effective charm in the clubhouse or the courtroom, and it had been more or less that way since kindergarten. But Arthur McHenry knew that the charm was less effective when he was not around. Whenever he returned from a trip of long duration Arthur McHenry could see that Joe Chapin's frown had become set; a few days later, with their hours of confidings and revelations, the frown would begin to disappear. "We've missed you, Arthur," Joe would say—and never understand that he was uttering more than a politeness. With realization Arthur McHenry became more comfortable in the relationship. It was quite enough for him to have the consciousness of his indispensability to the only man he loved.

The man who might have done more than he did to expedite Joe Chapin's ambition was not a fellow to waste love on anyone who would not return it. Mike Slattery was easy to define; too easy. He was Irish, second generation, and he had the pleasant, unlined face of a well-fed, successful parish priest. He had the look of a man who spent a great deal of time with the barber, the manicurist, and the bootblack.

He had small, hairless hands, and small feet that in another time and land would have been expert in step-dancing. He was exquisitely tailored, always in dark blue, and always wore a black knitted necktie with a pearl stickpin. His Irishness was a secret weapon. He was frankly and proudly Irish, but the Irishness was actually a means of allowing the non-Irish to succumb to self-deception. He could tell a funny story, and he had a quick wit, and no one would ever have mistaken him for anything but what he was, racially. He was good company, not to be ignored. But where the non-Irish made their mistake was in assuming that that was all he was; a jovial man from the Emerald Isle. He didn't fool the Irish; they saw through him while yielding a sort of loyalty to his accomplishments. But the non-Irish had to learn through associations and battles that he was a realistic, crafty, treacherous politician. He was contemptuous of the common Irish, and they sensed it, but he was the man to go to for favors, which whenever possible he granted, and with the favors and their pride in his prestige he kept them in line. As soon as he suspected that Joe Chapin was beginning to act like a man who wanted to be President he decided that Chapin was not presidential timber, and from that moment on Joe Chapin never had a chance. And Mike Slattery liked Joe Chapin. Joe Chapin was a gentleman, generally predictable in his actions and reactions and thus not likely to be troublesome. Also, he had a boyishness about him that was attractive to Mike Slattery, the father of four girls and one of them a nun. Much of what he did for Joe Chapin he did because he used him as a son, without being responsible as Joe's father. And some of what he did for Joe Chapin he did because he admired Edith Chapin. "If I'd been a Protestant I'd have married Edith Chapin," he once said, leaving no room for doubt that Edith would have accepted him.

Funerals were a part of Mike Slattery's life, and they might have been as much so even if he had not become a politician. This one was going well, predictably well. He looked over to the pew in which Edith Chapin, heavily veiled, sat impassive with her son and daughter and her own brother. At a Protestant funeral someone might faint, or have a heart attack, but there never was as much weeping, quiet or otherwise, as at a Catholic funeral. Mike Slattery did not weep at funerals or anywhere else; he had not wept twice in his entire manhood. This one time he had wept was on the day that Margaret, his daughter, had come to him and told him quietly that her mind was made up; she had a true vocation and was joining the Sacred Heart nuns. And it was not sadness that had made him weep that day; it

11

was for fatherly joy, that this plain girl had found a life for herself in which she would be happy. And there was pride, too. The Sacred Heart were an aristocratic order, and if a daughter of his was going to be a nun, it was nice to be able to think of her with the daughters of the best Catholic families. If Edith Chapin had been a nun, she would have been a Sacred Heart nun. The presence of her son and daughter beside her in the pew detracted not at all from Mike Slattery's fancy of Edith Chapin as a nun, and the veil she wore gave a realistic touch to the fancy. In his life as a politician he had had to hear and make use of many intimate facts about many people, including what he called their bed life. He had used the secret homosexuality of one political opponent to advantage; he had told an associate to get out of politics long before the nymphomania of the man's wife became common knowledge. No one had any information that could be used against Mike Slattery, but there were no peculiarities, perversions, excesses or denials that were unheard of by Mike Slattery—and nothing shocked him. But he never had been able to imagine Edith Chapin without her clothes on, nor Edith and Joe Chapin in the positions of bed life. He could not picture Edith Chapin getting out of her tub, drying herself. She was always to him a rather tall woman who was always fully dressed, who had a bosom without nipples. But along the way he had learned a thing or two about Joe Chapin, and what he had learned contradicted the notion that Edith Chapin was no more than a head on a virginal torso. Mike Slattery's repeated inability to illustrate in his mind the thought of Edith Chapin with her legs spread, ready to receive her husband (or any other man), was, he had sense enough to know, a part of her attraction for him. And she attracted him; always had.

Not so Ann, her daughter, a young woman who had been loosely called beautiful when people would enumerate the beauties among the girls of the Gibbsville upper crust. No one ever had called Edith Chapin beautiful, but in Mike Slattery's estimation she came closer to beauty than Ann did. His standards were his own and never stated, but Mike Slattery never had been known to call beautiful a woman who had any connection with sin. Ann Chapin Musgrove had been more or less vaguely connected with sin as far back as Miss Holton's School. The four Slattery girls had gone to Miss Holton's and the stories the girls brought home from Miss Holton's had sometimes given Mike Slattery useful leads for subsequently useful information. Ann Chapin's smoking was not extremely useful, but it had prepared Mike Slattery for the later news that Ann Chapin and one of the

Stokes girls had gone for a ride down country in a butcher's delivery truck. The girls had left the school after the eleven o'clock geometry class, wearing their school uniforms. As part of the adventure the truck had had to get stuck in the spring mud, "miles" from the main highway. It was seven o'clock in the evening before the girls got home. At eleven o'clock in the evening Mike Slattery had persuaded Joe Chapin not to have the boy fired. "Get him fired and you'll never hear the end of it," said Mike. "You handle the people at Miss Holton's. I'll take care of the boy." There was no traceable connection between the frolic with the Chapin and Stokes girls and the boy's departure. The boy left town and, as Mike said to his own wife, never knew what hit him.

Nineteen years ago, that was.

Not so long, at that.

Still, pretty long, when you consider that Edith Chapin was only forty when it happened. A woman forty is only a year out of her thirties, and Mike Slattery had three daughters in their thirties and he considered them young girls.

For no more than a second or two he was tempted to turn around and see if he could find his wife's face in the congregation. He quickly conquered the temptation; it would not look well, and besides he knew she would be somewhere in the church. Peg Slattery didn't have to be told twice which funerals to go to and which not. Her attendance at a funeral was to some extent a measure of the importance of the deceased or the survivors. She attended all politicians' funerals, regardless of party; practically all lawyers' funerals; all clergymen's funerals, and nearly all funerals for doctors, bankers, merchants, officers of fraternal orders and veterans' organizations; and popular freaks, such as old athletes, crippled newsdealers, Chinese laundrymen, canal-boat captains, aged Negro waiters, retired railroad conductors and enginemen, and children of unusually large families (ten or more). Joe Chapin came under several classifications and was in addition a personal friend, although Peg Slattery never had been inside his house. At the funeral Peg Slattery and her daughter Monica sat where they could be seen. With long practice she had mastered the impersonal bow for funerals and other state occasions: if someone looked at her, met her eye, she would nod, and if the person chose to take it as a bow, a bow it was. If the person was not someone to be bowed to, she would quickly turn away, and the person could think, because she had turned away, that no bow had been intended. In any case it was an unsmiling bow, or nod, or mere inclination of the head, quite suit-

13

able for use at funerals and other solemn occasions. The bow, or nod, was a part of her awareness of her position as the wife of Mike Slattery, a man to whom powerful people came for favors, who was powerful enough himself to grant the favors—and who discussed everything with her. No bridge was built over an obscure creek, no boy got an appointment to Annapolis, no reassessment of valuable property was put through without a discussion between Mike Slattery and Peg. It had taken some men thirty years to realize that fact, during which time they had antagonized Peg Slattery by ignoring her. She wanted no attention from the men, but she badly wanted their wives not to forget for one minute that she was the most powerful human influence upon one of the most powerful men in the Commonwealth. Edith Chapin had not forgotten; she had never known.

Peg Slattery did not know the name of the man who was conducting the funeral service. She had read it in the paper that morning, and the previous afternoon. Whoever he was, he pronounced his words like F. D. R., in whose single person were contained most of the features that Peg Slattery hated. The man in the cassock, surplice and stole did not resemble F. D. R., but because he enunciated as he did, he became a temporary symbolic representative of Mr. Roosevelt. She hated Roosevelt because he was a more successful politician than Mike Slattery; because he was a Protestant, an aristocrat, a charm-boy, a socialist, a liar, a warmonger, a double-crosser, and the husband of Eleanor Roosevelt. One of Peg Slattery's few witty remarks of record was her widely quoted comment that the only thing she liked about the Roosevelts was that they were Democrats, and she hated Democrats. She had no pride of authorship, but the remark itself made her hate the Roosevelts a little more when, a year or so later, she heard it repeated and attributed to some Republican committeewoman from New York. New York was where this man was from, who was quoting the Bible and sounding like an actor. A classmate of Joe Chapin's at Yale.

"The minister was a classmate of Joe Chapin's. At Yale." Peg Slattery whispered the information to Monica Slattery McNaughton. Peg had selected her second daughter to accompany her to the funeral because Monica was almost the same age as Ann Chapin Musgrove. Monica liked Ann well enough, but she had gone with her mother because she knew there would be almost an hour between the end of the service and lunch, and her mother might get generous and buy her a hat. The ceremonies preceding burial of the dead sometimes had that effect on her mother, Monica well knew, and Monica herself regarded a free hat as an earned fee for spending an hour in a strange church with a lot of people who did not interest her. She knew most of them, but they did not interest her. Like her sisters, Monica had been brought up to conduct herself at all times with courtesy to all comers, and politeness was drummed into the Slattery girls until it became practically instinctive. Their white gloves were maintained in spotless condition, their white teeth were under constant supervision and the parishioners of SS. Peter & Paul's would have backed the Slattery girls against any family from Trinity Church, for politeness, neatness, and all-around presentability.

Monica could execute the Peg Slattery nod, in slightly different form. When Monica and the other Slattery daughters did the Peg Slattery nod they added a gentle smile, a continuation, in maturity, of the smiles they had been commanded to give throughout childhood. Because of the added smile, the Slattery girls' nod differed from their mother's. Monica, Marie, Michelle—each was pretty in her own way, and a pretty girl's smile, even when given through an error of recognition, is welcome the world over. Even another woman has trouble resisting a pretty girl's smile when it has asked nothing in return. People who really knew better, who had had experience of life, had been known to remark that the Slattery girls made you feel that your troubles would soon be over. Others, slightly less cynical, had said that it was easy to see that the Slattery girls had never known a moment's unhappiness. Then there were others who, until Margaret took the veil, declared that the four Slattery girls were the best vote-getters Mike Slattery had. It was a not quite accurate judgment, since Mike Slattery did not get votes in the sense of persuading voters. The individual voter as such was not a concern of Mike's; he seldom made speeches, and he had abandoned door-to-door nonsense after his second term as assemblyman. He delivered a county, not a voter; the voter was the responsibility of the captain or the ward leader. But it would be accurate to declare that the four Slattery sisters had not *cost* him any votes.

Monica finished her inspection of the women's hats; women were not likely to wear anything interesting to a funeral anyway. The clergyman talked on, pronouncing his words in the same manner as some of her old schoolmates at Manhattanville; the New York ones. It was not a Boston accent, but it was not Brooklyn either. It was just the way certain of the New York girls spoke. Some of their brothers went to Fordham and some went to Yale, and they had the same accent. Just like this clergyman.

And now he had stopped talking and the professional pallbearers were sneaking up the side aisles. Johnny Loftus, the taxi driver; Matt McGowan, who was some kind of a railroad policeman; George Longmiller, who had some job at the courthouse; Frank McNaughton, a distant cousin of Monica's husband James and a helper for the Railway Express; Jack Duff, who ran a candy store on the East Side; and Ed Cresswell, a salesman in one of the men's clothing stores. She had never noticed before that Johnny Loftus and Frank McNaughton were almost exactly the same height. She had always thought of Frank as taller than Johnny. There was six dollars apiece in it for the pallbearers, she happened to know, and could not remember how she happened to know. Probably Jim had told her. Yes, Jim had told her. They had to be strong and sober, clean-looking, about the same size, and have jobs that they could get away from for a few hours on funeral days. It seemed strange to see Matt McGowan in a Protestant church; he usually took up the collection at the seven o'clock Mass in SS. Peter & Paul's, and seeing him here was like being in Paris, France, and seeing someone from home. She wondered—but of course Monsignor Creedon approved. Johnny was a Catholic, Matt was a Catholic, Frank was a Catholic, and Jack Duff was a Catholic. They wouldn't have taken work of this kind without Monsignor Creedon's approval.

Now the honorary pallbearers were coming out of their pews. Her father. Mr. McHenry. Henry Laubach. A very tall man from out of town that she had never seen before. Mr. Hooker, the newspaper editor. Mr. Jenkins from the bank. The Governor. J. Frank Kirkpatrick, the lawyer from Philadelphia. An admiral. Dr. English. Whitney Hofman. The Mayor. Judge Williams. Mr. Johnson, the new Superintendent of Schools. A man with two canes who was new to her. Paul Donaldson, from Scranton. Sixteen altogether.

"Sixteen honorary pallbearers," said her mother.

"I noticed that," said Monica.

"The out-of-town people went to Yale with Joe Chapin," said Peg Slattery.

"I never even knew he went to Yale," said Monica. "You could fill a book with what I didn't know about him."

"Hmm?"

"Nothing," said Monica.

The church was slowly emptying and Monica and her mother moved into the crowded aisle.

"Very beautiful service, Mrs. Slattery, didn't you think?" The speaker was Theodore Pflug, assistant cashier of the bank, stopping to hold up the departing worshippers and make way for Peg Slattery and Monica.

"Thank you. Very beautiful. Very beautiful indeed," said Peg Slattery.

"You notice the man with the two canes? That was David L. Harrison, a partner in J. P. Morgan and Company," said Pflug.

"Yes, I know," said Peg Slattery. "He went to Yale with Mr. Chapin."

"Good morning, Mrs. McNaughton."

"Good morning, Mr. Pflug."

"Can I give you ladies a lift or do you have your car?"

"Very kind of you, I'm sure, but we have some shopping to do," said Peg Slattery.

"Yes, I guess I'll go back to the bank. We're closed in honor of Mr. Chapin, but I *imagine* I can find one or *two* things to do. One or *two*, putting it mildly."

"Well, nice to have seen you," said Peg Slattery.

"A pleasure, I'm sure. Good-bye, Mrs. Slattery, Mrs. McNaughton. Good day."

"Good-bye," said Monica.

She paused with her mother at the foot of the stone steps. "You got that, didn't you?" said Peg.

"What?"

"I'm supposed to tell Dad Ted Pflug didn't take the day off, even though he was entitled to it. All right, I'll tell him. Now what do you want to do? Shall we go take a look at some hats? I'll treat you to a hat if it isn't too expensive."

"How high can I go?"

"Thirty-five. I'm feeling flush."

"If I like one for twenty-five can I have the difference?" said Monica.

"All right, and I can see where this is going to cost me a hundred and five. I can't buy for the one without buying for the others, is my motto."

"Oh, I thought this was a special for me," said Monica.

"No, I couldn't do that, but I'll take you to lunch at the hotel. Dad and the others are having lunch at Edith Chapin's. I was invited but I got out of it. Me sit around and watch Edith queening it over the Governor and the others? It's a wonder she didn't ride in the Governor's car."

"I think I'll call Ann up tomorrow."

"Don't you do it. Stay out of it."

"Stay out of what?" said Monica.

"Well, not exactly stay out of it," said Peg Slattery. "But don't start getting mixed up with those people. You never see Ann any more, and when you used to I always knew nothing would ever come of it. Joe's dead now and we don't have to pretend we're friends of the Chapin family, because we're not."

"All right," said Monica. "I wish I'd worn my tan. I want to get a hat to go with it and this dress is so completely different."

"You can always exchange it. We buy enough hats from Sadie, I never had any trouble exchanging one. Just as long as you don't wear it to a party, or publicly, then she doesn't mind."

"I could buy two fifteen-dollar hats."

"You wouldn't wear anything she has for fifteen. Buy a twenty-five now and exchange it later, is my advice," said Peg Slattery.

"I'd almost rather have a pair of shoes."

"No, you buy your own shoes. Let Jim pay for your shoes. They're a necessity. Hats are a luxury."

"All right," said Monica.

The day had turned cold and clear after the previous day's threat of snow and there was in the near-noonday traffic, augmented by the big black cars of the funeral and the politicians and the important, a festive air. The shiny limousines and the many strange chauffeurs and the low-number license plates and the stars and flags of the military motors were enough to make a man have some respect for Joe Chapin. The town was accustomed to big funerals; they were no novelty. But these big cars carried big men, who had made an effort to attend Joe Chapin's funeral. Big, busy men from all over the state and Washington and New York were in Gibbsville because Joe Chapin had passed on. You could not get a room at the hotel; there was a private car in the Reading Railway shed; members of the Gibbsville Club and the Lantenengo Country Club had been asked not to use the club restaurants at lunch that day, in order to accommodate the many visiting notables. The scene outside Trinity Church, upon conclusion of the ceremonies, was described in a special fifteen-minute program broadcast over the local station WGIB by Ted Wallace. Ted was a comparative newcomer to town, an expert in finding a connection between a popular song title and Kaufman's Kredit Jewelry, and with an unquestioned flair for making a high school basketball game seem exciting. He was assisted in identifying the celebrities by his good friend Al Jellinek, of the *Standard*, who had a list of the prominent. But Al was unable to keep his good friend Ted from identifying the deceased as Joseph B. Chaplin. The WGIB switchboard received eighty-four telephone calls, topping the previous Wallace record of fifty-five calls on the occasion of his crediting Frank Sinatra with a Vic Damone disk. It was the only time Ted had been placed in charge of a WGIB Special Events Program; indeed, it was the first time WGIB had broadcast a Special Events Program under that name. Ted was somewhat comforted by the fact that the station also received sixteen letters complaining against putting on a funeral instead of the customary Luncheon Siesta.

After a fairly serious tie-up lasting twenty minutes, traffic thinned down to noonday normal. The horns of protest during the twenty-minute jam were not able to drown out the tolling bells of Trinity. Those noble bells had been tolling while those motor cars were still buried in the Mesabi Range, and they would continue to toll long after the last of those cars was junk. But the battle of the decibels made Gibbsville, at least for part of an hour, sound like a city. And Joe Chapin, the cause of it all, was made to seem like an extremely important man.

His wife, the new widow Edith Stokes Chapin, likewise was made to feel an extremely important woman. All that day and into the night, until her retirement shortly after ten o'clock, she was the beneficiary of the small kindnesses that the big people know how to give. The graceful stepping aside as she took her place at the grave, the little glances in her direction by the clergy, the firm restraint of any emotional display at the inevitable mentions of Death in the burial service.

A civilian airplane, a blue Aeronca, was doing 8's around pylons during the burial service, and the gentlemen pallbearers to a man tried to stare the craft out of the air, but not one of them was heard to murmur displeasure at the ignorance of the pilot. The noisy little engine introduced a sporty sound to the unsporty occasion and the pallbearer who was an admiral frowned over at his two-striper aide, who nodded in comprehension. The aide knew that there was nothing that could be done about it, and the aide understood perfectly that the admiral felt he had to make some token sign of disapproval as senior officer present. Actually any action in the direction of the Aeronca and its pilot might not have been desirable, since the airplane held the attention, almost throughout the ceremony, of Joe Chapin Junior. There was nothing on Joe Chapin Junior's face to indicate displeasure or disapproval of the blue aircraft. He stood beside his heavily veiled mother, close to her in body, but his cold blue eyes followed the plane's exercises with a calm curiosity, and the set of his mouth told nothing. Joe Chapin Junior was alive and present, but it would have been easy for anyone else present to imagine that Joe Junior was only standing alone on a hillside, on a clear, cold spring day. And yet a stranger would have known that Joe Junior very much belonged at graveside. His attire, of course, proclaimed the mourner: his black knitted necktie in a starched collar; his black topcoat, blue serge suit, black shoes and black homburg were all of superior workmanship and material and did not show professional wear. No article of his attire had been bought for the occasion; all came from a complete wardrobe, items to be worn on other, dissimilar occasions but available for occasions like this one. Then there was the point of resemblance between the principal figure at the ceremony, the widow, her daughter, and her son: the Stokes mouth. The lips themselves were prominent, but not thick. The illusion of thickness was caused by the stretching of the lips, through the years, over the large front teeth. It was a remarkable resemblance, especially in the day of the orthodontist. The mouth and the now unseen teeth behind it were the same for the woman born in 1886 and the young man born in 1915. The mother's mouth was so unpretty as to be described as masculine, but with the mother present the young man's mouth seemed voluptuously feminine. The mouth was the sole point of resemblance, but it was so prominent as to be unmistakable and immediately apparent. The son had a thin nose and eyes buried deep and a large forehead, not bulging, but a continuing part of the face rather than a beginning part of the head. He was half a head taller than his mother, but his bones apparently were no larger than hers, which made him, for a man, slender to the degree of slightness.

The daughter looked more like the mother. If it had been possible to recreate a younger and prettier version of the mother, and place her at graveside, she would have been the daughter. The daughter's looks were a refinement of the mother's, a refinement and a softening, so that the mouth, in the daughter, became inviting, the eyes were lively, the teeth were for whitening the smile. The daughter was smaller than the mother and, beside her, dainty. It was a commonplace comment in Gibbsville: "How can Ann look so much like her mother and still be pretty?" Ann was remarkable, too, for something else: she was the only person at the funeral who was weeping.

There was a ton and more flowers and wire and foil at the graveside. Beside it stood two workmen, leaning on spades—gravediggers. They kept their caps on during the service and stared like innocently rude children at the members of the funeral party. To show any respect was not expected of them, and they showed none. Their only connection with the funeral party was their recognition of Mike Slattery and they nodded to him but they were not offended when he did not return their nod. They had not even done the work of digging the Chapin grave; they were only waiting for the removal of the floral tributes so that they could begin digging to prepare another grave in another plot. To that extent the Chapin funeral was in their way, holding them up, but gravediggers are well paid and there were a lot of grand people to stare at. In a little while the grand people would be going away and they could start work, spading out the correct number of cubic feet of earth to make a hole for the person who would be laid away the next day. Their stony, weather-beaten faces gave back in dignity the same austerity that they saw in the faces of the Chapin mourners.

Soon it was over. The immediate family got in their aging Cadillac while the others of the funeral party stood by, then the honorary pallbearers and the few others who had been invited back to the house followed in their own and assigned limousines. The ceremony at the grave took less in time than Peg Slattery's luncheon treat to her daughter. The honorary pallbearers in their limousines began looking at their watches and studying slips of paper on which their efficient secretaries had written train times. All of the out-of-town men had things to do later in the day, and at distant places. The sad duty to Joe Chapin had been performed; a bourbon, a spot of lunch, a few words with Edith and they would be gone, in many cases never again to see Gibbsville. Time was important to all of these important men, and most of them had learned the lesson that if you kept busy you lived; lived, at least, until you were caught dead. Not one of them liked what had brought him to Gibbsville, and not one of them wanted to stay and be further reminded of what had brought him. A drink of whiskey, a slice of rare roast beef, the clasp of Edith's hand and a kiss to her wrinkling cheek, and they could hurry back into the live worlds they lived in. There was nothing here for the admiral, whose postwar civilian services had been arranged for. The Governor was not running for re-election. Editor Hooker, the only man who knew the exact degree of importance of each pallbearer, was in such a state of glorious confusion that he gave up and relaxed. David L. Harrison, suspicious of any man he had not known for thirty years, hung on to Arthur McHenry, whom he had known for thirty years, and no valuable new contact was made by any two men as a consequence of their service to the memory of Joe Chapin. The very tall man who had gone to Yale with Joe Chapin had a private fortune much greater than David L. Harrison's, and any time he wanted to see David L. Harrison he could drop in at The Links, their common club. Henry Laubach transacted a good deal of business with J. Frank Kirkpatrick, but the two men did not like each other. The new Superintendent of Schools, Mr. Johnson, had boned up in his *Who's Who* for his information (and they were all in it, except Whitney Hofman and Mr. Jenkins from the bank), but he never became quite certain which was David L. Harrison and which was J. Frank Kirkpatrick. Mr. Jenkins from the bank had eyes only for David L. Harrison, but David L. Harrison made certain that Mr. Jenkins would not come up to him at any future bankers' convention. He did it by calling Mr. Jenkins "Doctor," a title and an occupation he was well aware did not fit Mr. Jenkins. Huddled together by the protection of the police, the sixteen men appeared to the public to be a close group, but they were not. Indeed, they did not all know the same Joe Chapin.

Of the sixteen pallbearers only one, Arthur McHenry, had known all of the Joe Chapins, and after him Mike Slattery knew more Joe Chapins than the rest. The Yale Joe Chapin was a friend of David L. Harrison and of the tall man, whose name was Alec Weeks. The legal Joe Chapin was a friend of Kirkpatrick's and Judge Williams'. The political Joe Chapin was a friend of Mike Slattery's and the Governor's and the Mayor's. The Old Gibbsville Joe Chapin was a friend of Dr. English's and Whit Hofman's and Henry Laubach's. Editor Hooker, the admiral, Banker Jenkins, Superintendent Johnson—they were not so much friends of Joe Chapin's as fellow members of committees. Paul Donaldson from Scranton, who was always referred to as Paul Donaldson from or of Scranton, was the kind of man of consequence who was admitted to the circle of men of consequence that has representatives in most of the states of the Union and several provinces of Canada. He was a rich, rich man who looked right and talked right. He was the only citizen of Scranton who was known to many rich and powerful men; all they knew about Scranton was that Paul Donaldson lived there. In the list of directors of his New

York bank his name was down as Paul Donaldson, Scranton, Pa., instead of Paul Donaldson, attorney-at-law, or the name of his firm. He was a member of the bar, but only incidentally a member of the bar; he was president of Paul Donaldson & Company, and he *was* Paul Donaldson & Company. In one respect he was the most important pallbearer, in that his absence from the pallbearers' roster would have been, to the knowing, a most conspicuous one. His handshake with Dave Harrison was perfunctory; after all, he had seen Harrison less than a week ago in New York, saw him all the time, and what's more, he was not a Morgan man. He was personally acquainted with Arthur McHenry, Mike Slattery, Alec Weeks, the Governor, Dr. English, Whit Hofman, and Dave Harrison. Arthur McHenry was a Pennsylvania gentleman, and they all had known Joe Chapin and each other at Yale. Dr. English and Whit Hofman and Henry Laubach were Gibbsville gentlemen, the kind of men Paul Donaldson of Scranton would know in any city in the country. Joe Chapin had been a Yale friend and he was a Gibbsville gentleman, and those were the reasons for Paul Donaldson of Scranton's being at Joe's funeral. When he had said, a few days earlier, "I have to go to Joe Chapin's funeral," he was speaking a simple truth. As Paul Donaldson of Scranton he had to go to the funerals of men like Joe Chapin of Gibbsville. There were no new Joe Chapins coming up, and nobody knew that better than Paul Donaldson from Scranton. He had no use for first-generation money or first-generation millionaires. He had no use for artists, authors, advertising men, Texans, musicians, or Jews. "Had no use" was his own expression; actually he used or dealt with all of them. But when he had got his use out of them, he dismissed them from his life. He would not have them in his house, he would not go to *their* funerals, not even jubilantly.

In the limousine on the way to Frederick Street he sat beside Mike Slattery. "They gave Joe a nice turnout," said Paul Donaldson of Scranton.

"Very," said Mike Slattery. "He'd have appreciated your coming."

"Oh, balls," said Donaldson. "Tell me about the son. I hear he's no damn good."

"That's about the size of it, I guess," said Mike.

"What about him, Whit? You know him, of course," said Donaldson.

"Oh, sure," said Whit Hofman. "I haven't seen him much since he was a kid, but we all get a lot of funny reports on him."

"What kind of reports?" said Donaldson. "Is he a Commie? One of those?"

"No, at least I haven't heard that. Have you, Mike?"

"No, although he may well be," said Mike.

"What else then?" said Donaldson.

"Well, I heard he was kicked out of your alma mater for being a fairy," said Whit Hofman.

"I can tell you *that's* not true," said Donaldson. "If we started kicking them out for being fairies . . . God, when I was there I don't think there were a half a dozen known ones in the whole university, but now I understand the place is full of them. But it's not only Yale. Every place. Harvard always had them. Princeton, full of them. Where did you go, Whit? You went to Williams."

"Right. Never any fairies at Williams. We used to send them all to the Big Three."

"You may think you're kidding, but you're not. My boy went to New Haven for two years and he was glad to get out and go in the Navy. He hated it, and I can't say I blamed him. You go to Yale nowadays and if your father wasn't a jailbird or an immigrant, you go around feeling you owe somebody an apology. I guess it isn't *quite* as bad as that, but things are going in that direction. Mike, where did you go?"

"Villanova to college and Penn to law school."

"Well, I guess Villanova's all right, but Penn, I hear that stinks too. But getting back to young Joby Chapin. You think he's a fairy, eh? I knew Joe was disappointed in him, but I didn't know that was the reason."

"That was one of the stories when he left Yale," said Hofman.

"Well, wasn't there somebody from Gibbsville there at the time? This was always a pretty good Yale town," said Donaldson.

"There must have been," said Hofman. "Who? Can you remember, Mike?"

"I was just trying to think," said Mike. "Young Ogden. Wasn't he at Yale about then?"

"Oh, no. Later," said Hofman.

"How did young Chapin stay out of the Army? He looks healthy enough," said Donaldson.

"He *was* in the Army for a while, wasn't he, Mike?"

"I can tell you about that," said Slattery. "He got a medical discharge for something to do with the inner ear, and then he got in that O.S.S. outfit. That was one of my contracts. They made him an instructor in code work at one of their secret camps."

"Overseas?" said Donaldson.

"Virginia somewhere," said Slattery. "I think that's where he is now, or at least he's still with the cloak-and-dagger boys to the best of my knowledge."

"What about Ann? Where was her husband? She's married to some fellow named Mugridge," said Donaldson.

"Musgrove," said Hofman. "Divorced. She's been living at home —how long would you say, Mike?"

"The best part of a year. Close to it," said Slattery. "I understand she's back and forth between here and Philly, but mostly at home."

"She have any children? No children, if I'm not mistaken, unless she had one lately," said Donaldson.

"No children," said Hofman.

"And she was married once before, wasn't she?" said Donaldson.

"To an Italian fellow that played in an orchestra. We had that annulled. Not many people know about that," said Slattery.

"Oh, the hell they don't, Mike," said Hofman.

"They may know about it, but they'd have one hell of a time proving it on any record," said Slattery.

"You fixed that, did you, Mike?" said Donaldson.

"I was instrumental, put it that way," said Slattery.

"Good old Mike. Instrumental," said Donaldson.

"We politicians have our uses," said Slattery.

"If they were all like you we wouldn't have anything to worry about," said Donaldson.

"Thank you, sir," said Slattery.

"I mean it. I often wish to God Almighty that we had you in Washington."

"What could I do in Washington that I can't do right here in Gibbsville? As long as I pay my phone bill."

"Well—yes. Whit, why don't you run for office?"

"Whit's very active behind the scenes," said Slattery.

"I see. Beg your pardon," said Donaldson. "Just so a good man like Whit isn't going to waste."

"He's not going to waste, you have my assurance," said Slattery. "He does more for our crowd than a lot of fellows that get more credit."

"Glad to hear it," said Donaldson. "Now, one more question. What about Edith? Is she going to be all right?"

"Financially, you mean? Financially, in the neighborhood of a million and a quarter," said Slattery.

"Besides financially. Her disposition, temperament," said Donaldson.

"Sound as a dollar," said Slattery.

"Not this God damn Chinese dollar, I hope," said Donaldson.

"No, not the Chinese dollar," said Slattery.

"Is she going to take this hard, Joe's death?" said Donaldson.

"You never know what goes on in a woman's mind, but Edith— well, you know her as well as I do," said Slattery.

"Yes, and I think she'll be all right," said Donaldson. "I was just wondering whether you had any particular information, any signs of anything."

"Edith wouldn't let on to me," said Slattery.

"Possibly, but you're one of the sharpest observers I ever knew," said Donaldson.

"Not sharp enough to penetrate that mask," said Slattery, "when it's the same face day in day out, year in year out. Ask Whit. He's her cousin."

"I'm her cousin, but I was Joe's cousin, too. Joe's mother was my aunt, my father's sister. I could never figure Joe out. I guess I'm not awfully good at that sort of thing. If I couldn't figure Joe out, I'd have one hell of a time with Edith. They're just my cousins, and I always more or less took them for granted."

"Now that's interesting," said Donaldson. "Your saying you couldn't figure Joe out. Why not? What was difficult about that?"

"One of the smartest things he ever said," said Slattery. "Who did know Chapin? Arthur McHenry knew him better than anyone else. Then I think I did. But I'll tell you this much, Paul. We knew exactly what Joe wanted us to know. And believe me, that wasn't much. You were a friend of his, sure. But did you know him? Do you think you knew him well? You didn't. I admit I didn't. I don't think Arthur did. And as to Edith—I wonder."

"Are you hinting that Joe had a secret life?" said Donaldson.

"No, but I am hinting that he could have had a secret life without any of us knowing about it."

"Oh," said Donaldson.

"Joe was like a young fellow that never grew up. In many respects that was what he was. But if you let it end there, you wouldn't have the full picture of the man. I can't believe that what I was allowed to see of Joe was all there was. If that was all there was, he was a dull man, perhaps a stupid man. But then that would make me a stupid man for taking so much interest in him, and while I may be a lot of things, I'll never admit that I'm stupid."

"Nobody could ever call you stupid," said Donaldson.

"Correction, Paul. They have called me stupid, but they usually found out different. I've been wrong, but not stupid. So, now we have these two people, friends of ours. The one is a woman, painfully shy and retiring, and we all right away credit her with a lot more gray matter than she ever admitted. Then the other, the man, he isn't shy or retiring. Enters politics. Gets around and meets people, so we never bother to wonder, maybe there's more to this man than we see. I've always thought there was a great deal more. In fact, Joe was a much more interesting study than Edith. We think, we conceded that the woman had more because she showed practically nothing. We don't bother to think the same thing about the man. Why? Because we think we've seen it all. I say we missed the boat on Joe Chapin, and I was one that missed it by a mile. Maybe I *was* stupid. Maybe I was."

"Mike, it sounds to me as though you were thinking a lot of these things for the first time," said Donaldson.

"Paul, you are absolutely right," said Slattery.

"Well, here we are," said Whit Hofman.

"I want to add one thing," said Slattery.

"What's that?" said Donaldson.

"I may have been stupid about Joe, and he's dead. But I won't be stupid about Edith."

Donaldson was using the hand loop to pull himself out of his seat. He paused. "You sound as though you might have plans for Edith?"

"It's too early to say," said Slattery. "Or is it?"

"Keep in touch with me, Mike. I'll be interested to see what develops." He patted Slattery's knee. "You know, you're the most stimulating Irishman I know."

"If I am, why limit it to Irishmen? We're a very stimulating race of people. So much so that the rest of you can only take us in small doses. Or so it would appear."

"You're an arrogant old son of a bitch, too," said Donaldson.

"Now that's more like it. There we meet on equal terms."

"You see why I love this fellow?" said Donaldson to Hofman.

"I sure do," said Hofman.

"Let's save the rest of the compliments for the deceased," said Slattery. "With my swelled head and your big bottom we're having a hard time getting out of this chariot."

They descended from the limousine and the chauffeur addressed Mike Slattery. "About what time will I be back for you, sir?"

"An hour and a half," said Slattery. "No, I'll tell you, Ed. Be back at four. That'll be soon enough."

"Yes, sir," said Ed.

"I hope you notice I'm using my own car, Paul," said Slattery. "The Commonwealth doesn't pay for this ride."

"Senator, your concern for the economy touches me," said Donaldson. "Whit, you know this house. If I don't empty my bladder this minute I'm going to have a childish accident."

"Then let's head for the garage. There's a can back there," said Hofman. "Mike?"

"Everything under control. See you inside," said Mike Slattery. One of Mike Slattery's gifts was that he knew when to leave, and he knew that Paul Donaldson had had a pleasant time with him. The moment to separate had come and he was glad that Donaldson had supplied the excuse.

The Chapin house was the only one on Frederick Street that had a stoop of three chaste brownstone steps. The other houses of equal age and proportion had marble stoops, originally chaste but soiled by time and traffic. The front door was a massive fixture, four inches in thickness, with a brass plate the size of a playing card, in which had been cut the name Benjamin Chapin. The patina from years of polish and rubbing left the name barely distinguishable. The plate was screwed into the door at a point sixty-eight inches from the bottom, or eyes' height as measured to the full height of Benjamin Chapin. Beneath the name plate, exactly halfway from top to bottom of the door, was a letter-slot of brass bearing the word Letters. (It had not been used in many years, a fact known to the regular letter carriers, but confusing to the occasional extra carrier, who did not know that the slot was permanently closed to keep out draught and dust.) Above the door was a fan light into which was etched the number 10. The outer side of the light had not been washed—"hopeless," was Edith's word for the task of keeping it clean—but the inside was comparatively free of dust. The doorknob and the bell-button assembly were of figured bronze, the latter a later copy of the design for the knob, made by hand at the time of the substitution of the electric bell for the bronze pull. The knob of the bronze pull still served as a paperweight in Joe Chapin's study, mounted on mahogany in which had been picked out the date of the installation of electricity in the Chapin house.

The entrance was in the center of the street floor. On each side of the entrance, on the western elevation, was a pair of windows, plate glass, separate but twins. The window sills were high enough above the street level to make it impossible for the nosy to peer in, and in any event there usually was nothing to see but furniture, since the rooms were seldom used in the daytime and the shades lowered, the curtains drawn, every night.

It was now possible to see human beings moving about in those rooms; the shades were raised, the curtains tied up. The crape of mourning had been removed from the front door and a curious passerby might have imagined that he was having a glimpse of a reception—which, in a manner of speaking, was the case. The front door was slightly ajar, intentionally, so that the invited would enter without ringing the bell, and the vestibule door was fully open and held open by a carpet-covered brick. There was a quite level tone of conversational exchange, animated enough by the animation and relief of the living who have just been burying the dead, but still suitably subdued for the occasion and by the fact that the company did not include enough of the very young to make a substantial difference. This was an older crowd, recessing now from a duty that was more frequently repeated every year. Joe Chapin, not the oldest of this group, was gone and most of the men and women present had good reason to expect that he or she would be the next, and soon. A month? Too soon. Ten years? Too much to expect. Five years? Three years? It got closer when you thought about it, and the best thing now was not to think about it. One knew, or could guess, the principal complaint or weakness of one's friends and contemporaries. This man, one knew, had a sixteen-inch-long scar on his belly. That woman was under the x-ray three times a week. That man would never smoke another cigar; that woman was never more than an hour away from her next whiskey. You bought a suit of clothes, knowing it would outlast you. You kept clean wherever soap and water could reach. You controlled the growth of hair on your face and head. You had the small grime removed from the settings of your diamonds and the lenses changed in your spectacles. You remembered everything you had ever known about your acquaintances, but sometimes you put a true sin or a true scandal in your record of the wrong person. Friends were beginning to bore you as much as enemies, and the one quickly became the other over nothing more important than a near-sighted revoke at bridge. But a gathering of this kind briefly took on a party atmosphere because there were so many like you present. No matter how truly you believed that you wanted to be alone, a gathering of this kind did stay off loneliness.

The front room at the right as you entered the Chapin house was the dining room, connected through a swinging door with the butler's pantry and the kitchen. Off the hall, on that side of the house, was also a lavatory, and in the hall was the front stairway. The front room at the left of the hall was the sitting room and beyond it a room that Edith Chapin called the library or den but that before her marriage had been called the back sitting room (and which was so indicated on the signal box in the pantry, with the letters BSR). As the invited entered the house they were greeted by Mary the maid. "Gentlemen will put their hat and coats upstairs and to the right. Ladies upstairs and to the left." It was a chant. The invited did as instructed, delaying upstairs for the bathrooms to be unoccupied and their turns to come. Otto, the steward, and two waiters from the Gibbsville Club took care of the drink needs expeditiously, asking the preferences of some, knowing from experience the tastes of others. For all to see, in the dining room on the large table—all extra leaves in place—was food, kept hot over alcohol burners, and on the sideboard a club coffee urn and china. The drink ingredients were not in evidence; they were in the kitchen. The largest call, as Otto had anticipated, was for bourbon-on-the-rocks, with the ladies who drank favoring slightly the dry martini. The admiral asked for, and got, brandy and ginger ale; Alec Weeks required Scotch and Saratoga vichy, without ice, and it was supplied. Otherwise the company taste was simple and predictable, as the excellent Otto was sure it would be.

The early arrivals accepted their drinks and sat down to rest, staying out of the dining room to make polite, irrelevant conversation, and greeting each other (whom they had last seen less than thirty minutes ago at the graveside) with a reunion heartiness, nicely modulated. No one wanted to be the first to attack the food; consequently, when the greater number were arrived, there was a sudden crowding of the dining room and some well-behaved confusion. The gentlemen soon gave up their attempts to serve the ladies first, and the ladies then forthrightly helped themselves and were fed first anyway. Some few more than sixty persons had been invited back to the house, and provision had been made for eighty. At the high point of the luncheon seventy-one men and women were served, including those who asked only for a plate of saltines and a glass of milk. Twenty or more of the company took pills before eating; a smaller number took pills after eating. It was not a group (nor was it an occasion) for sitting on the floor, a condition that resulted in half the men remaining on their feet. Cigars were not passed, but they came out before most of the ladies and gentlemen had finished their food. The time elapsed between the serving of the very first morsel and the last was under an hour; dessert, apple pie or ice cream or both, was generally declined, and a remarkable number of persons went without coffee because it was not Sanka, a detail that had been overlooked by the embarrassed Otto and the unaware Edith.

The widow's representatives among the invited callers were her son Joby and her brother, Carter Stokes, Junior, who was four years younger than she and therefore closer in age to most of the company. Carter Stokes was a not unpleasant little man, a bachelor who lived at the Y.M.C.A. because it was cheap and respectable and offered the facilities of the swimming pool, the cafeteria, the barber shop, the New York and Philadelphia newspapers, and all of the standard American and English magazines. He was a member of the Gibbsville Club (an annual Christmas present from Edith) but he seldom went near it for club life. The drinking and gambling at the Gibbsville Club were, he declared, too rich for his blood. At the "Y" he enjoyed the status of a full-fledged but democratic member of Gibbsville society, who preferred the company of a good bunch of fellows like the ones that lived at the "Y." He made $7,500 a year as assistant cashier at the bank, which enabled him to buy his clothes at Jacob Reed's in Philadelphia and maintain a Plymouth automobile and give one small party a year at the Gibbsville Club to repay hostesses for the free dinners he earned as extra man. It was generally agreed among his friends of both strata that he was not a homosexual, although no proof could be offered by those who brought up the question or those who defended against the suspicion. Men liked old Carter, who was called old before he was out of his forties, and hostesses found him useful at quarter-a-corner and twentieth-of-a-cent bridge parties, on which a large part of Gibbsville social life was based. As an alumnus of Haverford College he qualified as an educated man; in his case the college education figured in his past and his present in much the same way as the straightening of his teeth; in youth the teeth had been straightened, the education provided, and for the rest of his life he was a college man and straight-toothed.

Carter was not exactly a snob. He really had more fun with the fellows at the "Y" and his associates at the bank, and it was not because they were so different that he enjoyed their company. They put no great demands on his intellect and they even gave him a snobbish respect for his social standing. But he was not by any means ill at ease among the callers at his sister's house. He was impressed by the Governor's governorship and the admiral's admiralcy (Carter had been an ensign in World War I), and as a man in banking he was conscious of the Morgan partnership of David L. Harrison. He was not hurt when Paul Donaldson of Scranton did not remember him, although this made their fifteenth, possibly their twentieth, meeting. Carter had nice manners and a friendly attitude, which made him just right for his duty as Edith's representative, and the old, old fact that Joe Chapin could not stand him made no difference now. He had come to this house a hundred times, for Christmas dinner, Thanksgiving, Sunday suppers, and almost without fail his brother-in-law would say to Carter: "Well, Carter, what have you been doing?" And the tone of the question implied that the answer would be so awful or so dull that it was not to be waited for, so the question seldom got an uninterrupted answer. For years he had known that Joe despised him, and in his quiet way he hated Joe too. None of that showed as he went around seeing that people were eating, drinking, and comfortable. "I was afraid we'd have snow . . . Edith's taking it very well . . . Let me get you another cup of coffee." He was much more helpful to his absent sister than her only son.

Joe Chapin Junior was making mistake after mistake—the same mistake over and over again. He would go up to one of the sixtyish ladies, asking her if he could get her anything, and then allow himself to be held on to so long that his boredom would show and the lady would be antagonized. Then he would repeat the ordeal with another lady. His cousin Whit Hofman was the only person in the crowd he wanted to talk to. Knowing Whit, an affable, kind man who liked women, whiskey, and golf, Joby was sure that his cousin would have liked to join him in the pantry over a bottle of Scotch. Joby had no illusions of the esteem in which his cousin held him, but cousins they were, without any history of unkindness or quarrel. But a quiet drink with Whit was not possible now; Joby had his chores to perform, and Whit seemed to be having a good time. Whit had the social graces.

Joby excused himself from Mrs. Henry Laubach and made his way to the pantry and his second drink of the day, a straight Scotch with a water chaser. It had no immediate effect, but he knew it would do him some good in a few minutes, and he returned to the spot beside the newel-post which he had been using as his headquarters. There he was approached by Paul Donaldson from Scranton.

"Joby, I wanted to ask you—"

"Yes, Mr. Donaldson."

"What about your mother? I'm motoring back to Scranton in a few minutes and I wondered if I could see her for a moment or two. Is she seeing people?"

Joby looked at his watch. "I don't like to seem mysterious, but can you wait a few minutes? Oh, hell. I wasn't supposed to tell anybody, but almost any minute Mother's coming downstairs. She didn't want to have people coming in her room two or three at a time, so what she's going to do is, she's coming down and sort of wander through and say hello to people. Unless there was something special and you wanted to see her alone. Then I'd have to go up and ask her."

"No, I just wanted to be sure and see her," said Paul Donaldson. "She's all right?"

"Oh, yes. She's all right. Ann's been sitting with her upstairs. She hasn't been alone, if that's what you mean."

"I see," said Donaldson. "How are *you*, Joby?"

"Why, I'm all right, thank you. It came as no surprise to me. We'd had some warning."

"I wasn't thinking about your father. I understand you're in the O.S.S."

"Yes," said Joby. "In a very obscure capacity."

"Harry Reddington's an old friend of mine."

"Is that so?"

"Don't you know Harry Reddington?" said Donaldson.

"I may know him slightly."

"Now look, Joby, I'm not a German spy. Everybody in the O.S.S. knows Harry Reddington. You don't have to be as security-conscious as all that. That's like pretending you don't know Bill Donovan. Another friend of mine, by the way."

"As a matter of fact I *don't* know Bill Donovan. Mr. Donaldson, you appear to know a lot about the O.S.S., so you must know we're under instructions not to talk about it."

"Are you by any chance trying to snub me?"

"No, sir," said Joby.

"As a friend of your father's I thought I might be of some help to you, but apparently you don't need any help."

"I need all the help I can get, but as I say, I'm in such an obscure job, routine work."

"Psychological warfare?"

"Routine work, very unimportant," said Joby.

"By God you *are* snubbing me," said Paul Donaldson.

"All right then, for Christ's sake, I *am* snubbing you. You asked for it. Now why don't you shut your silly mouth and stop trying to show off how much you know. You want to be in on everything, don't you?"

"I'm in on a lot more than a snot-nose like you would know about. Good day!"

"Good—here comes my mother, if you want to be courtly. Be courtly, Mr. Donaldson. Bow from the waist." Joby turned to his mother, who was halfway down the stairs. "Mother, you remember Mr. Donaldson, from Scranton? Mr. Paul Donaldson?"

"Why, of course, Paul. What on earth do you mean, Joby? Remember Paul Donaldson."

Joby smiled at Donaldson, who did not return the smile, and moved away, circuitously but determinedly in the direction of the pantry. His mother could now take over.

He prepared a double Scotch and water and a large gin and ginger ale, and with them in his hands he mounted the back stairs to the back bedroom on the second story. A maid whom he did not recognize was in the room, and no one else. He looked in the other rooms, then proceeded to the third floor front, his old bedroom. His sister was sitting on the cedar chest, smoking a cigarette.

"Do you want this?" he said, extending the gin drink.

"Do I ever!" said Ann. "Thanks. What is it? Gin and ginger ale?"

"Yes," said her brother.

"Did you get anything to eat?" she asked.

"I didn't want anything."

"I wasn't hungry either, but I'm getting there. Do you suppose we could get them to send up a sandwich on the dumbwaiter?"

"I somehow doubt it. There are so many strange maids, if you blew the whistle they'd jump as though they were goosed."

34

"Probably," said Ann. "Jolly good show, what?"

"Horseshit."

"Too tebly steef uppah leep. Honor of the family, old bwah."

"Yeah," said Joby. "Well, I took care of one of them."

"Which one?"

"Paul Donaldson."

"Oh?"

"He tried to give the impression that one word from him and I could have Donovan's job."

"Who's Donovan?"

"Oh, the high muckalorum at O.S.S."

"And?"

"Oh, I took as much of his patronizing as I could and so when he asked me if I was snubbing him I said yes, I was, and told him—oh, I don't remember exactly what I said, but I don't think I can count on him for an electric train next Christmas."

"When was this?" said Ann.

"Just now. Why?"

"Pretty good. You held out till just now?"

"I was the little boy in the velvet suit and lace collar. You should have seen me. You'd have been proud."

"I probably would have thrown up," said Ann.

"How about you?"

"Well, I didn't have to mingle with the populace. And I had another advantage over you. I wore a veil."

"Was she noble?"

"Yes, she was noble. Oh, sure."

"How in the name of Christ can she keep it up for four days?"

"Listen, this is nothing."

"How do you mean?"

"I have a feeling that this is just a rehearsal."

"Oh, no," said Joby.

"Oh, yes."

"God pity you."

"Oh, I'll be all right," said Ann. "It's not bad. If she counted on me for anything, then it might be tough. But as a matter of fact she hardly knows I'm in the room. I'm kind of like a duenna. A duenna for a very well-behaved señorita, of course."

"What does she do?"

"The duenna?"

"No. Madam."

35

"Well—you mean when we're alone?"

"Yes."

"Well, when we're absolutely alone, no chance of being disturbed, she starts working on the lists. The lists of people that sent telegrams and letters. It's really quite a list, too. Well over a thousand. And she's going to answer every one of them."

"Do you help her?"

"I offered to, but she declined."

"Why do you object to her working on the list? I think that's rather—nice."

"I don't object to her working on the list. What I object to, she does it to kill time, and she won't do it if anyone can see her."

"What's wrong with that?" said Joby.

"Stupid. If there's anyone around, she wants to be the new widow, grief-stricken but stiff upper lip. Unable to do anything as worldly as making out a list. But when there's nobody around but me she works away, copying names and addresses, so she won't have to do it later. It's so insulting to me, or would be if I gave a damn."

"You mean she's going to write a thousand letters?"

"Over a thousand. I'm sure it'll be two thousand. No, I don't think she intends to write them all letters, but she's ordered cards and she's going to sign and address every single one in her own handwriting, and little personal notes on most of them."

"Joe would have liked that."

"Joe would have liked that."

"I want to do everything the way Joe would have."

"Yes, I want to do everything the way Joe would have."

"Do we have to put in another appearance downstairs?" said the brother.

"I'm not going to," said Ann.

"I wonder if I'm supposed to."

"Uncle Cartie's there."

"And having the time of his life," said Joby. "How long do you think Madam plans to stay down?"

"There's quite a crowd, and she'll have to speak to every one of them. Can't miss any."

"Seventy-one, according to Gibbsville Club Otto. A minute for each one. That's well over an hour."

"Why?" said Ann.

"Well, what the hell, if she's going to be there an hour or more, I can sneak us another drink."

"Operation Plastered," said Ann.

36

"No, but we might as well be comfortable. You go stand at the dumbwaiter." He left her and went downstairs. In a few minutes she saw the dumbwaiter rope quivering, then heard the rumble as the dumbwaiter was raised. She removed the bottles, ice, and glasses and carried them to her brother's room.

"I'm not as young as I used to be," he said on his return. "I used to run up those stairs fifty times a day."

"Who is? Thirty-four. What an age."

"Yep. You're through."

"You're not kidding," said Ann. "When do you go back to Washington?"

"Seven-five, tomorrow morning. I must say, this is the first time I ever wanted to go back."

"How much longer is this war going to last?"

"You hear all sorts of guesses. Five years. Three years. I think it all depends on the Navy."

"Five years. I'll be thirty-nine, one more year till forty. I thought thirty was bad enough, but forty!"

"I don't mind thirty," said Joby.

"Well, why should you?"

"Yes, that's right. Why should I? For that matter, why should I mind forty, or fifty, or twenty-eight. None of them seem to make much difference."

"That isn't what I meant," said Ann.

"I know it wasn't," said her brother.

The Chapin children were momentarily silent, not looking at each other, but together.

"This should be the start of some new life for us," said Ann.

"Why?"

"I don't say it will be, I didn't say that. But the death of your father should be some sort of a milestone."

"Maybe it is," said Joby. "Oh, sure it is. Sure it is. Father's dead, so he isn't here any more. We'll miss him. Is that enough for a milestone?"

"I have a feeling it should be more."

"Money. We each get a hundred thousand dollars apiece. Kinda nice to have a hundred thousand dollars—that is, if he didn't change his will."

"Yes, but bear this in mind. I know about the will, too. We each get a hundred thousand dollars, that's true. But maybe that's *all*."

"What are you hinting at?" said Joby.

"The income from a hundred thousand, what's that?"

"Varies. Could be three thousand, could be six."

"Let's suppose it's *four*," said Ann. "That's less than what you and I've been getting."

"So it is," said Joby. "I hadn't thought of that. You mean Madam can say to us we each have the hundred thousand capital and we have to take a cut."

"Exactly," said Ann. "And a thousand a year would make a big difference to me."

"Not to me, though. I'll make it up for you. I have a job, and I guess I always will have, so if you get four instead of five, I'll make it up. I lead a very simple life."

"Thank you, Joby," said Ann. "On the other hand, she may make it up herself."

"But you and I doubt that," said her brother.

Ann laughed. "I doubt it very much. She'll probably tell me I can live here and actually save money."

"Which you could."

"Which I could if I could live here."

"Well, don't let the thousand difference worry you," said Joby. "At any rate, dearie, you have your milestone."

"Yes, I guess I have. Although when I started out I wasn't thinking of money. I just feel as though something ought to be happening inside. It isn't, though. I don't feel older, or younger, or any great sense of loss, or even pleasure."

"Too soon. Too many things to do the last few days."

"Probably," said Ann.

They were silent again.

"What are you smiling about?" said Joby, presently.

"Was I smiling? I guess I was thinking about when we were children, I was always so much older than you. Then I guess I must have stopped being older and you passed me on the way, so now *you* seem older."

"I am older," said Joby.

"I wonder how you got older," said his sister.

"I'm not sure. Maybe you stayed young and I didn't."

"Yes, partly. I had love affairs and stayed the same age."

"I had love affairs, too. That doesn't explain it," said Joby.

"You're always so secretive about your love affairs."

"And I intend to remain secretive," said Joby.

"I wasn't prying."

"A little."

"Well—a little, yes," said Ann. "But isn't that all right? You wouldn't like it if I showed no interest whatever."

"I don't mind your showing an interest. Just don't get carried away. I had a session with Madam yesterday. As usual she has a couple of prospects lined up."

"Who?"

"Well, Sallie Morrison."

"Who happens to be in love with a doctor in Philadelphia."

"Jean Wildermuth."

"*Jean Wildermuth?*"

"Jean Wildermuth," said Joe. "And some girl in Easton. She couldn't remember the name, and of course I couldn't either. A girl who used to visit Elsie Laubach."

"I know the one she means. I can't remember her name either. I think her father's a judge. Sallie Morrison, Jean Wildermuth, and Elsie Laubach's friend. Who else?"

"That was enough for a starter. But that's interesting. Madam certainly doesn't give a damn whether I get married or not, as far as *my* comfort or happiness is concerned. But she would like to see her only son tucked away."

"Tucked?"

"I got it," said Joby. "It would *look* better to have me married. *Filed* away, let's call it. What I really think is she thinks that one Uncle Cartie in the family is enough."

"And she's quite right," said Ann. "Exactly one Uncle Cartie in every family, but not two."

"Ann, see if you agree with me. If you don't, don't agree just to be polite."

"All right."

"Am I imagining things, or is Madam planning some sort of a career for herself?"

"You know, I was going to ask *you* that. In one of her wistful moments the other day she asked me if I ever thought of patching it up with dear Mr. Musgrove. I couldn't believe my ears. I looked at her with horror. After all, she knows all about that. So I said to her there was a better chance of my going back to Charley than patching things up with the other gentleman. That shut her up."

"Charley. I hardly ever think of him. What's happened to him?"

"He's in the Coast Guard. A what-do-you-call-them, petty officer, leading a band. He's married and lives in New Jersey."

"Do you see him?"

"I've never seen him. I gave my word and I've stuck to it. Not that that's been difficult. Charley was nice, and he was the first. My first. And when they had it annulled they filled me full of dire warnings. If I ever saw him he'd be arrested, go to jail, and so forth. Not true, but I believed them. After that I was more careful. I didn't marry the boy. But you were wondering about Madam. Yes, I think she's planning a career. If I went back to Mr. Musgrove, the son of a bitch, that would erase the separation, and if you married Sallie Morrison, you'd be married too. Looks nice to have your children comfortably married. And why so many political people for pall-bearers? She could just as easily have had more inconspicuous friends. What was Robert Hooker to Father? And that lawyer from Philadelphia. And the Governor. Mr. Slattery I can understand. But Johnson, the school superintendent. He didn't even know the Chapins had a daughter. For that matter, Paul Donaldson wasn't *that* close to Father. Yes, she's making plans."

"Annie, my girl, she's always been making plans. If I weren't so comfortable here I'd be tempted to go downstairs and watch her in action."

"Please don't leave me," said Ann.

"I won't," said her brother.

Their mother in action was a lesson in graciousness under difficult conditions. By the time she made her appearance the invited callers had finished their food (no accident in timing; she had been so informed by Mary). She allowed Paul Donaldson the distinction of bringing her into the sitting room, but she did not allow him to monopolize her. She put her hand on his forearm and adroitly steered him to the first, the nearest group of five persons. She addressed each person by name, and she was of course assisted in this accomplishment by her deliberate manner of speech. Since she spoke slowly and precisely at all times, the hesitation had become a familiar personal characteristic, and it enabled her to gain that fraction of a second that was necessary for the recalling of some of the names. Her children's estimate of the length of time she would spend with her guests was wrong; their formula was wrong. If she had spent one minute with each of the guests, an hour and eleven minutes would have been devoted to her task of greeting. But by repeating her device of speaking to groups of four or five rather than to each guest singly she made the personal contact with all seventy-one with half an hour to spare. No one was slighted. Each man, each woman got a personal, usually a first-name, greeting, and a handshake; and they all had at least a brief opportunity to examine her close to, an essential part of the custom of calling on the bereaved.

With her veiled hat off, and in her beautifully cut black silk dress, she looked much younger than her age and much fresher than her friends had anticipated. The hat and veil had hidden her features almost completely for the hours at the church and cemetery, so that when she made her appearance unmasked, as it were, a general gloom was lifted too. It was not, and never had been, a pretty face, but now at least it was alive and smiling.

For each group she had one special thing to say, a general comment or observation that would reach every man and woman in the group. In one group it would be the weather: the snow had not fallen. In another, the text of the clergyman's words; in another, the flowers; in another, a full pardon for the ignorant aeronaut of the blue Aeronca; in another the music at the church; in another, the perennial beauty of old Trinity itself; in another, how much Joe would have loved it all. Each group was created, and skillfully. She would greet five, four, six people by name, then stop greeting them and say her words about the weather, the music, or the flowers. Then she would move on, again addressing four or five by name, halting the identification to make her comment on the next topic. Thus each group was automatically limited to those she addressed by name, and did not become outsize and unwieldy and impersonal.

It was a remarkable performance, for not only did it achieve its obvious objective, which was to greet each man and woman who had come invited to pay respects to her husband and sympathy to her; but the maneuver also succeeded in putting an end to the luncheon, and thus an end to the whole funeral. There was, after Edith had spoken her personal word, nothing to do but go. And that, too, was planned that way. She whispered to her brother: "Have I spoken to everybody? I haven't missed anyone?"

"Everybody. Didn't miss a one," said Carter.

"Good," she said; then, not too hastily and not at all abruptly, she went through the back sitting-room door, into the hall, and up the front stairs, leaving her brother to acknowledge the farewells. She continued slowly to her sewing room on the third floor, tired but not exhausted from the climb. The excellent Mary was waiting there.

"A nice cup of tea, ma'am," said Mary.

"Oh, well, yes," said Edith. "Who was that? Is there someone in the front room?"

"Mrs. Musgrove and Mr. Joby, that's all," said Mary.

"I see," said Edith. "Now, Mary, don't you bother any more. Put the tea on the dumbwaiter and have a cup yourself, in the kitchen. You must have gone up and down these stairs . . ."

"Very well, ma'am," said Mary. "Thank you."

Mary left on her errand, and presently Edith got up and went to Joby's bedroom. The door was open, but she was inside the room before Ann or Joby saw her.

"Mother," said Ann.

"Hello, Mother," said Joby.

"Well, we're together, just the three of us," said Edith.

"Would you like a drink? There's Scotch, and gin."

"Hardly," said Edith. She sat in the desk chair. "I hope it hasn't been a trying day for you two."

"Not at all," said Ann.

"You don't think you ought to be downstairs?" she asked Joby. "The people are leaving."

"I noticed the cars. No, hasn't Uncle Cartie got everything under control?"

"Yes. But I'd feel better if you were down there. Finish your drink, of course."

"I will," said Joby.

"Ann, what is that you're drinking?"

"Gin and ginger ale," said Ann. "Why? Would you like some?"

"No, thank you," said Edith. "Someone ought to be downstairs. To thank Otto and the people from the club. And the extra women."

"I thought Mary would do that," said Ann.

"She can, but it would be nice to have somebody from the family. I'm paying all these people by the hour, with the exception of Otto. He volunteered his services, but I'm giving him something. But I think it would be nice if you thanked him, Joby."

"Well, it's too late now. There he is, getting in somebody's car. Mike Slattery's. Otto and the other men from the club."

"That's too bad."

"Oh, I don't know. He didn't do it for us. He did it because he liked Father. And the others did it for money. Extra money, come to think of it. The club pays them, and so do you. I wouldn't let it worry you, Mother."

"It doesn't. I am a little worried about one thing, though."

"What's that?" said Joby.

"Why, your determination to stay here when you knew I wanted you to go downstairs and put in an appearance. I don't think that was very considerate of you."

"But I didn't see any necessity for me to go down after you'd been talking to them. As a matter of fact, I might have—they might have felt they had to stay longer if I was there."

"I don't think they'd have thought that," said Edith. "Did you have some sort of—did you and Paul Donaldson have words? Or any unpleasantness?"

"How do you mean?"

"Did you say anything to him, or he say anything to you, unpleasant?"

"Not that I recall," said Joby. "Why?"

"I was just wondering. When I came downstairs I thought his expression was—angry. And then you *introduced* him to me, a man I've known for thirty-five years or more, and you *know* I've known him that long. You sounded sarcastic."

"I'm sure I didn't mean to," said Joby. "What reason would I have for any unpleasantness with Paul Donaldson? Or anyone else, for that matter."

"He appeared to be angry about something," said Edith.

"Well, Paul Donaldson must have a lot of things on his mind, a man as prominent as that. More than likely thinking of some big deal involving millions, billions. You mustn't underestimate Paul Donaldson, Mother. Just because he came to Father's funeral, that doesn't mean *he's* not important. Father, I'll grant you, Father was a good solid Yale type, the type we Yale men are all very proud of, but without any great distinction. But Paul Donaldson . . ."

His mother watched him as he spoke, continued to watch his eyes and mouth after he finished speaking, then she turned to Ann. "What did I do with my fountain pen? The silver-mounted one. I had it this morning, but I can't remember where I put it."

"Isn't it on your desk? That's where I last saw it."

"Here, take mine," said Joby.

"No thank you, Joby. I've taken quite enough from you for one day," said Edith. She rose.

"That has all the earmarks of a double meaning," said her son. "Was there a double meaning in that?"

"Oh, now, Joby, how could *you* think a thing like that." She left the room.

"Pretty rough on her," said Ann.

"I thought I showed admirable restraint."

"I don't think you showed *any* restraint. But she did."

"She showed restraint, or she thought I did?"

"She showed restraint," said Ann.

"She always does. She always gets credit for showing restraint, being ladylike, shy. But after all, what's restraint? If the hate is there, or the bad temper, it's better for all concerned to get rid of it than store it up."

"She's had a tough time, lately, and she *isn't* a young girl. She's fifty-nine years old, remember."

"She wouldn't thank you to remember *that* fact," said Joby. "All right, I was sarcastic."

"Heavily. I don't think she minded what you were saying about Mr. Donaldson, but calling Father a nobody . . ."

"But a nice nobody," said Joby.

"That made it worse. Implying that Father was nice and she wasn't."

"Did I imply that? Yes, I guess I did."

"You know perfectly well you did," said Ann.

"How would you have had me do it? Play straight while she played the gracious widow?"

"You could go easy for a few days, for a little while. *Let* her put on her act. Let her enjoy putting on her act, because after all, Joby, when you stop to consider, who has she got? You, and me, her son and daughter, and Uncle Cartie. I'm perfectly willing to let her play games for a while."

"Who has she got? Well, you left out the most important one of all."

"Who?"

"Herself," said Joby. "She has herself, and she's been having herself for years and years. The one person she cared about. Made plans for. Regulated our lives for. You think of her as the dutiful, retiring wife of J. B. Chapin Senior? Some day I'll tell you a thing or two about that. Do you know why the biggest day in Joseph B. Chapin's life was his funeral? With all those big shots and so forth? Because she, his dutiful, retiring wife, kept him from being anything but what he ended up as. You don't like her because she interfered with your life, and you saw her interfering with mine. But are you aware of what she did to Father? The reason she didn't hit back at me now, just a minute ago, is because she didn't dare. She knows that I know. Let me tell you, Annie, she'll let me get away with all the sarcasm I care to dish out, just as long as I lay off what she did to Father."

"What did she do to Father?"

"Poisoned him," said Joby.

"Oh, now wait a minute," said Ann.

"I'm waiting."

"I refuse to believe that," said Ann.

"You refuse to believe that Mother killed Father with a slow poison?" said Joby.

"Oh. A slow poison. Oh, I get it."

"Now you get it," said Joby.

"You mean she did something to him that was like a slow poison."

"You get it," said Joby.

"I can see that," said his sister.

"And that's easier to forgive," said Joby. "She didn't put little drops of arsenic in his dessert, or give him cyanide in his cocktail. So that's easy to forgive. You don't believe that there are other forms of poison that don't come out of a bottle."

"Oh, stop talking like an I Don't Know What. A preacher. You're talking like a preacher."

"What do you think of a woman whose husband is an alcoholic, and she puts a drink in front of him every night?"

"Father was cert— I know what you're going to say."

"Yes. You'd agree that a woman like that is a murderess in one form, wouldn't you?"

"Yes."

"Poison—arsenic or cyanide, they're evil. The booze to tempt an alcoholic. You'll agree that that's almost as evil. But why does it have to be whiskey or iodine or something tangible?"

"I think you've had too much of something tangible called Scotch."

"Well, at least I'm drinking it of my own accord. Deliberately. The poison Madam gave Father was much too subtle. But it wasn't so damn subtle that I didn't catch on. And she knows it."

"Is that all you have to go on? She poisoned his mind in some way or other?"

"No, it isn't all I have to go on, Annie, but it should be enough. You loved Father, and anything destructive to him you should have hated. There's more, old girl, but I shall save it for another time."

"You say things to shock me," said Ann.

"Nothing shocks you. Surprises, maybe. But not shocks. I'll bet there isn't an evil, a sin in this world that you haven't heard about."

"Probably not, and that's why you're wrong. Nothing surprises me, but a lot of things shock me. I'd be really shocked if I thought Mother could slow-poison Father over a period of years."

"You would? Why? She hasn't had much time to work on you these past few years, but she's been successful in one thing."

"What thing?"

"She's blinded you."

Ann stood up. "You're getting pretty blind yourself, and not from Mother."

He smiled. "Annie, if you weren't my sister you might solve a lot of my problems."

She smiled back at him. "Dear old boy, you've forgotten about incest."

"That's where you're wrong. That's one of my problems."

"Thanks for the compliment."

"Well, don't think it *isn't* a compliment."

"I'm going back and see if Madam has recovered her fountain pen," said Ann.

"You do that," said her brother. "I think I shall just sit here and consume some more of the Joseph B. Chapin Estate Scotch."

"Dearie, that Scotch does not belong to the Joseph B. Chapin Estate. It happens to be mine."

"So much the better. I shall sit here and think vile thoughts of you."

"As long as you can think, which won't be long."

"Which won't be long, but longer than I care to think. God damn it, I hate to think. Thinking stinks."

Ann nodded. "Yes," she said.

Her mother was sitting with a copy of the county edition of the Gibbsville *Standard* in her lap. "A nice article about Father in the *Standard*," said Edith Chapin.

"Oh, naturally," said Ann. "Mr. Hooker."

"I don't think I care much for the heading. 'Notables Attend Chapin Funeral.'"

"Why?"

" 'Notables,' " said Edith. "Be so much better if they'd just said 'Funeral of Joseph B. Chapin,' without putting that word in the heading. And the article itself starts right out with 'Prominent figures in government, legal and business affairs attended the funeral of—' and so forth."

"But how else would you say it?" said Ann.

46

"Oh, I suppose it's all right," said Edith. "I'm rather weary, we all are, after these past few days. Now there's a letdown. You and Joby and everybody, you've all been a great help to me, and now that the excitement's over, naturally I can expect a letdown."

"Thank you, Mother," said Ann.

Edith acknowledged the thanks with a nod. "I've been wondering what to do, where to start," she said.

"With what?"

"Everything, everything," said Edith. "I'll keep this house. I always intend to live here, the rest of my life, and you and Joby will always have this as your home to come back to. There won't be as much money as with Father alive and earning—substantial fees. But I'll have enough to run this household *pretty* much the way I have. You know how we've always lived. Well within our income except for the money Father—uh—disbursed while he was active in politics. That was costly. Very costly. But it was Father's money, he earned it or inherited it, and I knew he'd never do anything that would jeopardize our welfare, you children's and mine. Twice he dipped into capital, entirely with my approval and consent. And I don't think it would be fair for me to tell you how much, because as it turned out, Father's investments became more valuable during the war, so in the end the, uh, increase in value just about made up for what he spent on politics. Possibly a little more than he made up. He had some very good advice from Paul Donaldson and also from Dave Harrison. And I think Alec Weeks, but not as much from Alec."

She looked up and at a distant, imaginary point. "I never liked Alec Weeks," she went on. "I was very much surprised when he said he'd be a pallbearer."

"Why didn't you like him? I thought you did."

"Ah, you thought I did because I wanted you to. Your father never knew I didn't trust Alec either."

"You didn't trust him?" said Ann.

"That's it. I didn't trust him. He always seemed to me to be one of Father's college friends that—oh, a link with the past, bright college years, but they really had very little in common. Wolf's Head. I've never been able to understand why two years together in a college club should continue to mean so much after a man has grown up. Those dinners in New York, year after year, taking too much to drink and singing those ridiculous songs, and I suppose a lot of toasts to the men who died since the last get-together. I suppose Alec Weeks will propose the toast to your father, next time, and Alec will be looked upon as the true brother who ventured into the wilds of Pennsylvania."

"Well, he can't, because what about Mr. Harrison and Paul Donaldson?"

"They were not in Wolf's Head. I think they were both in Skull & Bones. Anyway, Dave Harrison was, I know. Maybe Paul Donaldson was in the other one, Scroll & Keys."

"Key. Scroll & Key," said Ann. "Why don't you trust Alec Weeks?"

"All that charm, that superficial charm. I'd never met him before our wedding, so there was no reason for him to pretend I was any great belle. I wasn't, and knew it. And when a girl knows that about herself and a man makes a great to-do over her, it's really insulting. Unless the girl is a fool."

"But he might have been sincere."

"No, he wasn't. I knew all about him. Chorus girls and all sorts of women. He left Oxford because he was having an affair with an Italian countess, much older than he was."

"Alec Weeks," said Ann. "You never know."

"Yes, you do. You might not see it now, when he's sixty-three, but anyone with any sense could have told then."

"Do you think I could have, Mother?" said Ann.

"Your—difficulties weren't caused by your not having any sense. You simply allowed your heart to rule your head."

"My head couldn't have been very strong."

"Don't disparage yourself," said Edith Chapin. "Your life hasn't been lived yet, and I'm sure that a lot of good things are in store for you."

"I hope you are right."

"You'll have to help, of course. They won't just happen to you. You've learned, for instance, you've learned that love can be very deceptive. We often use that word when we mean something else. A warm-hearted girl like yourself can talk about love, about being in love, before she knows the meaning of the word. She has no other word to express some deep feeling, so she uses the word love, when actually it isn't love at all. Sometimes it can be pity."

"You still think I pitied Charley."

"Well, at least I don't think you loved him. If you had, your father and I would have known it. We'd have known it from you."

"I tried to tell you."

"And failed, and you wouldn't have failed if it had really been love, Ann. Charley felt passionately toward you and you felt pity for him, his helplessness. Men can be helpless under those circumstances, and a nice girl thinks it's her responsibility, or even her fault. A girl who isn't what we mean by a nice girl wouldn't feel that responsibility. She'd let him suffer, helpless. But that's exactly what you didn't do, and your kindness very nearly ruined your life."

"Very nearly."

"I know. I understand the irony in your voice. You still think we ruined your life, or you like to think that. But you must know when you're being honest with yourself that a marriage with an Italian boy in a jazz band wouldn't have lasted a year."

"If you had let me have the baby, if you and Father had given the marriage a chance. Done half as much to help it as you did to stop it."

"The baby was out of the question, Ann. A baby five months after you were married? How would the child itself explain that in later life? On legal documents, where you have to put down the date of your parents' marriage? To say nothing of your own friends, and for that matter, the father's friends. You know, people of that—class— are just as conservative as the more well-to-do, if not more so."

Ann got up and went to the window. "The last time we talked about this we ended up having a very stormy scene."

"Yes, and you went away and didn't write to me for months."

"I don't want to do that again," said Ann.

"And I hope you don't."

"Then let's stop talking about it now. There isn't a single detail of it I haven't gone over a hundred times. —Oh, not only with you. Stuart never stopped talking about it."

"I'm sorry about that. But it was part of—"

Ann turned quickly and looked at her mother. "Shall we stop now?"

"Why, yes. Of course. I was going to."

"No, the minute you said that a lot of good things were in store for me, I knew what else was in store for me first. A rehash of my first marriage."

Edith Chapin was silent. She waited until her silence became the most noticeable thing in the room, the dominant thing that would have been apparent to a person newly entering the room. When the silence reached that magnitude Edith Chapin ended it. In a higher tone that indicated a new topic of conversation she spoke again to her daughter. "Did we have a cablegram from Cousin Frank Hofman?"

"Not that I know of," said Ann. "Where is he?"

"He's in Buenos Aires. Whit Hofman sent him a cablegram. He was always so fond of Father, and Whit thought he'd want to know."

"I've completely forgotten about him. What does he do?"

"I forget. It must be at least fifteen years since I've seen him."

"I don't even remember what he looks like," said Ann.

"He's very different from the rest of the Hofmans. He's short, and when I last saw him he was quite stout. And I suppose living abroad all these years, someone who has a tendency to put on weight and cares a lot about food and wine—I imagine he's quite portly now. Although that's just a guess on my part."

"Is he married?"

"Not that I know of," said Edith Chapin. "Isn't Whit a dear?"

"Yes, he is."

"It's so seldom you see anyone with all that money who can be so utterly un-self-conscious. He's one of the people I want to have for dinner later on, when things get settled. Next fall. When the summer's over I'm going to start having people in for dinner, once a week. Not more than four or five people at a time."

"I'm glad to hear it."

"Sometimes I'll have to deal in the black market, but I don't see that it's worse to deal in the black market than to take your friends to the club or the hotel. Father didn't agree with that point of view, but he was more or less in politics and that made a lot of difference."

"Everybody buys in the black market," said Ann. "And gas rationing's a joke. Where did that roast beef come from at lunch today? And all those cars."

"The roast beef was perfectly legitimate. The club has always had a catering service."

"Now, Mother," said Ann.

"But it's true. You know that. Whenever we've had a big party we always had Otto, as long as I can remember. He asked me what to serve and I told him I'd leave that entirely up to him. And as far as the cars were concerned, weren't they mostly the undertaker's?"

"Not at our house."

"Well, I thought they were," said Edith Chapin. "But I agree with you. However, what else can you expect from the people in Washington? The waste and extravagance and dishonesty. Your father said it would happen, and it has. And it will continue as long as Roosevelt keeps his power."

"And that will be forever."

"Well, at least until the war's over."

"Five years from now," said Ann.

"At least. Unofficially, the admiral thinks it may be ten years before we finally win in the Pacific."

"Well, I hope he's wrong," said Ann. "Joby thinks five, and even that's too long."

The small talk had not been a complete success and they both were conscious of it. They had been able to agree that Whit Hofman was a dear. The choice of Frank Hofman as a conversational topic had seemed inspired at the moment, but certain aspects of Frank Hofman made him something of a misfit, an irregular, like Ann herself and her brother Joby. The talk of black marketing and the war allowed them to release their bad humor on a nonpersonal subject, but guesses as to the duration of the war took them into another undesirable area. In a war the men are away, and that postpones the chances of courtship and marriage; traditional, conventional courtship and marriage, which meant more to Edith than they did to Ann.

"Much too long," said Edith. "I wonder if I ought to lie down for a few minutes. I'm not tired, but I'm afraid I will be this evening."

"Who's going to be here this evening?" said Ann.

"Uncle Arthur and Aunt Rose McHenry, and Uncle Cartie and you and Joby. That's all. I think I'll just stretch out for a few minutes. I may not sleep, but I'll relax."

"Don't you want to take off your dress?"

"Yes, but I think I'll go down to my bedroom."

"I'll turn down the bed," said Ann.

"Thank you, and then will you tell Mary to come up?" said Edith. "Why don't you have a nap too?"

"I might try," said Ann.

"Then don't bother to come down. Call down to Mary and tell her to come to my room."

"All right, Mother," said Ann. She whistled into the speaking tube and at Mary's "Yes, ma'am," she said, "Mary, will you go to Mother's bedroom, please?"

"I will," said Mary.

Ann saw her mother to the stairs, then went to Joby's room. He was asleep on the counterpane, breathing deeply two notes in a minor key. She put a comforter over him and he did not stir.

W. Carl Johnson, new Superintendent of Schools, had no trouble walking home from the post-funeral lunch. His house was only a block

—a "square," it was called in Gibbsville—from the Chapin residence, and some indication of the intimacy existing between the Chapin and Johnson families was the fact that Edith's note inviting W. Carl Johnson to be a pallbearer was sent to the superintendent's office in the Gibbsville High School building. From Number 10 North Frederick Street to the Johnsons' rented house at Number 107 was actually less than a block, but Edith Chapin had first known Number 107 as the Lawrence property, then as the Reifsnyders', and after that it had been occupied by a succession of clergymen, educators, and engineers who brought their families to Gibbsville during some extended construction work. The house was the property of the Lutheran church, which made for a continuing respectability of tenancy.

The 100-block in North Frederick Street (there were no dwellings on South Frederick, which was only a block long) was abruptly steep after the flat of the block in which the Chapins lived. Cars parked on upper North Frederick were turned toward the curb. An advantage of upper North Frederick Street was that it provided children with a fine hill for coasting during the rather long Gibbsville winter, but that could be said of many Gibbsville streets. In the whole town there was not a street that was level for more than a single block. The Johnsons' neighbors in the 100-block were a railroad engineer, two railroad firemen, a young chiropractor, a Civil War veteran and his maiden nieces, a pharmacist, two salesmen for clothing stores, an insurance adjuster, the manager of an absentee-owned bakery, a state forestry official, a freight clerk for the Pennsylvania Railroad, and a newspaper man. Most of the neighbors were married and took in roomers, who were usually carefully screened. The rooms were rented to men, never to women, and the relationship between landlord and roomer was kept businesslike. Some of the landladies referred to the paying guests as boarders, but meals were not provided, no cooking was permitted in the rooms, and specific arrangements were always made in the case of men who wanted the privilege of getting their own coffee in the early morning. Sometimes the boarder, or roomer, would go for two or three weeks without encountering his landlord or landlady. So long as he left his weekly payment (always in cash) in an envelope on the hall table he was not disturbed, and two weeks was the outside limit for delinquency in rent payment. A testimonial to the screening of roomers was the record of North Frederick Street: fewer than a dozen men had been locked out in thirty years. There had been two suicides, three deaths from natural causes, and one arrest for embezzling, but only nine or ten men had lost their rooms through nonpayment of the modest rates. The record likewise testified to the character of the householders of North Frederick Street.

W. Carl Johnson and his wife Amy had not yet taken in roomers. Johnson's job paid well—$9,000 per annum—and since Amy was quite pretty, without her glasses, and only thirty-seven years of age, extra care would have to be taken in the screening. It was not that Amy was fearful of rape; but appearances still counted for a great deal in Gibbsville, Pennsylvania, and the school superintendent's wife was expected to be so high above reproach that the sex question never must come up. The ideal roomer for the Johnson establishment would have been old and ugly, but there the Johnson daughters became a consideration. Carlotta, eleven, and Ingrid, nine, were pretty children, and as experienced schoolteachers the Johnsons were acquainted with the problem of elderly degenerates.

Amy Johnson was not cognizant of the distinction she had attained as she and her husband made their departure from the Chapin house. It would be days or weeks before she fully realized that there were Gibbsville women—and men—who had wanted all their lives to see the inside of the Chapin home, and she had eaten a meal there in her first year. She took her husband's arm as they walked northward.

"Who was the little man that talked to everybody? He must have been some relation."

"Her brother. Mrs. Chapin's brother," said Carl Johnson.

"The younger man. That was her son."

"Yes. Joseph B. Chapin, Junior," said Carl.

"And the daughter, she never came downstairs, or at least I never saw her."

"I was surprised that Mrs. Chapin herself came down," said Carl.

"Oh, she was a tower of strength, I thought."

"Yes."

"There must have been at least a hundred people there, and she spoke to every one of them. She even remembered my name."

"Well, don't forget she knew most of the people there. We were practically strangers."

"But she didn't make me feel like a stranger. Very friendly. Nice."

"It's an art. I've always said so. I guess I haven't got it."

"Why not?"

"Well, I knew I was out of it in that group, the pallbearers, but I'm as important as Jenkins, or Hooker, or even Judge Williams. At least my job is. I'm the only superintendent of schools. Hooker isn't the only newspaper editor, and Judge Williams isn't the only judge.

And yet when one of those men said a kind word to me I was like a kid being patted on the head."

"They ought to see you with a bunch of teachers."

"Do you know something? Most of those men would seem just as important among a bunch of teachers. That Donaldson. Did you ever hear of him before? No, and neither did I. But I don't know whether you noticed the Governor. When Donaldson said something, the Governor hung on every word. When you get a group like that together they take one look at each other and they know right away who belongs and who doesn't. Maybe they never saw each other before and don't even know what the other does, but there's an American type, or maybe fifty American types, and they're all used to having authority."

"You have, too. It's just a different kind."

"It's so different that I'm damn glad I don't have to exert any authority over any of those men. They'd tell me to go to hell. And I'd go."

"By a different kind of authority I meant that men like that recognize your ability in your field. It isn't a question of whether you can boss them around or not."

"Oh, that. Well, I'm good at my job, sure."

"That's all your supposed to be. If the Governor rushed across the room to light your cigarette—I saw him do that for the lame man—it wouldn't make you feel any better, or more important. You're responsible for the education of almost three thousand kids and your budget is almost half a million dollars, for teachers' salaries alone."

"If you only knew it, honey, you aren't making me feel more important. You're making me feel less. *I'm* not responsible for the education of three thousand kids, and nobody knows that better than you. And as far as my budget is concerned, there were men there today that have incomes, personal incomes, as big as my whole teaching salary item. So calm down, honey. I'm just sore at myself for saying I'd be a pallbearer for a man I hardly knew. I don't like to be used."

"Well, they didn't invite *you*, Waldemar. They invited the Superintendent of Schools. They thought old Chapin was that important, and why complain? You're just as annoyed when people like that *ignore* the school system."

They were at their front door. "Naturally I left my door key in my other suit," said Carl.

"I have mine," said Amy. She took it out of her purse and handed it to him and he opened the door and allowed her to precede him. When he had closed the door he put his hand under her bottom and squeezed.

"Stop goosing me!" she said.

"You thought you were getting away with calling me Waldemar." She smiled. "I wondered if you noticed."

"I warn you, one of these days—right out on the main street. You'll call me Waldemar, and I'll give it to you."

"You do and you'll be sorry," she said. "I wonder how long we'd last here if you ever did."

" 'Why did you leave Gibbsville, Pennsylvania?' Well, you see I was walking along the main drag and my wife called me by my real first name, so I goosed her. She has a nice little ass, only it's not so little any more."

"All right, all right. Do you want a cup of coffee, with saccharin?"

"Yes. I'll go upstairs and change my suit. Do you know why superintendents get more money? Because they have to wear suits all the time, and teachers can wear slacks."

"And change your tie," she said.

"I'll be down in a minute," he said.

"Black ties remind me of funerals."

Amy Johnson put the kettle on, stashed away her coat and hat, and got out the cups and saucers, the spoons, the top-milk, the saccharin bottle. Carl appeared in the kitchen as the water came to a boil. He was carrying his coat and vest, which he draped over the back of a kitchen chair.

"If you weren't a Phi Bete would you wear a vest?"

"If I had a dollar for every time you've asked me that."

"But you always have a different answer," she said.

"Well, let me think of one for this time," he said. "If I didn't have a Phi Bete key, maybe I wouldn't have a vest."

"I've had that answer before."

"I was afraid so," he said. "Well, would I wear a vest if I weren't a Phi Bete? *You* don't wear a vest, you never wear your key. Would *you* wear a vest if you didn't have a Phi Bete key? There is a switch. You have a key, you never wear a vest. If you didn't have the key, would you wear a vest?"

"Have some coffee," she said. "Are you going to the office right away?"

"As soon as I drink my coffee and smoke one cigarette."

"Why don't you hang around a little while longer? The children will be home shortly. You'll probably work late and this would be a good chance to see them."

"Maybe I will," he said.

"You might as well," she said. "You've already put in a day's work, but nobody's going to consider it a day's work, going to an important funeral. Most people would say a schoolteacher should consider himself darn lucky to be with such important people."

"In a way they'd be right," said her husband.

"I refuse to give luck much credit. We've worked hard."

"So have a lot of other men and women we know. Let's just say I'm lucky to have got this far, but not lucky in that I don't seem to have the knack of using people. Brice Conley. Think of what Brice Conley would have done today, with all those big shots."

"Don't forget, part of it would have been Dot Conley. She'd have had them all back to her house."

"Can't you see us entertaining that group? The Governor of the state, the partner in J. P. Morgan and Company, and so forth and so forth."

"No, but I can see Dot and Brice Conley doing it."

"Well, they like to do it, and Brice's job pays twelve thousand and mine pays nine. We're doing what we like to do, and they're doing what they like to do. Three thousand a year difference in their favor, so from the financial point of view what they like to do is three thousand dollars better than what we like to do."

"You'll pass Brice and leave him way behind."

"Maybe, but on a day like today I wish I had more of what Brice has and fewer principles."

"No, you don't."

"No, I don't," said Carl. He inhaled his cigarette and examined it. "What did you have to do to get a pack of Philip Morrises?"

"Mm. Wouldn't you like to know? I got two packs."

"You had to do it twice."

"No, just once. Anybody can get one pack. I got two."

"Oh, proficient," he said.

"Very," she said. "Tomorrow I'm going to get three packs."

"All right," said her husband. "But when he starts giving you a carton, I'm going to complain."

"Why should you complain? You're the one that smokes most of them."

"I know, but it's the principle of the thing. If I could only go out and earn my own cigarettes."

56

"You poor man," said Amy. "You want some more coffee?"

"All right," said her husband.

She poured the coffee and he watched the fragment of saccharin dissolving.

"All right, what's on your mind?" she said.

"What's on my mind? Well—Gibbsville, at the moment. It's an interesting place."

"Why?"

"Of course any town is interesting, but this place is getting to be an interesting experience. It's the only place where we really started from scratch. In college we knew a lot about college beforehand. Columbia, we'd heard about New York and knew quite a little about it. And the other towns where we've worked, either you had some previous connection with it or I did, or both of us did."

"Mm-hmm."

"I'm finding out about this town. It's kind of a bastard town. It's supposed to be a coal town, or at least that's how it was always described for us. But you never see any miners on the streets."

"It's a coal capital, like Scranton."

"Yes. But so many of the so-called first families, they don't seem to have anything to do with coal. Some of them own farms, some own timber land. Small factories. The steel mill. Silk mill. Shirt factories. It's a highly skilled town. The other day I saw a list of college graduates that live here, and there isn't a major college in the East or Middle West that wasn't represented—with one exception. Do you know what that was?"

"Yale."

"Lord, no. It's full of Yale men, but you were close. I couldn't find one graduate of Harvard College. Penn State leads, then Lehigh, because of so many men with engineering training, I guess. Then the University of Pennsylvania, then Yale, and after Yale I think Lafayette or Muhlenberg."

"Anybody from Illinois?"

"Yes, I told you, all the Western Conference."

"Who from Illinois?"

"A man named Sanders, works for the Power & Light Company. He was in the class of '22. I haven't met him yet. He was a Zeta Psi."

"What was this list for?"

"Oh, they're thinking of starting a University Club. They tried it once before, years ago, and it didn't pan out because anybody that could afford a club joined the Gibbsville Club. But now the Gibbsville Club has a waiting list as long as your arm and some fellows would like to have a place to go that isn't the Elks."

"To get away from their wives."

"Very likely, among other reasons."

"And you're going to join this University Club?"

"I haven't said anything either way. In one way the Gibbsville Club would be better for me, but the new one has its advantages too."

"As the Superintendent of Schools you join the Gibbsville Club, but as a nice guy you join the new one. Right?"

"I've been told I can get in the Gibbsville Club through a special dispensation."

"Does the dispensation dispense with dues and initiation?"

"It does not," he said. "But there's a possibility I might not have to pay anything to be a member of the new club."

"Then join that," said Amy.

"No, seriously."

"I'm being serious. That's the one you can afford, and it'll look better for you to be in a club you can afford than one that everybody knows is too expensive."

"You know, you're right," said Carl. "And tell the Gibbsville Club people—"

"That you're getting in the new club for free."

"No, then they'll think I'm hinting for a free membership at the Gibbsville Club."

"Well?"

"No."

"If the Gibbsville Club will make it easy for you to join, they must want you, but you can't afford the expense."

"Maybe I can't afford not to join."

"You weren't a member when they hired you. Problems, problems. But I can't get too excited over this one. How much does the Gibbsville Club cost?"

"I think it's two hundred initiation and a hundred a year."

"Well, that solves that problem. Unless you want to make a few speeches and get paid for them, and then join."

"They'd probably want me to make speeches after I became a member."

"And without paying you. They want you in other words to shell out three hundred dollars to deprive yourself of the opportunity of making yourself a few hundred dollars. The more I think of it, the less I like the Gibbsville Club. What was originally on your mind when we started to talk about Gibbsville?"

"Let me see. Way back?"

"Yes, before we got onto this club stuff, which I can tell you I don't like any part of. Three hundred dollars. Let's make a list of things we could do with three hundred dollars and see how far down the list this club would be. Insurance, dentist, medical bills, clothes for growing children, vacation money, ten dresses for me, four suits for you, income tax, war bonds, new washing machine after the war. The longer I make the list the lower down the club gets."

"They want us to join the country club."

"After the war, if we're still here, then we can discuss the country club. The country club makes some sense. The children can swim there, and play tennis, but let's wait and see if we stay in Gibbsville, this interesting town."

"That's what I was saying."

"I know. We finally got back to it. You were saying something about its being a highly skilled town."

"It is," said Carl. "I imagine Schenectady, New York, is highly skilled, all those electrical engineers and practical men. But this place is interesting because it's diversified, and we weren't led to expect that. Do you know how many breweries there are in this town?"

"A lot."

"Five."

"That is a lot, isn't it?"

"It sure is," he said. "What I've been thinking about is that this town ought to be going places after the war. There'll be a let-down. There always is after a war. But not as bad as if the coal business were the only thing they had to depend on. There'll be a big building program, all over the country, and right here. And what does that mean? How does that affect us? Schools. Bigger and better schools, and being superintendent is going to be a bigger and better job. And it's going to be better, if not bigger, in our field, because with such a high percentage of college-trained and skilled men, education is going to be terribly important. If we were living in a mill town, with most of the people working with their hands, the laboring class—well, you know what that would be. Less interest in education. But every college man wants his children to be college men, and won't settle for less. And they'll take an active interest in education."

"And think they can do it better than you can."

"Let them think it, if they'll let me do it," said Carl.

"This is the first time you've waxed so enthusiastic about Gibbsville. How come? Has it been gestating, or is it sudden?"

"Both. I've been looking, studying, taking walks and talking to people. But I guess what got me started today was going to that funeral. A man that never did much, never really accomplished much, and from what I gather wasn't terribly popular—nevertheless you saw that funeral. Really impressive. I said to myself, 'What if I died? What kind of a turnout would I get?' Put aside the morbid aspects, and by gosh it was a stimulating experience. This is a good town, Amy, and we could do a lot worse than spend the rest of our lives here."

"Maybe."

"Well, can't you show a little enthusiasm? I don't expect much, but a little."

"I'll save my enthusiasm for when you need it. Right now you don't need any extra."

"Oh."

"I did a little thinking today, too, if you want to hear about it."

"Of course I do," he said.

"Well, I put myself in her place, Mrs. Chapin's. A big, respectable turnout, a lot of important people, crowds in the streets, and everything but a brass band. But what has she got? She has no husband, she has a daughter that I understand is a bit of a nymph, and a son that hasn't amounted to anything and probably never will. You were stimulated, but the whole thing depressed me, if you want to know."

"Oh."

"And the worst of it is, I didn't feel any sympathy for her at all."

"I wonder why."

"I know why," she said. "It's because without knowing her at all I got the feeling that she was the strongest person in that family, and that whatever happened was her own doing."

"Her undoing?"

"Her—own—doing. Her fault. I wouldn't like to have her for an enemy, but I also don't want her for a friend."

"Well, I guess that's the girls," said Carl. He called out: "Carlie? Ing? Come give your father a kiss."

"We're in the kitchen, girls," called their mother.

In the kitchen at Number 10, Mary Loughlan was engaged in conversation with Marian Jackson, the cook, and her husband Harry Jackson, butler-chauffeur-manservant. Harry was sitting back in the Morris chair, the most comfortable seat in the room, smoking a semi-bulldog pipe and sipping a well-diluted whiskey from a teacup. He was wearing the trousers of his chauffeur's livery and a white shirt and black necktie. His wife was sitting with her hands crossed at one end of the large table, and Mary Loughlan was at the other end, turning and turning an empty teacup over and over in her hands. "She hasn't shown a sign of strain that I've been able to detect, which is remarkable considering," said Mary Loughlan. "True, she's usually sound asleep the moment her head touches the pillow at night, but—"

"How do you know that?"

"How do I know that? The years I've been in service. I can tell more by the crushings and the contours of a pillow in the morning how a person slept than most people that occupied the same room and indeed the same bed. Ask Marian if that isn't true."

"It's true," said Marian Jackson.

"There's very little a person can't tell if she uses her powers of observation that the good Lord gave her. The condition of a bed in the morning holds very few secrets, and since I've been with her and the late lamented, the years were very interesting ones from that point of view."

"You should have been a house detective," said Harry Jackson.

"In a manner of speaking, that's what I have been," said Mary Loughlan. "Ask your wife if that isn't so."

"Yes," said Marian.

"I could almost put a date on when they discontinued the relation between man and wife."

"Put a date on it," said Harry.

"I can't now, but I could of then," said Mary. "And it wasn't when they took to the twin beds. It was some time after."

"Did you know that?" Harry asked his wife.

"Mm-hmm, at the time."

"How often did J. B. get up in the night to make his water?" said Harry.

"There's no necessity to be vulgar, Harry," said Mary. "No necessity for that, at all. But I could of told you that, too."

"Come on. How many times he got up during the night?"

"I knew he was having trouble with his kidneys, didn't I, Marian?"

"Mm-hmm."

"You could tell that from the condition of the bed?"

"I didn't say that, but Marian and I knew, didn't we, Marian?"

"How?"

"Let Marian tell you when I'm not present. I don't care to continue the discussion," said Mary. "Early breakfast for Joby. He's leaving on the seven-five train in the morning. He won't want much in the way of solid food, but strong coffee."

"The drunken pup."

"Well, it's a wonder to me it didn't happen long before this," said Mary. "At that it's better upstairs in his own room away from everybody than as if it was the Gibbsville Club or the hotel bar or other places I could think of. And at least it put him to sleep instead of giving him the prowls. Him prowling about the town on this night of all nights, that would be the last straw. Then he *would* hear from her. This way she's putting up a great pretense of total ignorance of his condition. She knows, but she won't let on. She doesn't have much to rely on—though credit where credit's due. Ann Chapin is the pleasantest surprise I've had these past four days. I give her full marks for proper conduct."

"What did you expect her to do?" said Harry.

"What I expected her to do is so far different than what she's surprised me by doing that the two don't compare. Yes, Ann Chapin Musgrove, I give you credit. There's good stuff in you after all, even if it takes a thing like this to bring it out."

"Good stuff, good stuff. I've known this family all my life. Sure there's good stuff on both sides," said Harry.

"Did you hear me say anything to the contrary?" said Mary.

"I don't like you criticizing," said Harry.

"Who was it only a moment ago called the boy a drunken pup?"

"I'm talking about Ann. It took you since you been working here to find out about her," said Harry.

"Ann's his soft spot," said Marian. "Never say anything against Ann when Harry's around."

"It's my recollection that I gave her credit for having good stuff in her," said Mary.

"The first time you ever said anything good about her, the first time since you been in this house," said Harry.

"Relax yourself, Harry Jackson," said Mary.

"I'm glad I got something better to do than look at bedsheets," said Harry.

"Now, now. Now, now, now, now, now. Don't get too personal there, my man. Don't get too personal. Have your favorite, if you like, and all well and good. But no personal remarks, and don't try to deprive me of my right to express my opinions, because nobody is going to tell Mary Loughlan to shut up, and nobody's going to tell Mary Loughlan how she's going to think about a person. Right, Marian?"

"Everybody should calm down," said Marian.

The speaking-tube whistle sounded. "Now what?" said Mary Loughlan going to the outlet. "Yes, ma'am," she said.

"Mary, will you go to Mother's bedroom, please?" said Ann.

"I will," said Mary Loughlan.

She looked at the Jacksons. "Speaking of the devil, or I should say, speaking of the angel," she said. "I'm wanted up on high."

Number 15, which usually left Gibbsville for Philadelphia at 4:10 in the afternoon, was held for fifteen minutes because of the unscheduled visit of Edith Chapin with the luncheon guests. The Messrs. Weeks, Kirkpatrick and Harrison and the admiral were taking Number 15, onto which was coupled the private car of the president of the line, and in which they were riding to Philadelphia. Kirkpatrick, the only Philadelphian, invited Harrison and Weeks and the admiral to dine with him at the Union League, but Harrison and Weeks said they were going to New York and the admiral was proceeding to Washington. The admiral was met by a Navy car; Kirkpatrick took a taxi home, and Harrison and Weeks were greeted by a personable young man whom they did not know, but who knew them. He escorted them to a black Lincoln limousine in which Weeks was first driven to the Broad Street Station, after which Harrison was taken to the Philadelphia Club. Harrison joined two Philadelphia friends, and the personable young man, who was a member, went upstairs and whiled away the time in a game of Sniff.

Weeks arrived at his apartment in East Seventy-first Street at the end, the noisy end, of a cocktail party. As chance would have it, he was acquainted with none of the eight or ten men and women in the foyer of his apartment, and those who looked at him gave him the blank look that greets the strange late-comer to a party of that sort. He went up the winding stairs to his bedroom. The door was closed. He opened it and a man in his middle thirties was standing beside Weeks's dressing table, changing his clothes. He was wearing a white shirt and a black four-in-hand tie, and the trousers of a tuxedo.

"Oh, hello, Mr. Weeks," he said.

"Oh, hello, there."

"Mrs. Weeks said it would be all right if I changed my clothes here."

"Sure, by all means," said Weeks. There was an oddly shaped piece of luggage on the floor, besides the calfskin Gladstone on the bed.

"I told her I could work if I didn't wear my uniform, so I brought my tux and changed here."

"I see," said Weeks, and he did see. Now he recognized the man as an accordion-player frequently to be encountered in New York and on Long Island.

"Nice party."

"Glad to hear it," said Weeks. "I guess I just about made it, myself."

"This looks good for another hour at least, but I told Mrs. Weeks, I gotta hit the sack early. She understood."

"Well, I'm sorry I didn't get here while you were still playing."

"A couple quiet choruses of 'Rose Room,' Mr. Weeks?"

"No, no thanks," said Weeks.

"How's Mr. Clark these days?"

"Fine, fine. Couldn't be better," said Weeks.

"You and Mr. Clark, you're the only ones that can stick me on those old tunes."

"Well, he's much better than I am."

"Oh, it's pretty close. You know quite a few he can't remember."

"Not so many. Would you like a drink before you go?"

"Uh—well, I'll have one with you."

"Scotch is all I have here," said Weeks.

"Well, I guess you know I'd rather have Scotch than anything else."

"I guess we'll have to do without ice," said Weeks. There was a cut-glass decanter on the dressing table and two glasses. They filled the glasses with whiskey and water from the bathroom faucet.

"All the best, Mr. Weeks."

"The best," said Weeks. He drank, and lit a cigarette. "Been to a funeral. I never go to funerals, or I say I never go to funerals. Seems to me I go to a lot of them these days."

"Yeah," said the man. His tuxedo was in the Gladstone and he was now in his uniform blues.

"All the way to Pennsylvania and back in one day. Not the best thing for a man my age."

"Pennsylvania. I've worked in that state all right. Plenty. And my first wife came from there."

"Is that so?" said Weeks.

"Practically a one-nighter, we'd call it in the band business. Nothing against the girl, but God, her family. God, did they give it to me.

But I don't want to talk about that." He put on his cap. "Shoving off."

"You've—been taken care of?"

"Oh—yes indeed, thanks. Mrs. Weeks, always there with that check, you know. And always generous."

"Good. Thanks for coming, and see you soon, I hope."

"Right, Mr. Weeks. And cheer up. *You* know."

"Absolutely," said Weeks.

The man departed, toting his bags, and Weeks sat down and took off his shoes and put on a pair of cracked patent-leather pumps. The hall door was knocked on and his wife came in.

"Hello, dear," he said.

"Hello, darling," she said. She kissed his forehead and cheek. "Are you going to join us, or are you tired? I heard you were home."

"I may stay up here, unless they know I'm here," he said. "Say, what's the name of that fellow, the accordion-player?"

"Charley. Charley Bongiorno."

"That's it. I was almost sure of the first name, but I can never remember the last."

"I told him he could change here. He's perfectly trustworthy, and nice."

"Oh, sure. I just couldn't remember his name. Nice fellow. What about dinner? Are there people staying for dinner?"

"I haven't asked anyone. I can."

"No, no."

"They'll all be gone very soon, and we can have dinner here, or would you like to go to 21 or some place?"

"I've got a lot of work."

"I'll get rid of those that are left and we can have dinner by ourselves. Was it an ordeal?"

"Well, it was no pleasure trip."

"How was Edith Chapin?"

"Oh—splendid, of course. Splendid."

"Aren't you being a little splendid too? About her?"

Weeks smiled. "Touché," he said. "Edith never liked me and never will, but at least I'll never have to see her again." Softly he whispered a few bars of "Rose Room."

The Governor, his private secretary, Henry Laubach, and Mike Slattery were having coffee and homemade doughnuts in the small cardroom at the Gibbsville Club.

"Mike, you're putting me on the spot."

"On the Chernowski matter?" said Slattery.

"I can't pardon him, and I should think you'd know that. Have you read everything on him?"

"No, I haven't," said Slattery.

"Have you read *any* of the testimony, or the appeal stuff?"

"No," said Slattery.

"Whose word are you taking?" said the Governor.

"Legally? A local man. Good lawyer. He said a pardon can be justified."

"I'm told the contrary," said the Governor. "Who wants this pardon?"

"A couple of our fellows. It's important, Governor. There's a second-generation Polish vote here, you know. You and I, we're liable to make the mistake of thinking the Poles are just illiterate miners. But that's not so any more. I saw the figures the other day for how many Polish boys are in the armed forces. I mean in this country, Governor. This was an accurate list, compiled from church records, so we didn't lose track of boys that Americanized their last names. We'd like to see Chernowski get a pardon. It'd be a great thing for our side."

"I'll have to think it over a little more, but I'll be frank with you, I don't want to encourage you."

"I see," said Slattery. "What about the Schneider matter?"

"That's the—" The Governor's secretary spoke.

"I know," said the Governor. "Motor Vehicles. I might be able to do something for you there, Mike."

"We'd appreciate that," said Slattery.

"Have we got anything we'd like to take up with *Mike?*" the Governor asked the secretary.

"No, sir," said the secretary.

"I was afraid of that," said the Governor. "Mike, you always have everything under control, or nearly always, so consequently when you ask for something it's difficult to turn you down. I'm sorry about this Chernowski business. Now then. When are you and Mrs. Slattery coming to dinner with us at the Mansion?"

"We were hoping we could get you to have dinner with us while you're in town."

"I have to be in Erie tomorrow, sorry to say, but you thank her for me. How are all your daughters?"

"Fine, thank you," said Slattery.

"Henry, anything I can do for you?" said the Governor.

"I don't think so, thank you. I'd like to put in an extra word for Mike on the Chernowski pardon, but I guess that's a lost cause."

"Well, not entirely lost. The man's in for life, so don't give up." The Governor had a habit of patting his knee rapidly when annoyance was setting in. He now patted his knee rapidly. "Joe Chapin pretty well fixed?"

"Edith'll have over a million," said Slattery.

"Net?"

"Net," said Slattery.

"Well, she's lucky. It would have taken that and more to elect Joe to the job I have. Why did he want it so much?"

"The honor," said Slattery. "And there was a lieutenant governor in his family tree, back in 1830, 1840, somewhere around there. Joe had other ideas, too, I think."

"Such as?"

"What every American boy aspires to," said Slattery.

"Not this American boy," said the Governor. "When I finish my term I'm going back to Erie and *stay* there."

"Don't like to hear that kind of talk, Governor," said Slattery.

"Mike, you don't have to horseshit me. I want to live a little while longer, watch my grandchildren grow up. I'll have a roomful of souvenirs, and my name on some iron tablets, and I'll be in the record books as Governor. All I have to do is keep out of prison a little while longer and then I can sit back and relax. Any son of a bitch that thinks he'd like to be President of the United States ought to try being Governor of Pennsylvania for a few years. Tom Dewey may like his job, but I don't understand him anyway. So Joe Chapin—did he think he had a chance?"

"He never came right out and said so," said Slattery.

"I didn't realize he had such ambitions," said Laubach. "Governor, yes. But President?"

"Well, at least he had as much chance of being President as he did Governor," said Slattery.

"Amen," said the Governor. "I guess Mike's right, even though he was being sarcastic. I guess this country's full of guys that secretly wish they could be President. I wonder why I never did. I guess the governorship looked so far away that the White House was way out of sight. You know something? This conversation relaxes me. I'm beginning to realize, really realize, that I actually did fulfill my life ambition. Very relaxing. Yeah, but now I'll start thinking maybe if

I'd had an ambition to be President, maybe I could have made that. Gentlemen, you have just seen a man bitten by the presidential bug, and if you call yourselves friends of mine, you'll see to it that I never even get a favorite son nomination. I mean it."

"We may not respect your wishes in the matter," said Slattery.

"Now, Mike," said the Governor. "Now, Mike."

"The party may need you," said Slattery.

"Mike, if you don't cut that out I may double-cross you on the Schneider proposition. I want to retire while I can still walk around a golf course and stand up in a trout stream. But imagine Joe Chapin. Gentleman Joe. Did Joe go to Harvard?"

"Yale," said Slattery. "Penn Law School."

"Not even Harvard Law School. Always thought of Joe as a Harvard man, but I guess there are quite a few of the same type at Yale. Always polite, trying to have a good time, but always making you think perhaps your fly was open or your necktie was crooked."

The secretary spoke: "Governor, you asked me to remind you when it—"

"You're right. Gentlemen, a great pleasure to see you again and I wish I could sit here and chew the rag some more, but I have to move along. Henry, drop in when you're over in Dauphin County. Be sure and do that. And Mike, you going to be at that meeting in Philadelphia next week?"

"Oh, sure, the good Lord willing," said Slattery.

They shook hands and put on their coats. "Reed, get me a copy of Bob Hooker's paper to read in the car. Can we get one downstairs? I don't want to stop at his office, because that'll mean another hour and I want to take a nap in the car."

"They'll have a copy downstairs," said Slattery. "The club gets a half a dozen copies. Good-bye, Governor, and thanks again for coming over. I won't say Joe would have appreciated it, but on a more practical basis, it was a good thing for local solidarity."

"A very fine thing," said Laubach. "Joe was a real party man, and the rank and file like to see that fact recognized."

"That's why I did it," said the Governor. "So long, gentlemen."

"We'll walk to the car with you," said Slattery. "It makes us look good, you know."

"Mike, you're a smooth Irishman," said the Governor.

"Yep. One of those bright young immigrant boys," said Slattery. "If you don't look out, pretty soon we'll be running the place."

"What are you talking about? You do now," said the Governor.

68

He waved and was driven away. Slattery and Laubach watched the official limousine until it passed Sixth Street, two and a half blocks away, then they returned to the clubhouse.

"He'll take care of the Schneider matter, but on the Chernowski matter we're licked, and licked good. Somebody else got to him first. That's the kind of thing a man loses sight of when he gets to be Governor."

"What's that, Mike?"

"The implications, the far-reaching effects. I don't worry about Chernowski's own parish. I leave that to the ward guy. But I could sure use a nice big gesture to show the Catholic vote and so-called foreign vote. You know, Henry, by rights this ought to be a solid Democratic county. Working people. Foreign-born or second-generation. We've been *stealing* this county from the Democrats because we had an organization. But now *they* have an organization and it's on the move. By the way, that fellow in Washington, I hear he's a sick man."

"So I heard," said Laubach.

"This Harry S. Truman. I don't know much about him, and you can be darn sure if I don't, the people don't. Colorless. Inconsequential. We can worry about him when the time comes. Meanwhile, I'm asked to deliver without a heck of a lot of help from the Governor's Mansion, and it isn't easy."

"I appreciate that, Mike," said Laubach.

"Let's go over and say hello to Billy English," said Mike.

The old gentleman was sitting in his chair at one of the large plate-glass windows on the street side of the reading room. His arms rested on the chair-arms, his hands hung over the edges of the arms and opened and closed as though he were beating time to silent music.

"Good afternoon, Billy," said Henry Laubach.

"Ah, good afternoon. Who is that?"

"Henry Laubach, and Mike Slattery."

"Billy," said Slattery.

"Hello there, Mike. Henry. Take a seat," said the doctor. "Well, Joe's gone. Another dear face passed on. Since I've had this trouble with my eyesight I always seem to think of people as faces. I haven't been able to teach myself to recognize people by their voices. I'll miss Joe."

"Yes," said Laubach.

"Since I've been living here at the club, Joe and I took lunch together once a week, every Friday, unless he was out of town or in court. Kept me up to date on what was going on, and usually he used to read a few articles out of the *Time* or the *Newsweek*, items of interest I couldn't get on my little radio." He clasped his hands together, gently rubbing the signet ring with the indistinguishable crest that he always had worn (except when he was operating). "Once a month I'd go over to Frederick Street for dinner. About once a month, Edith'd have me. Always remember their kindness to me when Julian died. And of course Mrs. English. This trouble I have with my eyesight—I would have liked to have seen young Joby and Ann. I brought them into the world, you know."

"That's right, you did, didn't you?" said Laubach.

"Yes. Ann arrived a little sooner than we expected. She was what you might call an early bird. Three o'clock in the morning. Joby, I think Joby was sometime in the afternoon. But Ann, she cost me a night's sleep. I've said that to her many times. They had the same Marian working for them that's working for them now, and she telephoned me and said she'd keep an eye on Edith, and Harry, their man, he was at my front door with the car by the time I finished dressing. Big Pierce-Arrow with the headlights on the fenders. Do you remember them?"

"Yes," said Mike Slattery. "Yes, indeed."

"Mike, you had one of those," said the doctor.

"No, the first big car I ever owned was a Cadillac I bought from Julian."

"That's right, that's right. I remember."

"I had a Pierce-Arrow," said Laubach. "My father's."

"That was it, that was it," said the doctor. "Now that's interesting. I just knew, I was sure one of you fellows owned a Pierce-Arrow, and I gave it to the wrong one. I couldn't afford one. They ate up too much gas. Well, gentlemen, I think I'll go upstairs now for a minute. Henry, would you like to give me your arm to the elevator? I can find it all right, but as long as I have a friend here."

"Of course," said Laubach.

"Good-bye, Mike," said the doctor.

"Good-bye, Billy," said Slattery.

"Always like to listen to the news program," said the doctor.

Mike Slattery waited in the main hall while Henry Laubach escorted Dr. English to the elevator.

"Mike," said Arthur McHenry, coming toward him from the billiard room.

"Hello, Arthur."

"Would you be interested in three rubbers?"

Mike Slattery hesitated. "Not unless you need a fourth."

"We need a third and a fourth. I saw you and Henry, and Lloyd Williams and I thought we could get you two."

"See how Henry feels about it. I'll do whatever he wants to," said Slattery. "Henry, Arthur wants to play some bridge."

"Have you got a fourth?" said Laubach.

"Lloyd Williams," said McHenry.

"I think I'd better say no, Arthur. Thanks, but I'd like to stop at the office a minute and catch up on my mail."

"I don't know why it is, but whenever I try to arrange a bridge game for Lloyd Williams, my friends have to catch up on their mail. I wish somebody'd write to me sometime." Arthur McHenry smiled.

"Play him some pool," said Mike.

"I'm going to have to," said Arthur McHenry.

"Well, you got him in here. He's your responsibility," said Henry Laubach.

"I am well aware of that," said McHenry. He rejoined Judge W. Lloyd Williams, who was watching a pool game from a high chair. "No luck, Lloyd. Henry and Mike are off to their offices. It's pretty hard to pick up a game at this time of day. Most of the fellows play in regular foursomes."

"Play it off the six-ball," said the judge. "It'll kiss in."

"I don't think so," said the pool-player whom the judge was advising.

"Sure it will," said the judge. "It's practically dead."

"Dead?" said the pool-player.

"Well, not dead, but it's an easy shot. Use high right-hand English and you'll break up that pile. Do you want me to show you? I'll bet you five dollars I can make it."

"No bet," said the player. He took a shooting stance and played the shot. As the judge had predicted, the object ball kissed off the six-ball and into the pocket, and the pile was broken.

"See?" said the judge.

"You were right," said the player. "But now what do I play? I'm safe."

"Well, you didn't hit it hard enough. You should have slammed into it," said the judge. "What were you saying, Arthur?"

"No luck on the bridge game."

"What about Laubach and Slattery?" said the judge.

"They're leaving."

"Yeah. Don't feel like it. They wanted something out of the Governor, but they didn't get it, whatever it was. I think I know what it was, too," said the judge. "Play the twelve, play the twelve. Don't play the cock-up now. Save it."

"Pardon me, Judge, but this is a tournament match," said the player.

"Is it?" said the judge.

"I just want to call your attention to the sign," said the player.

"I didn't notice it. What does it say? 'Silence is Requested During Tournament Matches.' Excuse me. Come on, Arthur. We're too noisy." The judge got up and went to the reading room, followed by McHenry.

"How often do they have these tournaments?" said the judge.

"Once a year," said McHenry.

"I guess it's too late for me to enter this year, but next year, from what I've seen I could win it. Those fellows we were watching, I could spot them fifty to thirty easily. At the Collieryville Elks we had at least ten better shots than those fellows. Care for a cigar?"

"No thanks," said McHenry.

"A drink? I'll buy you a drink."

"No, I had two before lunch and I'll probably have one before dinner. You have one, though."

"Aah, I don't want to drink alone. I had three at the Chapins'. That's an old mausoleum, that house. I was never inside the place before. If the widow wants to get rid of it she won't have any trouble selling it for a funeral home."

"I don't think she plans to sell," said McHenry.

"Oh, she'll sell all right, if she gets her price. That's a shrewd woman. I know she's a friend of yours, and that's nothing against her. I see enough helpless widows, so when I see one that can stand on her own two feet, my hat's off to her. Edith. You know who she reminds me of? You remember the Basso case? That whore that got Basso to strangle his wife? I know the Chapin woman's respectable, naturally, but—well, she's a friend of yours. We won't pursue it. How old would she be, Edith Chapin?"

"Fifty-nine."

"She get Joe's money?"

"Most of it," said McHenry.

"Mm-hmm. Quite a little money for a woman as healthy as she

is. She won't just sit around, not for long. Now you know what a woman like that ought to do? She won't do it. She's too respectable, and this is too small a town. But if we weren't all such hypocrites what she ought to do is pick out some bright young fellow in his last year at law school. Some handsome young law-review guy. She sets him up, furnishes him with an office and books, secretary. Gets him off to a good start. If she wants to sleep with him, that'd be in the bargain. I've known a few young guys that went to bed with women twice their age for a lot less than what I'm talking about. And history—boy, history's full of them. And I don't see the harm in it. She gets her little thrill, and the young fellow doesn't have to struggle along on nothing. I'm talking about a brilliant young guy, not just a stupid hack."

"But a brilliant young guy wouldn't need that kind of help," said McHenry.

"That's where you're wrong. The brilliant young guys need it more than the others. The brilliant young guys, what happens to them? They get offers from big firms and they're swallowed up. I mean the kind of a guy that comes out of law school and ought to be trying cases before the Supreme Court, but instead of that he's buried in some big firm."

"I don't think I agree with you, Lloyd."

"I didn't expect you to. I don't expect anybody to, but I'm telling you, it's a fair bargain. All she does is support him till he gets established. Why is it so much worse for a young guy to sleep with an elderly woman than a young girl to go to bed with an elderly man? You look around this club. You know yourself, half the members of this club are giving money to young girls for some kind of satisfaction."

"Half? That's pretty high."

"Arthur, your own friends are doing it, and you know it."

"No, I *don't* know it," said McHenry. "I suppose there are two or three . . ."

"You think I have a dirty mind. Well, I don't give a God damn what you think, or anybody else. Nothing personal. I just see what I see and I don't shut my eyes to it. There were sixteen men pall-bearers for Joe Chapin today. What would you risk on how many of them never had a young girl after the age of forty? If you want to know what my guess would be, my guess would be that Doc English and Mike Slattery were the only ones that never went to bed with a young girl after he got to the age of forty. I don't think

Slattery was ever in bed with any woman except his wife. And Doc English—well, the old story of doctors and nurses. With me they're guilty till proven innocent."

"You can't include me in that list," said McHenry.

"I should have stated, present company excepted. I'm protesting innocence myself, too."

"Jenkins, from the bank."

"Jenkins! He's so holy that I suspect him automatically."

"I'm afraid you have a very low opinion of your fellow man."

"I was assistant district attorney three times, district attorney twice, Army in the first World War, and brought up in a patch, not to mention private practice and what I've seen since I was elected judge. My opinion of my fellow man is that the man that reaches fifty without ever doing time—has been lucky. I don't care who he is, and myself included. That fellow I was telling how to play his pool shots—how far away was he from second-degree murder? I've come to the conclusion that the safest way to live is first, inherit money. Second, marry a woman that will co-operate in your sexual peculiarities. Third, have a legitimate job that keeps you busy. Fourth, be born without a taste for liquor. Fifth, join some big church. Sixth, don't live too long."

"I know somebody that—"

"Sure you do. Joe Chapin. Who else did you think I had in mind? Seventh, figuratively speaking, carry a rabbit's foot. That includes Joe Chapin, too. Luck. There but for the grace of God go I. Sometimes I sit up there in my courtroom and a case'll come along and the defendant reacted so much like the way I would in the same circumstances—why, it's like a good detective story, I'm so anxious to see how it comes out. The people smell better in this club than they did where I learned to shoot pool, and they've learned some restraint. But there isn't a hell of a lot of difference between the guy that politely shut me up and some bohunk that would wrap a cue-stick around my neck. You know what's going on all over the world, right this minute?

"People are killing each other, and getting medals for it. First they're trained to do it, taught to do it skillfully, given enough time to learn how to be a bricklayer or some minor trade. Then they're ordered to kill. Kill, take away human life. Kill. I hate that word. And I'm not deluding myself. I kill when I send a man to the electric chair, and I knew I was going to do it when I ran for judge. Yes, I have a pretty low opinion of my fellow man. He's just as evil as I

74

am, and that's saying plenty. But I'm a judge, thanks to the kindness of my fellow man and Mike Slattery. My fellow man and Mike Slattery very wisely decided that they would be safer if they put me on the bench, where I couldn't do as much harm as I would running loose. I have to know what's in certain books, and go by what it says. That way the people are pretty well protected from my evil inclinations. Before a man is elected judge he ought to be examined for criminal tendencies, and if he has enough of them he ought to be qualified. Now you, Arthur, you'd make a lousy judge."

McHenry smiled. "By your standards, I hope so, thank you."

"I shall now proceed to break a law by getting moderately intoxicated. Clear head in the morning, remembering everything in the books. But I shall take in enough alcohol to cause me to be unfit to drive a motor vehicle, then while under the influence of the alcohol I shall drive said motor vehicle to my domicile in Collieryville. No one will know that I am intoxicated, but I'll know that my reflexes and my vision will not be unimpaired. If I were one of those show-off judges I would long since have signed an order taking away my driver's license. There's always a show-off judge in Los Angeles, California, or Toledo, Ohio, fining himself for violation of a parking ordinance. Arthur, have I given you any ideas to chew over?"

"A great many," said McHenry.

"Just bear in mind, I'm a patch lad exposed to book learning. That can make for a great deal of discontent, because now I'm a patch lad to the educated, and an educated man to the patch lads."

"Lincoln was a kind of patch lad, educated patch lad. That ought to be some kind of consolation."

"Take it from me, it isn't," said Williams. "Every self-made son of a bitch in the United States of America compares himself with Lincoln. It's an overworked comparison. But I *have* given you some ideas to chew on. That's good. If I can't be popular, at least I can make an impression. Court is adjourned."

"You're leaving, Judge?"

"Yes, and one thing more, Arthur. You got me in this place and I appreciate it. I always wanted to belong to this club. But don't think you have to take the rap for me. Now that I'm a member, you know, I can stand on my own two feet. If they want to kick me out, you let them. I release you from all responsibilities implied or real. Nothing like me has happened to this club since young English wrecked the joint, fifteen-twenty years ago."

"Perhaps they need a little shaking. What about that drink you were talking about?"

"The hotel bar. I'm told the place is full of twenty-dollar whores these days."

"So I've heard," said McHenry. He helped the judge with his coat.

Williams put his hand on McHenry's shoulder. "Arthur, you may not be the greatest lawyer since Fallon, but you always have one or two surprises up your sleeve. And you're a good fellow."

"Thank you, Lloyd," said McHenry.

The judge's car was parked free of charge in the lot across Lantenengo Street from the hotel. It was a small graft that the judge accepted as part of the honor of being judge, and in using the lot as his downtown parking place he considered that he had bestowed an honor on the place. He did not accept free gasoline, oil, car washing, tires, flashlights or other goods and services. The fact that the judge used that lot was an endorsement and an advertisement, and a mutually satisfactory arrangement. The same space was always reserved for the judge, and he did not have to tip the boys. A pleasant greeting was all that was expected. (It was not likely that the owners would ever ask the judge for a major favor, but if they did he would take his custom elsewhere, and if he were to do that the owners would lose prestige. And, of course, it was possible that a telephone call from the judge might remind the police department that the parking-lot owners illegally obstructed sidewalk and street traffic throughout the day and part of the night. A judge is the only official who is universally feared by police officers; the only official who can give them orders and even make fools of them with impunity, and at the same time remain vaguely on their side.)

Lloyd Williams was not on his way to look at the twenty-dollar whores in the hotel bar, but he was not unwilling to allow Arthur McHenry to think along those lines. Lloyd Williams was a calculating man. His dress, in an era of double-breasted suits and real or imitation hand-painted neckties, was conspicuously inconspicuous. He habitually wore a three-button single-breasted suit of dark gray worsted, including, except on the hottest days of summer, the vest. He wore plain white shirts with soft collar attached and neckties of black or blue, and black calfskin shoes of simple design. He wore no jewelry, of any kind, and his wristwatch was a gold one, cushion-shaped, that had a strap that needed a stitch or two. He never put his hat on quite straight, and the crown was changed in shape from wearing to wearing, and oftener than not a wisp or a lock of hair stuck out from under the hat at the forehead or the temple. His over-coat was a three-button model, dark blue, and half the time the collar was turned up on one side and wrinkled under on the other. All of his clothing was of good material and workmanship, all bought off the hanger at a Gibbsville men's store, none of it cheap or second-rate, and he achieved what he set out to do: through extreme care he gave the impression of a man who cared nothing about clothes; or for ceremony, or for side. It was hard to avoid dressing like a motor magnate, when the stores were offering cheaper versions of the motor magnates' suits and neckwear, but Williams managed it. And nothing he wore diverted attention from the man who was doing the wearing.

His car was a 1940 Buick four-door sedan, plain black and with a radio and a heater, but with no other optional equipment. The citizens had to know it was his car, and not guess it by any special license plate, by initials on the doors, or by official or other badges. The car was as carefully unpretentious as his clothes.

"Hello, Tom. Keeping you busy?"

"Pretty busy, Judge," said the parking attendant. He did not offer to start the car or move it from its accustomed place to open the door for the judge. He knew better. The judge unparked his own car and drove it away.

He carefully obeyed all ordinances. He was a good driver, con-siderate and well co-ordinated. At only one point did he depart from any rule or regulation involving courtesy or consideration: in the 1900-block on Market Street he sounded his horn: one long and two short. There was no apparent reason for blowing the horn.

But he did it every afternoon, in the 1900-block on Market Street.

As a young man, as a law student, and as a young lawyer getting started, Lloyd Williams drank with the boys, whoever the boys of the moment might be. He was able to take in more alcohol with less inebriating effect than spirits had on his drinking companions, and he was respected for that ability. He did not have to drink every day to maintain his reputation as a drinking man, but the reputation followed him through life. In cigar-store discussions he was held up as the example of the brilliant lawyer who drank, just as a couple of doctors were cited as drinking surgeons. In Lloyd Williams's case the drinking was a political asset; he was a man, not a hypocrite, and another part of the asset was his reputation for being quite a man with the women. In his youth the drinkers were the patrons of the better whorehouses, and Williams himself went along with the boys in that activity. In any single year he was likely to go to one of the better whorehouses often enough to be welcome and respected, but in no single year did his visits to whorehouses number more than fifteen. There were other men, less conspicuous men, who went to a whorehouse every Saturday night, or every payday, but Lloyd Williams was hardly ever an inconspicuous man, and whatever he did was magnified. He acquired his reputation for success with women on little more than a monthly visit to a whorehouse, but the reputation was not confined to association with whores. Men somehow believed that all women interested Williams, and many women joined the men in that belief.

His reputation as a hellraiser flourished and was helped by the fact that he married rather late in life. And yet no one ever bothered to inquire too deeply into the renown as drinker or womanizer. Men assumed that because they got drunk with Williams, Williams had been drunk too; they assumed that because he went to bed with whores, he was going to bed with mysterious mistresses who were not being paid. In fact, in the presence of non-whores, Williams was the shyest of men, but even that characteristic was taken to be part of tactics and great discretion.

When finally, at forty-one, he married, the choice he made did nothing to disillusion his friends. Lottie Williams was a childless widow of his own age, a Gibbsville girl whose first husband died in the great influenza epidemic of 1918 while serving as a sergeant in the Quartermaster Corps, Frankford Arsenal. Lottie Danner and Jimmy Franklin had been a high school romance and an ideal one: Lottie, a girl with a startlingly flawless complexion, beautiful teeth, and wavy auburn hair, and somewhat on the stout side, had a contralto voice that kept all other girls out of singing competition for the four years she attended high school; Jimmy had the quick reflexes and spare build of the natural athlete and starred in baseball, basketball and sprint events and was good enough to win two letters in football. After high school and his failure to make big league baseball, he played town ball, semiprofessionally, but devoted himself chiefly to beer, drinking it and selling it. He attended all sports events in the area, and in the beginning his brewery employers encouraged his interest with an expense account. But his usefulness as a good-will representative came to an end with a succession of fist fights. He was partisan to a degree; he bet large sums and did not always pay off when he lost; he was suspected of bribing a participant in a high-stake pigeon-shooting match. By the time he joined the Army he had been a bartender, house man in a poolroom, auto salesman, political hustler, bill collector, insurance salesman, sewing-machine salesman, and private detective. Most of his jobs had been obtained through the intercession of Mike Slattery, who had admired his athletic ability in high school and who even then was building a personal political organization. During the years of unsteady employment Jimmy refused to permit Lottie to take a job, but within a month of his death she was at work as a millinery saleslady and within two years of it she had her own shop on Second Street, just outside the high-rent district. The Danners were solid, respectable people; Lottie's father was a letter carrier, prominent in the anti-Catholic fraternal organizations. Lottie was called Lottie Danner for most of the years of her marriage to Jimmy Franklin; they were a small-town version of two theatrical celebrities who have married but retain their professional names, although Lottie called herself Lottie Franklin. Lottie lived at her parents' home, as she had done throughout much of her married life. When her father and mother died she inherited the house on Locust Street, but instead of taking in roomers, she converted the house into apartments, retaining the first floor for her own use. With the success of her millinery and the renovation of her father's house a new life began for Lottie.

Women, Lantenengo Street women, often dropped in at Lottie's shop merely to smoke a cigarette. The shop, in fact, became the younger women's idling place that corresponded to their husbands' cigar store. Only the oldest women of Lantenengo Street withheld their patronage from Lottie, and their absence was helpful. Lottie not only had the youngest hats; she had the young for customers. The men of Gibbsville, Lantenengo Street or not, remained totally unaware of the noncommercial aspects of Lottie's shop. All they knew was that their wives had dropped in at Lottie's and had, or had not, bought a hat. Whether they bought or not, Lottie made them feel welcome. She supplied cigarettes; she had a clean toilet; a box of aspirin and a carton of sanitary napkins; a telephone in her small office. And Lottie did not mind if a young woman closed the door of the office.

Lottie's first love affair as a widow was with a doctor, a newcomer to Gibbsville and a bachelor, who was six years younger than she. George Ingram was a University of Pennsylvania M.D., a native of Trenton who had heard that doctors prospered in Gibbsville, in spite of the seemingly large number of doctors in proportion to the population of the town. He was sponsored by Dr. English, who sent him patients and helped him socially, but George Ingram was not quite so ready to marry as the available young women of Lantenengo Street had hoped. He was twenty-nine years old and determined to repay the aunt who had helped finance his education. When Lottie Williams came to him with a torn fingernail and in pain, she was a patient and no more, but she knew a good deal about him through the talk at her shop. On her third, and what was to have been her final office call, she made sure to be the last patient of the evening.

"Won't need another dressing," he said. "You can stop at the drug store and tell them to give you a rubber finger to wear at work, but I wouldn't even wear that all the time."

"Fine," said Lottie. She smiled at him and made no move to go. She continued to smile at him, and he smiled back.

"You make me feel as if I forgot something. Did I forget anything?"

"No," she said. "Do you have a cigarette?"

"Why, yes," he said.

"Let's you and I smoke a cigarette then," said Lottie.

"Okay, let's. Do you smoke these?" He offered her a Fatima.

"Beggars can't be choosers," she said.

"What is your regular brand?"

"Lord Salisburys," she said.

"Sorry I can't oblige," he said. "I'll have some the next time."

"That's good news," said Lottie.

"Oh, I take good care of my patients."

"So's that, good news," said Lottie.

"What made you think anything different?"

"I didn't think anything different, Doctor. I meant it was good news there's going to be a next time, and good news you take good care of your patients. I guess you're pretty lonely in town."

"Oh, I don't know."

"All the young Lantenengo Street girls after you, but you're giving them the cold shoulder."

"Well, I don't want to get serious."

"I don't either," said Lottie. She smiled at him and said no more while she inhaled her cigarette. He smiled back uncertainly.

"Does that door lock?" she said.

"Mm-hmm."

"Would you care to kiss me? And lock the door first?"

He got up and turned the key.

"Do you want me to take everything off?"

"Yes," he said.

"You don't say much, do you?"

"We understand each other," he said.

She stood up and they kissed each other.

"Turn your back," she said.

"All right," he said.

"I wish you could outen the big light."

"I will," he said. He snapped the ceiling light. "I'd better leave the other one on."

"I don't mind the other one. It's the big one," she said. In a few minutes she spoke again. She was lying on his sofa, the front of her body draped with her petticoat, but she was wearing nothing. "You take everything off too."

"I intend to," he said.

Their love-making lasted not very long and she said only one thing, when he was inside her for the first time: "God, I needed this."

"So did I," he said.

When they had finished she said: "Will you let me have one of those Fatimas?"

"Mm-hmm."

"Where do you live? Do you still live at the hotel?"

"Yes."

"That's too bad," she said. "Do you ever go away? Philly or New York City?"

"Only once since I came here."

"I'd like to be in a real bed with you and we wouldn't have to be in such a hurry."

"But you're all right, aren't you?"

"Sure. You could tell. You're a doctor."

"Sometimes I'm not."

"I'm glad of that. What if I get in the family way?"

"Well, let's hope you don't."

"Let's hope I don't is right. Did you like me?"

"Yes."

"Enough to have another date sometime?"

"Sure."

"When?"

"Well—I don't exactly. You decide."

"A week from tonight?"

"That's a Monday? Fine."

"Will I come here with my sore finger, or what?"

"Get here a little later, after eight-thirty."

"Any time you say. Listen, I don't want anybody seeing me any more than you do. I'm a respectable widow and business woman. I don't want any talk either."

"That's good."

"And you're younger than I am. I always used to think a woman that—well, I guess it doesn't make much difference, does it?"

"No, I guess not."

"Give me another kiss and then I guess I'll get started on my way home."

He kissed her briefly on the mouth.

"It makes you feel how much you've been missing over two years. It isn't that long for you, though."

"No," he said.

"Men are lucky," she said. "If you have to go out on a call next Monday, will the Monday after be all right?"

"I'll be here."

"For sure?"

"Well, unless there's some accident or something on that order."

"I'm started wishing it was Monday already, and it's still this Monday. I wish I could go to the hotel with you."

"Where do *you* live?"

"With my mother and father. They're both ready to go any minute. They have a trained nurse."

For nearly a year Lottie and Ingram took care of their need of someone, with no one in Gibbsville the wiser. He was the first and for a long time the only man to come to her apartment, but she never had him present at the small parties she gave, poker parties with whiskey and beer. Love never happened to Lottie and Ingram and when he told her he was planning to marry a Lantenengo Street girl she was secretly relieved; his love-making had become routine, as had her own, and besides she was beginning to like to listen to Lloyd Williams, who was getting to be a frequent member of the poker sessions.

She was forty-one when she married Lloyd Williams, a man her own age, and it was a great surprise on their wedding night to discover how little Lloyd knew about making love. Indeed it was weeks before she finally and fully realized that with Lloyd she could never expect to have anything but the embellishments of love-making and never the ultimate love-making itself. She had known there were men like that, and she now had married one. For two years she submitted to his technique, which excited her but gave her no relief. "What's the matter with you?" he would say. "You like it, every woman does. Most women would rather." He would become angry and frustrated by her own frustration. Time was getting short for her, she knew, and she thought of leaving him, of reopening her shop, but she would have no explanation to satisfy public or even private curiosity; he was not a drunkard, he did not beat her, he gave her a home, he was—publicly—a much better man than Jimmy Franklin had been. Then accidentally, during one of his angriest outbursts, she learned something about him that was something of a comfort without being satisfaction.

"Didn't you ever have real intercourse with a woman?"

"Sure I did," he said.

"Those whores?"

"Yes, those whores."

"Then what's the matter with me?"

"I don't know," he said.

"I'm built the same way."

"I never liked it with them."

"What didn't you like?"

"The way I did it with them."

"The regular way?"

"Yes, the regular way."

"Then why did you do anything? Why did you do it at all?"

"I had to. A man has—desires. When I had mine I went to a whore. But it wasn't what I wanted to do. What I do with you was always what I wanted to do."

"Why can't you do the same thing with me that you did with the whores? It's what I want."

"I can't help it what you want. All I can do is what I do. Once a month I'd go to a whore and get satisfaction, quick. With you I don't want to have satisfaction, not the same kind. I want *you* to have satisfaction. Why don't you? You won't let yourself."

"Didn't you do the same thing with the whores?"

"No, I tell you. I hated them. I respect you."

"Is that what it is? Respect?"

"You'd never find me doing that to a whore. Never."

"I don't understand it."

"Can you understand this? You and the whores are the only women I ever knew. And what I always wanted to do I do with you."

"That's almost as if you only knew two women in your whole life."

"That's what it is. I only knew two women. The other woman was all the whores, and I hated them. And I don't hate you. I love you."

"My God," she said.

"Listen, I'm not half as queer as some people. You ought to hear some of the things in court."

"I don't want to."

"Well, then you'd know."

"I don't want to know."

"You ought to hear some of those things."

"Why don't you change? Why should I be the one?"

"Listen, I'll give you some books to read. Havelock Ellis."

"Aw, books. I never read a—"

"Not novels. Scientific."

"Doctor books. I don't want doctor books. I know what I am: a woman. And you're supposed to be a man. Are you a fairy, too?"

"Like hell I am. I wouldn't be in love with you."

"What kind of love do you call this?"

"It's a kind. There's all kinds."

"Huh. Well, I'm going to sleep."

"All right."

"You were supposed to have—you were supposed to be Rudolph Valentino and Wallace Reid rolled into one."

"If you knew more you'd understand better," he said.

"I understand enough."

"No. You don't."

"There's one thing I understand and that's there's some things I don't care if I don't ever understand."

So—he loved her; he used the word. What he meant by love was not what she had always meant by love, which was simple, irresistible, and satisfactory. At forty-three she was having to learn about a kind of love that was as distant as death without death's inevitability. Death was acceptable and postponable; this kind of love was not within her imaginable experience. And yet she was experiencing it. She made some compromises; her secret reading of Havelock Ellis was some help, and so was a furtive, embarrassed consultation with George Ingram, who was not a mental healer but who reassured her by telling her that she was not the only woman in the world, or in Gibbsville, who was experiencing dissatisfaction. What he told her was hardly more than what she would have discovered by listening to the court cases Lloyd had spoken of, but the difference was that coming from George it had greater value; George had been her lover; George was a medical man. The compromise she made was a difficult one and long in the making, but it was achieved. It was simple. She learned to be Lloyd's wife on his terms. And at precisely that moment she began to lose him. For a year they were happy. He had converted her, and she was a convert. Moreover their differentness gave her a hidden sense of superiority over other women. But he had won, and she was losing, and then there began to be nothing.

Ruth Jenkins had lived all her life in Gibbsville, never had been out of the Commonwealth of Pennsylvania except for two one-day excursions to Atlantic City, but in twenty-six years she had never been inside the courthouse. Every day of her life, practically, she looked at the courthouse clock and that ended it. Like many residents of Gibbsville, her attitude was that the courthouse was county, not town, and a place that drew to Gibbsville a lot of ignorant miners in trouble and a lot of lawyers trying to get them out of it. Nothing could have persuaded her to set foot in the place, nothing but the kind of thing that did: the legacy from her aunt, the papers to be signed, and Mr. J. B. Chapin the lawyer to accompany her up the hill. The business in the office of Register of Wills was brief and she would have been home in another hour had it not been for her casual mention to Mr. Chapin that it was her first visit.

"Well," said Mr. Chapin. "Wouldn't you like to see what makes the wheels go round? Court's in session. Let's have a look in Number 3 Courtroom. We might run across something interesting." She was unequal to the problem of how to refuse the invitation. He led her to Number 3, to a row of empty chairs inside the rail, and they sat down.

"This is assault and battery with intent to kill. The defendant is that Italian man with the mustache."

"I see," said Ruth Jenkins.

"The witness is being questioned by Mr. Williams, Lloyd Williams, from Collieryville. Assistant district attorney, and smart as a whip. Watch him tie that witness in knots."

"I object, your Honor!"

"That's defense counsel. Mr. Troutman from Taqua," said Joseph B. Chapin.

"And quite rightly," said the judge.

"Judge *Bramwell*," said Joseph B. Chapin.

"Mr. Williams, shall we read back to you so that you'll know better next time?" said Judge Bramwell. "Twice in the past four minutes I've sustained Mr. Troutman's objection to that same line of questioning and now you persist in continuing it."

"I apologize, your Honor," said Williams. "I am only trying to show—"

"I think I know what you're trying to show, Mr. Williams. Right now the clock shows the hour to be past my lunch time and I think we'll all be the better for a recess. Let us adjourn until two o'clock."

"All rise!" shouted a tipstaff.

They held their places during the confusion of adjournment. "I'm afraid this was a disappointment," said Joseph B. Chapin. "But let's go over and say hello to Lloyd Williams."

"All right," said Ruth Jenkins.

"Lloyd! Lloyd!" Chapin called.

Williams turned and saw Chapin. "Hello, Joe," he said, and it was another first-time for Ruth Jenkins; the first time she ever had heard anyone call Chapin, Joe.

"I would like you to meet Mrs. Jenkins. Ruth, this is Mr. Lloyd Williams, our eminent assistant district attorney."

"How do you do, Mrs. Jenkins," said Williams. They did not shake hands; his were occupied with papers and large heavy-paper envelopes. "You in the courtroom?"

"Just got here," said Joe Chapin.

"Bramwell's been like that all morning," said Williams, to Chapin, and addressed Ruth Jenkins: "Are you Mrs. Edwin Jenkins?"

"Yes, I am," she said.

"I thought so," said Williams. "Edwin has a very pretty wife."

"Oh, now," said Ruth Jenkins.

"He has indeed," said Joe Chapin.

"Your client, Joe?"

"I have that honor," said Joe Chapin.

"Well, you're in good hands, Mrs. Jenkins," said Williams. "Unless you get in trouble with the law and I have to be on the other side. Then you'd see me ripping Joe to shreds."

"Unless, of course, we were before Judge Bramwell," said Joe Chapin.

"Oh, him. He should have retired ten years ago while he still had possession of all his faculties."

"Uh—Lloyd doesn't—uh—"

86

"Oh, Mrs. Jenkins isn't going to report me, are you, Mrs. Jenkins?"

"What for?" said Ruth Jenkins.

"For saying what I think. That Judge Bramwell should have retired. That remark of his about knowing what I was trying to show. That kind of a remark might come in handy on appeal, in a different set of circumstances."

"I thought of that," said Joe Chapin.

"He knows I can't lose this case, so he's having some fun at my expense. Be glad your husband isn't a lawyer, Mrs. Jenkins."

"You wouldn't be anything else," said Joe Chapin.

"You're right, I wouldn't," said Williams. "Would you care to see my office, Mrs. Jenkins? As a taxpayer, you might like to see how some of your money is spent."

"I'm afraid we have to be running along," said Joe Chapin.

"Whatever you say," said Ruth.

"Come on, have a look," said Williams. "Then I'll ride downtown with you, if that's all right."

"Would you like to do that?" said Joe Chapin.

"All right," said Ruth Jenkins.

"But I can't give you a ride downtown. You know that, Lloyd. I always walk."

"Have you got a car, Mrs. Jenkins?" said Williams.

"Yes, I do," said Ruth Jenkins.

"Then she can give me a ride, that is if she wants to."

"It would be a pleasure," said Ruth Jenkins.

It was so arranged. They had a look at Williams' office, which he shared with other members of the district attorney's staff and which reflected no personality; then they parted from Joe Chapin and got in her Ford two-door sedan. "I'm having a valve job done on my wagon," he said. "Could I ask you to drive me out to Klein's Garage and see if it's ready?"

They drove to Klein's Garage; his car would not be ready until later in the afternoon. She heard him telling the mechanic that that was a hell of a note, and she heard the mechanic say that that was when they'd promised it. She wondered about that, but not disturbingly. When he returned to the car he said: "That's always the way."

"Where else can I take you?" she said.

"Do you have to be home right away?"

"No," she said. "Ed eats lunch at the 'Y' Cafeteria."

"I go there sometimes, I've seen him there. I guess he goes there every day."

"Just about, except Saturdays," she said.

"A day like this, I often just get in my car and drive around instead of eating."

"That's not good for you," she said. "You ought to eat!"

"Yes, but sometimes I get more out of going for a ride and getting rid of that courthouse air. I like fresh air, but my work keeps me indoors most of the time."

"I like fresh air, too," she said.

"But you're probably hungry."

"No, I'm not so hungry. I had a milk shake around ten. Milk shake and a couple pretzels."

"You wouldn't feel like taking a ride down Beaver Valley way?"

"I don't know. Maybe," she said. She turned and looked at him. "Just down Beaver Valley and back?"

"That's all," he said.

"I don't know. Maybe we better not," she said.

"You don't want to start anything?" he said.

"What is there to start?" she said.

"It's started already. You can tell," he said.

She nodded. "I was never out with anybody but Ed since we got married."

"What about before?"

"I used to go out with fellows, but not seriously."

"Do you have children?"

"No," she said. "Do you?"

"No," he said.

"That's right. You married Lottie Danner, didn't you?"

"Yes. And you married Ed Jenkins," he said.

"I think I better go home. I think that's best."

"Who is it best for?"

"Everybody," she said.

"Everybody in the world? Everybody in the world? Everybody in Gibbsville? Everybody we know? Or everybody that's going to know we went for a ride. And who will that be?"

"People would recognize you."

"You didn't, in court," he said.

"No," she said. "But you're well known."

"We were introduced to each other in the courtroom, by Joe Chapin. A lot of people saw that. You gave me a ride to the garage. If anybody wants to know why I'm in your car, Joe Chapin gave me

88

an introduction to you and you helped me out with a ride to the garage. How many people are going to see you, just *see* you? Then ask yourself, how many are going to see you and recognize me? Then ask yourself, how many of those people are going to think anything about it? And of *those* people, how many are going to say to Ed Jenkins, 'I saw your wife with Lloyd Williams'? All you have to do is tell your husband you took me to the garage, so he'll know I was in your car."

"Ed won't like it," she said.

"What won't he like? The fact that Joseph B. Chapin took you over and introduced me to you? Joseph B. Chapin is the one that introduced us."

"It'd be different if it was just some ordinary man."

"Why does it being me make so much difference?"

"Oh, quit your kidding. You know. You have a reputation. You know that."

"You mean, other than my professional reputation."

She laughed. "I'll say."

"Well, how does it feel to be alone with a man with that kind of a reputation. Any different?"

"Well—I don't know."

"So far no harm has come to you? So far I haven't said anything or done anything that would justify your alarm."

"So far."

"What do you think I *might* do, Ruth? What do you think I *could* do without your consent? You're a married woman, aware of the relationship between man and woman—"

"You're clever. You got talking and got me talking, and now we're practically out of town. You did that on purpose."

"To some extent. But at least we're now getting in the country and not so many people can see us."

She was silent.

"Are you alone a lot of the time?" he said, gently.

"Yes," she said.

"What do you do when you're alone?"

"When I'm alone? My housework."

"But you're very neat, I noticed that. And I'll bet you don't have to use up much time doing the housework."

"No, not much," she said. "I do my sewing."

"Oh, you can sew?"

"I like to sew. I make some of my own dresses. The ones at the store are too dear, and half of them don't fit right. I make some dresses for other girls, too. They give me the material but I do the dressmaking. Usually I select the patterns."

"Why don't you go in the business?"

"I thought of that, but Ed wouldn't let me. He says it wouldn't look right, a man at the bank's wife a dressmaker."

"There's money in it."

"Don't I know that? I can make around fifty a month just making dresses for friends of mine."

"How does Ed feel about that?"

"What he doesn't know won't hurt him."

"Oh, you don't tell him."

"He'd stop me," she said.

"What do you do with the money?"

"I've got it hidden."

"It's a wonder he didn't hear about it, one way or another."

"He won't, because the girls I make the dresses for, they get like twenty-five to buy a dress but I make one for around fifteen, and they keep the other ten, only they tell their husbands they bought the dress. They wouldn't want to spoil that for themselves."

"No, I guess not. Do you know what you are, Ruth?"

"What?"

"You're a kind of a bootlegger."

She laughed. "Another Ed Charney. I don't care. Every penny Ed Jenkins makes goes into investments. If I didn't make my own dresses I'd look like something the cat dragged in. He wants me to look neat and well dressed but he won't give me the money for it."

"What would he do if you told him you decided you wanted to go into business?"

"He'd say I couldn't."

"But what could he do?"

"What could he do? Why—he could forbid me."

"Yes, and then what, if you said you were going to."

"I don't get what you mean," she said.

"Yes, you do," said Williams.

"You mean how could he stop me?"

"Exactly."

"Well, I never thought of it that way."

"Then think of it."

"Yes, maybe you're right. But he's my husband."

"It isn't as if you had children to look after. You have plenty of time and ability. It isn't right for you to lose all that money on account of his pride. That's what it is, it's his pride."

"Well—I guess we better not talk about it any more."

"All right," he said. "Ruth, you told me some secrets."

"Yes. I don't know if that was such a good idea."

"Yes it was. I'm great at keeping secrets."

"Well, just so you keep those."

"Something inside you allowed you to tell me them. Is that right?"

"I guess so."

"You know so. I want to ask you something."

"Is it personal?"

"Yes, personal and secret. Shall I ask you?"

"Well—all right, if it's not too personal."

"It's very personal, but it's secret," he said. "No, I changed my mind. Do you want a cigarette?"

"I don't smoke," she said.

"I didn't think you did. It doesn't go with the rest of you."

"I just don't like it. I have nothing against it," she said. "What was it you were going to ask me?"

"I don't think you'd answer the question and I wouldn't want to ask it if I wasn't going to get an answer. It's a very personal question. Private. Secret."

"What kind of a question?"

"If I told you what kind of a question, that would be as much as asking it."

"Ask it."

"Does Ed thrill you when you're together?"

She made no answer. They drove in silence for a couple of hundred yards.

"I don't have any right to be sore at you. I made you ask me," she said.

"I don't want you to be sore at me, that's why I wasn't going to ask it."

"Why do you want to know?"

"I want to know all about you."

"There isn't much to know."

"As long as there's one thing I don't know, I'll want to know it."

"Maybe I don't know what you mean by thrill."

"Yes, you do."

"All right, I'll tell you. He doesn't believe girls are supposed to get the same thrill as men do."

"I could thrill you."

"Yes, I guess you could," she said.

"Do I now, just talking about it?"

"Yes."

"I am, too," he said.

"We'd better turn around," she said. "I don't like this. You shouldn't get me like this. You ask me those questions and I don't know what comes over me."

"It's all right, Ruth. Turn around."

"Don't ask me any more questions."

"I won't. Do you want me to drive?"

"No, no. I want to keep occupied."

They said no more until they were at the city limits of Gibbsville. "Will you let me off at the Reading Station? I'll take a taxi from there."

"All right," she said.

"Are you sore at me?"

"No. I was, but not now."

"I know you were."

"Well, you expected me to be," she said.

"I guess I wouldn't like you as much if you weren't."

"Don't like me, I don't want you to like me or dislike me. Because I'm never going to see you again."

"I don't blame you, Ruth. But I wanted to know."

"Well, you found out."

"I'm not going to phone you—"

"You better not!"

"I won't. But you may want to phone me."

"You're wrong."

"If you do, tell the girl that answers that it's Mrs. Jay. In our office we get a lot of calls that people don't give their names."

"Don't worry, I'll never phone you."

But she did; in two years, a hundred times, from the house in the 1900-block on Market Street. And he never let her forget the two years. The horn signal was his constant reminder.

In the comparatively brief period in which Gibbsville had had a mayor, a period dating from its changing from a borough to a third-class city, the office had been held by some scoundrels of varying degree, who had used money of their own in their campaigns, confident that after election their investments would be returned. The confidence was always justified, and in two cases so well justified that the confident men left Gibbsville to settle in California and Florida, never to return to the home town. Other men had invested in the office with less spectacular returns on their money, and they remained in Gibbsville. Conrad L. Yates was the only man to spend a large sum of money on his campaign and continued to spend his own money during his tenure of office. In that respect he was like the Lord Mayor of London, treating the position as a luxury he could afford and satisfied with the honor of the title. He liked being called Mayor; he liked better being called Mr. Mayor; and, in police court, Your Honor. He liked having letters addressed to The Honorable Conrad L. Yates. He liked having the radio and siren and blinker lights and city seal on the Cadillac he owned and equipped with his personal funds. He enjoyed making speeches and serving on committees. Like Fiorello H. La Guardia, a man whom he did not admire politically, he gave a weekly radio talk. His chauffeur, whom he called his driver, was a temporary special policeman, on the city payroll for a dollar a year, but entitled to wear a police uniform. (The driver's actual salary was paid by Yates.) "What's wrong with it?" he would say to his friends. "Some men want to be a general. Knudsen, the big man at General Motors. He's a general. I ain't a big shot like Knudsen, so I won't never be no general. But I can be Mayor. That I like. Mayor I always wanted to be. Now I am."

He was a short, stout man, fast-moving and quick-thinking. He always seemed to be doing two things at once; if he ordered a beer he drank it quickly and talked interestedly and incisively. It was as though he were telling his thirst to lie down now while he did his brainwork. When he made a speech the words came out, jovially and often ungrammatically, but he seemed to be one man making the speech and another man studying the individual members of the audience. He was surprised and delighted to be chosen as a pall-bearer for Joseph B. Chapin, a man he admired without reservation, but during the hours of actual service as pallbearer he was uncomfortable. Here were big shots who made his limited celebrity seem small indeed. The Governor knew him and he knew the Governor, but here were Mike Slattery and Arthur McHenry and Henry Laubach and Bob Hooker and Whit Hofman and Doctor English and Lloyd Williams, from town, who were more genuinely big shot than he was. The man named Weeks, the Philadelphia lawyer Kirkpatrick, the admiral, the Wall Street man Harrison and Paul Donaldson from Scranton were big shots who had no idea who he was. He could feel like Mayor and Big Shot only to Edwin Jenkins, whom he could buy and sell, and young Johnson, the new school superintendent. He realized that his selection as pallbearer was no tribute to him; that any man who happened to be Mayor would have been selected, so long as he was a Republican. No one thanked him for the expeditiousness of the movements of the funeral cars, or for the extra police, or for keeping nonessential traffic out of Frederick Street. If Joe Chapin had been alive, and a pallbearer, Joe Chapin was the kind of a fellow that would notice these things and remember to thank him. As a pallbearer Conrad was where he had always wanted to be, in a small group of important men, publicly recognized as a man of importance. But when it was all over and he returned to his office in City Hall he privately conceded his disappointment.

The office walls were covered with framed, signed photographs of himself and the prominent people he had met, however briefly. Movie stars and starlets, band leaders, politicians, the military, radio personalities, singers, lecturers, business executives. No man or woman of prominence was allowed to set foot in Gibbsville, whether for a bond drive or in ordinary business pursuits, without having his picture taken shaking hands or kissing Conrad L. Yates. And on his not infrequent visits to New York and Philadelphia night clubs his arrangement with the maitre-dee at almost any famous hot spot provided him with out-of-town photographs of himself with George Jessel, Frank Sinatra, Dorothy Lamour, Jack Pearl, a Royal Air Force wing commander, Ted Husing, Winthrop Aldrich, and a batboy of the New York Yankees; as well as one of the few photographs of Betty Grable taken from the front. They were precious souvenirs, usually dependable as a means of restimulating him when inevitably he felt a little tired.

He had come a long way from the farm, and up the hard way, with only seven years of schooling and in those years only a few months to the year. In his boyhood it had been a big treat to go to Gibbsville for a load of manure to be brought back to the farm in the wagon that had wheels or runners, depending on the weather. For boys in his position the escape from farming was a job on the railroad, either as a laborer in the roundhouses or to learn a trade. But he was too small to convince bosses that he was good laborer material, and he was too poor to become an apprentice, which paid nothing in the beginning. Nevertheless he left the farm, and at fifteen he was working in a Gibbsville livery stable, where he was given a cot, and subsisting on tips. He was too small to be a blacksmith, since most of a blacksmith's income came from shoeing horses. He saved the tips that the livery stable customers gave him, quit the job, got a job as a Postal Telegraph messenger boy, and enrolled in Gibbsville Business College night classes, which he would not have been able to do as an around-the-clock stable boy. His stenography and typing were a complete failure, but he was fascinated by bookkeeping in spite of his poor penmanship. His books were not the prettiest in his class, but they had the fewest traces of the ink eradicator.

He was eighteen years old and still a messenger boy when he first met Joseph B. Chapin, who had just started the practice of law with the firm of McHenry & McHenry. Two or three times a week the farm boy delivered telegrams to McHenry & McHenry, which were signed for by the handsome young lawyer. They made a good impression on each other, and not all of the impression the lawyer made on the farm boy was due to the lawyer's habit of giving the boy five cents every time a telegram was received. The money came out of petty cash, but the decision to give it was up to the young lawyer. Mr. Chapin was not too stuck up to walk part way down the street with Conrad, and without knowing it he became the first person of consequence to treat Conrad like a human being. Also without knowing it he became the first person Conrad ever loved.

One afternoon late they were alone in the office as the telegram was delivered and the nickel received. "Sank you, Mr. Shapin."

"You're welcome, Conrad."

"Mr. Shapin, excuse me vonce."

"What is it, old chap?"

"I vant to ask you your adwice."

"Well, that's what we're here for."

"Ach, now, you're making chokes wiss me."

"You want another kind of advice? That it?"

"Ja. Yes. I vant to stop work as messenchah poy."

"Have you inherited a million, Conrad?"

"Making chokes wiss me again yet, Mr. Chapin. People lige to make chokes wiss me. My sice is too small already."

"No more jokes, Conrad. What can I do for you?"

"Vell—I haf sree hunret dollahs safed up. Some say go to Philly, some say stay in Gippsville. Vhat do you say, Mr. Shapin?"

Joseph B. Chapin patted the tips of his fingers together. "Hmm," he said. "You want me to advise you as a friend?"

"Yes, sir," said Conrad, never having been called a friend by anyone.

"Hmm. Well, you've been in town how long?"

"Going on four years I vas here."

"You've made quite a few friends in that short time."

"Vell, I know some people, two hunret maybe."

"You've worked hard, saved a nice little nest-egg in Gibbsville, and now you are thinking of trying your luck in the big city," said Joseph B. Chapin.

"Yes, sir."

"But you've never been to New York or Philadelphia."

"I vas nefer to Reading down."

"Well, Reading is bigger than Gibbsville, three or four times as large, and Philadelphia is ten times larger than Reading. You probably are thinking that means that many more opportunities. Possibly it does. But let us take into consideration the fact that you have a pretty good job here, and no job in Philadelphia. Friends here, and no friends in Philadelphia. And I can tell you from experience, it's easy to get lost in a big city until you know your way. I daresay you've thought of these things."

"Yes, sir."

"Then there's one more consideration, Conrad."

"Yes, sir."

"Your English. Here in Gibbsville we're accustomed to the Pennsylvania Dutch manner of speaking. We're used to it. But in a place like Philadelphia or New York—they think it's funny, and they're liable to laugh at it. They wouldn't be laughing at you. They'd be laughing at your way of speaking."

"That is right."

"When they hear you speak, you or anyone else from the Pennsylvania Dutch country, they may think you're imitating a stage comedian. They have comedians on the stage that talk very much like Pennsylvania Dutch. They'd laugh at you and hurt your feelings."

Conrad nodded. "I vould srow somesing and get put in the lockup."

"Well, I don't know how bad a temper you have, Conrad. But if I were you, I'd stay in Gibbsville a few years longer and lose some more of the accent. And who knows? You may not want to leave in a few years. You're bright and hard-working. Gibbsville is a growing town, on its way to becoming a city. Many, many opportunities here for a young man. I know I like it."

Conrad stayed in Gibbsville and prospered. The same ingenuity and application in a larger city might have earned him greater rewards, but he never left Gibbsville. His block on South Main Street was a New Yorker's on Fifth Avenue, a Philadelphian's on Broad Street. His house out on Lantenengo Street was a New Yorker's in Glen Cove or a Philadelphian's in Ardmore. They represented his talent for taking over small, unprofitable enterprises and making them pay, either as going concerns or for their real estate position. He became known as "Wie Geht's Yates." As his English became better he discovered that his Pennsylvania Dutch was not entirely the liability he thought it was. There was plenty of German among the Main Street merchants and he even understood the Yiddish of the Jews. Chiefly he was a real estate man, a restrained speculator. "All real estate is good," he would say. "But the way you make money out of it is knowing when to get rid of it." He bought and sold parcels in the shopping district, in the middle-class residential areas, and on Lantenengo Street. He owned, and relinquished, farms and factory sites, but he would not touch mining properties. "If they want to sell it to me, it ain't much good," he would say. "I ain't no engineer, and they are."

His interest in politics was genuine but hardly idealistic. It had to do with assessments and with zoning ordinances. He bought votes, and everybody made money; the men who had taken the bribes, and Conrad L. Yates, whose assessments were kept profitably low or whose properties were made or kept more attractive. He donated land for a hospital with the understanding that the area be designated a zone of quiet. He happened also to own much of the surrounding acreage, which became a peaceful residential development. He had a zoning law changed so that a prospective tenant could install carpet-cleaning machinery, which is noisy. He watched real estate prices go down as the neighboring housewives began to lose their minds, and when the prices were low enough, he bought the houses and sold them to a man who wanted to put up a planing mill, which is even noisier than a carpet cleanery.

As a businessman mayor he protected the citizens from any too-raw or too-large deals. His vigilance was not appreciated; everybody was making wartime money and when everybody is making money, deals are overlooked, Conrad well knew. But he was making sure that nothing too awful would be charged against his administration in future, less cynical years. Conrad, Junior, and Theodore Roosevelt Yates were in the Army, and between them had provided the Mayor with five grandchildren, which gave Conrad a sense of responsibility to his town and country. Moreover, to his great surprise and pleasure he had discovered, or had had discovered for him, the fact, and it was a fact, that an ancestor of his had fought in the American Revolution and that he and his children were eligible for membership in the appropriate societies. The discovery caused some embarrassed confusion at the Gibbsville Club, which had quietly blackballed Conrad for many years, and which as quietly admitted him in the nature of a fiftieth-birthday present. When a man who had thought of himself as a lowly member of the community finds that he has enviable ancestry and living descendants for the future, and has made himself a millionaire, he likes to pay his respects to future and past by some gesture that will have permanence. It seemed to Conrad Yates that a term as Mayor of Gibbsville, the metropolis and county seat, would make him a desirable ancestor of his unborn great-grandchildren and put him in almost the same category as his own Revolutionary forebear. He accordingly went directly to Mike Slattery, not to the merely local boys, and arranged with Mike to be elected Mayor. To Mike he was a welcome visitor. Except for the men whom he had bested in business deals, Conrad was a popular figure and could have won the election at a considerably smaller outlay than he made, but he wanted to win big, and Mike was happy to see the faithful workers get the money. The respectable element of the party regulars, such as Joe Chapin and Henry Laubach, were more than willing to sponsor Conrad, and so were the church people, the business community, the former poor, the young voters, and a sizable number of citizens who knew him only as Wie Geht's Yates. He won handsomely without the endorsement of organized labor, which correctly suspected him of a tendency to sympathize with big business (several parcels of Conrad's land were available for factory construction); and he got only token support from the slot-machine and whorehouse factions, which correctly suspected him of good morals.

. . . Now, back in his City Hall office after the funeral and the luncheon, he was momentarily a little man again. But that, too, would pass. He sat in the high-back leather swivel-chair, which he had swung about so that he could see the row of photographs that included a cabinet-size likeness of Joseph B. Chapin, which Joe had given him after repeated requests. The inscription was noncommittal enough: "To Conrad L. Yates From His Friend Joe Chapin." Conrad had wanted to get Joe Chapin to add to the inscription something about how Joe had made him stay in Gibbsville, but now it was too late. It was too late for a lot of things. He had wanted Joe and Edith Chapin once, just once, to come to his house for dinner. He had hoped for and half expected some small Christmas present from Joe, especially in one year when he had paid McHenry & Chapin (formerly McHenry & McHenry) a respectable sum in fees. But that year, as in other years, Joe Chapin sent him a chaste seasonal greeting, from Mr. and Mrs. Joseph Benjamin Chapin. The electric clock which Conrad had in reserve was unpacked and ended up in Teddy Yates's bedroom. As he looked now at the photograph of the man he admired, Conrad Yates realized that it would not have been *like* Joe Chapin to write the kind of intimate inscription that was on the photographs of movie actresses and ballplayers; no more than it would have been *like* Joe Chapin to send him a Christmas present, or even, for that matter, come to his house for dinner. Earlier in the day he had heard a dozen men and women comment that it was the first time they had been inside the Chapin residence. From that observation Conrad proceeded to the admission that there were plenty of people *he* did business with that he wouldn't have in *his* house. He did give away a lot of presents at Christmastime, and enjoyed doing it, but that was one of the differences between him and Joe Chapin. Joe Chapin did things one way, he did them another. And it pleased him to find that he and Joe had that point of similarity on the question of who was invited to your house.

In the mood engendered by that thinking Conrad put his mind to work on a project to honor the memory of Joe. He flipped a key on his intercom. "Get me Bob Hooker at the *Standard*," he said.

Gibbsville's outstanding man of letters was reading the galley proofs of his next day's editorial page material. He glanced perfunctorily at the proofs of the syndicated columns, saw that they had been initialed by one of the proofreaders downstairs, and devoted his attention to what was sometimes called, but not within his hearing, his daily masterpiece. Bob Hooker's own editorials never were set in type lower than 10-point, whether they appeared on the editorial page or, as on certain occasions, page one. No other editorializing or reporting was set in the same type, a rule which made it less difficult for style detectives to guess when Bob Hooker had spoken. When Bob Hooker spoke, his readers knew without further questioning what to expect in the way of policy or action from the Coal & Iron Company, the Taft-Grundy-Pew-Slattery faction of the Republican organization, the Ministerial Association, the American Red Cross, the Shade Tree Commission, the Greater Gibbsville Committee and Clean-Up Week.

Since not everything he said was automatically popular, he was proud of the name Fighting Bob Hooker, and he lived in yearly expectation of favorable comparison with William Allen White and Ed Howe. Actually he had been so compared, but only locally, at luncheons, and he was waiting for similar word from New York. An article he sold to *The Saturday Evening Post* was a constant reminder to Gibbsville citizens that their man of letters was good enough for national publication; the inference, which was drawn and encouraged, being that Bob could do it any time he wanted to, but that the Gibbsville *Standard* and Gibbsville had first call on his talents. A later article, intended for the *Post's* Cities of America series, was returned to Bob with such reluctance that readers of the letter could not understand how the *Post* editors could bear to part with the article. It was not, however, wasted effort. The article was printed up as a leaflet for the Chamber of Commerce, for which Bob received an honorarium of $250.

Very little indeed of Bob's professional effort was wasted. His newspaper enjoyed quiet subsidies from the Coal & Iron Company and the Republican party war chest, which seldom differed on policy, and when they did differ, the differences were not irreconcilable. A citizen who wondered what kind of cars Bob owned would not have had to peer in his garage; he could make his deduction from the advertising in the *Standard*. Bob Hooker had learned his profession in the days when newspapermen were given passes on railroads. As editor and publisher he felt entitled to appropriate courtesies from hotels, steamship lines and any other enterprises that valued the good will of the press. If he wanted to obtain tickets for a heavyweight prize fight in a distant city, he sent his request through the United Press or the newspaper feature syndicates. He rarely sought these favors for his personal use, but a couple of seats for a World Series game went a long way with the right people. He and his wife signed all chits at the John Gibb Hotel, but practically none at the Lantenengo Country Club, which had no free list. But even at the club Bob Hooker had a minor arrangement with the golf professional, who got his name mentioned in all golf activities as a courtesy in exchange for free balls, tees, club-cleaning and all such goods and services. Nor did he forget that his wife was entitled to consideration by the merchants. He knew something about mark-ups, and when his wife bought a dress or a suit or a furry item, she paid approximately the cost price, not the wholesale price. The small loss to the merchant in the difference between cost and wholesale was also the difference between favorable mention in the *Standard's* society column and no mention at all. But all such courtesy arrangements took place between the publisher and the principal. Any reporter who was caught "on the take" was fired without warning. A bottle of whiskey or a box of candy at Christmas was permissible; but greater courtesies were restricted to the top level. "I want no grafters," Bob Hooker would say to every new member of his staff.

In another day Bob Hooker's office had been as full of photographs and souvenirs as the Mayor's office in City Hall. Not so in 1945. On his return a few years earlier from a trip to Daytona Beach he found that in his absence his wife had done over the sanctum sanctorum, laying down wall-to-wall carpet, installing bookshelves, and furnishing the room with a massive desk and leather club chairs. His old Remington Number 10 looked strangely out of place in the new elegance, but his wife was wise enough to know that the typewriter belonged in the room in the same way that a scale model of a Model T belonged in the office of Henry Ford, a tiny locomotive in the office of Samuel Vauclain, a speedboat in the headquarters of Gar Wood, a chest of machinist's tools in the office of Walter P. Chrysler. A couple of million of Bob Hooker's own words had been tapped out on the Number 10, the second typewriter he had ever owned and successor to his Smith Premier Invisible. It was one of the few objects retained from the old office. Signed photographs of Herbert Hoover and Calvin Coolidge, Andrew Mellon and Mike Slattery, Joseph B. Chapin and George Horace Lorimer, E. T. Stotesbury and Gene Tunney and Mrs. Robert Hooker (Kitty) were framed in blue pinseal and placed at strategic points in the office, where they would catch the eye of the visitor. The other photographs of political and sporting figures, of Bob Hooker's high school class and National Guard company, of coal breakers and high-tension towers and the starting of the *Standard's* R. Hoe press, as well as caricatures and cartoons and letters from important people—they were all removed from the office and stored in the Hookers' town cellar for future hanging in his little den in the farmhouse down country. The knotty-pine paneling had been built into the den, but the framed souvenirs rested in the cellar.

Bob Hooker, as literary man, permitted himself a few mild eccentricities. He was a pipe collector, for one. He shaved himself with a straight razor, for another. He wore high-laced shoes. He carried a hunting-case watch that wound with a key "for show," and wore a time-piece on his wrist. There was nothing dangerously queer about him, but as a man of letters he knew he was not expected to be like everybody else. Another of his gentle aberrations was his insistence on an old-style desk instrument for telephoning. It was distinctive, and it cost him nothing. At its ring he picked up the receiver. (At this hour of the day only important calls were put through to him.)

"It's the Mayor," said the switchboard girl.

"Okay," said Bob Hooker. "Hello, Mayor."

"Hello, Bob," said Conrad Yates. "Bob, I been sitting here in my office thinking about Joe Chapin."

"Yes, yes," said Hooker. "His memory will live with us a long, long time, Mayor."

"That's exactly what I wanted to speak to you. Exactly."

"How's that, Mayor?"

"His memory. Joe's memory. Did you ever know Joe Chapin kept me in Gibbsville?"

"Why, uh, didn't you tell me something to that effect, I believe so."

"Some thirty-five years ago I was thinking of moving to the city and Joe talked me out of it."

"Talked you out of it. Well, that was a good thing for you and Gibbsville, Mayor."

"Thanks, Bob. I appreciate what you say."

"It's the truth. You've been good for the town, and I guess the town's been pretty good to you."

"And if Joe Chapin didn't talk me out of it when I was a kid I would have been just a dumb hick from the country down in Philly."

"I see. And what did you have in mind? I know you're leading up to something."

"That I am, Bob. Bob, I want to organize a few fellows together and propose some kind of a memorial to Joe. You and Henry Laubach and Mike Slattery. Arthur McHenry. I don't want Jenkins or the new school fellow that was there today. But some of us old-timers that was acquainted with Joe as a friend."

"Mm-hmm. Just town fellows. No out-of-town men?"

"Town would be better."

"Not Paul Donaldson from Scranton, fellows like that?"

"Well, we can ask them for a contribution later on, but the committee ought to be us, from town."

"What did you have in mind for a memorial?"

"Well, I didn't decide yet."

"Talked to the other fellows?"

"No, you're the only one so far," said Conrad Yates.

"Well, I'm in favor of it, provided it's the right kind of a memorial. I'll speak to Edith about it when I see her. Let me think about it and I'll call you in a day or two. I'll be talking to Edith and I can sound her out, although it may be a little soon. But how'd it be if I just kind of sound her out a little first? Then I could call a kind of an informal meeting here in my office, you and the rest of the fellows, and we could discuss the broad outlines. How would that be?"

"Well—you want to have the meeting in your office?"

"Or your office. But in your office it kind of gets into politics more or less."

"Well, if you want to keep politics out maybe we better forget about Mike Slattery."

"He's a state senator, don't forget that."

Conrad laughed. "I do forget it, most of the time. I'm so used to him being a politician I forget he's a senator too."

Bob Hooker did not laugh. "And a mighty influential man, Conrad. I don't have to tell you that. You got to look at it from all angles. I understand you don't want to run again, so we better take into consideration you may not be Mayor when the campaign gets under way, the campaign for Joe's memorial, that is. The next mayor may want to stay out of something that was started when you were Mayor. That's the only thing I was thinking. And these things take time, you know. We don't want to get started too soon."

"No, and we don't want to get started too late."

"I understand that, Conrad."

"I'm ready to start with a thousand dollars right now."

"Mm-hmm. Naturally I'll get behind it as soon as we have a few meetings and arrive at some decision."

"Uh-huh."

"And I still think we ought to have the meeting here, or anyway, some place preferable to City Hall. You see what I mean, Conrad?"

"I guess so."

"I've got a nice office, and we won't be interrupted."

"All right," said Conrad Yates.

"You'll be hearing from me," said Bob Hooker.

"Or you'll be hearing from me, either one," said Conrad Yates, hanging up.

Conrad Yates kept his hand on his telephone while he thought out his next move. His next move was to flip the intercom. "Is Joe Raskin in the building?"

"I don't know, but I'll find out," said his secretary.

"I want to see him."

In less than a minute his intercom flashed. "I got Joe Raskin. He's on his way up."

Raskin entered the office. "Hyuh, Mayor," he said. "What's cookin'?"

"I got a little story for you," said Conrad Yates.

"I can use one," said Joe Raskin, who covered police headquarters and City Hall for the Gibbsville *Morning Sun*.

"I want it to get in tomorrow morning's paper."

"That'll be easy," said Raskin. "You decided to run again?"

"Nothing like that, Joe. But maybe if I like the way you handle this, maybe when I make the other announcement I'll let you have it first."

"Mayor, everybody knows you aren't running again, but what's the story?"

"For tomorrow's paper," said Conrad Yates.

"You sound as if you weren't going to give it to the *Standard*."

"I ain't going to give it to the *Standard*. They can copy it from you, if they want to."

"All right. What is it?"

"Well, Mayor Conrad L. Yates, Mayor of Gibbsville, announces that he is going to donate a thousand dollars, one thousand dollars, to start a memorial in honor of the late Joseph B. Chapin, the distinguished lawyer and citizen of Gibbsville because I always admired Joe Chapin for being a great citizen and true friend."

"A thousand bucks, eh?" said Raskin, taking notes. "What kind of a memorial? A statue, or something of that kind?"

"Haven't decided. In a few days the Mayor will gather together a group of representative citizens to form a committee to decide about the memorial. Maybe one of them things, a plaque? Anyway, something nice, and I'll start the ball rolling with a thousand dollars."

Raskin smiled. "What are you sore at Bob Hooker for?"

"Sore at Bob Hooker?"

"*He's* going to be sore at *you* if this is in the *Sun* before he can print it."

"No, I just want to make the announcement as soon as possible," said Conrad Yates. "Get things started."

"Okay by me," said Raskin. "Any more?"

"That's all, Joe. Thanks."

"Thank you, Mayor," said Raskin.

Joseph B. Chapin was finally dead. They had started fighting over him.

In 1909 there were so many old, quite old houses on Lantenengo Street that Gibbsville did not need to have the still older residences of North Frederick Street and South Main. Lantenengo Street had houses that were old enough for all sociological purposes, and in fact the more antiquated places of Frederick and South Main were not much older than the landmarks of Lantenengo. Five or six houses on Lantenengo antedated some of the South Main and Frederick houses. But even in 1909 there was already one marked difference between the people who remained on Frederick and South Main, and the people who lived on Lantenengo: it was the difference that no one coming up in the town's business and social life was moving to Frederick or South Main, while slowly (and even in 1909) the old Frederick and South Main houses were being given up by the families that owned them. A Christiana Street man began to amount to something in Gibbsville, and he moved to Lantenengo Street, to live with the other people who amounted to something. A move to Frederick Street or South Main would have been a move downward. In 1909 to build a house beyond 19th Street was considered foolish because it was too far out, and a house on Lantenengo beyond 19th Street was not considered an important symbol. "Anything to live on Lantenengo," people would say of their Christiana Street neighbors who built in the 1900-block or past it. A 1900 or 2000 Lantenengo Street address carried no more social prestige locally than a 1900 Park Avenue address in New York. Still it was Lantenengo Street and things were happening in Lantenengo Street; things that had to do with progress. In 1890 the social outpost had been 16th Street; in 1909 it was 19th. But in the Twentieth Century nobody wanted to move to North Frederick Street or South Main, and the people who did live in the two oldest residential parts of town were fond of two statements: "I was born here, and I'm going to die here," and "When I get my price, that's when I'll sell."

The money was older on South Main and North Frederick. And in some cases, there was more of it. But it was not the amount of money that mattered in the social scheme of things: Family X, living on Lantenengo Street, might be an old Gibbsville family with money, or might be a Gibbsville family with new money; but Family Y, living on North Frederick Street or South Main, belonged to the old *and* the rich of Gibbsville.

The abandonment of North Frederick Street and South Main Street in favor of Lantenengo Street and the "Roads" and "Places" and "Drives" that were developed on the West Side of Gibbsville during the Twenties, was almost entirely the doing of the young people, the young men and women who were coming to maturity in the second decade of the century. And their abandonment was, by the end of the third decade, so complete that the families that remained in the old houses were either mildly (or not so mildly) eccentric, or so old and conservative that their age and conservatism were themselves a kind of eccentricity. No children were being born in those houses, into those families that remained; the grandchildren were being born, but in the new or remodeled houses on Lantenengo Street and the roads, places and drives. (Or, worse, in one of the Gibbsville hospitals.) The desertion was so nearly total that even before Mr. Franklin D. Roosevelt and his ideas arrived in Washington, the old homes on South Main Street and North Frederick had become monuments of a passing way of life, reluctantly and fearsomely recognized as such by the sons and daughters who had deserted the monuments, and visited only at Christmas and family holidays.

The big westward movement paused briefly, but it paused, on October 14, 1909, and the temporary halt was caused by the marriage of two of Gibbsville's best young people. The marriage of Edith Stokes and Joe Chapin was important enough because of the bride and groom and the family connections involved; but it was in addition a source of satisfaction to those residents of South Main and North Frederick who were disturbed by the westward trend. Edith Stokes was South Main; Joe Chapin was North Frederick, and what was more, he was taking his bride to live at Number 10 North Frederick. It was just short of a rebuke to the other young people, those who had decided to build or buy on Lantenengo. If North Frederick was good enough for Benjamin Chapin's son Joe, it was good enough for anyone else in Gibbsville—so said the older ones. Joe's decision earned him their gratitude and their confidence; the gratitude and confidence of people who gave neither freely. It was especially gratifying to learn of Joe's decision because as a rich, handsome and young man, and the prince of an old Gibbsville family, he could have lived anywhere he chose and no one would have criticized him. He could have built a California bungalow in the 2100-block, and some excuses would have been found for him. Joe Chapin, as Joe Chapin, took on a sort of ready-made popularity among the friends of his parents, but when there were added to that the fact of his money, the fact of his good looks, the fact of his choosing to marry a Gibbsville girl, and the fact of his favoring North Frederick Street over Lantenengo, Joe Chapin established himself as a young man who could be relied upon not to confuse change with progress, and a young man who would not reject the good things of the past merely because they were of the past.

There were those who believed, without insisting upon it, that Edith Stokes was entitled to some of the credit for Joe Chapin's good sense. For of the qualities of her elders found in Edith Stokes, none was more frequently cited than her good sense. "Edith is a girl with remarkably good sense," they would say. Nor was it a remark made exclusively by the men; the women said it too. But among the men and women who were slightly inclined toward Joe as between Joe and Edith (there was, of course, no real controversy), it was always pointed out that Joe had had the good sense to pick a girl who had good sense. "Joe could have had any girl in Gibbsville, not mentioning any names," they would say. "But he had the good sense to pick Edith." There was no one in Gibbsville, at least no one who counted, who would have been so discourteous as to suggest that Edith's enormous good sense might make up for the absence of mere facial beauty. It was still the custom of the North to say of a girl that she looked very pretty today, with no intentional implication that the prettiness was not the case yesterday or likely to be tomorrow. Few girls seriously questioned the compliment, but Edith Stokes was one who never let it pass. "Oh, but I'm not pretty and I know it," she would say, saying it with such conviction and such complete lack of coquettishness that her honesty contributed to the general regard for her good sense. Just as it was somehow known, somehow common knowledge without its being discussed, that for Edith Stokes there never had been anyone but Joe Chapin. Most other girls would at least have gone through the motions of enjoying the society of young ladies and gentlemen, friends her own age. But Edith stayed away from the picnics and the boating parties at The Run, she found excuses to exclude herself from the sleigh rides and chicken-and-waffle suppers. She rode horseback and played tennis, sometimes with young men friends, but the only young man who had ever taken her to an Assembly was the young man whose name she would bear throughout her lifetime. It was never a question of breaking a date to be with Joe Chapin; when Joe Chapin was in town she would not make dates, so that when he would write her a note, or encounter her on North Main Street, he could always know that whenever he wanted to see her, she would be ready and free. "I don't consider it quite fair to pretend that you're keen on a boy when you're not, and besides, I wouldn't know the first thing about flirting," she would say.

A girl of great good sense, of honesty and simplicity, so much so that the young man whose approval of her virtues was sought finally approved. She waited for him all through the last years of prep school, of college and law school, hoping to *see* him, merely to *look* at him, when he came home for Christmas (that awful Christmas when he went visiting a college friend in New Orleans and never came home at all). She watched the face become more beautiful, the form more perfect, the manner and the manners so polished and easy through his associations and his travels to distant cities that were to her no more than stars on the map. She had no fully developed idea of what she would do with him if she were alone with him and owned him; her information on the possession of one human being by another was incomplete, based largely on hearsay and logical comparisons of her own body and functions with those of animals. But no man or boy had touched her skin under her clothing nor caressed her on the outside of her clothing, and the caresses she shared with a girl in her single year at boarding school were pleasant and even exciting, but had no finality, not, at least, to the degree that she knew would be possible if she could own Joe. She had owned the girl in school, had surprised herself by the ease and rapidity of her possession of her. The girl wrote love letters to her, did favors for her, performed menial tasks, and risked expulsion night after night by visiting her curtained bed in the dormitory, but the experience, aside from the immediate pleasure, only confirmed for Edith what she had always half known: that a girl would respond passionately to certain caresses that a man could give, and the man she wanted them from was Joe Chapin, who could also give more, but whatever more or less he could give, it would be Joe Chapin or nobody. Thus what passed for her shyness was actually restraint. Toward other girls it was restraint and superior knowledge and experience and lack of curiosity. The ease with which she had taken possession of the girl at school convinced her that it would be no more difficult with girls she had known all her life. With young men other than Joe Chapin the curiosity did not become as strong as the desire to own Joe, and in the years just preceding their marriage she became convinced that when she owned Joe she would be owning someone whom no one else had owned. She had acquired a special wisdom about Joe, and one night in her bed, alone with her thoughts, she realized that he had belonged to no one else. He was intact, virginal, uninformed, and innocent. Her own experience, which had taught her much because she was willing to learn, and the new realization of Joe's virginity, gave her an advantage that Joe could not suspect or overcome. After that she was careful, but there was a change in her, and Joe was proud of the change because, he declared, he felt that in a small way he might be responsible for giving her more confidence in herself. Which was, indeed, the truth. Joe, she was sure, would have had a talk with his father somctime before the wedding, and the mechanical techniques she could learn from him and with him, but what he did not yet know was that there were depths to passionate expression and when she owned him she would use him to explore those depths.

Such pleasures were worth waiting for, and the very idea of risking them for the honors and amusements of social intercourse was foolish and absurd. There were friends of Joe's and of hers who had had relations with women, but they had nothing to offer her. She was more than content to have them think of her as the virgin which technically she was, and the unsuspecting girl that she was not. Moreover, she was content to appear to be naïve because her naïveté kept them ignorant of her subtle efforts to make them and their bad habits unattractive to Joe. He had gentlemanly standards, but it would have been easy to compromise his standards if he were allowed to believe that affairs with women were an attractive feature of those of his friends who led that kind of life. She encouraged his friendship with Arthur McHenry, which needed no encouragement, but when she was asked to comment on other friends of Joe's—Alec Weeks, for example —she would say: "You mustn't ask me about people like Alec Weeks. He is your friend, and I don't like to say anything in criticism of your friends. Women see things in a man that other men don't . . . Well, if you insist, I can't help feeling that he's sneaky, and I like honorable men." The effect was as she wanted it to be. Joe did not give up his friendship with the Alec Weeks type of man, but the Alecs were made to seem unattractive and their conduct unworthy of emulation by honorable men like Joe Chapin and Arthur McHenry. She caused Joe to believe that he had chosen his own way of conducting himself, rather than the Alec Weeks way, because his own way was preferable, superior, more fastidious, and, of course, honorable.

They had many discussions about honor, in which she encouraged him to repeat so often the conventional observations on the subject that he came close to sounding like its principal champion, if not the inventor of it. Because of the layman's association of Honor with The Law, which causes an honorable lawyer to appear to be slightly more honorable than anyone else, she was able to speak with genuine conviction when she uttered her admiration for him as a custodian of the principle. She had no knowledge or understanding of the law, and was quick to say so, but in spite of her remoteness from it she theorized that the study and practice of law offered a fortunate young man the opportunity to learn and employ secrets about honor that were not available to the layman. Honor, indeed, became a secondary career in itself. From discussions of honor, in which they were in total agreement, they sometimes proceeded to discussions of religion, and in such discussions they were again in complete accord, even more so, if possible. And since honor could be illustrated with stories of dishonorable behavior, honor was discussed more frequently and at greater length than religion. Four years at New Haven and the years in the somewhat more inquisitive atmosphere of the Penn Law School had made no apparent change in Joe's religious belief, which was Episcopal, and Edith's acceptance of the same faith enabled her to avoid detailed discussion of a topic that is never settled anyway. Their over-all belief, which was not unique at the time, was that friends who professed the other Protestant religions were likely to be overconcerned with matters of theology; that Catholics (Roman) were people who had lost control of the beauties of ritual; and that Jews were strange Biblical characters in modern dress. The church they attended, Trinity, was comfortably Low and not vulnerable to little jokes about the Pope and incense. Attendance at Trinity was good numerically and afforded a by no means unpleasant opportunity for weekly contemplation of the relationship with God, in sanctified but not severe surroundings and in the company of persons of one's choosing. In Trinity you were in another world, where the first rule was silence, but you bowed and smiled to your acquaintances as though in that other world you were seeing friends from home. Religion was a comfort; Trinity was nice.

If they talked oftener than most young couples about religion and honor, it was not altogether an accident. During what might be termed the early days of Joe's courtship Edith was anxious to have him depend upon her for a companionship that she could offer and that would become a habit with him; a companionship that was not based on qualities that other girls had more abundantly than she. There was, first, her good sense, which everybody knew about. But what everybody did not know about was Joe's unsureness of himself, that had nothing to do with his good manners. His manners were exquisite even in a day when good manners were the rule. But she became convinced of his unsureness of himself when she had her instinctive realization of his virginity. With that knowledge she encouraged him to talk to her and to reveal himself without quite exposing himself. On matters pertaining to the law and honor and religion they were on safe ground; in her company he became an authority on everything they discussed, and above all they were not there to argue. They did not argue. More and more he would permit himself to say what he thought, either as simple statement or hope-lessly complicated theory. She listened to everything he said and her questions were slight rephrasings of his statements, which proved to him how attentively she listened and how respectfully she heard. For a year they had no physical contact beyond the clasp of hands, but what she provided was habit-forming and exhilarating and intoxicat-ing. When he left her of an evening she could hear him whistling a Yale marching song and she knew that he was already looking forward to their next meeting. She would wash her face with Roger & Gallet soap and brush her hair, and lie in her bed and want to own him. She did not yet know that there were degrees of technical profi-ciency in love-making between a man and a woman, as well as fum-blings and acute dissatisfaction; consequently in her imagination she gave little thought to his pleasure other than to take for granted that since he was a man, his pleasure would come. Her owning him was for her own pleasure; he would be hers. She never thought that *she* would be *his*. It simply never occurred to her to think of herself as his. What-ever he would do with her—caress her, lie on top of her, insert himself in her—was part of her wakeful dream of undefined sensuality, of which he was the essential and enormously desirable instrument. She was convinced that he never had seen a live nude woman close to, and she would lock her door and parade herself about her bed, wearing no clothing, and pretend that he was lying on the bed and looking at her for the first time. She had reason to be proud of her figure. It was a time of the long, tailored line, when ladies' outfits came in three pieces of skirt, blouse and ankle-length coat, following the natural waistline. The design was to make women look tall, with vertical stitching and piping to further the scheme. Edith was an ideal model for the suits and dresses, and even the hats, which were enormous and elaborate (and expensive), were, if not "becoming," effective in draw-ing the attention away from the face that was less than beautiful. No man ever had seen her unclothed, and that too was going to be part of the great sensuality when she owned Joe. She was quite aware that men of her class expected the girls of her class to be virgins, and in most cases the expectation was justified. Not knowing exactly what to expect, limited only by her unlimited imagination, she conducted orgies of the mind with herself after an evening with Joe, while at all other times maintaining a calm that was her public character. It was also the character she presented to Joe Chapin; calm, attentive, interested, sympathetic, eager to learn from him the things of the mind, the intellect.

After a while he became totally dependent upon her without realizing it. Gradually other girls had become, he told her, so frivolous and empty-headed that he was regretting invitations that would involve his having to be paired off with them. His own friends, too, his contemporaries, were beginning to appear in a bad light; they were not taking things seriously enough, not buckling down to work, not thinking things through. It was not exactly their fault, he said. They had no one to help them think things through. With this conversation Edith moved into the first stage of owning him. She began to let him do things for her. She would ask him to stop at a shop to pick up something she had ordered. She had him do little errands for her on his visits to Philadelphia. She asked for and took his advice on investing a small sum of cash. She had him read a letter of sympathy she had composed on the death of a far-off cousin. She sought his help in mapping out a trip to Europe which in truth she never intended to take. Then, so fortuitously that she would not have dared plan it, she was stricken with acute appendicitis and had to undergo emergency surgery.

At that time the appendectomy was years away from the routine operation it was later to become, and a stay in the hospital was likewise a matter for great concern. The newspapers of the day always spoke of a patient as going under the knife, chloroform was the usual anaesthetic, and the word hospital was considered to be suitable evidence of the extremity of the patient's condition. The horses drawing the ambulance proceeded at a walk or a slow trot, and the ambulance bell, pressed by a large pedal button, was more of an announcement than a warning signal. The doctor and the nurse rode inside with the patient and because of the comparatively slow pace of the team of bays, the citizens were able to have a good look at the faces of the professionals. The faces told little more than the seriousness of their mission. Nothing about the trip to the hospital or the hospital itself was likely to dispel fear or create optimism.

It was a social convention that visits to hospital patients were restricted to members of the immediate families. This was no less true for patients in private rooms, and it was especially true where the patient was an unmarried young woman. When Joe Chapin read in the paper that Edith had been taken to the hospital he first paid a call on Dr. English at the doctor's office. The doctor revealed that it had been a nasty operation and that Edith had been on the table almost three hours. In the tradition of his calling the doctor employed words of Greek and Latin origin that Joe Chapin was at a loss to understand, but in reply to the direct question Dr. English cautiously admitted that Edith would live, barring unforeseen complications.

"When do you think I can go to see her, Bill?" said Joe Chapin.

"Had you intended to go see her?"

"Well, I would like to, if possible."

"Well—not for several days at the earliest," said Dr. English. "And you understand, of course, you'd have to have permission from her family."

"Oh, of course."

"I don't as a rule encourage visiting, Joe. Edith has a day nurse and a night nurse. She's still on the critical list, and I should think it'd be a week before she'd be ready to see anybody except her family."

"I'll abide by your decision, but I'm really very anxious to see her."

"Yes. Yes. That hardly comes as a surprise; and very understandable. But for the time being I'm keeping a close watch on her to guard against any post-operative complications, you understand."

"Of course."

"And as a man of the world, you understand that a young lady doesn't always look her best in a hospital gown, so there's that to consider."

"Bill, I have to tell you this. I've never told anyone else, not even Edith herself. But I'm in love with Edith."

"I'm glad to hear that, Joe. Not altogether surprised, but I'm glad to hear it. I'll tell you what I'll do. I'll speak to her family and get their permission, and then I'll ring you up on the telephone, next four or five days. But you must bear in mind, if I do allow you to see her, it will only be for five minutes, and your conversation must be confined to cheerful topics, nothing to upset her or even—well, nothing of a romantic nature, either."

"I promise you, not a hint."

"When we have her all well again, time enough then, don't you agree?"

"By all means, Bill. By all means."

"When the time comes I'll tell her ahead of time so she'll have a chance to have the nurse brush her hair and pretty her up a little, but don't be surprised by her appearance. She's been through quite a siege. And above all, don't show that you are miserable or unhappy at the way she looks."

On the appointed day Joe Chapin walked to the hospital and stood in the waiting room until a probationer arrived to conduct him to Edith's room. The odors and the darkness of the corridor and the coughing and the walking patients and the grubby visitors to mining-accident cases were all new to Joe Chapin. But Edith's room was not unpleasant, with the bareness relieved by an abundance of flowers.

Edith looked up at him from her pillows and raised her lower arm. "Hello, Joe," she said.

"Edith, how good to see you again." He took her hand for a moment, then let it fall back to the bedcovers.

"This is Miss McIlhenny, my day nurse," said Edith.

"How do you do, Miss McIlhenny."

"Good afternoon," said the nurse.

"Your flowers have been lovely. There they are, do you see them? Recognize them?"

"I'm glad you like them," said Joe.

"It was nice of you to come."

"Nice of me? Oh, Edith, I've been trying to ever since you've been here. How do you feel?"

"Well, much better, thank you. I've lost track of the days."

"Bill English told me you're a very good patient."

"Did he? I don't think Miss McIlhenny will agree on that score."

"Indeed I will, she's been a darling, and never a whimper," said the nurse.

"I haven't much news for you, I'm afraid. I've been in court most of the time. Everybody's asked for you, but *I've* been asking *them*. Every little scrap of information I could get."

"Everybody's been so kind, especially here in the hospital. They've done everything for me, everything. I've never had so much attention, kindness. But naturally I'll be glad when it comes time to go home."

"Do you know when that will be?"

"In another week, I believe. Isn't that so, Miss McIlhenny?"

"That's what we're hoping."

"Miss McIlhenny is going with me. Shall I tell him about the belt?"

"Sure, go right ahead if it won't embarrass him."

"Did you know that you have to wear an enormous belt after you've had an operation for appendicitis?" said Edith.

"Yes, I guess I'd forgotten that."

"It has to be made especially, but even so I won't be able to ride or play tennis for at least a year. Isn't that discouraging?"

"Oh, no. A year isn't long," said Joe Chapin.

"Oh, I think it is. And I'm not even supposed to laugh very heartily."

"Very well, then we'll talk about nothing but serious subjects."

"Oh, Joe. You're a dear."

"Am I, Edith?"

"Yes, you are."

"Well," said Miss McIlhenny, taking her watch out of her pocket. "If Mr. Chapin wants to come again, he can't stay any longer this time."

"Then I'll go immediately, because I want to come back soon. May I?"

"Oh, I hope you do," said Edith. She held up her hand and he took it.

"Good-bye, Edith, dear," he said.

"Come back soon," she said.

"Thank you, Miss McIlhenny," he said, and went out. The nurse followed him.

"You done her a world of good," she said, in the corridor.

"I did?"

"And what's more, I'm going to say so to Dr. English. You gave her a lift in the spirit, and that's as good as medicine any day."

"Thank you, thank you very much. She's so pitiful, so weak."

"We almost lost her, you know, and that's a fine young lady. If she's your intended, you're a fortunate man, because I see all kinds and I know. I'll drop the hint to Dr. English. Good-bye."

"Good-bye, and thank you," said Joe Chapin.

At the first opportunity he went to Philadelphia, to the establishment of Bailey, Banks & Biddle, where he made the purchase of a solitaire. It remained in the drawer of his dresser until he had seen the convalescing Edith half a dozen times after her emergence from the hospital. Her strength returned quickly, in spite of a diet consisting chiefly of junket, and on the evening before his actual proposal she began to feel once again in command.

"When I was in the hospital do you know what I missed most of all?" she said.

"What?"

"Our evenings together."

"I hoped you would say that," he said.

"Before you came to see me, about a week before, they sent for my family one night. They were sure I was not going to—not last through the night. I don't know whether I overheard something or what it was, but I knew my condition was serious. And that was the only time I cried. I didn't cry with the pains or anything of that sort, but when I thought you and I would never have these lovely talks together again, I was so unhappy that I shed tears, and that isn't like me."

"Oh, Edith."

"And that was when I made up my mind that if I ever got well, I would tell you how much our evenings have meant to me. But then when you came to see me, Miss McIlhenny was there, and I was shy, and weak. But now I can tell you, Joe. Our evenings mean more to me than anything else."

"They do to me too, Edith. As I told you before, I wandered about in a daze. My life was nothing without you, and I was so *angry* and at the same time felt so futile, not to be able to *do* something. I slept badly and I ate hardly anything, and finally Arthur caught on and told me to ask for a postponement of the case I was trying, which I did. The other lawyers agreed, very kindly. Arthur's really a very understanding friend, you know."

"I know," said Edith. "I was sorry I couldn't see him when I was in the hospital, but I wanted to save my strength for your visits."

"Oh, he understood, Edith."

"I'm sure he did," she said. "But now that I'm getting well again, slowly but surely, I don't want you to think that you have to go on seeing me and no one else."

"I don't want to see anyone else . . . You mean other girls?"

"Yes. Our friendship—"

"It's more than a friendship, Edith. You must know that by this time."

"Must I, Joe? Remember I'm not going to be able to ride or play tennis or go bathing at The Run for an awfully long time, and I don't want you to think that our friendship, or whatever you wish to call it, gives me the right to monopolize you."

"Edith, you don't think the horseback riding and tennis are all that's important to me? It's being with you that matters, dear."

"It matters to me. Oh, Joe, I shouldn't say this, but sometimes in the hospital I longed for you."

"Edith, my darling," he said. He kissed her mouth and her eyes, and again her mouth.

"We mustn't now," she said. "My dearest."

"No," he said. "But now you know I love you."

"Yes," she said. "And I love you. That's what I was saying when I said I longed for you. With all of me, Joe. You are the only man that could make me happy, just being with you. You must go now. Please, darling."

"Yes," he said. "I know, my dearest."

"I won't see you to the door. Just let me sit here."

He got up. "Tomorrow evening, my dearest?"

"Yes," she said.

The next evening they greeted each other with smiles and when he sat beside her he took the solitaire out of its velvet box. "I want to show you something," he said.

"Oh . . ."

"Oh, it's a ring, of course. But I want to show you the box. Look at it."

"Bailey, Banks & Biddle," she said.

"Have you deduced anything?"

"You're going to propose, I hope."

"But the name of Bailey's, doesn't that tell you anything else?"

"I guess I'm not very deep."

"My dearest. You know I haven't been to Philadelphia. Now do you deduce?"

"You've had the ring?"

"Exactly, dearest. I bought it weeks ago, hoping."

"I'm waiting, dearest, and I think you know the answer."

"Will you marry me, Edith?"

"Oh, my darling, of course I'll marry you." She held back her head and he kissed her.

"Try it on," he said.

"It fits perfectly, perfectly, and how lovely, what a beautiful diamond. Exquisite. I have a present for you, too."

"Did you know I was going to propose?"

"Hoped. I've been hoping. Of course I've been hoping all these months that we would fall in love, and then we did. And when we did—I went out today, shopping." She got up and went to the spinet desk. She handed him a small package. "Open it."

He did so, and held up a moonstone stickpin. "Edith, what a beauty!"

"Do you like it?"

"It's—perfect. You've noticed that I needed one."

"Yes, you lost the one you got at graduation."

"Will you put it on for me?"

"Of course, dearest. I'm so glad you like it."

"Like it! I'll treasure it the rest of my life."

"And I my solitaire. Isn't this a happy evening, Joe?"

"It is, dearest," he said. She put on the stickpin.

"What are you frowning for?" he asked.

"Was I frowning? I didn't mean to show it. I just remembered my operation. I wonder how long before we can be married. I don't like very long engagements, do you?"

"I've never had one," he said.

"Oh, Joe, seriously."

"I'm sorry, dearest."

"I never thought of it, but we have to, don't we?"

"Yes," he said.

"That side of marriage is—a complete mystery to me."

"I know, dearest."

"You will have to—I must learn everything from you. Men always know, don't they?"

"Yes, we find out."

"Shall I ask Billy English? He's really not so much older than we are. I didn't mind his operating on me, that was different. But this is—do you think I could go to that new doctor, that woman? Dr. Kellems?"

"If you prefer, dearest. I could ask Bill English. He knows I'm in love with you. I told him while you were in the hospital. I could ask him how soon we can get married and we wouldn't have to go into details."

"I wish you would. That would make it so much easier for me. See him and ask him before we announce our engagement."

"Bill's a gentleman, but he's a doctor too, and he has to meet this situation every day. Look at all our friends that go to him."

"That's true," she said. "Oh, dearest, I'm so pleased."

"And I," he said.

"Mrs. Joseph Benjamin Chapin," she said.

"Mr. and Mrs. Joseph Benjamin Chapin," he said.

"Yes," she said.

In Gibbsville, in 1909, only a few men could tell with exactness the true wealth of the wealthy Gibbsville families. A family that had assets worth $800,000 could, and usually did, live in great comfort without spending much more money than a family worth

$200,000. It was a matter of pride with the best people of Gibbs-ville to live comfortably, but without the kind of display that would publicly reveal the extent of their wealth. A few families, whose names were given to large holdings in coal lands and to breweries and meat-packing houses, lived in American luxury. They were the owners of the early motor cars. They employed the larger staffs of servants. They had summer homes at distant resorts and led the lists of contributors to church and charity. Their wealth was a known fact and they were free to enjoy it. But behind them, obscured by the known wealthy, were the well-off, who possessed considerable fortunes and who quietly ran the town.

The Benjamin Chapins were one such family. They lived within their income, they bought only the best and they bought to last. They ordered the more expensive cuts of meat, but they watched their butcher bills and they would hold up payment over a single lamb chop. In their home was a kind of restfulness; all that was needed was there, and nothing would be changed and no additions made un-less the change or addition was required for permanent improvement. The lighting fixtures had been installed for gas; when electricity was decided upon, the fixtures were converted, not taken down. Every room in the Frederick Street house was given a good cleaning once a week, and repairs were made promptly and by men and women with special skills. When something went wrong it was rectified before it got worse, whether it was a broken breeching strap or a brick in the sidewalk. Woodwork, furniture, silverware and brasses were worn smooth in the Chapin household and everything was always in its place because its place had been carefully decided upon at the very beginning. The Benjamin Chapins made no compromise with taste as they felt it or quality as they understood it. With those principles to guide them, they also privately believed, privately but firmly, that the very fact that an object was owned by *them* made it all right, good enough for anyone and too good for most.

For the Benjamin Chapins were convinced of their own superior-ity, and when they compared themselves with other Gibbsville couples they always were able to reaffirm their self-appraisal. Benjamin Chapin's wife was born Charlotte Hofman, a Gibbsville, Penn-sylvania, Hofman, and therefore connected with the Muhlenbergs, the Womelsdorfs, the Montgomerys, the Laubachs, the Penns, the Boones, and the Leisenringers, the FitzMaurices, the Blooms, the Dickinsons, and the Pennsylvania Lees. Charlotte Hofman was only twenty when she married Benjamin Chapin, who was thirty-four, but she was quite aware that towns and counties had been named after members of her family and that noble German blood flowed in her veins. She was a woman with a live sense of her duty to the past and the future, a conviction that her body was the inheritor of elements that needed only proper fertilization for the breeding of a superior offspring. She was small, dark, and pretty, and rich, and had many suitors. She accepted Ben Chapin because he was old enough in Pennsylvania lineage to have connections almost as imposing as her own, and earlier New England connections that produced educators, soldiers, and governors. As to his own qualities, he was healthy and honest and well liked by the major stockholders of the Coal & Iron Company. She married Ben Chapin in 1881 and their son, whom they called Joseph Benjamin Chapin after Ben's father, was born in the succeeding year. The first was the only child to live; he was followed by two stillborn babies, the second of them badly deformed, and after the birth of the sub-normal child Charlotte Chapin withdrew almost completely from society and devoted herself to the fancywork at which she was proficient and the raising of her son.

Her son grew quickly and tall, and ever closer to his mother. He displayed admiration and respect for his father, but demonstrations of affection were reserved for his mother. As he grew taller she would make him sit on the footstool so that she could rumple his fine brown hair, which was silky and straight and unruly until he went to Yale and slicked it down. Throughout his prep school years in Pottstown, the four years in New Haven, and the time at law school in Philadelphia, Joe wrote his mother twice weekly without fail. His letters were slangy and largely in a humorous vein, often padded with scores of athletic contests and university notices that were extracted from the college newspaper, but also providing a fair chronological record of his social and scholastic activities, and keeping her informed of his friendships and what he called his hateships. He wrote to his father only when it was necessary, as for accounting purposes and for permission to change college courses and take trips, and to tell him that he was going to join Alpha Delta Phi, his father's fraternity. He went out for the freshman crew and for the varsity eight in his sophomore year and almost made the tennis team, but among his friends athletic prowess was not regarded as the thing, any more so than conspicuous brilliance as a scholar or success as a heeler of other extra-curricular activities.

In his letters from New Haven and from Philadelphia, Joe Chapin mentioned girls' names only when they were to be, or had been, hostess or guest of honor. In the hearty tradition of his college and his day, Joe referred to girls as women, making generalizations about women that characterized the entire sex as foolish or romantically cruel, and in any case to be avoided. The attitude, of course, pleased his mother. She seldom lost an opportunity to point out that she had married his father when Ben Chapin was thirty-four. Women, she generalized, aged more rapidly than men; a man ought to marry a much younger woman; a man of forty was still a young man, a woman of forty was well along in years. She did not touch upon the subject of the menopause as such, but she convinced her son that to marry before thirty was to take on burdensome responsibilities that could easily thwart a young lawyer's career, and unnecessarily at that, since a man had all his life in which to raise a family. Impersonally, without mentioning any names, Charlotte Chapin would remind her son that the girls he was seeing during his college years were not really a great deal younger than he was. There was, she said, all the time in the world before getting serious.

The campaign was enormously successful, not only in the way she had planned, but in a way she could not have thought of. Joe Chapin, fixing on no particular girl, increased his popularity because he was equally attentive to all girls. He was handsome, he had nice manners, he was graceful, he dressed well, he seemed to have money, he was a member of Wolf's Head, he was considerate of his elders, and he laughed readily. At the same time he was not a fop or effeminate, nouveau riche, or patronizing with the parents of the girls he saw. A few of the fathers dismissed him as a snob, but there was one New York mother who lightened that characterization: "But what has he got to be snobbish about? He's from Pennsylvania." Joe's own father had unintentionally prepared the way for his son. There were men in New York and Philadelphia who had known Ben Chapin at Yale, and remembered him as a worthwhile fellow who had made no enemies, had got into no scandal, and of whom they would say to Joe: "I think I must have known your father. Was he a Yale man, about the Class of '68 or '69?" It was easy, in those days of more difficult transportation, for a New York man to lose touch with fellows he had known in college, and it was especially easy with a fellow like Ben Chapin, who had left a favorable but not an indelible impression. Chapin, moreover, was not an extraordinarily uncommon name. Thus when the personable young man turned out to be the son of Ben Chapin, '69, the boy's attractiveness was of a safe kind: nothing dangerous could possibly have been sired by old

Ben, and if the boy wanted to be a bit of a snob, well, that was a more self-respecting characteristic than if he had chosen to be a rounder and a roué, or a worthless bohemian.

"Do you ever see any old friends of mine?" Ben once asked his son. "In New York, I mean."

"Yes, Father. Oh, yes."

"Who, for instance? Frank Garth, for instance? He lives in New York. And a doctor named Ralph Dole?"

"Dole, let me see. No, I don't think so, Father."

"What about Frank Garth?"

"Well, I'm not sure. Frank Garth. Mr. *Blaine*. I met a Mr. Blaine that asked me if you were my father."

"Oh, really? L. B. Blaine? *That* Blaine?"

"L. B.? Yes, Mr. Lewis Blaine."

"Is that so? I never knew him very well. I'm rather surprised he remembers me. He was in Skull & Bones. Family had a big place at City Island. Very well-to-do people. I haven't seen Lew Blaine in over twenty years. Guyon Bardwell. Ever see a fellow named Guyon Bardwell? He lived on Staten Island, and I imagine still does."

"Bardwell. No, I don't think so, although I did go to Staten Island this year. It's a beautiful place."

"Beautiful. I used to visit the Bardwells there. Guyon Bardwell had a sister Amy, married a classmate of ours from Chicago. My, it's a long time since I've thought about some of these people. Do you realize it was only a short time after the Civil War? If the war'd continued a few years longer, I'd have been in it."

"Yes, I know."

"Lew Blaine. He had a brother Ivan, and I've often wondered why they chose a Russian name. We had some very interesting fellows in our class. For two years I was the only Gibbsville boy at Yale. I think that's the only time that ever happened, that only one Gibbsville boy was at Yale. Scranton, Reading, Harrisburg. But I was the only one from Gibbsville. It just happened that way. Fellows like Lew Blaine had never heard of Gibbsville."

"They still haven't," said Joe Chapin. "I've often found it saves time and useless explanation if you just say you're from Philadelphia."

"You do? Why did you do that?"

"To save time and useless explanation."

"But I don't think it would have been useless explanation. There's such a thing as polite curiosity, you know, and if someone is curious enough to ask you where you came from, they probably are polite enough to, and curious enough to, listen while you tell them. Now how much more interesting you'd have been if instead of aligning yourself with the large crowd of Philadelphia boys, you told them you were from Gibbsville. All those people know all about Philadelphia, but they don't know a thing about Gibbsville."

"That's exactly my point, Father."

"Then you should have told them."

"What is there to tell? It's a small town in the Pennsylvania coal region. Not even as big as Scranton."

"Not even as big as Wilkes-Barre, either. But not the *same* as Scranton, not the *same* as Wilkes-Barre."

"If I started to expatiate on the glories of Gibbsville I'm afraid my audience would turn away."

"Then I'm afraid I have a low opinion of their manners, a very low opinion indeed. And if all they're interested in is New York and Philadelphia and Boston, then I won't give them much credit for their intelligence. It isn't where a man comes from that counts . . ."

"Yes, but Father, that's *my* point. Would you consider it polite if I were to bore my friends with a description of the town I happened to be born in?"

"And your mother and I, both your grandfathers and both of your grandmothers, and *their* fathers and mothers."

"But some of those New York people, and Boston, and Philadelphia, their families go back so far that I'd run out of greats."

"Well, in my day they were ladies and gentlemen, and if they asked a man where he came from, they had the good manners to let him answer their question. And they might learn something into the bargain."

"Well, I suppose I'll have to tutor in Gibbsvilliana. I'm not even sure of the population."

"No, you won't have to tutor, but you might brush up on your own manners, starting with more respect for your father."

"I'm sorry, Father."

"I trust you are, and I accept your apology."

"Thank you."

"And the population of Gibbsville is 17,000, mostly English, German, Welsh and Irish stock."

"Thank you."

"And it's a very good town to live in, as I hope you'll find out some day."

The conversation, which took place in the summer between Joe's graduation from Yale and entrance in the Penn Law School, was typical of the Chapin father-and-son colloquies. They would begin amiably enough, but nervous impatience would set in, followed by sarcasm and apology, and the father's attempts at humor usually came too late.

Ben Chapin away from his legal work was of the loneliest of men. The vigorousness of which his wife spoke to their son as being present in men of middle age was present in Ben Chapin, but after the second stillbirth she never returned to Ben's bed. There was no dramatic scene, there was no theatrical announcement, and there was only one conversation. "Charlotte," said Ben one evening, "can't we go back to sharing our room together again?"

"I don't think so, Ben."

"I miss you."

"I know, and I miss you, but you know what's bound to happen. And if I'm not there, it won't happen."

"But I'm not an old man, Charlotte. Not yet."

"No, and I'm not a dead woman. But I would be if I had to go through another confinement and the same thing happened."

"I see. Yes, I see."

For the next ten years Ben paid visits at irregular intervals to a whorehouse on Arch Street, Philadelphia, where he would get slightly drunk before going to bed with one of the women, and wholly drunk afterward. The place was expensive because of the vigilance of the man and woman who owned it. If a girl was known to be diseased, she was fired; if she spoke to a patron on the street, she was fired. And a new patron had to be introduced in person by an old patron. Young men in their twenties, no matter who they were, were not admitted, but there was no limit above thirty. The girls submitted to or participated in any perversion that did not involve the drawing of their blood or the burning of their flesh. Ben Chapin was a simple man, whose wants were simple, and after he had slept off his drunkenness he would return to his hotel for a day or two until he was able to go back to Gibbsville and face his wife without showing his hatred of her.

Then after ten years of the visits to Arch Street the need became less urgent and was dissipated in his dreams. He had one experience in a Washington hotel that put an end to his overt sexual life. He had gone to the dining room for breakfast and was again in his room, lying on the unmade bed and reading his newspaper. He dozed off, and was awakened by the chambermaid's key in the door. When the door opened he saw her, a handsome Negress of thirty or more.

"Come here," he said.

"I be back, sir."

"Come here."

"I can't. I be fired."

"I'll give you five dollars."

"No, sir. Ten dollars."

"All right, ten dollars. Lock the door and get on the bed."

"Wutta you goin' do to me?"

"You know what I'm going to do to you."

"You goina hurt me?"

"I'm not going to hurt you. Take off your clothes, quick."

She obeyed him, and lay on the bed. "You take off your clothes?"

"No," he said. He managed to get inside her a matter of seconds before it was over. "All right, now go."

"That all? I want my ten dollars."

"I'll give you your ten dollars, just go."

"Yes, sir. You want me to come back?"

"No, God damn it, just put your clothes on and go."

"Cap'n, I do' want you angry with me. I can't he'p it if you too quick. Quick or slow, I can still get in the family way."

It was the only completely uncontrollable surging he had ever had, and the possible consequences frightened him as nothing had ever frightened him. He was not afraid of blackmail; he knew that a blackmailing chambermaid had no chance. But there was nothing in his past experience that had warned him of himself as a potential rapist. His relations had been entirely with Charlotte, and with the Arch Street whores, and if anything Charlotte was more freely passionate than the paid women. He never had had to consider rape as a kind of trouble he might get into. But he knew in all honesty that if the chambermaid had not submitted for money, he would have taken her violently. It was a real danger now, and the risk governed his thinking in relation to all women. And thus the chambermaid became the last woman to receive the seed that reposed in the body of Ben Chapin. It was a secret he was often tempted to tell his wife.

But he was not altogether sure that he wanted to take revenge upon her. He knew that Charlotte was making him old and souring his final years. And he was subtle enough to realize that the reason was too subtle for her to discover; it was not only the fear of giving birth to an idiot or dead child; it was her obsession with her son and his life. Ben was acquainted with the crime of incest, and the absence of incestuous practice did not remove the possibility of an incestuous desire, no matter how monstrously preposterous the idea might seem to Charlotte (and, until the years of denial, to Ben). As Ben's hatred became a real and final thing he grew to see that Charlotte was a limited, if not a stupid, woman, and that the boy was a handsome and bright creature, but lacking in warmth. Joe was not cold, for the cold ones can be passionate too. But he was lacking in warmth. Some nights in his bed, trying for sleep, afraid to drink himself drunk because he was afraid to rape his wife—Ben would fancy that perhaps his revenge upon Charlotte would come through the boy himself, through his lack of warmth. He, Ben, might not be there to see it, but it might come. And when he discovered that ironic possibility, that the loving mother might suffer through the well-loved son, Ben began to sleep a little better.

A married couple always presents an absurdly untruthful picture to the world, but it is a picture that the world finds convenient and a comfort. A couple are a man and a woman, and what goes on between them the world never knows, could not possibly know, does not anxiously want to know, unless the man and the woman are so spectacularly unhappy that the private events become public knowledge. But what is conveniently and comfortably regarded as a happy couple is accepted as such so long as the couple appear as a unit and refrain from revealing the slightest disturbance. The mistake a couple can make is to let the outside world inside for a brief second's look at a brief second of unhappiness. Then the unity is broken and the world demands to know more, and if there is no more at the moment, a live man and a live woman, who can breathe and love, can breathe and hate as well, and as they do they provide the world with the satisfied curiosity that it demands before passing on to something else. Ben Chapin's whores and his chambermaid had an outside look at the inside of the Ben Chapin marriage, but the whores and the mercenary chambermaid were a special unhappy world of their own, and so deep and selfish in their unhappiness that they cared nothing about the misery of a stranger. In that respect Ben Chapin and his wife were fortunate; the uncaring whores and the chambermaid were the only ones who had been given an inside look. The rest of the world saw a happy couple, a long-established happy couple who might even be asked for recipes and formulas for the creation of a happy marriage. In their own small family, in the person of their only son, there was a candidate for happy marriage who wanted the benefit of their advice and experience. So carefully had the Chapins as a couple maintained the appearance of unity that their son, a not altogether insensitive creature, had not questioned the veracity of the picture. And in that respect the Chapins were entitled to their belief in their superiority; they kept their secrets from the world; they made the world believe what they wanted the world to believe. In worldly terms they had a highly successful, a model, marriage. Indeed, they appeared to demonstrate successful marriage in a day when publicly unsuccessful marriages were exceptional. Among their close acquaintances there were occasional evidences of infelicitous marital relationships, usually blamed on the husband's drunkenness; but divorce had not occurred in the American history of the Chapin and the Hofman families. Under the unwritten rules of the time, Ben could have beaten and raped his wife with impunity; the screams of violently abused women were heard not only in the poorer districts of the town, where, to be sure, they were heard more frequently. But in accordance with the superiority they felt, Ben and Charlotte Chapin adhered to the ladylike and gentlemanly code which regulated all social activity and personal behavior, even including, by extension, the act of procreation. A gentleman did not force his attentions on a lady; the lady protected the gentleman's pride by pleading a splitting headache or by telling him that it was her time of the month. In the case of Ben and Charlotte Chapin the code actually did regulate their conduct, had regulated it throughout the early years of their marriage, so that when Charlotte made the announcement that began the years of denial, Ben was already accustomed to acceding to her wishes. He conformed because that was what he believed; he never gave any thought to the fact, and it was a fact, that if he had disregarded her wishes, she would have had no one to turn to. She would not have confided in anyone, she would not have cried for help, she would not have left him. They were living in a time when it was unthinkable for a woman of Charlotte's background to confide to another woman that her husband had seen her breasts. More explicit confidences were more unthinkable. An admission of sexual incompatibility was fantastically unlikely.

And so, to all outward appearances, the successful marriage of the father and mother of Joe Chapin.

The demonstrated affection between the son and the mother was considered by their friends and relations to be a most desirable state of affairs. The love of a mother for her son was taken for granted; but while a son was expected to love his mother, only a few sons were so palpably devoted as Joe Chapin was to Charlotte. Other sons might be reasonably polite and respectful; Joe Chapin was courtly. Other mothers envied Charlotte and made efforts to inspire their own sons to emulation of Joe, but whenever the mothers started, they started too late. Charlotte was fond of saying that all the time she was carrying Joe she had known she would have a son and that he would be beautiful and brilliant (she did not go so far as to claim that she knew her next two pregnancies would be failures). An irreverent member of the household staff said that you would have thought it was Jesus and not Joseph that was getting circumcised, the day the child's foreskin was cut. Throughout Joe's boyhood Charlotte supervised every detail of his life; his health, his schooling, his playtime, his friendships. Nor was anyone else allowed to punish him. When he was small she spanked his behind; when he grew taller she made him hold out his hand for slaps with a foot-rule. But in spite of the corporal punishment the relationship was not endangered. It would have been a very stupid child who did not notice that corporal punishment was always followed by a gift, or by special privilege.

Charlotte's supervision of Joe's activities entirely relieved the boy's father of most paternal responsibilities, and particularly the responsibility of punishment. But as a consequence Ben was hardly more than a nominal, although an actual, father. He and the boy shared a roof and not much else, and after Joe went to boarding school, even the roof was less often shared. Joe's allowance was determined by Charlotte and sent by her. It was not rigidly held to. She permitted him to borrow on future allowances, and then in June, because he had passed to a higher grade, she would write off the borrowing.

"What do you do with your money?" she asked him in the prep school days.

"Oh—spend it."

"But what on? Do you treat the other boys?"

"I should say not—well, when it's my turn I do, but not like Fothergill. He's a boy from Chicago that always wants to treat everybody. He thinks he can buy people."

"I'm glad to hear you don't do that, my dear."

"I should say not."

"But what do you do with your money? Do you play cards?"

"Oh, sure I play cards, but not for money. They'd ship me home if they found that out."

"And you're much too young to drink."

"Don't be too sure about that, Mummy. I know other boys my age that drink."

"They do? At The Hill?"

"Oh, but I wouldn't tell you who they are."

"No, I don't want you to be a tattletale."

"I want to get the gold watch Father promised me, so you don't have to worry about me drinking till I'm twenty-one."

"When you go to Yale you may drink wine. You'll be invited out to dinner and they'll serve wine. I have to speak to your father about that. But no spirits."

"Can I drink beer?"

"I don't know. I've wondered about that. We'll see if it's the custom. I don't want people to think you're strange. Let's get back to the money. What do you spend it on? Your clothing bills come to us."

"Well, I bought two sweaters. One was two and a half and the other was three dollars. And pennants for my room."

"You bought those in Lower Middler."

"Well, things *like* that, I buy that *sort* of thing. Let me see, we chipped in to buy a present for the baseball coach."

"That was nice. What else?"

"It's really very hard to say. But we always have these little expenses. They take up a *lot* of *collections*. And when we have a spread. And sweaters and baseball gloves. And just ordinary gloves. I'm always losing gloves—or other boys swipe them."

"Well, I can see that I'm not going to find out what becomes of your money. Just as long as you don't spend it on the wrong things. That's really what I wanted to inquire. And always buy the best. There's almost no such thing as a bargain."

"Oh, I believe in buying the best."

"Your father and I have always believed in that."

"Father? I knew you did, but I often think Father doesn't care about the best."

"I don't know where you got that idea. Such as?"

"Oh—I don't know. We're richer than the McHenrys, but Arthur's house is nicer than ours."

"Don't *ever* say that *again*, do you hear me?"

"Well, they have newer things."

"I'm not objecting to what you said about this house. I am objecting to what you said about the McHenrys and us."

"But aren't we richer?"

"I don't know—yes, we are, but what if we are? Where did you hear that?"

"Arthur's father told me. That's what he always says when I have something and Arthur hasn't. He says we can afford things because we're richer."

"I've never heard of Arthur being deprived of anything."

"I know. It's just because Mr. McHenry is stingy and you're not. He's terribly stingy, Mr. McHenry."

"I don't like you to use words like stingy when you're speaking of your elders, I don't care who they are."

"But that's what he is."

"I *said* I don't like you to use that word."

"I didn't. I just said that's what he is, I didn't use the word."

"Joe, you're clever, you're very clever. You *are* going to be a lawyer."

"When I am I hope I'll be a better one than some people."

"Now! Not another word!"

"Why, Mummy? You don't know who I was thinking of."

The expression, the wrong side of the tracks, never caught on in Gibbsville. A Gibbsville citizen would know only too well that so long as a single Chapin lived on Frederick Street, "the wrong side" was much righter than the opposite side; the expression would have no meaning. The numbered and tree-named streets of Gibbsville, for example, never had been and never would be known as anything but the addresses of the middle-class and the poor. There were two kinds of people on Frederick Street; there were the old-rich, whose families had made it an important address—and there were the others.

The old-rich as well as the others had to pass through the same ugly part of the town on their way to shop, to the bank, to the doctor's office, to social engagements on the west side of the railroad tracks. It had been that way even before the railroads arrived; in the days of the Old Canal that part of town had been a section that a lady on foot did not linger in. As in every town, as in nearly every city, the railroad station area became a tough area, infested with thieves and procurers, whores and hoodlums. Gibbsville was like any other American town in that the first impression and the last impression it created was that the traveler would have been safer at home—except that in the traveler's home town conditions were identical with the conditions in Gibbsville. Railroad Avenue was the street of the dives; the intersection of Christiana Street and Railroad Avenue was the local capital of crime and violence.

Through this district Charlotte Chapin had to pass on her way to Main Street. Her visits to Main Street were infrequent; her visits on foot were rare, since she always had a carriage or a cutter at her disposal. And her walks past Christiana and Railroad, unescorted, were rarer still. But they did occur. She never forgot either one of them, and there were only two.

She was twenty years of age and a recent bride, in the spring of 1881, and on a certain warm and bright afternoon she announced to the coachman that she would *walk* to Mr. Chapin's office, and that Connelly, the coachman, could meet her there instead of following the original plan, which was for Connelly to drive her to the office, meet Mr. Chapin and from there drive to a wedding at Trinity Church.

"Will I folly you with the carriage, ma'am?" said Connelly.

"Follow me? Why? I'm not going to faint."

"Christiana and Railroad, ma'am," said Connelly.

"I hardly think I'm going to be accosted in broad daylight," said Charlotte Chapin.

"I'm always prepared for the worst contingency, ma'am," said Connelly.

"Thank you for looking out for me, Connelly, but nothing's going to happen." She smiled at Connelly, whom she liked.

"You're welcome, ma'am, but you won't mind if I do folly you. The Mister'd skin me alive if I didn't."

"All right," she said.

She set out on her stroll and all went well until she came to the corner of Christiana and Railroad, the northwest corner, which was occupied by Dutch Amringen's saloon. The swinging doors had been installed for the summer and there was a large picture of a billy goat on a weather-worn sign reading Bock Beer On Sale which was swinging at the entrance. The sidewalk on the Christiana Street side was roofed over in front of the places of business in that block, and while that was not an unusual condition in Gibbsville, it had the effect in that neighborhood of making the passerby feel he was closer to the inside of Amringen's and places like it than he ever might venture. The cigar butts and fresh tobacco juice on the brick side-walk were a peril to the long-skirted and dainty. It was too early in the day for the songs and loud talk that were to be heard nightly in that block on Christiana Street, but voices from the saloons could be heard, rough laughter and heavily masculine conversations. A few were in front of Dutch Amringen's, smoking stogies and spitting tobacco juice, while comfortably seated on beer barrels. And as always the foot traffic in that block was made to seem heavier because so many men stood along the curb and the building line, and others chatting in the middle of the sidewalk made passersby walk around them. It was an atmosphere in which every respectable citizen was regarded as a trespasser.

A well-built man in his thirties, obviously half drunk, dressed in his poor best and with newly trimmed red hair and beard, came out of Rinaldo's barber shop as Charlotte Chapin reached the entrance to Dutch Amringen's next door. At first he seemed to be trying to make way for Charlotte, but as he moved to his right, she moved to her left, and when she moved to her right, he moved to his left.

"Girlie's playing," said the man. "Give us a little kiss."

"Get out of my way, you disgusting man," said Charlotte.

"Get outa my way, you disgusting man. You got a pretty little pussy? Have you?" Now he was deliberately blocking her way.

"Get—*out!*" she said.

"Me see your little pussy," said the man.

She quickly turned and would have gone back toward home, but the loafing men had almost immediately noticed the scene and were laughing loudly. The red-bearded man was encouraged by their laughter and he reached out and grasped her arm. At that moment Connelly, who had been following Charlotte in the victoria, jumped from the box and brought the loaded end of his whip down on the red-haired man's skull. The man sank to the sidewalk, bleeding. Charlotte ran to the carriage. Connelly, brandishing the whip, backed to the carriage, remounted the box and they drove away. They reached Main Street before the loafing men could organize an attack on Connelly, and no attack was made. For many of the loafing men there was a police deadline halfway between Railroad Avenue and Main Street, and to go beyond the deadline meant automatic arrest, thirty days in the county prison, and dreadful beatings between arrest and sentencing. Consequently the deadline was carefully observed.

"I'll get Constable Morgan," said Connelly.

"You'll do no such thing," said Charlotte. "But thank you, Connelly."

"We better have him arrested. He won't be hard to recognize, with that broken head o' his."

"You may have killed him. Do you know him?"

"Never laid eyes on him in me life before," said Connelly.

"Don't go to Mr. Chapin's office just now. I want to think."

"You'll excuse me, ma'am, but maybe you've got too much spunk."

"I don't want you to say a word to Mr. Chapin, not a single word. Do you hear? I'll be very, very cross, do you hear, Connelly?"

"I hear, ma'am."

"You hear, but I want you to heed as well as hear. Now we can drive to Mr. Chapin's office."

Connelly did not report the episode until later in the evening, first extracting a near-promise from Ben Chapin that he would say nothing to Charlotte. Neither Ben nor Charlotte ever discussed the incident, but Connelly from that day on was never without a pistol, and the bearded man, a mule-skinner at one of the mines, was arrested and sent to the county prison for being drunk and disorderly. His absence cost him his job, although in time he was able to find employment elsewhere in the coal region. Connelly, too, moved away after a few years. He was a sober man, not given to frequenting saloons, but he and his wife found that many of their friends stopped speaking to them, and would not sit in the same pew at Mass if they saw the Connellys first. Connelly became known as a spy, a vague term but the worst thing an Irishman could call another Irishman.

Six years passed before Charlotte again walked beneath the wooden awning in front of Dutch Amringen's. In 1888 she was boarding the Gibbsville train at Philadelphia, and a car's length ahead of her on the platform she could see—and instantly recognize—the red-bearded man, carrying a satchel and apparently about to take the same train. The next day she walked past Amringen's saloon on her way to Main Street and on her way home from Main Street, but the man was nowhere to be seen. She was unable to admit to herself the real reason for her curiosity about the man. She was, however, able to deny that the real reason was deeper than curiosity. In the long run the denial amounted to the admission, for Charlotte Chapin was not a stupid woman.

She was a far from stupid woman. From among her numerous suitors she had selected the man who, besides all the obvious eligibilities of family and money, offered the least likelihood of opposition to what she wanted out of life. Ben Chapin was not likely to make demands on her person (and her guess proved correct), but he was physically fit to reveal to her the mysteries of the bed. She was the purest of virgins, but she could not accept the conventional belief that love-making was enjoyed by the man alone, a distasteful preliminary to the holy joy of motherhood. She believed in God, and it did not seem to be a part of the divine kindness to give the male sex all of the pleasure and the female sex all of the pain. More mundanely, she had been stimulated by touches of a young man's hand on her own hand, and when she relived the experience in her active mind, she conceded that the excitement was not confined to the hand. The desire to be touched again was something she felt in her body, between her shoulders and her knees. She was not given to exchanges of confidences with her contemporaries, and as a consequence she took in less misinformation than she might have. The logic of sexual apparatus was apparent to her in her girlhood, and the only major surprise she received from Ben was in the difference between a passionate living man and pictures of soft cherubim.

It was Ben's bad luck to be the father of the stillborn babies, and thus to become associated with the tragedies as wholly or partly to blame. It made little difference to Charlotte whether she blamed Ben or the act of love-making; the man and the act became the one thing, and it was an abhorrent thing. What was worse for their relationship, she cared not at all whether Ben's needs were satisfied with another woman, so long as no scandal was involved. In the first years of their marriage she had been possessively jealous when Ben would innocently flirt with another girl. She never quite loved him with the great finality of love, but there was in the beginning enough pleasure in his company and in the state of wifehood to make the relationship live. The mess and the pain of the second stillbirth likewise killed the relationship for her, and she had sufficient excuse to make her announcement.

Things had not turned out quite as she had planned when selecting Ben to be her husband, but now, after the second dead baby, she gave up her husband and devoted herself to her son. It was a new start, but she was getting what she wanted. She had her home, her position in relation to her fellow man, and she had her son. She had a husband who would complacently supply an official parenthood, without interfering in the upbringing of the son. She had picked very well indeed when she picked Ben Chapin, for in this houseful of good manners she encountered no resistance to her acts and methods. And just as though she had done it deliberately (which she had not), she destroyed any love between the boy and his father. The father was made to seem just short of a fool; the son was made to seem just short of sacred.

The years went by. Christmases would come and presents would be exchanged at a most elaborately festooned fireplace, and Ben instituted, but after two tries dropped, the custom of reading *A Christmas Carol* by Charles Dickens. On the Fourth of July they would go to Ben's office to watch the parade of the Grand Army of the Republic, and Joe would be taken to a children's picnic at The Run. Foley, the coachman who succeeded Connelly, instructed the boy in the arts of riding and driving and introduced him to strong language. The father helped the son with his arithmetic and algebra and first-year Latin, but the mother supervised the rest of his scholastic work. She would hear his spelling and listen to his reading, making him repeat the readings so that she could correct the Pennsylvania Dutchisms that occurred in his speech. Her own accent was refined and precise as a result of the influence of an English nanny, and she was determined to protect Joe as much as possible from the singsongy delivery that was more or less common to Gibbsville children who were not Irish. Ben's speech was plain, closer to New England-Yankee than any other influence, although he pronounced his r's. On such matters as the knotting of a cravat and gentlemanly jewelry Ben was allowed authority, but the only thing he ever really taught the boy was how to swim.

Ben came home from the office one July day when Joe was six years old. It was noon, time for dinner. "Good morning, Father," said the boy. "Mother has a headache."

"Oh," said Ben.

Foley's sister, Martha, entered the sitting room and announced that Mrs. Chapin had a headache and would not be down for dinner.

"So I understand," said Ben. "Tell your brother to put Blackie in the cut-under and bring him around to the front door. Right away, please, Martha."

"Will you be having your dinner now, sir?"

"No. Just do as I tell you, please."

"Where are you going, Father?"

"I'll tell you in a minute. Is your mother asleep?"

"I don't know. I guess so."

"Well, tiptoe upstairs and see, and come right down and tell me."

The boy was unaccustomed to orders, but he did as directed and returned to report that his mother was asleep. "We're going for a drive, you and I."

"You and I, Father?"

"Yes."

"I didn't ask Mummy."

"I'll leave word. I'll write her a note. She won't be worried."

"Yes she will, Father."

"Not after I've written this note."

"Where are we going?"

"It's a surprise."

Ben was writing the note to Charlotte.

"What kind of a surprise?"

"A nice one," said Ben. "Now don't ask me any more questions till I've finished this note."

"Are we going away somewhere?"

"Hmm?"

"Where are we going?"

"A place you like to go to," said Ben.

"The carriage is out front, sir," said Martha.

"Give this to Mrs. Chapin when she wakes up. Come on, son."

The father and son drove away in the cut-under and Ben refused to vouchsafe any information until it was unmistakable that they were driving to The Run.

"Are we going to The Run?"

"Yes."

"What for?"

"A surprise."

"A picnic, Father?"

"You'll see."

The Run was the name for a large reservoir owned by the coal company. The shores were lined with boathouses, elaborate and simple. The Chapin boathouse was not one of the simple places. Ben got out and lowered the horse's checkrein and knotted the tie-strap.

"What are we going to do?" said Joe.

"We're going for a swim."

"I can't swim, Father, you know that."

"Now's the time to learn." They entered the boathouse and went downstairs to the men's dressing room. Ben took off his clothes and put on his bathing suit. "Well, get undressed, son."

"I don't want to. I don't want to learn to swim."

"Now, just take off your clothes and hang them up over there."

"I want to go home!"

"All in good season. Shall I undress you, or can you undress yourself?"

"I don't want to get undressed. I don't want to learn to swim! I want Mummy!"

"She can't hear you, son. Now do as I say, or I'll do it for you."

The boy took off his clothes and laid them in a pile and stood waiting for the next move.

"That's a good boy. Now for a dip."

The water was eight feet deep in front of the Chapin boathouse. Into it Ben suddenly threw his son, then after a few seconds he lowered himself into the water and took hold of the screaming, thrashing child.

"See? Now you can swim."

In half an hour the boy actually could swim. When Ben said it was time to go home the boy asked to go in once more and Ben granted the permission. They dried themselves and got into their street clothes.

"See? Now you can swim. Isn't that splendid? Did you like it? Do you like being able to swim?"

"Yes. Oh, yes. Wait till I tell Mummy I can swim."

"It's the only way to learn. It's the way I learned. Sorry I had to take you by surprise, but that's the only way. And you'll never forget it. Once you learn to swim, you never forget. Isn't that splendid?"

They drove to the stable and went through the yard to the house together, the father with his hand on the boy's shoulder. "I hope Mummy's awake so I can tell her."

"She is. I see her at the window."

The boy looked up and waved and his mother waved back. "Come up and see me, dear," she called to him.

"I have a surprise for you," said the boy. He and his father went to Charlotte's room.

"Tell me *all* about it," said Charlotte. "I want to know everything you did."

The boy gave an accurate, excited account of the swimming lesson. When he finished his mother said, "Have you had any dinner?"

"No, Mummy."

"I thought not. Well, run downstairs now. Your father will be down in a minute or two."

The boy left the bedroom. When the door was closed they sat

until they heard his rapid footsteps on the stairs, then Charlotte got up and crossed the room and slapped Ben's face three times, four times. "I could kill you," she said.

"I understand that, Charlotte."

"You are a pig, a coward, a beast. Do you realize what could have happened? Hit his head on a stone? Heart attack from that freezing water? You are the worst son of a bitch that ever lived. Do you hear me? You are the worst son of a bitch that ever lived. You are a son of a bitch, a son of a bitch. You are a fucking son of a bitch, do you hear me? You son of a bitch. Oh, I'd like to kill you. I'd love to kill you so that you'd die in horrible pain, and I could watch you."

"I know that, Charlotte."

"And you did it to torture me."

"No," said Ben. "I wanted to teach your boy to swim, and I did."

"You son of a bitch."

"*You* can't swim," said Ben. "Now you can go to The Run with him and he won't drown. Before this you couldn't save him. Now he can swim. Now if you'll excuse me."

He went downstairs and from the dining room the boy called to him. "Is that you, Father?"

"Yes, my dear. I have to go back to the office. Good-bye."

"Good-bye, Father," said the boy.

Charlotte should have been—but was not—grateful to Ben if for no other reason than that Ben's drastic introduction to swimming put Joe on equal terms with Arthur McHenry. Arthur had learned to swim the same way, but earlier than Joe, and Charlotte did not like the idea that Arthur could be better at anything than Joe was. She had plans for Arthur even at that age: Arthur was a nice boy, a quiet, steady boy, well born and healthy, and devoted to Joe. The friendship between the boys was a natural and genuine thing and needed no more than propinquity for a start. But Charlotte gave it active and thorough encouragement. She wanted Joe to have a *suitable* friend; a boy with the same background but an ancillary personality. She was not convinced that at the age of six Joe was a brilliant boy in the things of the mind, but she correctly judged her son to have the makings of a brilliant personality. He had good looks that were not likely to suffer during the distortions of puberty and adolescence. (The fine thin nose, the beautifully formed thin lips.) His way with servants was something you were born with, almost never acquired, almost never lost. At a children's party he was the child whom, besides their own offspring, the other mothers looked at. He was accused of arrogance and insolence before he was ten years old, and in most instances the accusations were unjustified. But the mothers of lumps of children felt keenly the difference between their own scions and the Chapin heir. Joe, the most mannerly child, was subject to the severest scrutiny because his slightest departure from the conventional politenesses was automatically exaggerated by the very fact of his usual good manners.

At a party at the Montgomerys' when Joe was ten an incident occurred that affected various lives out of proportion to the words and deeds making up the incident. The game was Hide the Thimble. The thimble was hidden, and the children trooped into the parlor to search for it. Blanche Montgomery, the mother of the nominal host Jerry Montgomery, made the customary announcement: "When I say you're getting warm, that means you're getting close to it. When I say you're getting cold, you're getting farther away. Does everybody understand?"

Yes, they all understood.

They milled about until one little girl said: "Who's the warmest?"

"The warmest? Henry Laubach's the warmest," said Blanche.

"No he isn't," said Joe Chapin.

"Oh, yes he is, Joe," said Blanche Montgomery.

"Oh, no he isn't," said Joe.

"Please don't be rude, Joe. That's naughty," said Blanche.

"But Henry *isn't* the warmest," said Joe.

"Then suppose you tell us who is," said Blanche.

"Arthur is," said Joe.

"I *hardly* think so. Arthur's *very* cold."

"Ha ha ha." Joe laughed. "Are you cold, Arthur?"

Arthur laughed. "No, I'm boiling hot."

"Are you the boiling-hottest one in the room?" said Joe.

"Ooh, I'm scalding hot," said Arthur.

"Just a moment, please," said Blanche. She walked to the part of the room where a puzzled Henry Laubach was standing. "Someone has played a nasty trick, and I think we all know who it is," said Blanche.

Some of the children provided her answer: "Joe Chapin! Joe Chapin!"

"Have you got the thimble?" said Blanche.

"No," said Joe.

"Or Arthur McHenry?"

"Yes, I have it," said Arthur.

"Then hand it over, please, and we'll start the game again without you boys. No prize for either one of you."

"But I found it and I gave it to Arthur," said Joe.

"You played a deceitful trick on all the other children. You're a spoil-sport," said Blanche.

"But I'm not, Mrs. Montgomery. I saw it first, as soon as we came in the room," said Joe.

"That must have been before the game started," said Blanche.

"No, it wasn't. The game started as soon as we came in, I thought," said Joe.

"Well, you thought wrong."

"That's not fair. I found it first and I gave it to Arthur and he was the warmest."

"That is *not* the way the game is played, and you know it. And what's more, I don't like little boys to be impertinent."

"I wasn't impertinent," said Joe.

"Yes you were. You always are. You think you're a lot, but you're not."

"Then I'm going home," said Joe.

"Me too," said Arthur McHenry.

"You'll do no such thing. Kindly hand over the thimble and we'll start the game over again without you two boys."

Arthur handed her the thimble.

"You boys can sit here, and now, children, all the others go out in the hall and we'll hide it again. All others go out in the hall, please. No, Joe. Not you. Not you, Arthur."

"We're not going out in the hall, we're going home," said Joe.

"You'll *have* to wait for your carriage," said Blanche.

Joe stared at her for a few seconds, then suddenly he ran, followed by Arthur, out of the house, without stopping for cap and coat. The woman hurried to the porch, calling after them, but her voice only made them quicken their speed.

The Montgomery house was on Lantenengo Street, on the other side of town from the Chapins' on Frederick Street. The boys stopped running at Main Street and spent a half hour looking in the shop windows and otherwise disporting themselves, picking up some mud on their shoes and stockings and incidentally catching the beginnings of colds in the late-winter air. When darkness began to come each boy went to his own home.

Blanche Montgomery was with Joe's mother in the sitting room.

"Mummy?" called Joe.

"In the sitting room, dear."

"Don't track up the whole house with your muddy shoes," said Martha. "Let me wipe them off."

"Martha's taking the mud off my shoes," called Joe.

"Take off your shoes and come in here," said Charlotte.

The boy went to the sitting room. On seeing Blanche Montgomery he hesitated.

"I want you to apologize to Mrs. Montgomery for leaving her house that way."

"I apologize," said Joe, and turned to leave.

"Is that all, Mrs. Montgomery?" said Charlotte.

"I'm sorry this had to happen, and—"

"We're all sorry it happened. Thank you for coming over. Very considerate of you. Martha, will you see Mrs. Montgomery to the front door?" Charlotte emphasized *front* door only slightly.

Blanche spoke to Joe: "I'm sorry this had to happen, Joe. Next year I hope we'll—"

"Yes. Thank you very much," said Charlotte.

Blanche Montgomery left the house and Joe gave his version of the incident, a true one.

"And that's all? You hadn't been misbehaving before the game started?"

"No, Mummy. And besides, that was the first game. And we didn't even get any refreshments."

"You can hardly expect to get refreshments if you leave the party before it's time. I've told Martha to give you your supper in the kitchen. I'm very disappointed in you."

"But why, Mummy? She just as much as told us we were cheating and we weren't. I saw the thimble first."

"That's not why I'm disappointed in you. A gentleman doesn't make scenes. You were a guest in their house and you're supposed to abide by the rules of the house you're visiting. I've told Martha, no dessert."

"What is dessert?"

"Floating Island."

"But I love Floating Island!"

"I'm sorry, but that's your punishment, not only for forgetting you're a gentleman, but for not coming straight home. What if there'd been a runaway and the horses dashed up on the sidewalk?"

"I would have run inside the stores."

"Never mind the ready answers, please. I'm very disappointed in you, very, very disappointed. Now go have your supper and get ready for bed."

The Montgomerys of that day were on an equal footing, socially, with the Chapins and the McHenrys, although Blanche Montgomery was not a Gibbsville girl. She was a Reading girl who had come to Gibbsville as a bride. She was, in fact, a distant connection of Charlotte's, but Charlotte had not "done anything about her" when she came to Gibbsville, an oversight for which Charlotte was now glad.

"Have you anything pending with the Montgomery firm?" she asked Ben that evening.

"How do you mean, pending?"

"Well, any business negotiations?"

"No, why?"

She gave him her own version of the party incident.

"Well, if you mean are we on a friendly basis with the Montgomery firm, don't let that worry you."

"Worry me?"

"Aren't you planning some sort of reprisal, retribution?"

"Not exactly, not exactly. But I wanted to make sure."

"We're more likely to be in opposition to the Montgomery firm than otherwise. They handle cases that we have to refuse because of our Coal & Iron association. How are you planning to put Blanche in her place?"

"You're so *clever*," said Charlotte. "Well, I haven't had time to consider."

"I wouldn't like to be Blanche Montgomery," said Ben.

"She deserves whatever she gets. She has it coming to her. Of course it may take time."

"Whatever time it takes, Charlotte, she'll know why you're doing it," said Ben.

"Yes, but how much—simpler—if she *doesn't know* I'm doing it, whatever it is. Bess McHenry. If she had a little more character, and yet that's in our favor. She *hasn't* much character, therefore Blanche won't look for trouble from that quarter. Let me see now, is Bess Miller related to the Montgomerys? I don't think so."

"No, no relation," said Ben. "Before you go any further, ask yourself if the Montgomerys know any of our weak points."

"I wasn't aware that we had any weak points," said Charlotte. "At least that would be worth anything to the Montgomerys."

"In that case, damn the torpedoes, go ahead!"

"I'll need your help. You may hear of something they want to do

142

and we can prevent their doing. I'm glad I never called her when she came to town."

"Yes, it would look hypocritical now," said Ben, with a completely straight face. "You hadn't thought of giving a large party and not inviting them?"

"Oh, Ben. How un-subtle men are."

"I daresay. If Blanche were to take a lover . . ."

"Blanche? In Gibbsville? Nobody has lovers in Gibbsville," said Charlotte. "Where would she meet him?"

"I've often wondered."

"You have?" said Charlotte.

"Why, yes, and so have you, my dear, or you wouldn't have asked the question in the first place."

"Dear, dear, dear me. We're so deucedly clever. I know where they could meet. In the summer house. There was a famous case and you know it better than I do."

"Yes, and ever since then no respectable woman in Gibbsville ever goes to her summer house without her husband. Summer house became practically a synonym for house of assignation. Well, this kind of talk does me no good. You decide on your own form of revenge, my dear, but don't start the wheels going without consulting me. We may have skeletons in our own closets."

"I don't like that simile."

"It's a metaphor. I didn't think you'd like it, but do bear in mind that there is one thing about you and me that would make a nice morsel of gossip. The protecting mother that is no wife to her husband."

"You may come to my room tonight, Ben. If your desires are that strong, that you'd risk my life and unquestionably, unquestionably start a baby that isn't even a—that there's no name for. You have a son, healthy and beautiful and to be proud of. But you never saw the others, and I did. However, you have rights to my body, I suppose."

"Oh, don't talk about it, Charlotte."

"I never would, if I had my way. But I know this much, Ben. If you did come to my room, and I did have another of those—things, and that's what they are—I swear to you I'd take Paris-green, drown myself, anything."

"You're in no danger, Charlotte."

"I'm never sure when you talk this way," said Charlotte. "I think I'll drop a note to Bess and ask her to have a cup of tea. Now you, Ben dear, why don't you smoke a cigar? It always rests you."

"Yes, I believe I will, and a glass of brandy."

"Whiskey, Ben. The brandy gives you those heart palpitations."

Bess Miller McHenry was a large blonde Pennsylvanian whose fixed attitude was that of a woman who was attentively listening to each word of every speaker, following the conversation from speaker to speaker as though she were a speechless moderator, a powerless but conscientious judge. In so doing she always kept her mouth slightly open as if tentatively half-forming the speaker's words, but when she was included in the conversation she was invariably taken by surprise, and had nothing to contribute. She had an accompanying habit, which was to start nodding in agreement before her vis-à-vis had declared anything. She wanted to give no trouble, to receive no trouble, and her life was dedicated to the comfort of Arthur Davis McHenry, her husband; to Arthur Miller McHenry, her son; to Pansy McHenry, her daughter; to the house on South Main Street where she made her home; to Trinity Church; and to the canary birds which she talked to in terms and volume which she withheld from human beings. She belonged to the sisterhood that are commonly called *good* women.

Bess McHenry knew that the summons to tea at Number 10 Frederick Street was related to the incident at the Montgomery party. Her own inclination would have been to forget the whole matter. Her son Arthur had been punished for his participation by being deprived not only of dessert but of supper, and the reason for his punishment was that he had committed a breach of etiquette in leaving the party before it was time, a somewhat different crime from the subtler one of not behaving according to the rules of the house one was visiting. Things were simpler in the McHenry household.

Charlotte had assumed semi-invalid status among her friends and it was generally accepted that "Charlotte doesn't go out." A visit to Charlotte consequently was always opened with some remarks about her condition. It was for the most part an age of reticence and there was no need for specific anatomical report; Charlotte had some female trouble and no matter how curious her friends might be, none of them took the initiative in finding out what the trouble was—and Charlotte most certainly never volunteered anything.

"You're looking well, Charlotte."

"Thank you, Bess. And so are you. That's a perfect color to go with your eyes."

"Oh, this? I bought the material in Philadelphia last October and

I had Mrs. Hammer make it into a dress for me. I was going to get rid of Mrs. Hammer, but after she made this I decided to give her another chance."

"She needs the work so."

"She needs the work so, yes. Yes, she does need the work. What do you pay her, Charlotte?"

"Well, I haven't had her doing any sewing for me lately."

"Oh, she hasn't done any sewing for you."

"Not lately, but I've really had so little sewing that I haven't done myself. I like to sew."

"Yes, you've always liked to sew, haven't you? I wish I had more time for the *nice* sewing. I do the children's mending and some of Arthur's things, but that doesn't give me much time for fancywork."

"Yes, I do some of Ben's things too, and *all* of Joe's. The darning is the only part that I don't like."

"The darning, I don't like that either. Isn't darning a nuisance? I have a basketful at home that every time I look at it, it just seems to say to me, 'Bess, you're neglecting your darning.'"

"Boys' stockings," said Charlotte.

"Boys' stockings are the limit."

"But not really a chore, not for our boys. Arthur is such a delight. Ben and I often congratulate ourselves that Joe has such a fine boy for a friend. Best friend."

"Oh, dear. Joe is—I can't put it into words how much we love Joe."

"And so nice together."

"Aren't they? They're so nice together."

Charlotte sighed. "I wonder why a woman like Blanche Montgomery—now how can she call herself a lady?"

"Exactly."

"Our boys must have been to dozens of parties, dozens—"

"At least," said Bess, and then, as though she had counted: "Dozens."

"And behaved like little gentlemen, always. You know, Bess, we'll never get to the truth of what really happened at Blanche Montgomery's house. I most assuredly didn't believe the cock-and-bull story Blanche told me. You know she came to see me that very day."

"Did she?"

"Before Joe got home, spattered with mud from the street, and the start of a heavy cold. Oh, yes. Blanche was here making accusations against a ten-year-old boy, two ten-year-old boys. Arthur as well as Joe. Did Arthur catch a cold too?"

"A slight one, yes."

"That's what I thought. Something happened that made those children want to leave that house without waiting to put on their hats and coats. It may have *started* over the game of Hide the Thimble, Bess, but there must have been more to it than that. There must have been."

"Oh, I think so too, Charlotte."

Charlotte smoothed her skirt and folded her hands. "What can we do about Blanche Montgomery?"

"I don't know. Had you thought of anything?"

"We don't want people to think we're two mothers resenting the shabby treatment of their children. Humiliating them before all their little friends, and making it impossible for them to stay another minute. Of course we can see to it that our children never set foot in that house again. That we can take for granted, naturally. But that isn't enough. Blanche herself is responsible, and she's the one that ought to be taught a lesson."

"She might be kept out of the Assembly."

"Something like that, but not that exactly. The Montgomerys have belonged to the Assembly since it started."

"Yes, they have, that's true."

"She's *in* your sewing club, isn't she?"

"Yes. Last year. Too bad it isn't this year."

"And the Altar Guild."

"Oh, yes. Busy as a bee in that."

"I'm afraid it isn't a question then of keeping her out of things she'd like to push her way into. It would be more of a reflection on the Montgomerys than on her. Except there is one thing."

"What's that, Charlotte?"

"Well, the organized things, like the sewing club and the Altar Guild, we can't do anything about them. But there are other things that aren't organizations. There's that group you're getting together for next year, the little dinner club."

"Arthur's chairman."

"So Ben told me. Naturally in my condition we had to decline, but so far you haven't even got a name for it, have you?"

"No, we haven't even got a name for it so far. It's just an informal little dinner club. Once a month, November, December, January, February, and March."

"Just the kind of thing Blanche Montgomery's dying to get in. An upstart from Reading, and some nice people that have lived here all their lives won't even know about the club. After the way she treated our children I know *I* wouldn't enjoy sitting down to dinner with her. Well, I think that would do for a start."

"Oh, I can see to it that they don't get an invitation."

"You have so much influence, Bess. If she's quietly left out, without making any fuss, and if people don't accept *her* invitations, then she may come to realize that you simply can't humiliate small children and get off scot-free. She sat in this very room and I've never seen a woman with such a guilty conscience. And when I saw my little boy, spattered with mud, and chilled by the cold—well, Arthur must have been the same, and you must have felt the same as I did."

"Yes," said Bess.

"I won't say anything about the dinner club, not even to Ben. You take care of it in your own way, and perhaps Mistress Montgomery will learn that she can't ride roughshod over the feelings of some mothers. And if you think of anything where I can be of help, you tell me, Bess. It was our boys that were treated so shabbily, and that makes you and I even closer than ever."

"I promise you that, Charlotte."

"Ah, dear Bess, old friends are the best, aren't they?"

"Yes. Yes they are."

The exclusion of the Montgomerys from the informal little dinner club was not noticed until the unannounced twenty-couple limit had been reached and nominations closed. It was an informal club in that there was no clubhouse, it had no rooms, no place for a bulletin board, no stationery. Its name was The Second Thursdays, without the word club. When it was seen that the Montgomerys were not included (and when it became known they had not been asked), their social indispensability was at an end. Charlotte's strategy had included extra, direct snubs for Blanche Montgomery, but she need not have planned so carefully. The absence of the Montgomerys from The Second Thursdays lowered their standing in the eyes of non-members and members—and no one, or almost no one, ever knew what had happened. One day they were a First Family; then in a short while they were just another old family with money. And even Blanche Montgomery did not suspect Charlotte, who was not a member of The Second Thursdays; nor did she suspect Bess, a woman incapable of intrigue. In her tears and anger she blamed herself, but she never discovered the real reason for the snub. Perhaps she spent too much money on clothes? Perhaps she had flirted with someone's husband? Possibly they did not like the color she had chosen for the repainting of the old Montgomery mansion? She was fully aware of the enormity of her failure: not even being married to a Montgomery was enough to carry her, *but* being married to her was enough to hurt a Montgomery. In 1930, when her son was a lawyer for the big bootleggers and organized prostitution, dressed like a bootlegger and one of the prostitutes' best patrons—she still blamed herself, and wished that her boy could have turned out like Joe Chapin.

Charlotte observed in passing that Bess McHenry had done her work well, but Charlotte was too industriously Joe's mother to permit the Montgomery affair to become an obsession. There were other things to think about. Charlotte encountered no difficulty in persuading the McHenrys that their boy belonged in a boarding school. Arthur Davis McHenry had gone to Gibbsville High School in the Class of 1870 and to Dickinson College. A high school education was considered adequate; college, any college, was a luxury. Charlotte's way was made easy by young Arthur's wanting to do the things that Joe did, and Arthur D. and Bess McHenry were as enthusiastic as their son about boarding school. But the McHenrys were a Dickinson family, and to convince them that their boy should go to Yale was not so simple. It was not a question of money. The difference between having a boy at Yale and sending him to Dickinson, Lafayette or Muhlenberg was not important financially. But there existed a strong feeling in Pennsylvania in favor of the good nearby colleges, and a slight prejudice against Yale as a New England institution and Princeton as too strongly Southern. To Gibbsville the University meant the University of Pennsylvania, the traditional institution. But it was in Philadelphia, and many families preferred to have their sons in smaller towns—Easton, Allentown, Carlisle. Most of the boys who were sent to Yale had some pre-Pennsylvania New England background, as was the case with the Chapin family. It was always understood that Joe Chapin would go to Yale, but to win young Arthur McHenry's family over from Dickinson was a task that took Charlotte and Ben five years. The winning argument was based not on Yale's superiority as a college, but on the advantages of friendships that would help the boy if, as they predicted, he should become an outstanding lawyer. They had a point.

The Coal & Iron Company was owned in Philadelphia and New York, where Yale men were more numerous than in Gibbsville.

Charlotte's concern for young Arthur's future was real, but involved only his future as a roommate for Joe. Since it was impossible for her to accompany her son to Yale, she could do the next best thing: she could provide him with a trustworthy companion. It was fortunate for all parties that the boys were fond of each other. The senior McHenrys created no difficulty about law school. They sent their son to the University of Pennsylvania with Joe, ignoring the fact that Dickinson had a first-rate law school. But by that time Arthur and Bess "had a son at Yale" and they were committed to the Big Four.

It never occurred to anyone to ask young Arthur his school and college preferences, possibly because it never occurred to him to wonder what they were. His companionship with Joe Chapin was so much a part of his life that in making the big decisions he was nearly always guided by Joe's preferences. It would not have been an American way of thinking to say so, but the fact was that Joe occupied a position like that of royalty, with Arthur's relationship that of noble companion. But never in his own mind did Arthur occupy a servile or humble position. He was often a convenience for Joe, but he never regarded himself as that. He possessed complete self-respect and was not plagued by jealousy when Joe enjoyed the company of Alec Weeks, Dave Harrison, or Paul Donaldson. On his looks, his manners, and the fact that he was financially stable, Joe was invited to parties and into the homes of Yale friends who did not feel compelled also to invite Arthur McHenry. Joe could easily have become a New Yorker and been lost in the large and increasing body of New York Yale men. Arthur, on the other hand, was truly a Pennsylvanian-at-Yale and never anything else; never sought jobs or the entree to jobs in New York. To Arthur during his four years at New Haven and later at Penn, the big social event of the year remained the Gibbsville Assembly; the New York and Philadelphia parties were events at which he always felt like a guest; in Gibbsville he was a *member* of the Assembly (or would be when he reached the age of twenty-five). In his own way Arthur McHenry came close to matching the Yale career of Ben Chapin, with the notable exception that he was considerably more of a social success in point of organizations joined and friendships made. But Ben Chapin and Arthur McHenry were New Haven-Yale men, not New York-Yale men. Dave Harrison and Alec Weeks, New Yorkers, would have welcomed

Joe Chapin into their midst and he never had trouble picking up the relationship when he would reunite with them. Out of sincere politeness they would inquire for "McHenry" because he was known to them to be Joe's best friend, while Joe was one of their crowd who happened to live in a place called Gibbsville.

But Joe Chapin followed Arthur back to Gibbsville.

They had one discussion on the subject. "I sometimes think I'd like to work in New York," said Joe in their senior year.

"You'd do well there," said Arthur.

"Do you think I would, honestly?"

"I think so."

"Why?"

"Well, you like New York. You have a good time there. You like the people."

"Yes, but I wouldn't want to take a job there unless you did."

"Oh, I never would," said Arthur. "I belong in Gibbsville. I don't really like New York as much as you do."

"No, you never have, have you?"

"Once or twice a year, that'll be enough New York for me. But I'd never feel that I was a part of New York. Any more than Alec or Dave would ever feel he was a part of Gibbsville. But you could fit in in New York very easily."

"Maybe. But I guess I have the same feeling about Gibbsville that you have. It's where I was born, et cetera."

"As I look at it, our families spent a lot of money to educate us, Yale, and The Hill. But they gave us something else besides."

"What's that?"

"Well, all those years before we went away to school, we were learning all about the people and the geography, the streets, the names of the towns and patches. You might say we took a course in Gibbsville. Why throw that out the window? No, I'd never work in New York, not permanently. I'll go to work in Father's firm, get married, maybe run for judge some day."

"What about our partnership?"

"Can't have a partnership if you're going to be in New York."

"Oh, I wasn't very serious about New York."

"Well, I don't blame you for considering it."

"Dave and Alec have been broaching the subject, that's the only reason I considered it."

"Well, don't act hastily. We're not even in law school yet."

"And I'm not so sure I'd like New York if I went to live there," said Joe. "I don't like the idea of having to explain who you are. I don't know how many times this has happened to me, but I've met girls in New York and they say how strange it is they never met me before, and then when I tell them I'm from Pennsylvania they look at me. *Pennsylvania?* As though it were part of the Indian territory. Or else they take for granted I'm from New York and can't understand—well, the same thing over again. Why are they just meeting me for the first time? New York's supposed to be a big place, but among Dave's and Alec's friends it's just a small town like Gibbsville. The only difference is, I'm not part of it in New York, and in Gibbsville I am."

"You could be part of it in New York in no time."

"I'm not sure I could. When they start talking about things they did when they were children, I have to keep quiet. They all knew each other. I think it would take years before I got to be part of New York. And I don't think I want to marry a New York girl."

"Have you got over your case on Marie Harrison?"

"It was never a real case. I kissed her, but I'm not the only one that kissed Marie. And she'd have let me do more than kiss her. You may think it's a rotten way to talk about a friend's sister, but I found out. I heard a Princeton fellow saying how Marie was looking for a husband and didn't care who it was or how or what she had to do to get him. And when I stayed at the Harrisons' in February . . ."

"You don't have to tell me anything."

"I've told you that much, I might as well tell you what happened. I was given the guest room, on the same floor as Dave's mother and father. On the same floor, mind you. And I was asleep the second night I was there and I guess it must have been three o'clock in the morning. Sound asleep, and suddenly I woke up, or not suddenly. I woke up gradually. I thought I was dreaming this, but she was in bed with me. In her nightgown and in bed with me and rubbing her hand over my stomach and finally when I got altogether awake she put her hand over my mouth and whispered to me. 'Sh-h-h, darling.' I thought I was dreaming it, but I knew I couldn't be."

"Then what?"

"Frenched me."

"God! Really?"

"You know I wouldn't make this up."

"I know."

"The next day I could hardly face her, but it didn't affect her.

You would have thought nothing happened. That night we all went out together and I didn't know what to say to her, and half the time I still couldn't believe it was true, what'd happened the night before. But it was true, all right."

"Why? Did she say anything about it?"

"Not only said. On the way home in the carriage she whispered to me, 'Don't go to sleep.' I guess I couldn't have anyway, because by that time I was hoping she'd come to my room again. And she did. That time she didn't have to wake me up. I was waiting for her, over an hour. Closer to two hours. 'Darling, are you asleep?' she said. I said no, and she got into bed, but this time without her nightgown and I admit it, I didn't have anything on either. She stayed till about five o'clock in the morning."

"Good Lord, that's taking a chance."

"I know, and I wondered how I could face her mother and father, and Dave, one of my best friends. But it didn't worry her. She's like two people, two different people. You think of her as a pretty girl and good company, but like somebody's sister. Well, she *is* somebody's sister. Dave's sister. I'll bet if Dave knew anything about it he'd kill her, and me too. And in a way I wouldn't blame him."

"But you didn't make the advances. She did."

"But I should have had more sense."

"But what could you do?"

"Well, whatever I could do, I didn't do it. She's like two completely different people. But she's *not* two different people. I took for granted that she expected me to marry her and before I came back to New Haven I said to her, 'Marie, I have to finish law school before I can get married,' and do you know what she said?"

"No."

"She said, 'Well, don't let that stop you from visiting us again.' Never expected me to marry her. It meant no more to her than holding hands does to some girls. I was relieved, but then I changed. I fell in love with her."

"I *thought* you had."

"I wrote her letter after letter. I wrote her every day for a while, and got no answer. Then she wrote me. Oh, I might as well show it to you." Joe went to his desk and unlocked a black metal strong box. "Here it is."

" 'Dear Joe,' she says. 'I am writing to you because if I am to believe your letters I have led you on. Such was not my intention, much as I value you as a friend. Our pleasant moments together were not intended to convey that impression, therefore I can only say to you that I shall always think of you as a charming friend of Dave's and I shall always be glad to see you as a welcome visitor to our house. Please forgive me if I have accidently' (She spells it a, c, c, i, d, e, n, t, l, y.) 'given you any other impression. I am very much in love with a certain gentleman who must be nameless for the time being, otherwise I would be glad to tell you his name. I wish you every good fortune and I remain, Your friend, Marie.' "

"What do you know about that?" said Arthur.

"Well, she must have been in love with the other fellow when she came to my room."

"And yet it's hard to believe," said Arthur.

"The whole thing's hard to believe," said Joe. "I'm glad I don't know who the other fellow is."

"Would you care to know what I suspect?"

"What?"

"I suspect she's in love with a married man," said Arthur.

"You do? So did I. Why else be so secretive?"

"Exactly."

"Well, that's why I don't think I want to marry a New York girl."

"Why?" said Arthur. "They're not all like Marie."

"No, of course not, but she's the only one I had any experience with, that kind of experience, and I wouldn't want to be disillusioned again. Your father and mother, and my father and mother—that's what I think marriage ought to be. Marie's only twenty or twenty-one, and yet *think* of her."

"Yes."

"She's *old*, Arthur. What'll she be like when she's thirty? Not in looks, but experience. I'm sure it's a married man, and most likely there'll be—she'll be written up in the scandal sheets. And when that does happen I'll be thankful I escaped when I did."

"Yes."

"The man that marries Marie—how would you like to be in his boots?"

"Not me, thank you."

"True. But think of what I just told you. *I* was almost that man. I thought she expected me to marry her."

"But she didn't."

"Luckily. That's what it was, sheer luck. But do you know what the experience did to me? This doesn't apply to you, but I look at the fellows we know and I wonder how much they know about women. And I also wonder if it shows on me, my experience."

"Well, I knew there was something going on that you didn't want

153

to tell me about, but I don't know whether it would have shown itself to the other fellows."

"I hope not. I have no use for a rounder. I could never trust one in business, professionally, any more than I could socially. And I wouldn't want anyone to consider me a rounder, although of course I'm not one. But if my experience with Marie showed on my face, it would show a weakness in my character. My mother always said those weaknesses show up sooner or later."

"I believe that."

"Do you know that that's one of the few houses my mother fully approved of? The Harrisons'. One of the fine old New York families, according to Mother."

"Well, they are."

"But it shows that you can't always go by outward appearances or what you *think* you know about people," said Joe. "Arthur, do you still believe what we used to believe—about the husband? You remember, the husband should be just as decent as he expects his wife to be?"

"You mean bride and groom?"

"Yes."

"Yes, I believe that. I expect to be when I get married."

"But I'm not any more. Do you think that's something I ought to tell my wife when I get married?"

"Well—I wouldn't, if I were you."

"I was hoping you'd say that. I don't feel that I *belong* to Marie, and that's what counts. If you didn't really *belong* to somebody else before you're married. I can truthfully tell my wife that I never belonged to another woman."

"With a mental reservation."

"Yes, a mental reservation. Oh, I'll tell her a white lie for that matter."

"Unless another girl comes to your room some time. Then it might not be a white lie."

"I never thought of that. It never crossed my mind. I don't think it's liable to happen."

"Do you half wish it would, Joe?"

"Well—we don't lie to each other, you and I. So I'll tell you the truth. If I had the powers of the Almighty, and I could eradicate my experience with Marie—I wouldn't. I think if she came to my room again I couldn't resist her."

"Then you did belong to her, didn't you?"

"Yes, I did, Arthur. I admit it. When I get married I am going to have to lie to my wife about Marie. You know, I've lied to myself, but I couldn't lie to you. Isn't that odd?"

"You're truthful."

"It's best in the long run."

"No doubt about it," said Arthur.

The friends avoided Marie as a topic of conversation for almost two years. They were rooming together in a fraternity house at the University of Pennsylvania. Arthur came home one afternoon in the late winter and found Joe sitting in the Morris chair, still wearing his ulster and overshoes.

"What's the matter, Joe? Is there something wrong?"

"Yes."

"Your family? Your mother and father?"

"No. Marie. Here's what was waiting for me when I got home. It's from Dave."

Arthur read the letter:

Dear Joe:

Knowing your fondness for Marie and hers for you I am faced with the sad duty to tell you that she died last Thursday evening from peritonitis following an abdominal operation. The operation was performed at one of the private hospitals in the suburbs and the funeral services, which were strictly private, took place on Saturday. We had no pallbearers and we did not invite anyone but family to the funeral.

In going through her effects I found a small stack of letters which I recognized to be in your handwriting. I confess that I read one of the letters, although only one after I realized that they were love letters. I am returning them to you since I do not feel that they are for other eyes. It may console you to learn that Marie still had your photograph in a locket which she carried in her purse until the day she went to the hospital. I wish I had known that you and Marie had once been in love with each other. If your romance had been encouraged to completion there might be a different and happier story to tell today. But no more for the present . . .

Dave

"The poor thing," said Arthur.

"Is she, or am I?"

"I said it about her, but I don't know, Joe," said Arthur. "It sounds as though she'd been in love with you all the time."

"It sounds like more than that, too," said Joe.

"You're thinking of the operation?"

"I'm thinking of the operation in a private hospital in the suburbs, and strictly private funeral, and mystery, covering up. You must know what I'm thinking."

"That she died of an abortion."

"Yes. That's what poor Dave is trying to tell me. I'm going over to New York on the next train."

"Shall I go with you?"

"Thanks, Arthur. But I'll be back later this evening. I just want to talk to Dave. I'll send him a telegram and he can meet me at the University Club. I don't want to see the family if I can help it. Just Dave."

Joe returned from New York after midnight.

From his bed Arthur spoke to Joe. "I'm awake, if you want to talk."

"I don't know," said Joe. He was putting his things in the coat closet.

"Will you throw me a cigarette?" said Arthur.

Joe did so and sat in the Morris chair. "Dave asked me not to repeat any of this."

"I understand," said Arthur.

"On a slight technicality—everything we guessed from the letter was true."

"Everything *you* guessed," said Arthur.

"And what you guessed, too," said Joe. "You guessed that she was in love with me, remember?"

"Yes, I remember I did."

"Two nights before she died, or rather *the* night before she died, she mentioned my name when she was in a sort of delirium. When she came out of it they asked her if she wanted to see me, and she said no, no, she didn't want me to become involved in it. If I had shown up at the hospital—you know. Oh, Arthur, why couldn't I have known? Why was I so stupid about her? She *loved* me! She's the only person who ever did love me! And what did I think? What did I say?"

"Whatever you said, you only said it to me."

"Yes. I'm not so much ashamed of what I said to you as what I thought. I tell you everything, but that was evil of me, thinking she was no more than . . ."

"Listen, Joe, if we were all hanged for what we thought we'd all be on the gallows."

156

"I have a very strange feeling. I feel as though I'd been found guilty of something that happened so long ago that I've almost forgotten the crime I committed. I feel as though I ought to feel guilty, but I don't feel guilty. And yet I know that all my life I *will* feel guilty. The older I get, the more I'll feel the guilt."

"But you're not guilty of anything."

"I wasn't responsible for the abortion, no. And yet I was. If I had been wiser, more knowing—what do I mean?—more perceptive? What I want to say is, if I'd seen that she loved me she wouldn't have had the affair that ended the way it did."

"She sent you on your way, remember that, Joe."

"That's when I should have been—perceptive. I keep using that word. There must be a better one. Understanding. I don't know."

"How would you like a highball?"

"I tried one. I couldn't finish it," said Joe.

"Joe, you're making yourself feel what you don't feel, trying to. You're trying to make yourself feel what you think you ought to feel."

"Do you consider me as insincere as all that? I like *that.*"

"Not insincere, no. But as though you had a duty to feel badly," said Arthur.

"I don't think I like that. I don't think I like that at all, Arthur."

"But am I right?"

"No, I don't think you're right for one minute."

"Well—you misunderstand me. I'm trying to prevent you from upsetting yourself needlessly."

"Needlessly! A girl that loved me lies dead in New York City because I wasn't perceptive enough to realize. Needlessly!"

"Well—go to bed and try to get some sleep."

"Damn little sleep I'll get tonight," said Joe.

But he went to bed, and, as Arthur noted, sleep came quite soon.

In the succeeding months Arthur also noted that he had been unfair to Joe's capacity for feeling. On a fine day Joe would bring up Marie's name apropos of nothing. They would be at a University baseball game, or watching the rowing on the Schuylkill, and Joe would say, "I can't believe Marie is dead," or, "Marie would have enjoyed this day." He displayed no lachrymose grief, but it was not like Joe to bring up sad subjects, and Death was not a subject he brought up at all. Marie was the first of their contemporaries to die and the phenomenon which Death is to the young was brought even closer to them by the lively intimacy Joe had shared with Marie.

There was something else about Joe that Arthur noticed, observ-

157

ing it so frequently that he could predict it: at college dances and the larger Philadelphia functions and on visits to the seashore—where the two young men might be likely to meet girls they had not met before—Joe avoided the girls who were pretty and bright and gay. He would perform the duty dances, and his good manners were maintained, but he managed never to be alone with girls who might be—were—romantically intentioned. He seemed to prefer the company of spiritless pretty girls, who had only their prettiness to remind him of Marie, but even those girls were alone with him for no longer than the measures of a waltz, and it would amuse Arthur to watch Joe, at the conclusion of a dance number, guiding his partner to the safety of a group. For an outsider Joe was well received in Philadelphia. If he had been a Philadelphian he would have been a prospective member of the City Troop and the State-in-Schuylkill, but he approved of his own ineligibility. "I'd feel the same way about a Philadelphian that came to Gibbsville," he told Arthur. "You don't just walk in and join our Assembly or The Second Thursdays. If you could, things like that wouldn't mean as much as they do to us." Whatever Joe secretly felt about the organizations, Arthur was sure of one thing: Joe was not going to marry into them.

"I'll probably marry some day," he said to Arthur. "But it will be a Gibbsville girl, and it won't be soon."

Five hundred invitations went out, requesting the honor of approximately eight hundred persons' presence at the Chapin-Stokes marriage ceremony. In several hundred cases the invitations were the next thing to an insult: if out of the stiff envelope did not fall a card for the reception, a Gibbsville citizen and her husband were being reminded that they were not yet of consequence in the town. It was a local custom that silverware and china were not expected of persons who had been invited to the church but not to the reception. Nevertheless the purchasers of silverware and china were more numerous than the list of persons invited to the reception. A few women bought the items because they would not admit to their jewelers that they had not received the double invitation; and a smaller number of women bought the items because they were sure there had been a mistake.

Edith Stokes made no such mistakes. Her lists had been checked and rechecked long before the engagement announcement, so that when she took the list to Charlotte Chapin, the mother of the groom and the bride-to-be were in almost perfect accord. Names marked with an "R" for reception remained marked with an "R"; a few, but a very few, marked with a "C" for church-only, were remarked with an "R" because Charlotte felt that this husband or that husband was slightly more important in the business affairs of the town than Edith could be expected to know. "It will mean a lot to Joe later on, Edith dear. I'd have done just what you did, but if you let down the bars just a little bit, just in one or two instances, I *know* it will be appreciated. And they're worthwhile people, and in one more generation there wouldn't be the slightest question about their being invited. So don't you think we ought to be nice to them now?"

"It's remarkable, Mother Chapin, how you've kept up your interest."

"Well—you will, too, dear. Our dear old Gibbsville, we're very fond of our dear old Gibbsville."

Charlotte was genuinely pleased with the match. ("I wonder how Charlotte Chapin is taking the turn of events.") The engagement came as no surprise to her and caused her no displeasure. She confidently believed that there was nothing about Edith Stokes that she did not know, and the very fact that Joe had selected Edith as his bride was reassurance to Charlotte that her son knew nothing about women. He would have some surprises and some excitement from this girl, surprises and excitement that an inexperienced boy would have with any girl. After a time the surprises would end and during some of the excitement they would create a grandchild. But no girl with a face as plain as Edith's could inspire a love or even a passion that would cause a son to reject his mother. It would be a safe marriage for the son, and it would present no problems to the mother. "You are going to have this house eventually," said Charlotte, during the engagement period. "So why not from the very beginning? I hope that you'll live here all your lives, and your children too." Edith had agreed so quickly that Charlotte was not compelled to make the concessions she was prepared to make if Edith had resisted. Instead of having a whole story to themselves, or a suite, the bride and groom were given a bedroom and their own bath and some extra closet space.

It was a six o'clock wedding and the chimes of Trinity and the long striped canopy down the terrace and across the sidewalk had given notice to the uninvited that something was up—and there were few who were unaware of what was up. A wedding in Trinity was always a favorite free show for the poor, who arrived early and stood against the inside of the canopy walls, defying the routine efforts of the two constables to chase them away. The carriages of the bride and her bridesmaids began to arrive at ten minutes before the hour and when Edith with her father passed through the double line of the poor and up the carpeted stone steps there were remarks suitable to to the occasion: "Ah . . . Pretty . . . Lovely . . . Lace . . . Satin . . . Isn't she? . . . Ah . . . Bouquet . . . Her father . . . Ain't she? . . . Did you ever? . . . Good luck . . . Lovely . . . Isn't she? . . ." Her father produced a cut-glass, silver-capped vessel shaped like a cornucopia and offered it to Edith. "It's smelling salts, dear."

"I know, but I don't need them," said Edith.

"Well, I do," he said. "Any of the girls need them?"

"No, of course not, Father," said Edith.

"Well, give me a kiss, Miss. The last one as a miss." He kissed her and the march to the altar was begun.

Joe was as pale as his tie, but his responses were audible in the good acoustics of Trinity, and when the now married pair turned their back to the altar and commenced the recessional they walked briskly and smiling. It had gone off well, without the breaking of a bridesmaid's garter, a fainting, a coughing spell, a flatulent report, an apopleptic stroke, a child's vomiting, an upset candelabrum, a bass *gaffe* by the organist, a popping of an usher's shirtfront, a case of hiccoughs, a dropped walking-stick in the aisle, a weeping spell, a Socialist's protest. It was as nice a wedding as anyone could hope for, with none of the disturbances that sometimes occur as a result of nervousness, anger, or jubilance. The reception, on which foolish expense had been spared, was in the best of good taste, dispensing with such ostentatious features as out-of-town caterers, florists, and orchestra, and taking on some of the spirit of a large family party. The secret of the principal couple's destination was well kept and when they departed in a closed carriage there was no vulgar attempt to follow them.

They were driven ten miles down-country to the Laubach farm, which had an owner's house separate from the quarters occupied by the hired farmer's family. In the late morning they were to be driven to the railroad station and the train to Philadelphia and White Sulphur Springs; meanwhile the Laubach country house, warm and comfortable, lit by kerosene lamps and candles, was theirs. It was a house with which the bride and groom were familiar and when the Laubach coachman deposited their overnight luggage in the hall Edith and Joe were completely alone.

He kissed her. "My wife, my love," he said.

"My dearest one," she said. "My husband."

"Isn't it nice of the Laubachs?"

"Sweet of them. I don't know what we would have done."

"It would have been awful to take the sleeper."

"Oh, I couldn't have stood that," said Edith.

"Everything went so beautifully, don't you think?" said Joe.

"I expect so, dear."

"I know, you must have been, as my Aunt Jane used to say, in a tizzy."

"I hope I remembered everyone's name."

"You did. You were positively splendid. Much better than I was."

"Well—it's over, and we'll have the rest of our lives to think about it."

"The happiest day of *my* life," said Joe.

"And of mine," said Edith. "Shall I—go upstairs?"

"Do you feel like it? We can sit and talk awhile, if you like."

"No, my dear. I want to start our life together."

"Yes."

"Shall I call you?"

"Yes."

"When I turn out the light, will you come in?"

"My dearest," he said.

"But you—I almost forgot. *Dearest*, what will you do?"

"Let's go upstairs together and see."

They climbed the stairs and went to the room which they knew to be Mr. and Mrs. Laubach's. The bed was turned down.

"You can change in the next room," said Edith.

"And then when I see the light go out, I'll come in?"

"Yes. I'll try not to be long."

She took fifteen minutes while he got into his pajamas and heavy dressing gown. When he saw the light go out he tapped on the door and she said, "Come in." He walked directly in the dark to the bed and removed his dressing gown and laid it on a chair. She was under the covers and they kissed and embraced. He put his knee between her legs and she made a sound like a moan.

"Do you want me to stop?" he said.

"*No!*" She said.

He felt her breasts and she pulled up her nightgown.

"Do it to me, do it to me," she said. "Hurry." She made it difficult for him to find her; she was already in the rhythm of the act and could not stop. "For God's sake," she said. "For God's sake."

"I'm trying, dearest."

"Do it then," she said angrily.

The moment he entered her she had her climax, with a loud cry. His own climax followed and immediately she wanted him again, but when she realized it was impossible she lay calmer, while he stroked the hair of her head and kissed her cheek.

"I've been waiting all my life," she said.

"Doesn't something happen to you?"

"Not what you think."

"I thought it did."

"Not always. Am I the first for you?"

"Yes."

"I hoped so. I knew it. And you'll never be anyone else's, will you?"

"No."

"You won't have to be. Unless you think I'm too much this way. Do you think I am? Would you like me better if I were cold? Did you think I was cold because I'm shy?"

"I wouldn't want you to be cold, heavens," he said.

"Oh, dear . . ." she said.

"What?"

"It has happened. What you thought. Oh, dear. When it didn't hurt, I thought—but it has happened. Now you have to marry me."

He laughed.

"Am I altogether different than you thought I'd be?"

"I don't know what I thought. Except that I love you."

"I love you too, Joe," she said.

"We must love each other for the rest of our lives," he said. He put his head between her breasts and before she fully realized it he was asleep.

"Are you asleep, Joe?"

He did not answer, his breathing was an answer.

"I own you," she said. "At last." But he was asleep, and even in her glowing she wondered and doubted. He had let himself get completely possessed by her, and as different from the man she had always known as he could be, and expressing himself into her and with her as he surely had with no one else in the world. But what she owned now was not enough. It was incomplete and he was asleep and distant from her, and the fire they had lit had gone out. And then she began to understand that he was going to take a lot of owning and that she had been wrong in thinking that owning him was going to be so quick and simple a matter as she had hoped and believed. She might own him as completely as anyone else had owned him, and more and more as the years would pass, but she was beginning to see that what she had wanted was a bigger possessing than she knew could exist. She had been naïve in her simple want: the ceremony of matrimony, the consummation of it with their bodies. Now, with his head on her breast, she saw that the desire to own him was not to be so easily satisfied, or possibly ever satisfied. It was not Love; Love might easily have very little to do with it; but it was as strong a desire as Love or Hate and it was going to be her life, the owning of this man. He was going to have to be more than a part of her, more than a child she was carrying or had given birth to, more than a dear friend or an essential of life. It was going to be as though she had covered him with a sac and as though he depended on her for breath and nourishment. And it was going to take forever and it never, never could be achieved because if it ever ended the ending would mean incompleteness, and the kind of owning she wanted was continuing and permanent and infinite.

Now as she lay there, enjoying the experience of her body, she was beginning to see that she could possess him through his body and the sharing of tactile pleasures inside herself and on her skin and on his skin (and there would be many such pleasures). But time itself was going to be as much a part of what she wanted as the kisses and the touches. Now she was pleased that he had gone to sleep so quickly, although at first she had not been pleased. Sleep would renew his strength for the tactile, neural pleasures which she planned to enjoy. But easy sleep also meant to her that he was a simple man who could be as nearly owned as she wanted him to be. Yes, it was impossible to own him as she wanted to own him, but that was because infinity was impossible, and as long as she had life she would be owning him just short of completeness, and there would be no resistance from this simple, now sleeping man. At first this new discovery of the enormity of owning him had alarmed her; but as she put her hand on his cheek and let it slide from his cheek to her breast she enjoyed the future. She would give him anything he wanted and she would even teach him to want more than he knew, because all that he could ever want would be so little in comparison with what she would be taking.

She thought of her friends and of marriages she had known, and the details of marriage: the giving of shelter and warmth and food and clothing, the creation and bearing and raising of children; the problems of money and outside relationships; the compatibility and the incompatibility; the ordering of the meals and the choice of curtains; the separations and quarrels and reuniting; the effect of public opinion; the small business of whom to invite and where to educate the young and the suitability of an Easter bonnet. And she smiled. They were all so easy, such insignificant problems when they were problems, and ambitions and hopes and short-lived desires. Now in herself she felt greatness, not mere superiority but greatness. It took greatness to want to own a human being and to come as close to achieving it as she would with Joe. And it was nothing to tell anyone else; no one else could ever understand. She owned the idea itself, she accepted the inevitability of its incompleteness, and the knowledge of her greatness and that she had a life with a great plan were already starting her on a new and unique serenity. And suddenly she laughed at infidelity: what a foolish admission of inferiority to want to squander time with more than one man when the owning of one man was going to be such a fascinating passion! What did it matter if the owning were inevitably unachievable? She had a life with a plan.

There came a time when at last the Chapin-Stokes wedding was a part of the social history of Gibbsville. The town dearly loved to talk about its weddings and its funerals, its Assemblies, and its rare crimes involving members of the elect. Assemblies occurred twice a year and they provided conversational topics throughout the succeeding months; funerals occurred when necessary, which was oftener than Assemblies; crimes involving the citizens of prominence occurred so infrequently that they were unfamiliar conversational exercises to the uninvolved. There was a pattern to discussion of a Chapin-Stokes wedding; the invitation lists were dwelt upon; the conduct of the guests; the women's clothes and the men's when there was some freakish departure from conventional attire; the wedding presents; the luck of the weather. The details of a wedding continued to be good conversational material until it became known that the happy bride was expecting, and at precisely that point the wedding took its place in the social history. It could always be revived, and would be revived so long as any guest survived to talk about it; but as a conversational topic of the first rank it ceased to entertain when once the bride's delicate condition was whispered to her cousins.

In its way, a first pregnancy was a social event; it provided social conversation. There would be speculation as to the sex of the unborn child; there would be impromptu statistical researches based on the record of the bride's family for producing sons, the groom's family record for producing daughters. It was a by no means generally accepted theory that the sex of the child had been determined early in the pregnancy. As the happy swelling became publicly noticeable there were guesses as to how high the unborn infant lay, a vital point to those experienced mothers and observant virgins who held that the sex of the child could be predicted by its location in the belly of the mother.

When more than two good friends were present there never could be a discussion of the act which caused the pregnancy, but it was the only stage which was not considered fit for conversation, so long as the conversation was conducted in discreetly euphemistic terms. Edith's hip measurements came in for repeated discussion and the previous regularity and painlessness of her menstrual periods, and the size of her bust. The single, almost boisterously unuttered hope was that the child she carried would be a boy, or, if a girl, would look more like the father. A boy's looks didn't matter; but for a girl to look like Edith—it was phenomenal how no one seemed to say it but everybody seemed to think it.

At 10 North Frederick Street the possibility of a girl baby was acknowledged, but only because it was a God-fearing household. If God in His infinite wisdom was seeing fit to make this child a female, He must have some reason, and with the Deity one did not argue, one did not question. But the physical and mental preparations were carried on in a frame of mind that admitted the possibility as no more than a possibility and an extremely unlikely happening. Ben Chapin sounded what he intended to be a humorous warning that girls were, after all, being born every day, but in the sitting room and backstairs his slight hedging was treated as though he had defied an established superstition. The expectant mother and the expectant grandmother were in a state of domestic felicity that was more than anything Edith had dreamed of and which proceeded from the moment Joe was permitted to announce the coming event. All her life Edith had had to make her own bed and tidy up her own room; her mother had seen to it that she learn to sew and cook. Likewise, her father had seen to it that she learn to rub down her own horse and hang the tack on the proper pegs. Now in her waiting months she was so much under the benevolence of Charlotte Chapin that Dr. English had to insist on her taking short walks to relieve her constipation. The fact that she had never ceased to hate the chores she had been compelled to do at home made Edith a willing subject of Charlotte's benevolence. And the arrangement was satisfactory to the two women because they mutually understood that it was impersonal, or at least as impersonal as it could be in view of the circumstance that one of them was actually carrying a child. Edith opposed no suggestion or rule or order that Charlotte set up. The rules were all made with Edith's comfort a factor, which made them easy to honor; and because she knew that her mother-in-law was thinking primarily of the grandchild, Edith did not wish for more warmth and less imperiousness in the stating of the rules.

Charlotte was too clever to let Edith suspect her of the truth, which was that she regarded the younger woman as an incubator. Charlotte was as far from being a Roman Catholic as a Christian woman could be, but she devoutly subscribed to the belief that in a choice between letting the mother or the infant survive the accouchement, the mother must die, the child must live. The pregnancy affected Charlotte's attitude toward Joe in gradual and subtle ways that she did not herself immediately observe, but since Joe seemed not to notice the changes, Charlotte, when she became aware of them, was not frightened of their possible effect on his love for her. If she had been caused to believe that there was a danger of diminished love for her, she would have rejected the baby and restored her son to first concern. But Joe too was behaving as though the child were the first ever to be conceived, and his attentiveness to his wife was a mixture of courtliness and platonic love that all but denied the vigor essential to the creation of Edith's condition. He came home for every noonday meal, and in the evenings he would read to her (and to Charlotte) until nine o'clock, and then he would stay one step behind her as they mounted the stairs. A second bed was placed in their room and he occupied it during the entire time of Edith's known pregnancy because neither Joe nor Edith thought to ask the doctor's advice in the matter. What they both quickly forgot was that neither of them had ordered the second bed; it had appeared in their room without specific comment by Charlotte, and had been accepted by them as evidence of practical delicacy on her part.

Someone in the household was always remembering that a baby was on the way, and the someone was not always Edith. Halfway toward her time the luxurious ease that Charlotte arranged for the young wife became monotonous; Edith was not tempted to forsake the comforts or to complain, for each little attention was welcome for the momentary pleasure it gave, but Edith was a strong young woman who was being overprotected from the simplest routines of living as well as from rainy weather, the slightest exertion, rich foods, tobacco smoke, ordinary household noises, and even the comparatively small number of Gibbsville women who were her friends. Charlotte encouraged Edith to have visitors in pairs, never singly, on the theory that a single visitor would talk and talk without restraint, while a party of three was somewhat less inclined to the intimacy of a party of two and its long-winded long-lasting visit. Such visits, Charlotte said, were all right when they were not exhausting, although she never had asked Edith to define the limit of her exhaustion. A visit that lasted more than fifteen minutes was likely to be terminated by Charlotte's entrance with the candid remark that "we" must rest. The visitors would put down Edith's mild protests to conventional politeness—and go. As a consequence Edith saw little of anyone who was not a member of the Chapin family or its servants. The servants were among those who never let Edith forget that she was with child, *Chapin* child. In point of fact Edith was physically stronger than any of the female servants, but they had been sternly commanded not to allow Edith to lift anything or to ascend the stairs without being followed, a safeguard against a backward fall. Under this regimen Edith took on weight to such a degree that her figure could fairly be described as voluptuous. Watching her come in from the bathroom one evening Joe smiled and said: "Sweetheart, you are a lot of woman."

"I don't know that that's a very pleasing remark," she said.

"I meant it to be," said Joe.

"It doesn't make any difference how you meant it. I don't want to be fat. I hate being fat."

"I didn't say you were fat, dearest."

"You didn't have to say it. I know I am. What else have I got to do but notice how fat I'm getting?"

"Dearest, I only meant that—your figure is very desirable."

She got into her bed and he went over to tuck her in.

"Lie down," she said.

"Do you think I ought to? I don't think I'd better," he said. For a while they limited themselves to gentle caresses, stroking of the hands, kissing of the cheek, but it could not last that way. He got out of the bed but she held his wrist tightly.

"You can't stop now," she said.

"But we mustn't," he said.

"You fool, you can't leave me this way."

She had never been so unrestrained, or so noisy in her demands. When they finished she lay there with her eyes closed and a grin of pleasure on her mouth.

"Edith, darling, I'm ashamed of myself," he said.

She said nothing, appearing not to have heard him.

"I promise never to do that again," he said.

She opened her eyes and smiled. "Stay here," she said.

"I can't. You know what's liable to happen."

"What?"

"It may affect the baby. I might hurt you. Maybe I have."

"Nothing's going to happen. I'm all right, and so is the baby."

"I'll have to talk to the doctor about it."

"You'll do no such thing. Other women make love while they're pregnant."

"Because their husbands are inconsiderate."

"Oh, what if they are? Do you think the miners and people like that don't have intercourse when the wife is pregnant? And they have hundreds of babies."

"But we're not miners and people like that. I'm supposed to be a gentleman. I'm ashamed of myself, and if anything happens it's my fault."

"Well, nobody will know it's your fault."

"I'll know," he said.

"But nobody else will, so stop worrying about it."

"I'll never stop till the baby is born and you're all right," he said.

"Oh, don't talk like that. We're not so different from other people, and I've been wanting this for months. And I'll go on wanting it. Good heavens, nobody ever lets me forget that part of myself. Your mother, the servants, you. I think about myself all the time, and you. Everybody's trying to make me think pretty and holy things—it's quite the opposite, I assure you."

"It's a very difficult time."

"You don't know the first thing about it, so stop saying things you've heard other people say."

"Good night, dearest," he said. He kissed her forehead.

"Good night," she said. She heard him getting into bed and rustling the bedclothes, finding a comfortable sleeping position. She had no clock to tell her accurately, but she was sure he was sound asleep in less than 360 seconds. She heard the courthouse clock strike for hours.

It was so for many nights and days until the child was born. She was regulated not by the Gregorian calendar but by one of her own devising based on lunar months and confusing even to herself. The clock meant no more: there was a grandfather's clock on the second-floor landing, a grandmother's clock in the sitting room, a banjo clock in Edith's bedroom, a cuckoo clock in the kitchen, all kept wound and all signaling the time on the hour and the half-hour; but Edith never knew what time it was, and cared not at all. She was drowsy a great deal of the time, at least partly because she had been broken of the habit of doing things. When her time, the infant's time, was nearing, the months preceding seemed to have flown by, and every hour, then every minute, began to count.

The first twinges of pain began in the early evening, but Dr. English had been in to see Edith in the afternoon, and told her no more than she already knew. In an attempt to lighten her mood he said: "I think we can say with positive assurance that you're going to have a baby."

"When?"

"Well, if you were one of my patients, a woman who lives out near the steel mill, I could tell you almost to the minute, and how long it would take. She's had nine and another on the way. She doesn't really need me. But with a first baby I don't like to make very positive predictions. You know. I want to be your doctor with all your babies, so I don't like to make a guess and be wrong on the first one."

"*All* my babies?"

"Yes. You may not think so now, Edith, but you and I are going to see a lot of each other, professionally. You're going to *want* them. Oh, they can be all sorts of trouble, I know. Julian's too high-spirited, for instance, but he's not a *bad* boy and if we had our way we'd provide him with brothers and sisters, but we can't always have what we want in this life. Now I'll leave you in the capable hands of Miss McIlhenny and I probably will drop in first thing in the morning."

He was more nearly correct than he knew. He was sound asleep when he received the telephone call, and he was dressed, if unshaven, by the time Harry arrived at his house with the Chapin Pierce-Arrow.

"Doctoring must be hard work, sir. Three o'clock in the morning and I wager it happens often."

"It happens very often, Harry."

"Marian put the coffee on for you."

"Good."

There was no one asleep at 10 North Frederick, and for the first time in thirty years someone other than Charlotte Chapin was in command. She had no more true confidence in William English than she had in any other doctor or any other man, but doctors are accustomed to giving orders and are in the habit of being obeyed, two related facts which produce in them an air of authority even when they are not authoritarian men. The manner, even when it is only acquired, inspires respect and confidence, and with William English it was not only acquired but inborn.

"Now if you don't mind, I'd like everybody to stay downstairs except Miss McIlhenny and Marian," said he, on the second-floor landing.

"Marian?" said Charlotte.

"Yes, Marian. We're not going to have time for Edith's mother to see her first, but that's just as well. Now, if you don't mind, will everybody clear out? Downstairs, please?"

He had some coffee and a cigar in Ben Chapin's bedroom and from time to time he would look in on Edith. Then Marian came in and said, "Nurse McIlhenny—"

"Well, sooner than I expected. Thank you, Marian. I'd like you to remain in the hall where we can call you if we need you." He had another look at Edith, who was beginning to show perspiration on the forehead. Now for the first of many times Nurse McIlhenny said, "Bear down," and the birth had begun. After two hours they put the aluminum mask on her face and dropped chloroform on the gauze. With the outrageous final pain she fainted into deep sleep.

"Tell Marian to tell them they have a daughter," said Dr. English. "Granddaughter, I *should* say."

Marian tiptoed down the stairs to the sitting room. The father and the grandfather were fully dressed; the grandmother was clad in flannel nightgown and a quilted dressing gown, bed socks and mules. Marian looked quickly at each person, and then from old habit she reported to Charlotte: "A baby girl, ma'am. A beautiful baby girl."

"Have you *seen* her?" said Charlotte.

"No, ma'am."

"How is my wife?" said Joe Chapin.

"Sleeping peacefully, Mr. Joe, sleeping peacefully."

"Really asleep, not—something else," said Joe.

"Really asleep, sir."

"What does the baby weigh?" said Ben Chapin.

"I wasn't told, sir," said Marian.

"Exactly what *were* you told, Marian? Without any of your own embellishments, please," said Charlotte.

"I was told to tell you that Mrs. Joseph Chapin had a fine baby girl—"

"Who said that? Who said fine?" said Charlotte.

"Miss McIlhenny, Nurse McIlhenny," said Marian.

"You have not spoken to Dr. English," said Charlotte.

"No, ma'am, but he was in the room when Nurse McIlhenny came out in the hall."

"And you were told to tell us—?" said Charlotte.

"That it was a beautiful, I mean *fine* baby girl, and Mrs. Chapin was sleeping peacefully, sir. Sleeping peacefully, Mr. Joe."

"Thank you, Marian," said Joe.

"That's not all," said Charlotte. "Marian, you march upstairs and find out when we can see the baby—and Mrs. Chapin."

"Billy English will let us know, I'm sure," said Ben.

"And again it may slip his mind," said Charlotte. "Do as I say, Marian."

"Very good, ma'am," said Marian, marching.

"Congratulations, son," said Ben, shaking Joe's hand. "Now you belong to the great brotherhood of fathers. Welcome."

"My boy," said Charlotte, kissing Joe, who bent down for the salute. "I'm sure everything's all right and you have nothing to worry about, although I should think William English might at least have told us himself."

"Shall we all have a glass of champagne?" said Ben.

"No, we shall not," said Charlotte. "Five o'clock in the morning is no time to drink champagne."

"It's no time to have a baby, either," said Ben. "But you didn't have anything to say about that, and you're not going to have anything to say about the champagne."

"Let's not, Father," said Joe. "Let's wait."

"I have no misgivings about the baby or about Edith. If there'd been any complications Billy English would have sent for you, not us, *you*. He didn't send for you, he sent Marian to tell all of us. I'm going to have a glass of champagne and toast my granddaughter, and I'm going to smash the glass in the fireplace. God damn it, I won't be around for her wedding, but I'm here now." He went out to the butler's pantry where there was a case of champagne in a bin.

"Oh, hello, Harry," said Ben, surprised. Harry was sitting at the kitchen table. "It's a baby girl. Is that tea, or whiskey you have in that cup?"

"I have to own up, it's whiskey, sir."

"Well, chop some ice. We're going to have a bottle of champagne, Mrs. Chapin and Mr. Joe and I. Three of Mrs. Chapin's best glasses and a bowl of ice. Bring them to the sitting room and I'll open the bottle."

"May I offer congratulations, sir?"

"Thanks, Harry, you may, you may indeed."

"It's too early to tell who she looks like?" said Harry.

"I haven't laid eyes on her. I'm taking her on faith and I love her sight unseen."

"Yes, sir," said Harry. He raised his cup. "To the new Miss Chapin. The only Miss Chapin, I guess, sir?"

"You are correct," said Ben.

Ben returned to the sitting room where Joe was sitting on the sofa beside his mother. "Well, any more news?" said Ben.

"Not yet," said Joe.

"Can't I persuade you two that this is a cause for celebration, not for long faces?" said Ben.

"It's easy for *you* to forget," said Charlotte.

"How *dare* you!" said Ben.

"Father, please," said Joe.

"Go upstairs and see your wife and your child," said Ben. "Do as I tell you."

"I'd better wait till—"

"Did you hear me?" said Ben.

Joe rose and left the room, and when he had gone Ben stood before his wife. "So—you've been filling him up with the horrors of it."

"I refuse to listen to you," said Charlotte.

"I know what you're doing, and you know I know it," said Ben.

"If you could see yourself," said Charlotte.

"I see *you*, all right," said Ben.

"Yes, and I see you. You look as though you were having apoplexy. If you are—too bad. Too—bad."

"You wish I were, but I'm not, Charlotte. I'm in the best of health and I'm going to stay that way, so I can watch my son getting to be a man."

"Your idea of a man," said Charlotte.

"Exactly," said Ben. "Now he's a father, and you're going to have to watch him getting to be a husband. He hasn't been, but he will be. The human being you ought to hate now is that baby. That baby is your rival now."

"Well, you never were," said Charlotte. "I never had to worry about you."

"Oh, I admit that. You ran his life, you got the affection and respect. But watching you lose it to a tiny girl, an infant, that's going to be some satisfaction to me. And there isn't a thing you can do about it, Charlotte my dear."

"We'll see," said Charlotte. "Or I will. As you yourself said, you won't be here for her wedding, and a lot can happen between now and then."

Harry came in with the tray. "Congratulations, ma'am."

"Thank you, Harry."

The man left the room and Ben picked up the champagne bottle, removed the foil and the wire and started to twist the cork. Suddenly he turned and fell onto the sofa, dropping the bottle. Charlotte jumped to her feet, away from him, and looked at him. His eyes had closed and he was breathing heavily, his cheeks puffing and vibrating his lips.

"Ben!" she whispered sharply. "Ben!"

There was no answer.

"Ben Chapin," she whispered again. That he was alive it was plain to see and hear. He was half sitting, half lying on the sofa, asleep as she had often seen him in his chair, but she knew that the suddenness of the overpowering sleep, the quick fall, were signs of a stroke. She jerked the bellpull and Harry responded. He went to Ben without speaking to Charlotte.

"A stroke?" said Harry.

"You'd better get Dr. English."

Dr. English came down to the sitting room in his shirt-sleeves. He examined Ben, and with Harry's help stretched him out on the sofa. He turned to Charlotte. "He's had a stroke. He mustn't be moved. And I'd like an ice pack."

"Some ice in the bowl, sir," said Harry.

"How convenient," said English. "Did he just keel over?"

"Yes," said Charlotte. "We were talking, and Harry had brought in the champagne. And Ben was opening the bottle and suddenly he fell, right about where I was sitting. What can we do?"

"For the time being, let him sleep. I'll give him some medicine. Harry, go upstairs and bring me my satchel, the small black one with the compartments for pill bottles. Bring it right down and don't stop to answer any questions. Mrs. Chapin, I think it would be better if you went to your room." Harry left.

"I don't think so," said Charlotte.

"Well, I do."

"I'm perfectly all right," said Charlotte.

"Yes, I know you are," said English. "That isn't what I was thinking about. And if you don't like being alone, take Marian with you, but not your son."

"What are you implying?"

"Now, Mrs. Chapin, please?" said English. "As soon as the registry's open I'm going to get a trained nurse. You understand that there'll be two trained nurses staying in the house?"

"Yes, I understand," said Charlotte.

"Then we *both* understand," said English. "A mutual understanding, and no more need be said."

She half smiled at him. "I think you're insolent, Billy English."

"Perhaps. Perhaps Billy English is, but this is *Doctor* English, Mrs. Chapin, and I think *you're* being impertinent."

"You will excuse me?" said Charlotte, and withdrew.

The presence in 10 North Frederick of two helpless persons and two persons who were professionally helpful brought about major rearrangements in the housekeeping and in the household. "I always seem to be passing someone on the stairs," said Joe to his wife.

"Well, we have life and death happening right here at home. It's like a small hospital."

"Doesn't seem so small, either," said Joe. "I went to see Billy English."

"What did Billy have to say?"

"I went to have a talk with him about Father."

"Yes, I gathered that," said Edith.

"Billy doesn't think that was the first stroke Father had. I don't suppose Father ever said anything to you?"

"Heavens, no."

"Well, it was a possibility. You and Father were getting closer," said Joe.

"Mostly because I was having Ann. He was being solicitous, that's all."

"He never said anything to me."

"And I shouldn't think he'd have said anything to your mother," said Edith.

"No. I haven't asked her, but I shouldn't think so," said Joe.

"If he had had a stroke before wouldn't somebody have known?"

"Not necessarily. It might have been a slight one and he didn't even know it himself. At least not recognized it as a stroke."

"Are you worried about him?"

"Am I worried about him? Perhaps not as much as I should be."

"Should you be?"

"Yes, I think so."

"Why?" said Edith. "Something Billy English told you?"

"What he didn't tell me, as much as what he did."

"What do you think he didn't tell you?"

"Well—he seemed to be implying that Father'd now had two strokes and the next one would be fatal."

"But he didn't say it in so many words?"

"No, not in so many words. Doctors can be like lawyers when it comes to making a positive statement. And I guess for the same reason. Self-protection. What you don't say can't be used against you."

"It's too bad your father isn't going to live a long time."

"It is, but why do you say it that way?" said Joe.

"Because he loves Ann and gets such pleasure out of her."

"So does Mother."

"Your mother is waiting for me to produce a son. Your father is happy that I produced Ann."

"Naturally Mother would like to have a grandson, but I don't think of her as waiting for you to produce one. She loves you very dearly. I've told you that."

"Yes, you've told me, quite a few times. But I think your mother and I understand each other. You don't understand us. You see—we don't have to love each other, your mother and I."

"Not have to, of course."

"Not have to, and don't. I am your wife, and that was all I was until Ann was born. Now it's all I am again until I produce a grandson. You mustn't insist on your mother and me loving each other. That's one of your notions. You have so many notions."

"I believe in certain things, yes."

"Notions. I'm talking about notions. You've had a notion for years that your mother and father love each other. They don't. They hate each other. Why can't you face the truth and admit that they hate each other? I hadn't lived in this house a week before I knew it. I guessed it before we were married, but after a week, I knew it."

"They often disagree, and—"

"Please don't deny it to me. That's the trouble with your notions. You deceive yourself."

"Sometimes it's better to deceive yourself."

"Oh, you do admit it."

"No, I don't admit it. Underneath it all Father and Mother love each other."

"You'd be happier if you admitted it," said Edith.

"Happier? To admit that my father and mother hate each other?"

"Yes."

"Edith, there are times when I don't understand you at all."

"I can readily believe that."

"How could I possibly be happier if I knew my father and mother hated each other?"

"I can explain that easily. If you admitted it, then you wouldn't keep on looking for signs of their loving each other. You never see any signs of it, but you go on looking because you won't admit the truth. The truth being, that they can't stand each other."

"Now how would that make me happier?"

"I've just told you," said Edith. "You spend half your life convincing yourself that they love each other and looking for proof, but the only time you get any kind of proof it's proof that they *don't* love each other, not that they do."

"But you haven't explained why I'd be happier."

"If you thought there was a gold mine in the back yard and dug for it and dug for it, but then some expert told you there was no gold within a thousand miles, wouldn't you be happier not wasting your time?"

"The expert might be wrong."

"Meaning I might be wrong?" said Edith.

"Yes. You might be."

"When you were a little boy, you believed in Santa Claus."

"Till I was five years old, I think."

"But not now," said Edith.

"No."

"Because believing in Santa Claus is a childish notion."

"It may be a childish notion, yes. But it's a good one."

"For children."

"Yes."

"Did the stork bring Ann?"

"Oh, now, Edith," said Joe.

"Did the stork bring Ann?"

" 'Answer yes or no'? No."

"You and I made love and your seed stayed inside me and grew and finally very painfully I gave birth to a child. Not the stork flying over Gibbsville and bringing a baby to 10 North Frederick Street."

"Yes."

"When you were born, did the stork bring you?"

"No."

"Your mother and father made love, and so forth."

"Yes."

176

"Your mother eats three meals a day."

"Yes."

"Your father eats three meals a day."

"Yes."

"Does your mother go to the bathroom?"

"Yes, and so does my father."

"Do they drink water?"

"Yes."

"Do they breathe air?"

"Yes."

"Does your mother like anybody?"

"Of course."

"Does she dislike anybody?"

"Yes."

"Does she hate anybody?"

"Oh."

"Please just answer me. Does she?"

"I don't know that she hates anybody."

"Do you believe it possible that she *could* hate anybody?"

"Could, that's a big word. Yes, I suppose she could."

"Could she hate your father?"

"She could, but I don't admit that she does."

"Will you admit that she could hate him and that he could hate her? You don't have to go into the reasons why they do, just admit that they could. If you admit that much, for the first time in your life, then that'll be a start toward getting rid of one of your notions. You know of law cases in which the husband and wife hate each other, even kill each other. Your notion is that it couldn't happen to *your* mother and *your* father."

"That's what I prefer to think."

"You're afraid that if you think something people will know you're thinking it. Don't be afraid of that. They won't have to know. But if you deceive yourself, you'll know it. You'll be more successful and happier if you don't deceive yourself. I'm happier than you are because I don't deceive myself. I know all the good and the bad things about myself."

"I don't think you're any happier than I am, and I don't know any of the bad things about you."

"You might not be so happy if you knew the bad things about me."

"What are they?"

"They're my secret, and I hope you never find out. You won't if I can help it."

"Would you like to know some of the bad things about me?" said Joe.

"No, I'd rather not."

"Ah, then you practice self-deception too."

"Perhaps I do, perhaps not. But it doesn't suit my plan to have you tell me the bad things about yourself."

"You'd rather find them out on your own hook?"

"Oh, perhaps. I'm only a woman, so don't expect me to be consistent."

The crying of their daughter brought an end to the colloquy. The nursery was on the floor above their room and in the hall they saw Joe's father standing in the doorway of his own bedroom, clad in nightgown and bathrobe and leaning on a snakewood walking stick.

"Time for her little drink, eh?" said Ben.

"Time for her drink, yes," said Edith.

"Time for you to stay in your chair, Father," said Joe. "You know that."

"Oh—bother my chair," said Ben. "Come in, I want to talk with you."

"I'll be right down after I've seen Ann," said Joe. He followed Edith up the stairs and was allowed to hold the hungry baby while her mother prepared to nurse her.

"I hope you don't mind if I have notions about *her*," said Joe.

"What kind of notions?" said Edith.

"Childish ones, I guess. I want her to be the happiest girl that ever lived."

"So do I," said Edith. She held up her hands for the baby.

"I didn't finish," said Joe, placing the baby in her mother's hands. "I want her to be happy without thinking her mother and father hate each other."

"I do, too. Now would you mind leaving while I feed her?"

"I like to see you feeding her."

"I know you do, but it makes me feel ill at ease, so go have your talk with your father."

Ben was lighting a cigar as Joe opened the door of his bedroom. "Father," said Joe.

"I believe it does me more harm to sit here and wish I could have a cigar than smoking it does. Besides, what difference does it make? Have one?"

178

"No, thanks," said Joe.

"Where I'm going, there'll be too much smoke to enjoy a cigar."

"Oh, now, Father."

"Too early in the day for you to have a drink, I suppose. There's a bottle of whiskey on that closet shelf. Pour me a half a glass, will you please? And fill it up with water. Half and half. Always reminds me of an old English story. A fellow'd been out carousing late at night and he came to his favorite tavern, but it was closed. So he banged on the door and banged on the door till the innkeeper stuck his head out the window. I can just see him, with one of those night-caps, putting his head out the upstairs window and saying, 'What do you want at this hour?' And the drunken gentleman said, 'I want me half and half.' 'You'll get your half and half,' the innkeeper said, and poured the contents of the chamber pot down on his head. 'Half the old woman's, and half mine,' said the innkeeper."

"Here you are," said Joe.

"I first heard that story when I was a junior in college. I suppose they still tell it."

"Yes, they do."

"Old stories die hard," said Ben. "Well, there are several things I want to talk about. First, I want you to find out how much it will cost to buy a full partnership in Arthur McHenry's firm. I want you to find out right away, tomorrow, if possible. When you do, I'll write you a check."

"I know the amount. It's fifteen thousand dollars."

"Is that all?"

"That's all, but I don't want you to buy it for me, Father. I want to buy it myself and pay for it year by year."

"I know you do, and that pleases me, and I would have let you do that if I hadn't had this stroke. But now I'd like to see you a full partner before I die. It isn't much money, son. If you were going to open a grocery store on a good corner you'd have to spend that much before you were through. And you're not opening a grocery store. You're becoming a partner in one of the best law firms in the eastern part of the state. With their name and our name, there won't be any better."

"Why do you want me to become a partner in another firm instead of continuing your firm?"

"That's a delicate question. I'll tell you why. I have friends, but I also have enemies. The McHenrys have friends and enemies too. My enemies, that you may inherit, they may take their business to the firm with the understanding that Arthur handle the business. And the same is true the other way around. And two unrelated young fellows are stronger than any one fellow, especially carrying on a family business. There's still another reason. A little healthy competition between you and Arthur will be good for both of you. Keep you on the alert, friendly rivalry, better all around. New blood for the McHenrys, new blood for the Chapins. Now I'll tell you something else."

"Yes," said Joe.

"In about five years you're going to be so successful, you and Arthur, that either one or both of you are going to be offered partnerships elsewhere. Philadelphia, and New York. Stay where you are. You will make more money here, you'll have the outstanding firm, and the New York people and the Philadelphia people, they'll have to come to you. You won't be working for them as a junior partner, or any kind of partner. You will be able to fix the terms and conditions you want. You will be the one firm in this part of the world that the big fellows in New York and Philadelphia will want to do business with."

"Hmm."

"A lot of people are going to ask the same question you did. Why do you and Arthur form a partnership? Well, it's obvious that you can get along without Arthur, and Arthur can get along without you. So since that's the case, people will say, well, those two young fellows must feel that they're even stronger together than apart. Therefore why not do business with the two strong firms in one? Later I'll speak to the McHenrys as a courtesy and then we'll make out the check."

"Father, I don't know how to thank you."

"I'll tell you how, Joe. Be the man I wish I'd been and didn't turn out to be. I don't have to tell you not to do anything crooked, but I hope you can get through life without doing anything cruel, or dirty, or mean. Now then, I've made a will. Your mother gets the bulk of what I have. The income while she lives. The bulk. I've left you a hundred thousand dollars and I suggest you invest it and forget about it. Pretend you haven't got it. Earn your own money and live on what you earn. I've left twenty-five thousand outright to Edith."

"Excuse me, Father. You're spilling your glass," said Joe.

As Ben was speaking he tilted the tumbler so that the whiskey and water dripped on the Brussels carpet. "Waste not, want not," said Ben. "I don't know why I said that. It doesn't apply. But as I was saying, I've left Edith twenty-five thousand dollars. I'd like to remember Ann too, but of course you'll have more children and it doesn't seem fair to mention Ann and leave out the others that haven't been born. So you take care of them for me. I know you will."

"This talk, Father, this information you're giving me."

"Yes?"

"I hope it doesn't indicate pessimism on your part. You aren't in that frame of mind, I hope. A man who's had a stroke doesn't go out and play tennis, but he can live for years."

"He can, but this one isn't going to. Yes, I consider this one of our final talks, Joe, and since we're about it, I have another request that I haven't made a condition in my will, but I can say to you, I hope you hold on to this house. Everything's following the westward trend, Lantenengo Street. And if you buy any real estate, buy property as far out Lantenengo as you can, hold on to that too, as long as you live. Don't sell. But this house, don't let it fall into other hands. If you decide to sell, tear it down. I don't want anyone but our family to live here. I hate to see that happen to a house. Our family built this house, and I wouldn't want another family to—to live in these rooms, go through our front door. I was born here, you were born here, and now my first grandchild. I hope *you* have grandchildren born in this house. I love this house."

"I'll never sell it, or at least I hope I never have to," said Joe.

"If I had my way I'd be cremated, so that what's left of me could stay on in this house, but I guess that's impossible in Gibbsville. I never heard of anybody being cremated in Gibbsville. And yet it's so much more sensible."

"But cold-blooded, I think. I'm not in favor of cremation."

"I don't know, it seems much more sensible to me," said Ben. "Joe, this is a very unpleasant ordeal I'm putting you through, talking so morbidly, but I have a reason. I'll tell you a secret. I don't think this was the first stroke I had. I think it's the second. I think I had one about two years ago. Not as bad as this one, but enough like this to make me feel pretty sure it was a stroke. Of course it may not have been a real stroke, but I was in Philadelphia, forget what the business was. And came back to the hotel late in the afternoon, got to my room, and fainted. Lay there till the chambermaid came to turn down my bed and she had the doctor. The hotel doctor. He asked me if I had a doctor in Philadelphia and he wanted to have him in, but I didn't want to make any fuss, so I came home the next day. I never told your mother or anybody else, but I tell you now. It may have been a slight stroke."

"You mean it *was* a slight stroke."

"Well, it may have been. The hotel doctor didn't use that word. He may have been confused because I'd had quite a bit to drink. Wasn't intoxicated, but quite a few drinks. Well, what difference does it make now? I've had the real genuine article, diagnosed and so on. Oh, this is a hell of a life, Joe, and sometimes I sit here and wonder what makes us want to hang on to it. But then I think of little Ann, and I have my answer. I want to give you one last piece of advice about her."

"Please do, Father."

"Spoil her."

"You mean, don't spoil her."

"No, I mean spoil her. Give her everything she ever asks for, everything you can. Edith won't let you, of course, but you give her as much as you can. First and foremost—love. When she wants a pony give her a pony. Dolls, dresses, toys. It never hurt a little girl to have her father spoil her. It never spoiled her, in fact. I once knew a girl, her father did the opposite of spoil her. And when she grew up she hated men, because her father didn't as-they-say spoil her."

"I don't know that I can promise you that, Father."

"I didn't ask for your promise. I merely gave you a piece of advice. I'll give you another piece of advice that you don't have to pay any attention to."

"All right."

"When you have a son, and you'll have a son—don't try to get too close to him. It isn't in the nature of things for a father and a son to be very close."

"I think you and I are."

"Oh, no, Joe. No. But we're close enough. I can wish we'd been closer, but I see now that we were just right. Not too close, and not too far away. You're a good boy. Honorable. Stayed out of trouble. And reflected credit on your mother and me, and now you're a father. Independent of your parents, and that's a good thing. I have one regret, one big regret."

"What's that, Father?"

"Well, it seems a pity that we had to wait all this time to have such a frank talk. But I suppose that's not very consistent. One minute I tell you a father and son can't ever get close, the next minute . . ."

"I've always felt very close to you, Father," said Joe.

His father touched Joe's hand. "D'you know, Joe, I believe you have."

182

Joe was so fully prepared for the death of his father that he was totally unprepared for the death of his mother. Ben Chapin stayed around until the infant Ann was almost a year old. As is so often the case, he had said his good-byes and had created in the minds of his household an acceptance of what was not yet an accomplished fact, but a fact that was only awaiting the final, confirming incident. Ben sat in his chair, smoked his cigar, drank his little whiskey, read his newspaper, fed himself his thrice-daily morsels, suitably greeted his family and servants, accepted their greetings in kind. Age and death were upon him and his life was over, and it was as though his body knew it and was afraid. His body was not resisting death but giving in to it. The voice that communicated the industry of his mind was still hard and masculine but if the words had been fearful the voice could have been called a croak. Instead it was a manly voice, speaking no whimpering words, and making liars out of his eyes which only told what was happening to his body. The eyes had become weak and unrevealing of the soul of the man. They were sick eyes because they could not help it any more than his skin could help what was happening to it. One night he died.

Harry Jackson was the first to notice that Charlotte was beginning to die.

He saw her rather less frequently than did the other members of the household. He had a whipcord livery with black leather puttees, which he wore when he was acting as chauffeur, and it was his public dress. He had another uniform, black trousers and waistcoat and black alpaca jacket, which he wore when answering the doorbell. But most of his duties were in the stable-garage and in the yard and in the cellar. Harry was not a butler, or a chauffeur, or a coachman, or a valet. He was The Chapins' Harry, who could prepare a meal or fix a toilet trap or plant the peonies. Sometimes five-day, six-day stretches would pass in which he didn't lay eyes on Charlotte Chapin. In his own words, he stayed out of the way as much as possible, and his love for the big Pierce-Arrow kept him close to the stable, which he had begun to call the garridge. An hour after the car had been returned to the garage a man could have run a white-gloved finger under the fenders and found them spotless. All six cylinders were treated as individuals, and his principal reading was the Pierce-Arrow manual furnished by the Foss-Hughes firm in Philadelphia. The radiator petcock was as ready for inspection as the lap robe, and frequently Harry would sit in the car happily when he could have been sitting comfortably in the kitchen with a spiked cup of tea. Sometimes when Charlotte sent for him he would send back word that he was all greasy when such was not the case.

But he would wipe off real grease and change his shoes for any summons that gave him a chance to see the infant Ann. His love for the child was so early and staunch that Marian's early attempts to explain it were futile. It soon seemed a sufficient explanation to say that Harry wanted a little girl of his own, and indeed it was the only explanation that anyone offered. No explanation ever became as important in the household as the fact itself. He simply loved the child. He had no fondness for her mother, and because they were so close in age, while distant in position, his feeling for Joe was neither deep nor warm. But when he began to realize that Joe's feeling for the child was strong and true, Harry felt that on that score he could share a warm interest with Joe. If Joe said anything about Ann, Harry would smilingly watch the workings of Joe's face and the pleasure in his eyes, and he would listen without interrupting to everything Joe had to say about his daughter. Harry was never heard to say, to declare, that he loved the child. It was so far from necessary that the declaration would have been too moderate.

There was hardly anything that could be said *against* a child that was not yet a year old. But Harry was present when Charlotte made the mistake of blaming the child for her own weariness. It was shortly after Ben's funeral. Charlotte's visitor was Bess McHenry, who in all her niceness and stupidity had been telling Charlotte how well she had stood up through her ordeal.

"I mustn't let you believe that, Bess," said Charlotte. "You mustn't go on believing that. These past months, if I could have gotten away from an invalid husband and a screaming baby, I'd have gone."

"Oh, no, Charlotte. Not you," said Bess.

Charlotte ignored her; now she was talking to herself: "I don't need much sleep, but I must have what I do need, and I don't know when I'll ever get it. I just don't know. Do girl babies cry more than boys? It seems that way to me. Oh, here's Harry to drive you home, Bess. You can't walk in this rain. How I envy you being able to go for a quiet stroll. I envy you."

Harry was one of the McHenrys' friends' servants who were always remembered with a $2.50 gold piece at Christmas, and he liked Bess McHenry, but on the drive to her house he made sure she was set straight on Ann Chapin. "I overheard you talking about the baby," he said, pretending not to have heard everything. "Ah, that's the bright spot at that house, that baby. The best in the land, an angel from heaven. A real comfort in every way."

"I imagine she must be," said Bess McHenry.

"A real princess, you might say," said Harry. "If all babies were as good as her . . . Well, here we are, ma'am."

He returned to the house satisfied that he had corrected any wrong impression left by Charlotte, and rather pleased that he might even have created a new impression of Charlotte herself. At least, he felt, he had planted a doubt in Mrs. McHenry's mind. But Charlotte was not going to be let off so lightly. She had made her mistake and Harry never gave anyone a second chance. He became aggressively protective of the child against her grandmother.

After Ben's death the nursing staff was cut down to one member, Miss McIlhenny. She was a trained nurse, not a baby nurse, and she was being paid one hundred dollars a month and room and board, but Joe decided it was worth the expense to keep her on; she gave Edith a sense of security and Joe himself said he felt better about his mother with Miss McIlhenny in the house. Her presence meant extra work for Marian; she ate her dinner and supper off a tray, since her position in the household was, in Marian's words, "too good to eat in the kitchen and not good enough to eat with The Family." There was no resentment against her, backstairs. She did add slightly to Marian's chores; at the same time she took care of the baby work and she became a combination companion and personal maid to Mrs. Ben. And she had sense enough not to try to lord it over Marian and Harry, who could have made her life so miserable that she would not have stayed. She was obviously more at home having a cup of tea in the kitchen than watching Charlotte having her cup of tea in the sewing room.

"It looks to me like it'll only be a question of time before we get another visit from Wagner Brothers," said Harry, one afternoon after Bess McHenry's call.

"The old lady?" said Miss McIlhenny.

"There may be nothing the matter with her, nothing for the doctors to find, but if you want to know what I think . . ."

"What?"

"Well, her and the recently departed, I never heard them say a civil word to one another," said Harry.

"*That's* wrong," said Marian. "There you're wrong."

"Am I? All right, then. They never said anything excepting a civil word to one another."

"Now you're right," said Marian. "All politeness and none of the milk of human kindness."

"Exactly," said Harry. "Exactly, Marian. They *hated* one another! By Jesus—"

"Not the name of the Lord, please, Harry," said Miss McIlhenny. "Excuse me."

"I don't mind a little cursing and swearing, but not J. C.," said Miss McIlhenny. "But go on with what you were saying. I find it interesting."

"Well, what kept her alive, the old lady, was she hated *him* so much that it give her something to occupy her mind. Now she don't have nobody to hate and I swear to you, I notice it taking effect on her. The daughter-in-law, she never mustered up a good hate for the daughter-in-law because the daughter-in-law's just too anxious to please, she wants to have everything right. As long as it don't cost her too much effort. She's a lazy one, isn't she, Marian?"

"Not lazy, exactly. I never said she was lazy," said Marian. "She'll do what she has to do, but she'll never go out of her way. You know how some of them are?"

"Oh, do I indeed!" said Miss McIlhenny. "They'll make their own bed, but they won't put on fresh sheets for fear they'll have to reach up on the top shelf of the closet. I could give you dozens of examples, but I know what you mean. But Harry, I don't understand why you think we'll be getting another visit from Wagner Brothers. She's only a young woman compared to her husband. Still, I guess that puts her in her late sixties."

"The poison, Miss Mac," said Harry. "The poison. The poison she cooks up inside herself, now she don't get the opportunity to rid her physique of it, it runs through her system till her whole system is saturated with it like she was a sponge in a bottle of iodine. You two, you see her more oftener than I do, so you don't have my advantage of noticing how she's changed since the old man passed away. I took notice the other day when I was in the sewing room. This old lady, I said to myself, she don't have long."

"Well, she don't complain of anything," said Miss McIlhenny. "So I can't call the doctor."

"If I was you I'd tell you one thing I'd do," said Harry.

"What?"

186

"Don't let her handle the baby. In her present weakened condition she's liable to drop little Ann—"

"Oh, now," said Miss McIlhenny.

"Yes, oh now," said Harry. "And if that happened—"

"If that happened," said Marian. "Harry'd strangle you with his own two hands. Maybe you wouldn't have anything to fear from the baby's father, but Mr. Harry here—oh, my."

"You shut up," said Harry. "I was talking to Miss Mac, not you."

"Be careful who you're telling to shut up. I'll have none of your impoliteness to *me*," said Marian.

"Now, the two of you," said Miss McIlhenny.

Harry's warning, where it concerned the baby, took effect, although it was no cruel or unusual punishment for Charlotte to be deprived of the hefting of her granddaughter. Insofar as the warning was a prediction of Charlotte's early end, it had little effect. Miss McIlhenny was not receiving any medical information from unqualified diagnosticians, for she was in fact frequently skeptical of the diagnoses of the qualified. Consequently Harry was the only member of the household who was able to say I-told-you-so when Miss Mac one morning came out of Charlotte's bedroom with the news that Charlotte was dead. It could have been said of her, in the words of one poet, that she died of nothing but a rage to live; her passing was otherwise described in the Gibbsville press: she passed away peacefully in her sleep.

By the very nature of things the lives of young married couples are likely to become complicated and simplified by the death of a couple's four parents, as well as by the birth of their own children. In less than two years Joe Chapin's parents and Edith's father died, leaving Edith's mother as the sole grandparent of Ann Chapin. The death of Edith's father had remarkably little effect on Edith's life. It made her no richer; Carter Stokes, Sr., left all his money to his wife. Emotionally, it caused no void. As to responsibility, Edith turned that over to her brother Carter, who was the kind of young man who almost seems to have been born to take care of a widowed mother. Mrs. Stokes was an old bore, a bore before she was old and a worse bore as she aged. It is possible to take a second, more penetrating look at people who have the reputation for villainy and evil, and sometimes the second look makes for a reappraisal of the naughty ones. But the public judgment on bores is seldom to be appealed. In the first decade of the Twentieth Century the word "bore" was still a Society word, borrowed from the English and not in general conversational use in the United States of America. For that reason Mrs. Stokes was not often *called* a bore, but her qualifications to the dubious distinction were known to her friends and acquaintances. She was never quite well, she was never quite ill. She was without distinction in appearance, without prettiness even in young womanhood, with a bosom that was almost flat but not firmly flat, with ankles that were not noticeably heavy or trim, and no one ever remembered or argued over the color of her eyes. She was conventionally addicted to cleanliness but at the Assemblies she exuded the odor of perspiration without having to waltz. This woman had had some participation in the act of copulation and had given birth to two children; had cooked edible meals, knitted shawls, gone to church, discharged servants, attended the opera, read the newspapers, cashed checks, purchased hats, skinned her kneecap, stayed at the Bellevue-Stratford, written letters, trimmed her toenails and lit a fire. And yet she was a bore. No experience and no total of experiences had excited her or made her the least bit exciting. She was a denial of the meaning to men of the word "woman." The tone of her voice was ladylike and her enunciation was correct, but in all her life she never had said anything memorable or memorably. When Edith got away from her, she stayed away from her, and Mrs. Stokes even caused a strain on Joe's unfailing politeness.

What her father's death did do was to fix Edith firmly on North Frederick Street. With Ben Chapin dead and Charlotte Chapin dead, and her own mother waiting out her time in the South Main Street house and looked after by Carter, Edith became the lady of the house at 10 North Frederick. Now she no longer had any sense of impermanency; there was no old woman upstairs who could give and rescind the orders; when Edith gave her address as 10 North Frederick Street, in the shops of Philadelphia and New York, she gave it with conviction, assurance, where in earlier months she often was afraid that the salesgirl doubted her right to say that that was where she lived. To Edith the house was a symbol of her improved station in life, and for that reason she was more than content to leave it as it had been. It pleased Joe that she did so, but that was no more than a happy accident. It never occurred to her to repaint, to redecorate, to refurnish. The house and its contents intact were the symbol, and any big change would have altered its symbolic value. Another woman might have waited impatiently for the moment when she could begin to replace the lighting fixtures and the stair runners and the purely decorative objects. Not so Edith. The only changes she made were in the den, and they were changes to gladden Joe's heart: his school and college pictures, his diplomas, his fraternity and club shields, his other youthful souvenirs were brought down from the bedroom and given space in the little room. The transfer was, of course, a subtle announcement of the new fact that it was *Edith's* husband who was now head of the house, but hardly anyone thought of it that way, and even if anyone had, was it not the truth?

Joe, with the death of his parents, was a rich man, much better fixed than many Gibbsville men who had retired, and for a time Edith considered Joe's retirement as a possibility. The world beyond the borough limits of Gibbsville was not too well known to Joe, and known barely at all to Edith. On Joe's income they could have traveled to the far places and seen the strange things, the lands and people that they knew through Stoddard's Lectures. But who in Shanghai, China, would know that in Gibbsville, Pennsylvania, U. S. A., Joseph B. Chapin was an aristocrat of unassailable standing? If a Chinese prince were to come to Gibbsville, he would be entertained by the Chapins, but if the Chapins were visiting in Pekin, would the reverse be true? Closer to home, to take up residence in Philadelphia or New York was not a prospect that attracted Edith. It would require much, much greater wealth than Joe possessed to get established in the big American cities. Joe could, of course, continue his legal career, but that was not to live as a retired gentleman. He could *work anywhere.*

Thus Edith came around to the basic question of retirement itself. She knew precious little about the law, and not much more than that about Joe's ability as a lawyer. But she did know that he was a member of a firm that was bound to be successful if only because of the business that would come its way through connections. From her brother Carter, who was no fool, she learned that a great deal of the work performed by a firm like McHenry & Chapin was simply a matter of looking it up in a book. Arthur McHenry and Joe Chapin were not likely to save a man from the hangman's noose through a dramatic courtroom strategy; that kind of performance was in the Montgomery tradition, which was being maintained by Jerry Montgomery. The very fact that the brilliance, the fireworks were *not* a McHenry & Chapin specialty was an invitation to the less spectacular but continuingly profitable kind of law business. Until her conversation with her brother, Edith had had the conventional idea of a corporation, the cartoonists' fat man in the silk hat and with the dollar sign in his ascot necktie. Carter pointed out to her that the small meat-packing firm of Schneider & Zimmermann, the local planing mills, the brass foundry, and most of the Main Street stores were, technically, corporations, requiring legal services that were completely unrelated to murder and rape. McHenry & Chapin not only attracted that kind of business: they were in a position to accept or reject clients. For the first time Edith understood that law was not all lawsuits, that the McHenry & Chapin kind of firm preferred to stay out of courtrooms. Moreover, by keeping out of courtrooms, McHenry & Chapin acquired a kind of prestige that they carried into a courtroom when circumstances forced them into one. They almost never took a criminal case; if for one reason or another they became counsel for the defense, they automatically conferred on the client a sanitary seal that put the plaintiff at an immediate disadvantage.

The law firm, then, gave Joe something to do, and he seemed to like it. If he had had an interest in book collecting, or polo, or even if he had been the kind of young man who could go to his club every day and while away the time in card playing and modulated drinking, Joe would have had Edith's encouragement. Her own father had been a quiet souse, which did not interfere with his functioning as an owner of timber lands and a vestryman in Trinity. But her father was not a handsome man, and Joe was handsome; her father was not a rich man, and Joe was rich. And her father was not her husband. She did not own her father. She had never been able to direct her father by order or by guidance, subtle or overt. She did not consider herself lucky to have Stokes as a father; she never had had ambitions for him; he never had been an instrument of her pleasure. And she was quite sure, without being bitter, that her father had not loved her; as sure as that she never had loved him.

Edith did love Joe, as an adjunct, as a part of herself and a mechanism in her life. That Joe loved her she never for two seconds doubted. In her alone, she was sure, reposed the power to awaken and continually reawaken whatever of lust there was in Joe. Sometimes it was as though she had been present with Joe every minute of his life from birth, and when the time came—on the night of their wedding—he was at last ready, and she was, as always, there to share this new experience. Before their marriage she had so finally convinced herself of Joe's virginity, and on their wedding night she had been so much more convinced by his awkwardness—that she suffered no curiosity about his relations with other girls. Accordingly, she never inquired; consequently, the lie he might have told her did not come up for a test.

Her appraisal of his love for her, in those early years of their marriage, was no more complicated than such a simple emotion and such simple circumstances demanded. There was, for instance (she believed), the fact that he *told* her he loved her. Then if that had not been enough, the fact that he depended on her completely for sexual pleasure. They were living in a time when it was popularly remarked that "he never looked at another woman." Joe did look at other women, handsomer women—but never strayed from her. There was a point in politeness beyond which Joe did not go, and that was mild flirtatiousness. If, indeed, he ever reached that point. He was a gentleman, and the art of the fan was being practiced by the women they knew, which meant that some of the women appeared to be flirtatious; but Joe would participate only to the extent that nonparticipation would have been loutish. Aside from such politenesses, Joe gave Edith not the slightest reason to have the minutest doubt of his love for her.

In a town that was populated—at least in their set—by happy couples and only happy couples, they stood out as a happy couple for other happy couples to use as a model. There was some slight uneasiness among the other happy couples that was caused by the Chapins' failure, deliberate or otherwise, to produce a second child. But the worries were set at rest when, along about the time the Germans were invading Belgium, it became known that Edith was going to have another baby.

The British and German propaganda machines went quickly to work, although the British efforts were not as a rule characterized or even recognized as propaganda. In Gibbsville, where propaganda was not needed, the old German families responded as any such group might be expected to respond. The nice people, exclusive of the German-descended, and regardless of origin, immediately went to the assistance of the Allies. The German-descended were put on the defensive and some of them said and did foolish things when provoked that provoked reprisals, and in several cases enmities originated that not only outlasted the first World War, but were easily recalled upon the outbreak of World War II. Edith's pregnancy and the European hostilities postponed any further discussion of travel abroad—postponed it for more than ten years. The war in Europe did a curious thing: it provided a topic of conversation (except when the German-descended were present) which was dotted with European place names such as Louvain and Metz and the Argonne woodland; the men, at least, were talking about places they never had talked about in their lives (Metz had occasionally been in their conversations because there was a motorcar by that name); but the conversations were only "for show"; the European war was not understood and the reporting of it was meager, so that the question, "Can we stay out of it?," was not being asked during the months that saw so much death in Europe while Edith was transfusing life to her child. Two, then three, then more of Joe's Yale friends or acquaintances were reported to have joined the British and the French, but in conversations with Arthur McHenry the war remained a European affair, not brought any closer to home by the volunteering of their friends. One of the volunteers had earlier gone on big-game-hunting expeditions in Africa, and to Joe and Arthur his signing on with the British was precisely of a piece with his firing rifles at lions. It was a chance for adventure and no more. When another classmate was killed in the first battle of Ypres he was conceded not to have been a big-game hunter or a mere adventurer; but an explanation for his being with the British was not hard to find; he was working for the London branch of an American bank and probably had a great many English friends. In every way the war was such a distant thing that Joe and Edith could hope for a son without any thought of his ever becoming cannon fodder.

It happened that Ann was sitting on her father's lap, being read to, when Miss McIlhenny, who had been re-engaged for the occasion, came to the den with the news that Edith had given birth to a son.

"Did you hear that, dear? Mummy—you have a brand-new baby brother," said Joe.

"What's his name?" said Ann.

"Well, I think his name *will* be Joseph Benjamin Chapin, the same as mine, except that he'll be Junior. Aren't you happy? Aren't you pleased?"

"Everything's fine, Mr. Chapin. Fine," said Miss McIlhenny.

"Thank you, Miss McIlhenny, thank you ever so much," said Joe.

"Why did you say everything is fine? Do you mean there's something wrong?" said Ann.

"Not a bit of it," said Joe.

"Can I see him?" said Ann.

"In a few minutes," said Miss McIlhenny.

"Why does Mummy have to get sick to have a baby brother?"

"It isn't really a sickness like—measles."

"She had to go to bed, she had Dr. English. Dr. English is still upstairs," said the child.

"It's because babies have to stay in bed so much when they're tiny, and she wanted to be there when Dr. English brought him," said the nurse.

"How did Dr. English bring him?"

"In that little black bag," said Miss McIlhenny.

"Why didn't he stuffocate, if he was in the little black bag? He couldn't breathe. He must be very tiny."

"Oh, he is, very tiny," said Joe.

"Not so very tiny, at that," said the nurse. "He's over seven pounds."

"What if I don't like him?" said Ann.

"Oh, you'll love him," said Joe.

"I haven't even seen him, I'm not sure I'll love him."

"But you will love him, I'm sure of that," said Joe. "Just as we all loved you when you were born."

"Where is he going to sleep?"

"Why, I suppose in Mummy's room, for the time being. In his crib."

"My crib," said Ann.

"Well, it was your crib when you were a tiny baby, but you don't mind if he sleeps in it now, do you?"

"Yes I do," said the child. "Somebody took my dolly out of my crib and put her on a chair. That wasn't nice."

"But they did it for a real, live baby, your new baby brother," said Joe. "I know you'd rather have your baby brother sleep in the crib than your dolly."

"No I wouldn't," said the child. "What if somebody puts him in my bed?"

"Nobody's going to put him in your bed," said Joe. "You have your own bed as long as you want it. Then some day you'll grow so big that we'll have to buy you a bigger bed."

"What color?"

"Any color you like."

"Without a fence? I want one without a fence."

"Oh, by that time you surely can have one without a fence."

"But then you'll give my brother *my* bed."

"Well, maybe. Maybe not."

"Buy me a new bed and he can have mine with a fence. I mean please."

"Well, we'll see."

"Father? Will you carry me upstairs to see my brother?"

"Carry you? My big girl?"

"I'm not a big girl, I'm a little girl."

"Tell you what I'll do. I'll go up first and have a moment or two with Mummy, *then* I'll come down and carry my big little girl upstairs to see her brand-new brother. Does that sound like fun?"

"Yes, Father."

"Splendid. Now you go find Margaret and you and she can wait here for me."

"Margaret's in the kitchen with Marian."

"Very well, you go tell her what I told you."

"Will you please tell her? She won't obey me."

"All right. We'll both tell her."

"Father?"

"Yes, dear."

"Will you pick me up and give me a hug and a kiss first?"

"Why of course I will," said Joe. "You bet I will."

"And will you carry me out to the kitchen, please?"

"Sure I will that," said Joe.

"You sound like Marian," said the child.

"Sure and do I sound like Marian?"

"Father, you're funny."

"Sure and am I funny?"

"Sure and you are," said the child. "Am I funny?"

"Sure and you are, and the sweetest, loveliest—you're my big little girl. Up we go!" He picked her up and they started for the kitchen.

"Do Marian some more," she said.

"Sure and I better stop if I know what's good for me," said Joe.

"Do her some more," said Ann.

"Oh, that's enough for the time being."

"Will you be right down?"

"Two shakes of a ram's tail."

"Will you carry me downstairs after I see my brother?"

"Well, I don't know. It may be your bedtime. But we'll see."

"When you say 'we'll see' you do it. When Mummy says it, she doesn't."

"Hmm. We'll discuss that some other time. All right, my dear, dismount."

"Please carry me into the kitchen."

"All right, into the kitchen but then I must go upstairs and see the rest of our family."

Later that evening, and after the well-intentioned Mrs. Stokes had departed for her own home (after telling Ann that the stork had brought her brother and carried him down the chimney), Joe had a visit from Arthur McHenry.

"I'm glad you don't like champagne any more than I do," said Joe.

"It all tastes like Rubifoam to me," said Arthur.

"Rubifoam?"

"It's a liquid I use to brush my teeth," said Arthur.

"Never heard of it," said Joe. "Lot of things I never heard of."

"Well, welcome to the new arrival."

"Welcome to the new arrival," repeated Joe. They drank their whiskey neat, and without another word or a signal they hurled the glasses into the fireplace.

Next they toasted Edith. "I don't think we have to be so destructive this time," said Joe. "It seems to me I remember paying a damn big bill for that dinner I gave my ushers."

"How is Edith?"

"Well, somewhat exhausted, naturally, but Billy English says she's fine. How is Mildred?"

"I'm discouraged," said Arthur. "I'm going to take her to Philadelphia next week to see a specialist. Do you know what she weighs? A hundred and five."

"Goodness, Arthur. A hundred and five?"

"A hundred and five pounds, and the worst of it is, they don't seem to know what's the matter with her. She weighed close to a hundred and thirty when we were married. Or maybe even a pound of two over that. Billy says it isn't cancer, he seems certain it isn't that. But he doesn't offer any opinions about what it might be, so I'm going to have this man in Philadelphia take a look at her and maybe he'll be able to diagnose it."

"What kind of a specialist is he?"

"It's something to do with the blood stream. The white corpuscles and the red corpuscles. You know how little I know about medicine. I was thinking of letting Malloy examine her."

"No, he's a surgeon."

"I know he is, but at least it would be another opinion."

"I don't think Billy would like to call him in for a consultation. Billy doesn't like Malloy."

"Well, what Billy doesn't like is too damn bad. If I hadn't made the arrangements to take Mildred to Philadelphia, I'd call Malloy myself."

"He wouldn't come. That's medical ethics. Not as long as Billy's your doctor. And Billy will do everything for you that Malloy can do. Malloy'd probably send Mildred to a specialist too. Probably the same specialist."

"Well, probably. I'm impatient because I don't see any improvement at all."

"Is she in pain?"

"Well, not acute pain, but she's so God damn weak, Joe. So God damn weak. You know for Mildred to weigh a hundred and five— well, there isn't much left on her bones any more. She doesn't complain, but sometimes I think when she looks at me that she was begging me to do something. And what is there I can do?"

"What you're doing. Take her to a specialist. Cheer up. He may discover what's wrong with her right off the bat."

"Rose is going along with us, and if the examination takes more than a couple of days she's going to stay there with Mildred."

"Rose is a fine girl, fine."

"Devoted to Mildred. It's the way sisters should be but they damn seldom are," said Arthur. "Nothing new at the office today, or of much importance. Karl Schneider was in. He wants to find out if we can sue the Pennsy for delaying putting in that spur. You know their new building, where they want some new trackage to take the place of the old siding. I told him to make haste slowly. If we went into court every time that wild Dutchman had a grievance."

"I agree with you. Has he paid his bill?"

"He paid it yesterday. I'd be inclined to tell him to find another law firm, but they're going to get bigger and bigger, Joe. And I understand the British are buying all the beef they can get their hands on, so let's humor him for another couple of years."

"Yes, and there's the vague possibility, only a possibility, but worth considering. We *could* be maneuvered into this war."

"If we were, would you go?"

"If we were invaded, of course I'd go. So would you."

"It may not take an invasion to get us into it."

"What else would get us into it?"

"Well, suppose the Germans invaded Canada," said Arthur.

"Canada? That would be the same as invading us."

"Or Mexico."

"Why would anybody want to invade Mexico? I consider the Germans a stupid race of people, but who would be that stupid?"

"It would be a good way to invade us. Mexico first, then us."

"They'd never get across the Rio Grande."

196

"The Mexican bandits do."

"But not a Mexican army. Not in a real war. And by the time the British and French are through with the Germans they won't have enough men left to—invasion? Out of the question, Arthur."

"Well, you said it was a possibility."

"Yes, but highly improbable. About as unlikely as the Chinese invading California. We're protected by two oceans and by Canada on the north, and to the south—well, we have nothing to fear there either. All the same, I wonder what I'd do if I'd just got out of college and had no matrimonial plans. What would you do?"

"I think I'd enlist, in the Canadian Army."

"If you did I'd go with you."

"I wouldn't go without you."

They laughed lightly. "It would be ridiculous, wouldn't it?" said Joe. "And yet, you can't deny what the Germans did in Belgium. Especially to the Belgian women. Putting them in whore houses for the troops. When you hear things like that you wonder if it would be so ridiculous after all. You have to admire the British and the Canadians for going to the defense of the Belgians the way they did. What must a Belgian father or husband feel when he hears what they did to his wife or daughter? And they say the British are just as angry at those atrocities as the Belgians. Well, of course, the British sense of fair play. Code of decency and all that sort of thing. Have you thought of joining the National Guard? Some of the fellows at the club were talking about it."

"I'd rather wait awhile and see what happens. I don't want to have to drill, and go to camp at Mount Gretna, and march in parades every time a Civil War veteran dies," said Arthur.

"No, that could be tiresome," said Joe.

"Drudgery," said Arthur.

"Well, we're worrying about nothing. I'm convinced that Woodrow Wilson will keep us out of it. Not that I like Wilson, but he doesn't even look warlike. And of course he was a college professor."

"Yes, but he was also a football coach," said Arthur, smiling.

"He was? I didn't know that."

"At Wesleyan."

"Wesleyan? The Wesleyan at Middletown, Connecticut? That Wesleyan? I thought he was Princeton through and through."

"I'm sure he is, but he taught at Wesleyan," said Arthur. "How about the young man upstairs? Have you entered him at New Haven?"

"No, I never thought of it. Took it for granted. He'll be the fifth

197

in line to go to Yale, fifth generation, and maybe more. I'll tell you what I *have* thought of: I've thought of entering him in Groton."

"Groton? Why not The Hill?"

"I have no strong feeling about The Hill. I was sent there because it was close to home, and it may be all right if you're going to Penn or Princeton, but if my boy goes to Yale or Harvard I want to prepare him for Yale or Harvard. You don't like the idea."

"Well—no."

"Why not?"

"Why don't you send him to Eton?"

"Eton's in England."

"Well, if you're going to send your boy to a place that tries to be Eton, why not send him to the real thing instead?"

"Oh, I don't think Groton tries to be Eton."

"Maybe not, but the fellows we knew that went there . . ."

"Dave Harrison went there. Alec went to Groton. You liked them."

"Did I?"

"Didn't you? Now don't tell me you didn't like Dave and Alec."

"How often have I looked them up in New York?"

"You were an usher for Alec."

"With sixteen other fellows, or eighteen, or whatever it was."

"He wasn't one of your ushers," said Joe, remembering. "Why wasn't he?"

"He wasn't asked," said Arthur. "Alec got married as soon as he got out of college. You and I waited a couple of years, and by that time Yale didn't mean quite as much to me as it had—if it ever did. I'm not convinced that going to Yale was the best move I ever made. I'm not sorry I went there, but I think I would have learned just as much at Lafayette. I'm sure I would have learned more at Harvard. I was so damn busy being careful so I'd make a senior society, and I didn't really give a damn about it except that I knew you were sure to make one, so I had to too. If I had a son, which I never will, I'd send him to Gibbsville High and Penn State."

"You're joking."

"No, I'm not joking. I don't recommend that for your son. Your father's people have all gone to Yale and they were New Englanders. My family are all Pennsylvanians on both sides. You can get just as good an education at Muhlenberg as you can at Yale, and maybe better with all those Pennsylvania Dutchmen and fewer distractions."

"Why, you don't even know anybody that went to Muhlenberg."

"Yes I do. Old Judge Flickinger went to Muhlenberg. He studied law at Penn, but he went to Muhlenberg. Dr. Schwenk, the pastor of the Lutheran church. And half a dozen other men that I consider as well educated as any Yale men we have around here."

"You never see them. I've never seen these educated men at your house."

"More's the pity, Joe. I wish I knew some of them right now, to get an educated German-American's views of this war."

"I'm afraid they'd be more German than American."

"Well, what if they were? We're making them feel like bastards, and some of them go back to pre-Revolutionary days."

"Maybe they are bastards," said Joe.

"Judge Flickinger?"

"Well, I wasn't thinking of him. I hardly know Dr. Schwenk. But we know men in this town that are sending money to Germany secretly."

"Well, we know others that are sending money to England openly. I happen to be one. I have cousins in England that I never saw, never expect to see, and if they knew I was talking like this I'm sure they'd return my money. But I'm really tempted to send some money to the Germans too."

"You're talking through your hat."

"Aren't we neutral? Aren't we?"

"Officially, because Woodrow Wilson wants us to stay out of it."

"Very well, then if my sympathies cause me to send money to England, my belief in strict neutrality, the policy of our country, ought to cause me to send money to Germany."

"Well, don't do it, because no matter what we are officially, if we get into this war you know darn well whose side we'll be on."

"Yes, and the Germans know it too."

"Well, they started it, and they're going to be very sorry they did."

"Joe, that's exactly the attitude that may result in your donning a uniform and fighting for your country."

"All right. If I have to."

Arthur helped himself to more whiskey and whistled an unrecognizable tune. They had the kind of friendship that permits quiet as well as argument, without nervous searching for conversational topics. Always the one who happened to be the visitor knew he could leave when he felt like it, comfortable in the knowledge that visits were only incidental to the whole relationship.

"Edith asleep?"

"Mm-hmm, I think so."

Joe picked up the afternoon newspaper. "They had quite a big fire in Fort Penn."

"Yes, I saw that," said Arthur.

He sipped his drink.

Joe read the newspaper.

"Are those the shoes you bought at Wanamaker's?" said Arthur.

"Hmm?" said Joe.

"Are those the shoes you got at Wanamaker's?"

"These shoes? No, I got these at Frank Brothers about two years ago. They were hard to break in, but now I like them."

Joe went back to his newspaper and Arthur smoked his pipe, sipped his drink, whistled in between. Perhaps five minutes went by. Then Arthur stood up, but Joe did not ask him if he were leaving. He was not leaving. He went to the dictionary, spent a minute with it and sat down again.

"What were you looking up?" said Joe.

"Parturition."

Joe laughed. "Oh," he said. "I looked it up myself about eight months ago."

In a little while he finished with the newspaper. "What's the name of the man Mildred's going to see?"

"I don't remember."

"Not Deaver or d'Acosta or one of those?"

"No, I'd never heard the name before. He has an office on Walnut Street."

"Well, I hope you remember the number, on Walnut Street."

"I have it all written down, and Billy telephoned him long distance last week."

"I'd like to drop in and say hello before she leaves."

"I'd rather you didn't. She—"

"You're right, you're right. It might alarm her. You're absolutely right." Joe nodded. "Make it seem like—nothing very serious, nothing to get alarmed over. I'll send her a book to read on the train."

"That would be nice."

"Something light, humorous," said Joe. "Would she like some candy? You know Marian's homemade candy."

"She loves Marian's candy."

"You know, Arthur, it's awful how much of our lives we spend just waiting, isn't it?"

"Yes."

"Edith and I, first waiting to be sure she was going to have the baby, then waiting for her to have it. Now you, waiting to take poor Mildred to Philadelphia, and waiting there for what the doctor has to say."

"I *know* what he's going to say, Joe. And that's when the worst waiting begins."

"Oh, no. You don't think it's that bad. Do you really?"

Arthur nodded. "Whatever it is, it's gone too far. And Mildred knows it too. We pretend, but we know."

"Oh, Jesus, Arthur. Here I am, so God damn happy, with my son . . . Arthur, I feel like a shit. I've been no help to you at all."

"Oh, yes you have. Yes—you—have."

"Don't be ashamed to cry."

"I'm not ashamed. I was just hoping I wouldn't."

Joe rose. "I'm going upstairs. You stay here as long as you like, and don't bother about the lights. I'll turn them out when I go to bed."

"Thanks, Joe."

"And I'm right here every night, you know that."

"I know," said Arthur. "Congratulations. That's really why I came."

Joe smiled and left him.

Newness lasts longer in a small town than in a big city, whether the newness is on a private residence, a store building, a new baby —or, for that matter, a corpse. A new baby remains a fresh conversational topic long past his first birthday, just as a house that has sheltered a family for a full generation may continue to be referred to as a *new* house. And in the same way a man who has lost a loved one in March is still being told, in December, that "I'm sorry for your trouble," if the speaker is Irish, or the conventional expressions of sympathy if he is not. Joe Chapin thus was receiving expressions of sympathy (and sorrow for his trouble) while accepting the early congratulations on the birth of his son.

As an example there was the case of Mike Slattery, when the two men had a chance meeting on Main Street. "Good morning, Joe," said Mike.

"Good morning, Mike," said Joe.

"The last time I talked to you was right on this very spot," said Mike. "Only that time it wasn't to congratulate you."

"I remember," said Joe.

"Very pleasant news. The mother and child both doing well, I trust? I've heard nothing to the contrary."

"Yes, they both seem to have benefited by the experience."

"Glad to hear it. I always admired Edith greatly. A fine woman. And little Nancy, is it?"

"Ann," said Joe.

"That's right, Ann. I fancy she's pleased to have a little brother in the house."

"Oh, yes. And your little girls. You have three, haven't you, Mike?"

"Margaret, Monica, and Marie. In that order. All M's, but no Michael so far. I told Peg, I said the next one is going to be Michael no matter what."

"Michelle's a pretty name, in case you have another daughter."

"Thank you, thank you," said Mike, with mild sarcasm. "But if you don't mind, I'd like a straight, plain Michael. A stem-winder, as the fellows say. Your boy is Joe Junior, I understand."

"Yes, Junior. We're both named after my grandfather."

"Uh-huh. The Joseph B. Chapin they named the school after."

"That's the one. I guess they're mostly little pickaninnies going to that school, but my grandfather would have been pleased with that. He was bitterly opposed to slavery."

"Oh, is that so, Joe? Was he in politics?"

"Oh, yes. He served one term as lieutenant governor."

"Lieutenant governor of Pennsylvania. I didn't know that. Your father was never active."

"No, Father never became interested in politics. I don't know why, but I suppose because Mother was a semi-invalid."

"Of course. Well, Edith's a fine, healthy woman."

"Yes."

"Edith isn't a semi or any kind of an invalid."

"No."

"Do you get what I'm driving at?"

Joe smiled. "Possibly."

"It'd be nice to have another Joseph B. Chapin in public life."

Joe smiled again. "Well, you might talk to my son when he gets old enough."

"I'll talk to him when the time comes, but I'd like to put the bee in your bonnet too."

"I'm afraid not, Mike. Nobody knows me."

"And nobody knows anything against you. Seriously, the party's always desperate for the better-type young man. If fellows like you took a more active interest, politics wouldn't have such a bad reputation."

"Thank you, Mike, but I'm a lawyer."

"I never heard of that being a hindrance, not in politics. Invite me over to your house some evening when Edith can be present and I'll tell you a few things about politics that you may not realize."

"You don't think *Edith* would want me to go into politics. Why, Edith is one of the shyest girls I've ever known."

"Well, I didn't say I was going to ask Edith to run for anything. I'd just like you and Edith to know that politics can be the most respectable thing in the world. Don't forget, Joe, the men we all look up to the most—Washington, Lincoln, Teddy—they were politicians, and darn good politicians."

"Mike, you're too persuasive already."

"Just promise me you'll speak to Edith, just tell her what I've told you. Now I've got to go and play some politics. Help a man get a pension that he's entitled to, but on account of some red tape he's on the verge of starvation. That's politics, too, Joe. A lot of it is helping people get what they're entitled to. Billy English can tell you some of the things we politicians do that you never hear about."

"Mike, you're a scoundrel and I've listened to too much already. Give my kindest regards to Peg."

"Thank you, Joe, and the same to Edith and Joe Junior and *Ann*," said Mike. "I'll never call her Nancy again."

When Joe came home that same evening Edith was at his desk in the den, writing letters. "I don't think I'll ever catch up on my correspondence, and yet before we were married I didn't write six letters a year. By the way, who do you think sent me the biggest bouquet of flowers today?"

"I don't know, dear. Who?"

"The Slatterys. Mr. and Mrs. Michael J. Slattery. Michael James Slattery. No message, just the card. I looked under the envelope and the card is from Bailey's. What ever possessed them to send me flowers?"

"Well, they've always been friendly. I've known both of them all my life, and Mike was in my class at law school. We used to see each other there, and ride home on the train together at Christmas time."

"Oh, I know them, I know them, but they don't know me well enough to send me flowers. To tell the truth, I can't stand her. That round pretty face and those clothes. I've never seen her in the same thing twice—not that I ever see her much. But she always looks new and *painted*."

"Painted? Peg Slattery?"

"I don't mean like a bad woman, but cheap. *New*. And there must be at least six dollars' worth of roses. Now I'll have to write to her, and I don't want to write to her. I have no idea what to say to her. And what on earth does she want? Her oldest child is in Miss Holton's and I think she goes to dancing school. What else does she want?"

"They're Irish, and the Irish are very kind people. Generous. And you've just had a baby."

"I hope I don't have to keep track of all their babies. They have three girls and I think another child on the way. Oh, she wants something, of that you may be sure."

"Well, let's wait and see what it is," said Joe.

The invitation Mike Slattery sought was not forthcoming, and he did not press the point, either of the invitation or of Joe's more active participation in politics. In time, but not immediately, Peg received a note from Edith Chapin:

> Dear Peg:
> I would like to offer my belated thanks for the beautiful flowers you sent when our son was born. They were exquisite.
> I hope this finds you and your family all well.
> Sincerely,
> Edith S. Chapin
> (Mrs. Joseph B. Chapin)

Peg Slattery read the note aloud to Mike, a custom they both followed even to household bills. "When did I send exquisite flowers to Madam Chapin?"

"I forgot to tell you. When you went to Scranton for Sheila's First Communion?"

"Yes?"

"I happened to meet Joe Chapin on Main Street and we had a chat and I got an inspiration. It wasn't an inspiration, meaning the first time I ever thought of it. I've been thinking of it for quite a while. But while I was talking to him I planted the bee in his bonnet about him getting into politics. And what a lucky coincidence! Because it came out in the conversation that his grandfather and namesake, Joseph B. Chapin, was once the lieutenant governor. Did you know that?"

"How would I know that?"

"Well, I didn't know it either, and it makes it so much easier. I told him the party needs young men like him, and if ever I spoke a true word in the form of flattery, that was it. A good old name, plenty of money that wasn't stolen, at least stolen outright, and a handsome fellow with a good education. Married. Two young children. Protestant, but not an A.P.A. No scandals anywhere in the family."

"Edith's father liked the bottle."

"But was he ever in trouble? No."

"Joe's mother. A long, long time ago she got in some mix-up on Christiana Street when they used to have all those saloons there. Mom told me about it. Charlotte Chapin was—oh, dear, now—there was something about a man lifting up her skirts and—the Chapins had a coachman—he horsewhipped the man that got fresh with Charlotte."

"I never heard *any* of this," said Mike. "It sounds crazy."

"It isn't, I can assure you. I haven't got it right because it's so long since I thought about it. But I'm pretty sure the coachman beat up the man . . ."

"Did the man climb in her carriage and get fresh?"

"No. She was walking."

"Oh, come on now, Peg. Charlotte Chapin would never walk through that section."

"Ah, she never did again, but this one time she was walking—"

"Accompanied by the coachman with a whip, of course," said Mike.

"Never mind the sarcasm," said Peg Slattery. "It all happened just about the way I'm telling it. And *after* that, shortly after that, Charlotte Chapin took to her bed and stayed there the rest of her life. Or at least hardly ever left the Frederick Street house."

"It couldn't have been much if I never even heard of the incident," said Mike.

"Maybe not, but I'd find out who the man was that the coachman beat up."

"Yes. This was what, about thirty years ago?"

"I couldn't say. But around that," said Peg. "So you sent some exquisite flowers to Edith Chapin—Mrs. *Joseph B.*, that is, just in case I might get her mixed up with the old lady who's dead. You're going to get at Joe through her, is that it?"

"More or less."

"It won't be hard."

"You think not? What makes you think so? According to Joe, she'd have a horror of public life."

"Proving that Joe knows his wife no better than many husbands know their wives. I don't say Edith's a suffragette or one of those kind of women, but if she'd been pretty she'd make a good Dolly Madison. She has two children, four years apart, so it doesn't look to me like she's out to increase the population. And her house doesn't take much to run it—time, I mean. Harry and Marian run that house to perfection or Old Lady Chapin would have sacked them long ago. Edith isn't interested in clothes. She dresses like someone that got her clothes at Cohen's-North Main. She doesn't do much church work or charity. I'd say Edith Chapin would relish being the wife of—what? You wouldn't start him as an assemblyman."

"At first, I wouldn't run him for anything. Just get him acquainted around among the boys. Then later spring him on the public, and if they took to him, fine. He's not going to cost anybody anything—"

"Far from it."

"And you know he's so gosh-darn respectable. And I *like* Joe."

"Well, why shouldn't you? I do too. He's never done anything, good or bad, that I can see. Everything he is or has, he inherited. His good looks, his money, his name. The one thing he didn't inherit I consider a handicap, but maybe that's because I can hardly look at her, she's that ugly."

"Oh, you and Edith could never be friends in a thousand years," said Mike, amiably.

Peg looked at him straight. "Hmm," she said.

"What do you mean, *hmm?*"

"Never you mind, Mr. Michael James Slattery. I see through you," said Peg.

"I never said you didn't," said Mike. He kissed her on the cheek and she pretended to suffer the kiss.

"She'd be no fun that way," said Peg.

He laughed, and she pushed him. "Go 'way from me," she said.

Joe Chapin's political career could have ended with a word from Peg Slattery. If she had expressed an instinctive dislike of Joe, Mike Slattery would have said no more about Joe to her or anyone else. If she had wanted to punish Joe for Edith's shortcomings, Mike would have so punished him. Mike in the first instance would have been relying, as he usually did, on Peg's sound reactions to candidates. In the second instance he would have been no more than a loyal husband. But Peg, an equally loyal wife, was deeply and intensely interested in her husband's business, which was politics, and she was above personal pettiness when it might affect that business. For her there was only one man in the world, and if other men were hurt or honored in the process of her man's advancement, she was more than willing to dole out the honors and inflict the injuries. By the way that older men were coming to rely more and more on Mike's judgment and delegate authority and responsibility, a duller woman than Peg could have told that Mike was already accepted as a senior member of the gang. His religious affiliation would keep him from the highest public honors—Governor of the Commonwealth, President of the United States—but the compensation there was that governors and presidents get defeated and the mark of defeat is upon them, while politicans are often at their most powerful after a defeat. When a candidate has taken a licking the party needs the professionals like Mike, the full-time noncandidates, to reorganize for the next campaign. It is a simple enough rule, and it explains the mystery that sometimes baffles the public (and defeated candidates): why, after a defeat, are the same old politicians still eating the big meals and smoking the expensive cigars? Peg knew the answer to the mystery; the best answer was her man, who was a full-time politician who would be eating the big meals and smoking the big cigars (although he personally did not smoke) no matter how many times Woodrow Wilson got elected president.

Mike had laughingly turned down opportunities to become chief burgess of Gibbsville, county clerk, sheriff, register of wills, and other offices that were as high as some men could aspire. Mike, when asked to run for such offices, would always reply that his committee work was more important, which indeed it was. It was more important to the party, and it was much more important to Michael James Slattery, who did not want to be marked with an early defeat for a minor office. In the beginning, as soon as he got out of law school, Mike did work that demanded the qualifications of a moderately industrious office boy, not a man with a law degree. But he soon proved his ability and his dependability: a couple of times he was given sums of money to hand over to ward leaders. It was only a venial political sin to pocket some of that money on its way from the committee to the ward leader: but when Mike was given $400 to deliver to a ward captain, the ward captain received $400, not $375. There would have been no comment and no disillusionment if Mike had paid himself a $25 delivery fee, but he early showed that he was not a $25 man. The $25 men are indispensable, but they invariably remain $25 men, and it is worth a great deal to a political organization to find out who among their younger workers are above nervous larceny. The wiser old politicans were also pleased to note that Mike was not in any great hurry to go into the street-paving business or make premature demands for his share of legitimate county legal fees. The paving business and the receiverships came later, along with Mike's partnership in an insurance firm and directorships on the boards of farseeing corporations. In the beginning Mike was content to wear out a lot of shoe leather and pay for it himself while building up what eventually became a personal organization without its becoming publicly identified as the Slattery gang.

In his entire career Mike was never once indicted. No ambitious district attorney could ever have shown that Mike had handed a man two dollars for his vote. Mike did not even buy the barrel of beer for a volunteer fire company. The beer got there, and it was well understood that Mike had seen to its arrival, but he was careful to mask his connection with it. And of course it is not illegal for a citizen to slake the thirst of a group of unpaid smoke eaters; nor is it illegal for a public-spirited citizen to provide the ice cream and pretzels for a Lutheran Sunday School picnic; nor is it illegal for the wife of some such citizen to make an appearance at the African M. E. Church for the funeral of a popular waiter, and if she happens to be accompanied by her husband and is the only white woman present, she and her husband may be kindly remembered by the members of the congregation. (That particular funeral took place in 1915, and Mike might have attended it without political intent, since he was genuinely fond of Clarence Whitehall. Twenty years later the Slatterys' attendance at a 1915 funeral was recalled by several important Negroes who were being invited to forsake the Republican party for the greener pastures of the New Deal.)

There were men and women who availed themselves of Mike's services while withholding approval of his activities, and among them were many members of what was always called the Lantenengo Street crowd. There were two things the snobs did not know and never could believe: first, that Mike and Peg were reconciled to their social status, and wanted social preferments only for their children; second, Mike's activities as donor of ice cream and charitable intermediary were successful for one reason: he *liked* to do things for people. He was shrewd and perceptive and capable of ruthlessness, but he was also a man who took pleasure in administering kindnesses. He did many kindnesses automatically, instinctively, and without time for hope of reciprocal favors. On visits to the big cities he performed acts of generosity and kindness and politeness among strangers who could not possibly know who he was and whose only way of returning the kindnesses was to acknowledge them with the words, "Thank you."

He was also quite capable of killing anyone who hurt his wife or his daughters. By killing is meant depriving of life. Mike could and did use the telephone, tie a necktie, read the bass clef, speak French and translate Latin, explain the Dartmouth College Case, handle a pair of hackney ponies, understand the principle of the internal combustion engine, keep his temper, eat in moderation, outbox a stronger fellow, and observe all rules of personal cleanliness. He had come all the way with civilized man. But he was also quite capable of killing anyone who hurt his wife or his daughters. In all other matters he was tractable and sometimes eager, sometimes willing, to compromise. Moreover, he knew that about himself; his ability to size up other men began with a rather thorough understanding of his own personality, an understanding which in part was traceable to frequent examinations of conscience before visiting the confessional. Because of his awareness of his extreme concern for his family, he was carefully slow in adjudging offenders against their happiness or well-being. But when a man or woman was found guilty, Mike was thorough in his punishment. The negative fact that he did not commit murder was less valuable in an estimate of Mike Slattery than the unproven fact that he was capable of it.

After Peg had begun to understand Mike's fierce protectiveness, her discovery taught her to exercise caution in reporting slights and wounds. Mike did not always agree with her estimates of men and women, but he believed everything factual that she told him. Her lesson was learned in the second year of their marriage. They were sitting at home one evening after supper, and Peg, in her recital of the events of her day, mentioned, casually, she thought, a happening that had annoyed her. ". . . I was buying the groceries and I had my arms full, and on my way out the door that Paul Tristram let the door swing on me and I dropped everything."

"He what? He let the door swing on you?"

"Yes, it made me furious. I had to stop and pick up all my bundles off the floor."

"He didn't even help you pick them up?"

"No, he just looked at me."

"He knew he'd done it, though."

"Oh, of course he knew. I said to him, 'What's the matter with you, anyway?' "

"And he could hear you?"

"Sure, he turned around, and then he kept on going."

"He did, eh?" said Mike. He got up and put on his coat and hat and while walking to the door he said, "I'll be back."

"What are you going to do?" said Peg.

He did not answer her.

He first walked to the north side of town, where he knew Paul Tristram lived. He turned the handle of the doorbell, and Tristram's wife opened the door. "Hello," she said.

"Is your husband in?"

"No, he ain't. He ain't in. I think he's over't the hose company."

Mike nodded and left. The Perseverance Hook & Ladder Company was three blocks from the Tristram house. Mike knew it well. He went upstairs to the social room, where there were a bar, a pool table, a poker table and chairs. Mike was not a member of the Perseverance, but he was greeted by the half-dozen men present, among them Paul Tristram. He went directly to Tristram and slapped his face. "You gotta learn some manners, Tristram," said Mike. He then closed his fists and attacked Tristram with punches to the face and body, hammering him until he fell, and when he fell, Mike gave him a kick in the ribs. Mike for the first time addressed the others: "Let him tell you why I did it," and left.

It was not a fight; it was a beating. Even Tristram's friends suspected that it was a deserved beating, although they could not be sure what had provoked it. If it had been a fight they might have felt called upon to take Tristram's side, during the fighting and in the years that followed. But when a sober man goes to so much trouble to track down and punish someone who has insulted his wife, the sober man is given the benefit of the doubt. The incident may have cost Mike six votes, but no more, and it gained him that many among members of the Perseverance Company who until that time had had no feeling about him one way or the other.

The story got around Gibbsville in three or four days. It annoyed Mike, and he kept it out of his conversations by refusing to discuss it. But it remained a part of the Mike Slattery legend. It did not reach the ears of the ladies of the Gibbsville upper crust, although there was hardly a man in the Gibbsville Club who did not hear of it. Among them were some men who were just beginning to hear of Mike, and when they were told that it had not been a typical Irish brawl, Mike suffered not at all in their estimation. As to Peg, she cared little enough about what other women thought, and the incident embarrassed her not in the slightest. But it made her think twice before saying anything that might arouse her man.

Opportunities to influence Edith Chapin were not often given Mike Slattery and he decided to create one. He considered the various men friends of the Chapins, immediately ruling out Arthur McHenry as too obvious and too close. Next in the friendly relationship—although a distant second—was Henry Laubach.

Henry Laubach belonged to a family that was accustomed to hearing its name pronounced two ways: among the Lantenengo Street people, Laubach was pronounced Law-back. All other citizens of Gibbsville pronounced it Lah-bock. Henry belonged to the first generation to use the American pronunciation, which was considered less Dutchy. The family dated from pre-Revolutionary times and intermarriage had bred out most of the obvious German characteristics, so that Henry could easily have called himself Lowell and no New Englander would have disbelieved him on account of his cranial or facial details. Born the same year as Joe Chapin, Henry was literally a boy Joe had grown up with. When Joe went to The Hill, Henry's family sent him to Mercersburg and then to Lafayette, where he was popular among the students, and Phi Beta Kappa. He worked for the golden key because his father, who had retained a few of the old German traditions, believed that a boy went to college to learn something. The key was satisfactory evidence of Henry's obedience, and earned him a present of $2,000.

Laubach & Company was a family firm, wholly owned by Laubachs and first cousins, which invested Laubach money and made Laubach profits; collected Laubach rentals, clipped Laubach coupons, and protected the Laubach name. The embossed letterhead contained no more than the name, in script, and the address, in Roman, and revealed nothing of the powers and activities of the firm or of the sub-corporations owned by Laubach & Company. It was not generally known, for example, that the firm was entitled to function as a private bank and agent for several steamship lines, rather more for the convenience of the firm than for the public. Visitors were not encouraged at the firm's offices: the window in the main entrance had the firm's name, the word Private, and the request, Please Knock, to indicate the firm's attitude toward casual callers. The firm was so set in its ways that when someone did knock, it was extremely likely that he had no business there, and was stared at accordingly by the officers and staff. Joe Chapin, Arthur McHenry, and a very few other men could drop in for business or non-business chats. But most men, including the Chapins and the McHenrys, were seen by appointment. Henry believed in his father's motto that an office was not a *Kaffeeklatsch*. In the office of Laubach & Company there was not so much as a family portrait on the walls.

Henry Laubach answered his own telephone, and when Mike Slattery asked him for ten minutes of his valuable time, Henry was already deciding how much financial support he would give the party before Mike hung up.

Mike, as always, was punctual, arriving in Henry's office at two minutes before three o'clock. Henry signaled to him to come to his glass-partitioned space.

"How are you, Mike?" said Henry.

"Very well, thank you, Henry. And all goes well with you, I trust?"

"About as usual," said Henry. He opened a mahogany humidor and held it out to his visitor. "Offer you a cigar?"

"Never use them, Henry," said Mike. "Never use them. No bad habits except politics."

"Well, I hardly ever indulge, myself, except after a heavy meal. I *like* a good cigar, but sometimes a week'll pass without one."

"No doubt you must be thinking I'm a little early this year, Henry."

"A little early?"

"For a campaign contribution."

"Well, it is a little early, isn't it?" said Henry.

"I'm squeezing in an extra visit because this time I'm not here to ask you for money."

"Well, it's always a pleasure to hear that," said Henry. "What else is on your mind?"

"It's a difficult problem, political problem. I know you're a busy man, so I won't take up too much of your time with a lot of beating about the bush."

"I'd appreciate that, but not because I don't enjoy your company."

"Thank you, Henry. Well, it boils down to this: I have been weighing all the pros and cons, and I've come to the conclusion that we ought to try to persuade Joe Chapin to take a more active interest in party matters."

"Joe Chapin, eh?" said Henry. "Joe Chapin."

"How does that sound to you?"

"Well, I know he never *has* been active in politics. But of course that's no reason why he shouldn't start now. His father never ran for office, but his grandfather was lieutenant governor. Long before our time, of course, but that was as close as Gibbsville ever came to having a governor. What I'm wondering now is why you came to me. Joe's one of my best friends, but I don't think I'd like to try to influence him in a matter of that kind. Granting I *could* influence him."

"This is the hard part, Henry, and I don't want you to refuse me out of hand."

"Oh, I never do that. I always listen to whatever the other fellow has to say."

"Fine. Now don't be surprised, what I'm going to say."

"Can't promise you that, not knowing what you have up your sleeve," said Henry.

"All right, then. I believe you're a cousin of Edith Chapin's, are you not?"

"Not a first cousin, but I'm related to Edith. You could say I was related to Joe, too, but I'm a little more closely related to Edith."

"And you and your good wife are friends of hers, are you not?"

"Oh, yes. Yes indeed."

"Good. Good. Now here is where I need your help. I think—and I believe I'm right—that if her friends could convince Edith that it would be a good thing for Joe to take a more active interest in party matters, Edith could do the trick."

"Oh, I'm afraid—Mike, that's the kind of thing I always stay out of. Family matters. No, that's none of my affair."

"I'm not a bit surprised, Henry. I respect you for that, but I haven't asked you to do anything yet, have I?"

"No, but you're going to, I have a feeling."

"For the time being, if the subject comes up, of Joe going into politics *and if you believe it's a good idea*, will you tell Edith you think it's a good idea?"

"Well, I might do that, yes. I see no harm in that. But you're going to want something else."

"You're right, I am. If the subject comes up, and you tell Edith you think it's a good idea, and she asks you any more about it, will you say to her, 'Why don't you ask Mike Slattery?' "

" 'Why don't you ask Mike Slattery?' I'd have to think about that, Mike."

"But if she wanted to know, there'd be no harm in saying that to her."

"No, I suppose not. All right, I guess I could say that much without incriminating myself. If she asked me, it wouldn't be sticking my nose in her family affairs. Yes, I guess I can do that much."

"I'd appreciate it, and I know it would be a good thing for the party. I'd also appreciate anything else you did that might influence Joe in the right direction. Men like you and Joe—"

"Now, now, Mike! I won't have you mention my name in any political connection whatsoever. I mean that."

"Henry, I wouldn't think of it. I know exactly how you feel. That's why I didn't ask you in the first place."

"Just as long as you understand that. If you ever get me mixed up in politics, I'll send my contributions to the Democrats, and I mean that, too. Joe's a lawyer, and if he wants to go into politics, that's his business. But not me. We want to stay anonymous. We always have, and we always intend to."

"I'll respect your wishes to the letter, and thank you for these few minutes of your valuable time. So long, Henry."

"So long, Mike," said Henry.

Mike had no difficulty in respecting Henry's wishes. He would have had, as he told Peg, trouble getting Henry elected dog-catcher, even if the Gibbsville table of organization had included the office. Moreover, dog-catcher had been an appointive, not an elective, office. It disappeared from the municipal table because for several terms nobody wanted the job. When the function was restored, in 1920, it was under the auspices of the Gibbsville chapter of the Society for the Prevention of Cruelty to Animals, with a full-time employee who was sworn as a special constable, but not as a public servant on the public payroll. Interestingly enough, one of the leading supporters of the Society, and thus a contributor to the dog-catcher's salary, was Josephine Laubach, Henry's wife. The dog-catcher selected by the Society was a man named Pierson, a distant cousin of the Howard Pierson who later married the Slatterys'—in 1916—unborn daughter. In a small town the most casual remark can have constant repercussions.

The threat of Woodrow Wilson made for a revival of interest in politics that was somewhat stronger than the usual reanimation which occurs in a presidential year. Mr. Hughes, with his whiskers, made a lot of people think of Father; Mr. Wilson had the appearance of a man who had a schoolteacher's switch hidden in the folds of his Prince Albert. Mr. Hughes was a Republican; but Mr. Wilson was a Democrat who had kept us out of war and who was not a horse to swap in midstream. Mr. Hughes was not in the least warlike; Mr. Wilson had sent the National Guard and Black Jack Pershing to the Mexican border, ostensibly to punish the bandits, but actually to train an army and to show the Central Powers that we were getting ready and would have no nonsense. But if we were having no nonsense, was it not time that we stopped sending Notes when our ships, flying our flag, were torpedoed on the high seas? Mr. Wilson was pussyfooting, keeping us out of war and hurrying us into it with his warlike gestures. There was no argument in favor of Wilson that could not be answered with the countercharge of inconsistency, and as the people of Republican Gibbsville turned out their lights they were able to go to sleep with the comforting knowledge that Mr. Hughes would soon take over and Woodrow Wilson would be politely banished to Princeton.

Joe Chapin was more bitterly disappointed than Arthur McHenry. "Those people out in California," said Joe. "They're so far away from everything they have no idea what's happening."

"It's a long distance away," said Arthur. "As far from us as we are from Europe."

"With one big difference. What's next to California? Nevada. There are no German submarines in Nevada, but there are off the Jersey coast. That's how much closer we are than those Californians."

"Well, like it or not, we have four more years of Mr. Wilson."

"Yes, and the prospect—it makes me want to do something."

"Well, you did something in this campaign."

"What, Arthur? I gave some money, and I had my name on some letterheads."

"Don't underestimate either. Your name is worth a lot. So's your money, but your name plus your money—it's the first time you've ever let them use your name. Speaking of which, I meant to tell you this before. You'd better give Bob Hooker a better photograph of yourself. The other day, just for the fun of it, I drew a pair of glasses on your picture—Joe, that picture makes you look like Woodrow Wilson."

"You're not the first one to tell me that. Edith mentioned it. I never take a good picture."

"Well, you'd better get a different one if you're going to be in politics."

"I'm not going to be in politics. I'm a partner in McHenry & Chapin, attorneys-at-law. But I'm interested in good government and the future of the Republican party, and as Edith says, if Vance McCormick can stand up for the Democrats, I can stand up for our side."

215

"We're soon going to have to make a decision about the firm, by the way," said Arthur.

"To get bigger or not to get bigger?"

"Exactly," said Arthur. "I don't think you had this in mind, but if you should become influential in politics, very influential, we're going to be attracting a lot more business. Some of it we won't want. That'll be the people who will want us to handle their legal affairs because we may, just may, have political influence. Then of course there's the other side. There will be some clients who will leave us because we're mixed up in politics."

"I've had occasion to think about that lately," said Joe. "I met a man in Philadelphia the other day. When he heard my name he asked me if I were the McHenry & Chapin Chapin, and when I said I was he gave me his card. He has a construction business. I have the card at home. Name I never heard of."

"Why did he give you his card?" said Arthur.

"He said if I ever came to Pittsburgh to drop in and see him. I said, well, if he ever came to Gibbsville to drop in and see us. That was all."

"That was all for the present," said Arthur. "How did you meet this fellow?"

"The day I had lunch at the Union League. You know, with Kirkpatrick. Kirkpatrick introduced me to him."

"Well, I had a chat with Henry Laubach yesterday, at the Gibbsville Club. Henry never comes to the point if he can help it, but I can usually tell what he's thinking. I would say, reading between the lines, that Henry tried to tell me that if we became a political law firm, we'd have to struggle along without Laubach & Company. Joe, I think we ought to go easy on this whole thing. I don't like your friend from Pittsburgh, whose name you don't remember. You don't remember his name, and the only thing we know about him is that he's in the construction business. But we also know that Council is going to ask for bids on paving South Main."

Joe smiled. "I spied that connection right away," he said.

"I hoped you would," said Arthur. "Laubach & Company were almost our first clients, and they were my father's clients before you and I hung out our shingle. Now we may decide that we want to get bigger, expand. But let's not take the first business that comes our way. And let's be very careful about taking on construction companies from Pittsburgh. If they're any good they have their legal business taken care of by a Pittsburgh firm. If they're not taken care of by a Pittsburgh firm, they're probably fly-by-night."

"I agree," said Joe.

"You may want to run for office, and that might be a good idea. But without talking like Henry Laubach, I want to say here and now that I'm always going to oppose taking new business that looks as though it came our way through politics, or your political connections. You don't need the money, and while I haven't got as much money as you have, I don't need the money. We're doing very well now, and we'll continue to do very well and better as our firm gets older."

Joe nodded slowly and seriously. "I'll tell you what my ambition is, as far as money's concerned. I would like to be able to leave my wife and children each a million dollars."

"You have quite a way to go," said Arthur. "But we ought to be good for many more and prosperous years. You could do it. But you're going to have to do it through investments and the stock market. Not through our profits as McHenry & Chapin."

"Let's have this talk again a year from now," said Joe.

"Why, of course. Let's have it every year," said Arthur. "You may want to go out after that big business—and maybe I might change my mind."

"I doubt it," said Joe, smiling.

"So do I," said Arthur. "But if I see you getting rich . . ."

"I know what you're thinking, Arthur," said Joe.

"Yes, I imagine you do," said Arthur. "Am I thinking that I have no children to leave it to?"

"You don't want to talk about Mildred," said Joe.

"You're the only one I do talk to."

"But not enough," said Joe. "Don't you ever talk to Rose?"

"Rose? Not about Mildred. Rose misses Mildred as much as I do. We don't even want to see each other."

"I think you and Rose ought to get married," said Joe.

"You what?"

"Don't hit me," said Joe.

"Is that Edith's idea?"

"It's my own idea, and I never thought of it till just this minute."

"Well, get rid of it quick, and don't ever repeat it. Don't ever say that again."

"I'm sorry, Arthur, but it's what I think. I think you and Rose would be perfect for each other."

"I thought you knew me. That is the most cold-blooded statement you've ever made."

"Why?" said Joe.

"Because it is. I shouldn't have to explain why."

"Even so, why?" said Joe.

"Mildred hasn't been dead a year, but you suggest not only that I get married, but that I marry her sister."

Joe looked away from him. "Well, I was in love with a girl, and she died. She died without my marrying her. And she was in love with me. Then I fell in love with another girl and did marry her. Love can happen twice, and it can happen very quickly. In some ways you're so much more intelligent than I am, but in other ways— Arthur, Rose has been in love with you for years. And I think it's damned unfair of you to let her become an old maid. She will, too, you know. Has she any beaux?"

"No. Or at least I'm sure I don't know."

"Yes you do. You know. Be honest. Rose White made the best of it when you married Mildred, but—let me ask you something, and give me a word-of-honor answer. Are you in love with Rose?"

"Yes," said Arthur.

"Now aren't you glad you told me the truth, Arthur?"

"No, I'm not, not a bit glad."

Joe took the receiver off the hook and spoke into the telephone: "Six-four, please."

"What are you doing?" said Arthur.

". . . Hello, Rose? This is Joe Chapin. Arthur wants to speak to you." He got up and transferred the receiver into Arthur's hand.

Frowning and bewildered, Arthur spoke: "Rose, this is Arthur . . . No, there's nothing wrong. He just called your number and handed me the phone. Will you be home this evening? . . . Could I drop in for a minute? . . . That would be fine . . . Good-bye."

"You're so punctilious, if that's the word I mean," said Joe. "So proper."

"Well, you're not, I must say. I was afraid you were going . . ."

"I thought of it, and I almost did. But it'll be more punctilious if you tell her yourself," said Joe. "This may change your attitude toward making money."

"What made you act as Cupid?" said Arthur. "It's something new for you."

"I wonder. I suppose when you have a daughter it starts you thinking along those lines. You're too old for Ann, and in fact you're getting too old for Rose, but you're marriageable."

"Are you sure Edith had nothing to do with this?"

"Edith not only had nothing to do with it, I don't want you to

218

ever say anything to her about this. Edith has altogether different ideas about me. In fact, I don't think anybody really knows me. If they did—oh, well.'

Arthur put his hand on Joe's shoulder, a display of intimacy he had never made before. "You know, Joe. You're a very kind man."

Joe looked at his own hand. "That'll be enough of that, please," he said.

Arthur smiled and left his friend without looking back.

On an afternoon in April of 1917 the partners met in Arthur's office. They talked for an hour and more, then Arthur summed up. "All right, one of us goes, and the only way we can decide it is to toss a coin."

"Here's my cartwheel," said Joe. "You toss it and I'll call it."

Arthur flipped the coin and while it was in the air Joe called, "Tails."

It was heads.

"I win," said Arthur.

"Wait a minute," said Joe. "What were we tossing for? We should have agreed on that first."

"The winner joins the Army," said Arthur.

"That wasn't agreed upon. I insist on another call. This time, if it's heads, you join the Army, and tails, I join the Army."

"Well—all right," said Arthur. He tossed again, and again it came up heads.

"I furnished the coin, but I lost anyway," said Joe.

"You lost twice, if you want to be honest about it."

"Oh, well, it may be over by the time you get there. Everybody says the Germans will quit now that we're in it."

"Sour grapes from a bad loser," said Arthur.

"They don't really want men of thirty-five."

"I'm still thirty-four."

"Especially people who are out of shape and never take any exercise."

"But I had a complete physical examination a month ago and Billy English says I'm in excellent condition, excellent. I think you forget, I took out more insurance for Rose."

"That was considerate of you, but I'm sure she won't need it. Take my advice and write a letter to the Judge Advocate General, that's where you'll be most useful, out of the way. You a soldier! *Hoch der Kaiser!*"

Some of the bitterness Joe felt was lessened by the assignment given Captain McHenry. They had agreed to abide by the decision of the coin: that one or the other was to stay at home and carry on the business of the firm until the Army called him. Arthur was sent overseas, but his duties consisted largely of desk work in Paris and Tours, where he saw war but engaged in no personal combat. Joe's bitterness, he admitted to Edith, changed to envy, which was somewhat easier to suffer. As the war continued into its second American year Joe began to make preparations to suspend the firm's activities and transfer some of its business to other firms. He had completed most of the arrangements when the Armistice was declared. Arthur remained at Coblentz until the late spring of 1919, and was one of the last Gibbsville men to return to civilian status.

Joe had done everything a healthy civilian could do, but the Army was forever out of his experience and conversation. It took a little time for Arthur, who had no delusions of heroism or sacrifice about his own service, to understand that in missing the experience Joe had been affected in much the same way as a classmate of theirs who had failed to make a senior society. At New Haven Joe and Arthur had tried to tell their friend that the failure meant very little, and now Arthur tried (but only once) to convince Joe that there was no shadow over his patriotism or manliness. Arthur accidentally made one consoling remark: "It's too bad we couldn't have made a trade. I could just as easily have been here half the time and you in Paris." He carefully never revealed to Joe that while he never fired a shot at the Germans, he had once been under fire, and machine-gun fire at that, when he and a colonel got lost in the forward area.

In re-familiarizing himself with the firm's affairs he was made to realize the amount of work Joe had undertaken, the money he had made for the firm, the money he had given to war campaigns, and the time he had put in in the militia and in investigating distress cases for the Red Cross and the Patriotic League. But the mere mention of these activities seemed to fill Joe with disgust, and Arthur refrained from mentioning them in Joe's presence. "I don't see how one man could have done so much," he said to Edith. "Joe did the work of four men."

"Yes, he did," said Edith. "But it will never make up for his not being in the Army."

"Do you blame *me*, Edith?" said Arthur.

"Tossing a coin wasn't the way it should have been done. No, I don't blame you, Arthur, but I wish you had both agreed that keeping the firm going was not as important as it seemed. It will take a long time before Joe feels right about the war, maybe forever."

"He did more than I did. I mean that."

"I don't doubt you for a minute. But you *were* in uniform, and you came back with those little striped ribbons on your coat."

"Well, they're not on my coat now, Edith."

"No, that's true," said Edith. "I have a confession to make. I tried to coax Joe to give up the law and *join* the Army, but he insisted that you would have kept your end of the bargain if you'd lost. I insisted that you'd do no such thing. And you wouldn't have, would you, Arthur?"

"No, I probably wouldn't," said Arthur.

"At least you admit it," said Edith.

Arthur smiled. "Edith, for the first time in our lives I'm beginning to realize that you don't like me. I've been very stupid."

"Oh, I don't believe you ever cared what I thought, whether I liked you or disliked you. All I ask now, Arthur, is that occasionally you remind yourself that Rose could be in my position and you could be in Joe's. You served your country in the Army, but it was all decided by a toss of a coin."

"I'll do exactly as you wish. It happens to be what I'd have done anyway."

"Very well, then the subject is closed," said Edith.

"Good. Now there's a subject I would like to bring up, if you don't mind."

"Please do."

"Are you in favor of Joe's going into politics?"

"Whether I'm in favor of it or not, his war record is against him, or would be if his opponent had been in the Army."

"I guess the subject isn't closed after all," said Arthur.

"Well, we have to face facts," said Edith. "And of course *you're* not unhappy. *You* don't want to see Joe in politics."

"No, you're damn right I don't," said Arthur.

"You can be emphatic without talking like a soldier. You never used to swear in my presence."

"I beg your pardon."

"*If* Joe should enter politics, I do think you ought to put aside your personal preferences in the matter, and do for him what he did for you while you were in Paris. That is, do all you can to support him and encourage him and assist him. Joe has all the money he'll ever need—"

"Not quite. He needs three million dollars so that he can leave a million each to you and the children."

"Oh, so you know that? Well, I'd rather have him feel happy in whatever he's doing than make a lot more money for the children and me. And the day may come when he does decide to do more in the field of public affairs, for better government and the good of the party."

"Mike Slattery," said Arthur.

"I beg your pardon?"

"Edith, we'd better not talk any more."

"Whatever you say," said Edith.

"Whatever I say will be used against me."

"Very clever tonight, aren't we?"

For most married couples who are parents, there comes a Children's Era. It commences with the parents' ceasing to regard the children as pets, toys, total dependents. There is no fixed age when the change occurs; the change in parent and child is too subtle for that. But in retrospect the parent sometimes can fix the time by recalling an incident, by a recognizable change in attitude of parent toward child, or of child toward parent.

In 1920 Ann Chapin reached the age of nine, and her small brother became five. Ann had her own room, she was at Miss Holton's School, she had a Shetland pony which she drove in a governess cart, on Saturdays she rode her mother's gelding, and on Saturday afternoons she attended dancing school, which she hated because it was full of girls and half full of boys who likewise hated it because it was full of girls. She fought boys with her fists and with her fingernails and teeth, but she liked to sit in the garage with Harry while he repaired and polished the new, the Chapins' second, Pierce-Arrow. She helped Harry: when he was washing the car he would tell her to turn off the hose, turn on the hose, bring him the sponge, hang up the chamois. When he finished he would take off his rubber boots and put on his old sneakers (which had belonged to her father) and they would go to the kitchen for a glass of homemade root beer. Marian would always protest that the root beer would spoil Ann's supper, but Harry would remind her that root beer contained herbs, and herbs were good for a person. Better for a person, Marian would say, than the smoke from Harry's pipe. "But Father smokes a pipe," Ann would say. "But he puts tobacco in it," Marian would say. "Not old hunks of rubber boots."

She liked the pungency of the garage, with its mixture of motorcar and horse smells, and the lingering sweetness and cleanliness of the kitchen and even the dankness and cleanness of the laundry, with its stationary tubs and inside wash-lines. When Harry was out she would watch Marian at her ironing or her baking or cleaning a chicken, and she liked Marian, but being with Marian was not the fun that being with Harry was. When she had a wound she would show it to Harry, when she needed money she would go to Harry.

When she needed affection demonstrated, she would go to her father, and she would go to him when she wanted to know the meaning of a word, or for permission to do something unusual, or for an appeal from severe punishment. It was not lost on her, even before she was nine, that her father reserved for her alone any outward demonstrations of affection. There was almost always room made for her on his lap; and in his den, at his desk, he would always break his concentration on a book or a letter when she entered and spoke. She had been told not to sit on her mother's lap, an order that was not satisfactorily explained to her during the time of Edith's second pregnancy, a time during which her mother also had stopped carrying her upstairs to bed or lifting her into her crib. Edith forgot to resume the tender acts after the baby was born, and the oversight cost Edith the opportunities for affectionate gestures that Joe made automatically. Thus inevitably home to Ann meant her father first, then her mother and Harry and Marian, then her brother.

"I don't think you ought to spend so much time in the garage and the kitchen," said Edith, during Ann's ninth year.

"Harry likes me to," said Ann.

"I wouldn't be so sure about that," said Edith. "You must get in their way."

"No I don't, Mother. I help Harry *and* Marian."

"I'm afraid you keep them from doing their work, and they're too polite to say so," said Edith.

Ann stayed out of the kitchen and the garage for a week. She spoke to Harry and Marian only when spoken to, and replied to them without looking at them. Then Harry, who was beginning to miss her visits, said to her: "Where you been keeping yourself?"

"I don't know."

"You don't know? Well, you better give that pony some exercise or she'll be sick."

"Why?"

"Because it isn't good for her to be standing in the stall without any exercise, that's why."

"I've been forbidden."

"You've been forbidden? Forbidden to what? Your father'd rather sell the pony than have her just stand there and founder. She'll get the bloat."

"My mother said I get in you and Marian's way."

Harry looked at his wife, who nodded and made a face. "Ah, you don't get in our way," said Marian. "We're only too glad to have you."

"That's not what my mother said," said Ann.

The situation was relieved by a conversation between Harry and Joe and a further conversation between Joe and Edith.

"Do you want her to grow up saying *ain't*? And I've heard her say worse," said Edith.

"What worse?"

"The word beginning with S. You know where she got that."

"I'm pretty sure I know where she *didn't* get it, Edith. Harry wouldn't use those words in front of a child."

"She heard it somewhere and that's the logical place. Besides, it isn't only the nasty words. It's *ain't*, and *me and him*, and bad grammar. And another thing."

"What?"

"Talking about Captain's big peter."

Joe laughed.

"I don't think it's funny, to have a nine-year-old child discussing a horse's private parts. And you know where she got the word *peter*. From Harry, of course."

"Well, it could have been worse," said Joe. "I'm glad Harry showed restraint."

"You seem to think the whole thing's funny. She said Captain's peter nearly touches the ground."

"Well, how old were you when you first rode a horse? About the same age. And you can't spend much time around them without noticing certain things. Harry worships Ann, worships her. You can be damn sure that no harm is going to come to her if Harry can help it."

"No, of course not. Except that she'll grow up talking like a stable-boy."

"You're not being fair to Harry, Edith. Decidedly unfair, in my opinion. And while I don't as a rule like to interfere, this time I think there's more to be lost than gained by forbidding Ann to visit the stable."

"Very well. I gave the order, if you wish to countermand it," said Edith.

224

"Couldn't you just say to her, something to the effect that she's been such a good girl lately, you've decided she could go to the stable again."

"I couldn't say *that*. She hasn't been such a good girl lately."

"Well, you know why," said Joe.

"Yes, I know why. She's been sulking because she was told to stay out of the garage. Or stable, which you prefer. She's been misbehaving, refusing to do her homework, refusing to touch her food. Very naughty. And you propose to have me tell her that as a reward for being naughty, she can do as she pleases. I'm very sorry, my dear, but I refuse to do it. If you want to spoil her, that's on your conscience. That's for you to decide. But in the future, perhaps you'd like to take over the whole responsibility. Oh, I'll relinquish it. But let me remind you that the time isn't far off when she'll need her mother more than her father."

"This isn't the crisis you're making it out to be," said Joe. "I said nothing about countermanding, or relieving you of your authority. However, when I think you're being overzealous—"

"Overzealous? Hmm."

"I reserve the right to intervene," said Joe. "I'm going to tell Ann that what we meant was that we were afraid she was interfering with Harry's work, but that Harry said she wasn't, so . . ."

"So?"

"Well, she could go to the stable, but perhaps not as *often*."

"Proving exactly nothing except that I was wrong, and she won't forget that."

"Well, I think you exaggerate that part of it. But that's what I'm going to do."

Joe followed out his plan and Ann's visits to the stable-garage were resumed. The episode—it was more than an incident—took place over a period of about a year, from Edith's ruling, through the restoration of Ann's visiting privileges, and into Ann's tenth year. The episode concluded with an unhappy occurrence.

Joe Junior—who was known in the family as Joby, a name which developed from the child's attempt to speak his full name—liked to do everything his sister could do. He played with her dolls, he imitated her speech, he screamed when he was kept out of her parties, and he attempted to achieve the same relationship with his father that his sister enjoyed. If he saw Ann sitting on her father's lap, he would climb on the remaining space and try to play the same games with Joe. The maneuvers made the father and the daughter uncomfortable, but they would try to make room for the boy. His mother would invite him to sit on her lap, and he would do so, but his attention remained on his sister and his father, so that Edith was made to feel excluded from the family play, and she ceased to try to participate. Which, in turn, left Joby out of it all.

Among his imitative activities was his following Ann to the garage, and he would try to beat her to the faucet when Harry told her to turn off the hose; to have the chamois in his hand for the moment when Harry would call for it. Joby was quick in body and mind and he sometimes annoyed his sister by anticipating Harry's commands. On one occasion Ann lost patience with him and turned the hose on him. She was punished, this time by her father, who ruled that she could not go to the stable for a week. She punished Joby by keeping him out of her room and taking away her dolls, privileges which were restored when she was allowed to go back to the garage.

But Harry had no warmth of feeling for the boy. "I can't get to like the kid," he told Marian. "I don't know why."

"He's a miserable little lad, you ought to try," said Marian.

"Miserable? What's miserable about him?"

"You don't see it, but I do," said Marian. "*She* don't know how to give him affection—"

"That I can believe."

"And Ann don't need *her*, with her father and my husband lavishing all the love a child can want."

"Well, it's the way some people affect you and some don't. He's such a snotty little prick, too. *He* don't hesitate to order me around. I don't pay no attention, but that don't prevent him."

"Oh, now."

"It's the truth. I get more orders from the boy than I do from him and her put together."

"What orders could a five-year-old child give you?"

"That five-year-old child can say *hello Harry* and make it sound like he was giving you an order. I wisht he'd stay out of the garridge and bother *you*, if you're so kindly towards him. That time he tattled on Ann—listen, if I had a dollar for every time I had a notion to give him a good dousing with the hose . . . And he's very mean to the stock."

"That I didn't know about," said Marian.

"Oh, I don't like that," said Harry. "He'll no sooner be in the cart than he grabs the whip and starts slashing away. Or did until I took the whip out. And that pony, you know a Shetland can be as mean a son of a bitch as walks on four feet. And this one kicks. One of these days, you mark my words."

It was one of not many days later. Ann was sitting in the governess cart, the reins in her hand. It was a rule laid down by her father that the pony was always to be *led* out of the stable and down the wooden ramp to the alley.

"I want to lead her," said Joby.

"Get in the cart," said Harry. "I'll lead her."

"Come on, Joby, get in," said Ann.

"I want to *lead* her!" said the boy. He made a quick movement to snatch the rein from Harry. The pony struck out and bit the boy's upper arm, tearing the cotton middy blouse and breaking open the skin. Harry slapped the pony's head.

"Get out, Ann, and take care of your brother," said Harry. The boy sat screaming on the cobblestoned floor while Harry removed the harness and put the pony back in her stall. He picked up the terrified child and carried him into the house. "The pony bit him, send for the doctor," he said to Marian. "Ann, you go tell your mother what happened." He poured some whiskey on a clean rag and soaked it on the wound. The child screamed without a let-up, raising his voice at every new development and every attempt to comfort him.

In the evening Harry was called to Joe's den for his version of the biting. He told it straight.

"Well, I'm afraid he got what he deserved," said Joe.

"It isn't that I'm thinking about, sir," said Harry.

"What *are* you thinking about, Harry?"

"Well, I don't know how to say it. It's hard for me to . . ."

"Go on, Harry, go on," said Joe. "You did everything that was right."

"Thank you, sir. It's more in the future."

"What is?"

"Well, it's in the past, too."

"Is it about Joby? Is it something you don't like to tell me about him?"

"Yes, sir," said Harry. "It's—some children don't understand animals. Ann could go in the box stall with the pony or the horse and nothing'd ever happen. But the pony had it in for the boy."

"And the boy had it coming to him?"

"Yes, sir, I'm afraid he did."

"And that's taking into consideration the all-around meanness of some Shetlands."

"Uh, yes, even taking into consideration."

Joe thought a moment. "Would you say he was cruel?"

"I don't like to say it as strong as that."

"You don't like to say it, but if you were under oath that's what you'd have to say, is that right?"

"Well—yes."

Joe nodded. "Well, what *about* the future?"

"I'll try my best, but I can't guarantee it won't happen again."

"In that case, I guess we'll have to get rid of the pony. We can find a home for her."

"No, Mr. Chapin. That ain't the solution," said Harry. "You got me saying more than I wanted to say, so I might as well be hung for a sheep as a goat."

Joe smiled. "We can't get rid of the *boy*."

"That's right, you can't, but if it was my son I'd keep him away from animals till he has a few more years to grow up."

"You think this is a, uh, part of his make-up."

"If it hadn'ta been the pony it'da been the horse. I never let him in the stall with the gelding, never. You know how when some people get near a horse it'll start pawing the ground and start snorting?"

"God, is it as bad as that?"

"I don't dare take my eyes off the boy the whole time he's there."

"I wish you'd told me this before."

"Mr. Chapin, I don't like to tell it to you now. I'm only doing it because we saw what happened today. It coulda been a lot worse."

"I appreciate everything you've said and done. And I'm well aware, Harry, that if it hadn't been for you, there might have been a runaway, with my daughter in the cart."

"God forbid," said Harry. "God forbid that."

"Well—it's a problem, no doubt about that. And don't you worry about it, Harry. Mrs. Chapin and I both appreciate what you did. Cool-headed. The right thing. Go on out and have a nice big tumbler of that whiskey, illegal or not."

"Much obliged, sir," said Harry.

For Joe Chapin the Children's Era had begun.

Gibbsville, in the first two decades of the Twentieth Century, suffered from a sense of shame because of its lack of a country club. The existence of the tennis club, which was, from the standpoint of exclusiveness, far superior to any of the country clubs in comparable Pennsylvania towns, did not make up for the fact that until 1920, Gibbsville gentlemen had to motor to the next county if they wished to play golf. Everyone who was a member of the tennis club was given the opportunity to become a charter member of the new Lantenengo

Country Club, and almost every tennis-club member did so. Anyone who belonged to the tennis club had made the club grade in Gibbsville. There were men in the Gibbsville Club who could not achieve membership in the tennis club because their wives had not come along in the social world to the same degree that the men had progressed in the business and professional world. Nor did membership in the Gibbsville Club automatically ensure an invitation to join the new, larger, more expensive golf club. Almost any sufficiently solvent Christian man, who had made his money in a sanctioned enterprise and did not habitually leave his car parked in front of whorehouses, could be reasonably sure of election to the Gibbsville Club within two years of proposal and seconding. The only large list of persons who were in effect automatically eligible for country-club membership was the invitation list of the Gibbsville Assembly, and every person on the list was sounded out before the officers of the new club considered other possibilities. A man or a couple who stayed away from five consecutive Assemblies could be dropped from the invitation list, but the rule was seldom invoked, barring extreme misconduct at or away from the Ball itself. Consequently the men and women who were not on the Assembly list were the rare exceptions among the possible members of the new country club. There were two Gibbsville groups that were immediately essential to the formation of the new club. Without the approval of a majority of the Assembly Board, the club never could have proceeded beyond the conversational stage, and the same was true of The Second Thursdays, a group that finally and ultimately possessed the greatest social power in Gibbsville. The very existence of The Second Thursdays was unknown to most of the citizens of the town and even to many who were invited to the Assembly. In its history it never had had a non-member guest, it had no charter, no constitution and by-laws, no rules, no officers, no dues (although assessments were permissible), no stationery, no headquarters, no waiting list other than the direct descendants of the original members. At their meetings the gentlemen wore two-inch-wide red ribbons diagonally across their starched shirt fronts and each lady was provided with the corsage of the evening. Among the persons who did know of the existence of The Second Thursdays none was socially so foolish as to mention the organization to one of its reputed members. The club roster never had been printed or made public, and from time to time young non-members would try to break the secret of the membership. The young blades would station themselves near the homes of reasonably likely members and keep track of the ladies and gentlemen who entered the homes. But no two reports had identical lists of names, and consequently the curious were not able to say with certainty that any single report did actually cover The Second Thursdays. They might have been mere dinner parties. The curious could have questioned the servants of suspected members, but the purpose of the questioning would have been apparent to any cook or maid, and the reliability of her answers would have been doubtful, since she might be lying out of loyalty or for deviltry. In the beginning the secrecy had had a rather kind justification: they did not want to hurt the feelings of the fellow-townsmen who had not been invited to the dinner parties. But as the years passed the secrecy acquired two other reasons for being: it was fun, and "it was nobody's damn business."

Joe Chapin became a member upon the death of his father, despite the fact that his father and mother never had attended a dinner meeting. It was decided that since the elder Chapins had been on the original list, membership should pass on to Joe regardless of the fact that his mother's illness had kept his parents from active participation. At her first visit (and Joe's) Edith was in an advanced state of curiosity and excitement. Although she had known everyone present all of her life, the members had taken on the importance that the long mysteriousness had created. She was thrilled to be among these people who but for her marriage to Joe would have gone on for years and years in their unrevealed superiority. It was almost like danger. "To think that Josephine Laubach could have been snubbing me without my knowing it," she thought. "To think that Whit Hofman isn't a member. To think of all the times I've sat with Arthur McHenry without being sure he belonged to this. To think what Peg Slattery would give to be here." She was reluctantly proud of Joe with his red ribbon and his easy manner, taking the whole thing in stride.

There were always three toasts: to George Washington; to Abraham Lincoln; and to The President of the United States. The conversation at table was no different from the conversation at any dinner party which included some or all of the people present. At no time during the evening was the name of the organization spoken. After dinner the gentlemen separated from the ladies, staying away for exactly thirty minutes. When the group re-formed, the host, at Edith's first dinner, Billy English, rose and knocked his ring on the taboret to gain attention. "Ladies and gentlemen," he said. "We are honored by your presence in our house." (Edith later was to learn that it was a set speech, to avoid long and flowery expressions of the thought by the various hosts.) He smiled and bowed slowly in a gesture that included everyone present. "It is my pleasant duty to welcome Edith and Joe, and it is my duty to relieve each of the gentlemen of twenty dollars. The purpose of this assessment is to alleviate the distress of a lady whom we all know, whose need is acute. For the information of our newest members, this money is delivered anonymously to the person in distress, with a note assuring her that it is a perfectly legitimate transaction and that it would be a waste of time for her to try to thank the donor. I assure you, Joe, that these assessments are not levied at every meeting, but I also must warn you that they are sometimes larger. Our next meeting will be on the twenty-first, at Henry and Josephine's. Thank you."

The business of the meetings was seldom more complicated than on that first evening. Edith soon learned that the ladies had nothing to say about the business affairs of the club which were discussed during the gentlemen's half-hour. An election to membership was announced with the unadorned statement: "At our next meeting we will be joined by . . ." and the names of the new members. It was not practicable to blackball a candidate, since the eligibility of a candidate was so rigidly established. No one ever had refused to join the club, and no one who had joined had had to resign for financial or other reasons. It usually took three years from meeting to meeting at any one house and all eligibles were able to afford their turns as host.

To Joe, who had always known he would some day be a member, The Second Thursdays was a social event offering good food and wine, among old friends whom one might not otherwise see as often as he might wish. It was a gathering of ladies and gentlemen in their best bibs and tuckers, where one felt free to speak without being careful not to be overheard. "We mean something in Gibbsville, besides meaning something to ourselves," he told Edith. "When the club was started, in 1892, it pretended to be no more than a congenial group of friends. But you notice now that the men who founded it made a pretty good guess as to the really substantial people. The reason the club is just as good twenty-eight years later is that it probably would have been just as good twenty-eight years before, if you see what I mean. They could just as easily have started the club in, 28 from 92, 1864. I think the exact same families would have been represented in 1864 as are represented now. There are a lot of nice people in Gibbsville that would be pleasant additions to the club. I'd like to see Whit Hofman a member, for instance. Rather, I'd welcome Whit Hofman. But the founding fathers, as you might call them, didn't see fit to invite old Mr. Hofman, and they must have had their reasons. Billy

English—his father was a crook who blew his brains out, but Mr. English was an original member, so Billy is a member and that entitles Julian to membership when his father dies, which I hope won't be for a long time. Julian would have to calm down quite a lot, but of course we can't hold people responsible for college pranks."

"Julian English is a bad boy and always will be," said Edith.

"Nevertheless, he is entitled to membership when his father dies. If he's kept out, or if someone new is taken in, then it's no longer The Second Thursdays. We might as well disband."

"I personally would like it smaller," said Edith.

Joe smiled. "It will get smaller. Death will take care of that for you. Originally there were twenty couples, but they didn't all have sons to inherit membership. And not all of the present members will have sons. The McHenry membership almost ended with Arthur, and will end if he and Rose don't produce a son . . . on the subject of clubs, I am going to take up *golf!*"

"You're going to stop playing tennis?"

"Not entirely, but I'm in my thirty-ninth year, remember. Next year, I'll be in my fortieth year, so I might as well start learning the old man's game."

"Are you going to wear knickerbockers?"

"I shall wear my white flannels. I had such a hard time persuading Mother and Father to let me wear long trousers, I'm not going to give them up now. Do you realize they kept me in knickerbockers until I was fifteen? And the same height I am now?"

"Yes, I remember."

"That's why I wore boots and breeches so much of the time. At least they weren't knickerbockers, and I didn't look like an overgrown oaf. What was it we used to say? A poor unsophisticated piece of humanity. 'Hello, there, you poor unsophisticated piece of humanity!' That's what we used to say to each other. Mortals who abide in vitreous edifices should not possess morbid propensities toward disestablishmentarianism. Do you know what that means?"

"No."

"People who live in glass houses shouldn't throw stones. Mortals who abide in vitreous edifices should not possess morbid propensities toward disestablishmentarianism. I wish I remembered important things as well as I do that."

"You have an excellent memory," said Edith.

"For some things, but not all," said Joe. "Well, are *you* going to take up golf?"

232

"I wonder. I'd like to get some exercise, and ladies have just about given up horseback riding in Gibbsville. I thought I might take some lessons from the professional and see if I like it. I could play in the mornings, while the children are at school. Rose thinks she'd like to take it up and in the beginning we'll all be dubbers—"

"Duffers."

"Except for the wives who play at the places where they spend the summer."

"Ah, another topic to discuss. Are we going to rent a cottage in Ventnor this summer? I had a letter from the real estate people this morning. You don't have to decide now, but I think we ought to let them know in a week or ten days."

"Oh, I've thought about it. I think it's good for the children to get away for the summer, and we all love the ocean. But I've never felt the same about Ventnor since they had that shark scare."

"Two *years* ago, wasn't it?" said Joe.

"Even so, they could come back. And I've always heard that there were more cases than were ever printed in the newspapers."

"But we never saw one. You never saw one, I never saw one."

"Thank heaven I didn't. I'd faint dead away. Their pictures are frightening enough, thank you," said Edith. "I'd like to go some place else."

"Martha's Vineyard? Maine? Where would you like to go?"

"The water's too cold for the children in Maine, and Martha's Vineyard—Pennsylvania people trying to make friends with Boston and getting absolutely nowhere with them. Oh, those Boston people looking down their big noses and waiting for you to say something frightfully gauche. Do you know that the Rieglers' farm is for sale?"

"Known it for some time. Why, would you like to buy it?"

"Well, it's self-supporting, and they have electricity and a telephone line, and a dam for swimming—"

"You talk about Maine cold water," said Joe.

"The dam is cold early in the morning, but the sun warms it up, and I must say fresh water is more invigorating than salt water, and the children will be much better swimmers. You can't really swim in the surf, and you know we often used the pool in Ventnor."

"Don't misunderstand me, dear," said Joe. "I'd like to learn how much you *want* to buy the Rieglers'."

"Well, it has many advantages. The main house is over a hundred years old."

"Just about," said Joe.

"It's cool inside for the hot days in August, and it would be a place to go for short visits all winter and fall. It's really lovely in the fall, down country. They want to sell it furnished and I happen to know they have some valuable old furniture. We could keep what we wanted of that. We could add on two sleeping porches for ourselves and the children, one at one end of the house and another at the other."

"Two hundred and forty acres of land, about sixty of it in timber. They have a herd of Holsteins they want to sell with the property, and all the equipment, farming implements. They're asking thirty-five thousand for the whole business, lock, stock and barrel. It's about seven and a half miles from the new club, although not all of that is improved road, remember. It's fourteen-plus miles from the center of town."

"Thirty-five thousand. They'll take less, much less."

"No, not a great deal less. Mr. Riegler doesn't need the money, and the only reason he's selling is his wife. Understand she had a heart attack."

"No, it wasn't a heart attack," said Edith. "She told several people that it was too lonely there."

"She took a long time to find that out," said Joe. "They've lived there God knows how many years."

"But then they had the children. Now their children are all grown up and married," said Edith.

Joe nodded. "I wonder what'll happen to us when our children grow up and marry. Suppose we did buy the Rieglers' place. Ann and Joby marry, we're a couple in advanced middle age. Would you want to sell the farm?"

"I'd wait and see how our grandchildren enjoyed it."

"Oh, you've thought about it?" said Joe.

"Of course I've thought about it. The years pass very quickly, and if you don't think about things, suddenly you're middle-aged, your life is more than half over, and you're left with nothing to do. That's why I'd like you to develop outside interests. You promised your father you'd never sell this house, and you promised him you'd never join one of the big law firms in Philadelphia or New York. Those two conditions, if that's what I should call them, they make it pretty certain that we're always going to live in Gibbsville."

"You have no objection to that," said Joe.

"Far from it. The very fact that I've been thinking about the Rieglers' farm proves that. I wouldn't care to live in a big city. But

234

you proved during the war that McHenry & Chapin doesn't take up all your time and energy. You actually proved that you could do the whole thing yourself, without Arthur. And now that Arthur is back, I've noticed that you get home promptly, and you can take your time over lunch. Your law practice really doesn't keep you too busy, does it?"

"Well, I don't work as hard as some lawyers do."

"You don't have to. You wouldn't have to anyway as far as the money is concerned. As far as the money is concerned, you really don't have to work at all. If you gave up the law, we'd still go on living on the same scale we do now."

"I know all these things you're saying," said Joe. "But I wonder why you're saying them."

"Because I want you to be happy."

"Why, I'*m* happy, Edith," he said. "Aren't you?"

"I am if you are, but you won't be if you don't have enough to do."

"In the South, I'd take three or four hours out for lunch and a nap every day. I do much more than a Southern lawyer, for instance."

"They're lazy, and you're not. They're affected by the climate and the local customs. I don't know anything about the South, but if it's true that they take four hours to have lunch and a nap, that's a local custom and everybody does it. Therefore, they don't transact business, nobody transacts business, during that period. That's the way they live, and that's why the South is backward. We're not Southerners and we're not living in the South, and our men are accustomed to longer hours and more work."

"But what's the use of taking on more work?"

"It doesn't have to be legal work. It could be a lot of other things. You could prepare yourself for the day when the children grow up."

"Ah, there you are. One reason I don't want to take on more work is that I'd like to devote more time to the children."

"Why?"

"Well, Joby," said Joe.

"What about Joby?"

"If we buy the Rieglers' farm I'd want to spend more time there, I mean a lot of time. With Joby."

"Doing what?"

"Oh, there are so many things to do on a farm, that a father and son can do together. I know if we bought the farm, I'd build a tennis court right away. That's not farming, but it is country life. I'd like to have us do things together."

"I see," said Edith.

"I've always regretted that my father and I didn't spend more time together. I remember when he taught me to swim. We went out to The Run one day, and he threw me in. Sink or swim."

"Well, Joby can swim without that kind of treatment."

"I know he can," said Joe. "But I wish I'd taught him, not some paid instructor in Ventnor, New Jersey. I'd like to take him for walks in the country, take sandwiches and milk in a thermos bottle."

"What about Ann?"

Joe smiled as he almost always did at the mention of her name. "Oh, Ann—Ann is so different from Joby. She's happy. But Joby needs us more. I don't mean that Ann doesn't need us, but she gets along more easily with people than Joby does. Oh, if we buy the farm the first thing I'd do would be to buy another saddle horse so I could ride with her. I look forward to that."

"When are you going to teach Joby to ride?" said Edith.

Joe stopped smiling and paused. "It's probably a little too early for Joby to ride. Some children shouldn't start too early. You know, their bones are still soft, and some people believe children can get bow-legged if they ride too early."

"Luckily that hasn't *happened* to Ann," said Edith.

"Yes, that would have been too bad," said Joe.

The market in farms suitable for "country homes" (which they were not called in Gibbsville) became active immediately upon the spread of the word that the Chapins had taken possession of the Riegler place. Three of the more recent Lantenengo Street families paid their first visits to the Riegler neighborhood, only to receive the disappointing information that the adjoining farms were not for sale. They were not for sale because the mortgages on them had been quietly taken over by Joe Chapin. Joe was thorough. He made a large deposit in the Swedish Haven Bank & Trust Company, which was the farmers' bank for that area, and let it be known that he was interested in the purchase of shares of the bank's stock when available. He had himself elected to the boards of directors of the Valley Water Company and the Valley Telephone Company. He informed Peter Kemp, the farmer who did the actual farming of the Riegler place, that he contemplated no change in personnel or policy, that everything would be the same as when Mr. Riegler owned it. Joe also had a visit with his old friend Conrad Yates, who was coming up in the world. From Conrad, who was born not far from the Riegler place, he obtained a list of the neighbors. On the list, Conrad wrote his comments on the honesty and reliability and efficiency of the men, and his opinions of some of their women. Joe thus knew which of the wives were getting regular beatings from their husbands, and which husbands bore scars inflicted by the wives (for in that country the women were often larger and sometimes stronger than the men). "This here one," said Conrad. "Four young ones and a son of a pitch if two of them hat the same datty. But she runs the farm, Choe. Not chust the milking and all like that. When it comes the haying season, I seen her. One of her fork-fuls equals two of his'n. I seen her. She'll fuck anybody anytime, but work! All he does is drive the horses. The work, she does. Now this next one, he's consumptive. He says it's the asthma, but my ass it's the asthma. He ought to be at Mount Alto but what'll happen to the farm, he says. What'll happen to the farm if he don't go, I say. A hard, hard worker, Choe, but too stinchy to take care of himself. Start looking for a new farmer there."

"I'll get you to look *for* me," said Joe.

"So," said Conrad. "Choe, you notice my English getting better?"

"Much better. You still have some trouble with some letters."

Conrad nodded. "I seen one of those comedian fellows on the stage. You don't remember, Choe. A long time ago, long long time. You sait I sounted like a comedian on the stage. Don't go to Philly, they'll laugh at you there. Stay in Gippswille. You had right."

"You *were* right," said Joe, correcting him.

"Thank you. I'm better off in Gippswille. Some laugh, but not many. And some wouldn't laugh so much if they see my pankpook."

"That's the way to talk, Conrad," said Joe.

"Who do I thank? *You*, Choe," said Conrad.

The Children's Era; the Year We Bought the Farm. The one as fixed as the other, but the second had a date on it—1920—and the other was only a period of family life that began on some obscure date and was never given a title, and would never have been called by so intellectual a word as *era*, by two such conventionally un-intellectual persons as Edith and Joe. They were not aware that they were living in an Age; a Jazz Age, or an Age of Lost Innocence; they took some pride in living in the Twentieth Century, and a little later they were gratified that they were living in the Harding Administration and normalcy after those long years with the sick professor and wars and rumors of wars. They drank of the dwindling supplies of wine at the dinners of The Second Thursdays; there was a very, very different kind of music at the country-club dances; the older sons of their friends wore tuxedos, not tailcoats, to the Assemblies; it was becoming a custom to give the daughter a roadster when she graduated from college; members of the Gibbsville Club were requested not to stand near the windows with highballs in their hands, where they could be seen by passersby on Lantenengo Street; the very spot where Charlotte Chapin had had her unfortunate encounter with a mule-skinner was now a hangout for a group of youngish men, whose Broadway look was as new to Gibbsville as the enterprises which paid for their flashy clothes; at ladies' bridge parties the cigarette was now out in the open, and parents were now promising their daughters, not alone their sons, rewards for abstaining from smoking; the sanitary napkin was being advertised as a discovery of Army nurses in France; Jack Woodruff, fourteen, made a legitimate, attested hole-in-one on the short seventh at the country club, thus becoming the first member to do so; Miss Holton's School opened its new building at 20th and Lantenengo Streets; Gibbsville Country Day School announced plans to remove from its building at 16th and Christiana to a new location at 22nd and Christiana; the boys' secretary of the Y.M.C.A. was discharged for homosexual acts; the upstairs girl employed by the Ogden family gave premature birth to a baby, which she buried in the Ogdens' cellar; coal gas took the lives of a family of eight on North Railway Avenue; Norman Stokes, a cousin of Edith Chapin, entered the sophomore class at the Sheffield Scientific School, Yale University; a shocking case of adolescent prostitution was being tried one day when Joe Chapin dropped in Number 3 Courtroom to kill some time. There were so many articles in the press, so many tidbits in polite conversation, so many items of gossip, that a bachelor could hear without more than passing interest, but which to the father of a small daughter and a small son were threats and promises. A man could envy the accomplishment of one man's son; he could thank God for protecting him from the sorrow of another man. A parent is sweepingly protective of his infant's existence; but after the baby days are over, the threats become single threats, calling for defensive measures singly, a measure to a threat; vigilance and defensiveness always, but each threat of harm dealt with individually. And, of course, each hope to be dreamed and planned over by itself. In the beginning years the father's fears are for bugs, and the less visible the worse the fear, but not much can be done about them. In the later years the bugs are still there, but now the enemy is people, and some of them no more visible than the most dangerous bugs, and as little to be done about them. But of course there are the good and the kind and the loving among the people, the serenely good, the impetuously kind, the continually loving, who trust their own goodness and kindness and loving without suspicious questioning or ultimately contemptuous analysis, or denying the positive, glorifying the evil, marketing the poison, or trading nothing for something, the gag for the joke, the sneer for the laugh, the fancy lie for the plain truth, the ophidian devious for the classic simple. But of course of the good, the kind, the loving, there are exactly too few, exactly, and among them are traitors as well as converts.

The enormous four-year-age difference between Ann and Joby was responsible for her adopting the position of third parent, a position she took as soon as her first early worries were over, her confidence regained, with the knowledge that her infant brother was not to supplant her in parental affections. At Ventnor she would keep an eye on him when he played near the ocean. In the stable at 10 North Frederick she protected him from the Shetland's kicks, and in the kitchen she took matches away from him. She would try to reason with him in the ponderously adult fashion of young child with younger child. "Matches are *bad*, Joby. *Bad*, do you hear? You mustn't touch matches, ever. Do you hear? You could set the whole house on fire with just one match. So don't ever let me see you stealing matches again, or I'll slap you within an inch of your life." Or, in other circumstances: "Joby, you were a very good boy to help Marian, a very good boy. Always try to help Marian with the laundry basket, and you'll grow up to be big and strong, like Harry and Father. Let me feel your muscle. Oh, that's a big muscle, hard as a rock, Joby. Oh, I wouldn't want to get in a fight with *you* when *you* grow up."

The east-side location of 10 North Frederick had disadvantages for the children of the Chapins. They had no suitable friends on the East Side, and arrangements had to be made for playmates; Joby or Ann would have to go to a friend's house on the West Side, or the friend would have to be brought to 10 North Frederick. There was little fraternizing with the children of the Chapins' neighbors. The Chapin children had not been fortunate in their selection of neighboring playmates. A William Street friend of Ann's, when Ann was not yet six years old, created a painful situation by her purloining of a dozen silver teaspoons, spoon by spoon. The child was acting under orders from her mother, and so admitted when questioned by Harry and Marian. Then when Harry went to the child's home to retrieve the silverware, the mother threatened to sue Harry and the Chapins, until

Harry said, "All right, then, I'll go get the constable and we'll see who sues who." And Ann lost a friend.

Joby had no friend so close. On East Christiana Street, around the corner from 10 North Frederick, there was a hose company, which contained a steamer and a hose cart and five horses, three for the steamer, two for the hose cart. It was a unit of the Gibbsville Volunteer Fire Department, of which each company had a paid hostler who usually lived in the building. The Nonpareil Hose Company Number 2 was the most attractive institution in the neighborhood for the small boys who would stand in the doorway and gaze at the fire engines. The boys were not allowed to set foot inside the house; Bart James, the hostler, terrified the boys with his threats. Every harness-snap was in perfect condition, the brightwork was unmarred by a single fingerprint from fire to fire, and he hated all small boys. To Bart James there were no individual small boys, and he did not know Joby Chapin from any other neighborhood brat. As a result of Bart's ignorance, Joby was "arrested."

One boy, not Joby, could no longer resist the temptation to ring the hose-cart bell. He waited until Bart was back in the hose-house stable and sneaked in and pulled the leather lanyard, which brought Bart from the stable. The boys who had been watching the adventurous one ran, all but Joby, who waited. Bart seized him, held him by the arm while he kicked the boy's bottom and pushed him. "You're arrested, you little bastard," said Bart. "I'm coming to your house tonight and take you to jail, and the rats'll eat your nose off."

Again it was Harry who represented the family. "You know whose little ass you kicked this afternoon?" said Harry.

Bart guessed. "Jesus Christ! The Chapin kid?"

"Yes," said Harry. "What happened?"

Bart told him.

"Well, you kicked the wrong ass. Hereafter don't be so free with your boots."

"What's Chapin gonna do?" said Bart.

"What he oughta do is come over and kick *your* ass. That's what I feel like doing."

"I didn't know it was his kid."

"*Any* kid, Chapin kid or I don't care who. You're a cranky old bully."

"What's he gonna do, Harry?"

"Wouldn't you like to know?" said Harry. "You'll find out."

The implied threats were Harry's invention; he had been sent to investigate and if necessary to convey Joe's apologies for Joby's mischief; but Harry had his own way of dealing with people, especially those he knew better than Joe did.

The next day, entirely on her own, and in a gesture which she never revealed to a living soul, Ann paid a call on Bart James.

"Are you the man that kicked my brother?" she said.

"Who are you?" said Bart James.

"Ann Chapin. Did you kick my brother?"

"What if I did?"

"*This* is what if I did," she said, and kicked his shin. "You terrible man." She turned and ran home and went to her room and closed the door. No one came to punish her for striking a grown person, and the next time she had to pass the hose company Bart James smiled at her and tipped his hat, but she did not return his smile. Bart James died long before she was able to understand why he smiled.

On the farm, during their first summer, Ann and Joby were together oftener and for longer periods than they ever had been before. Her parents and the servants always seemed to be trying to find something that was in another closet, another bureau, or left at home. "Oh, yes, I remember now, I didn't bring that," her mother would say, Marian would say, Harry would say, her father would say. Or, "I know I packed that, so it must be here somewhere." Her father bought a light Ford truck for the farm, a vehicle with a top and curtains on the side, with removable benches that ran along the sides, and a step beneath the tailboard. Ann called it the ice-wagon. The ice-wagon was more fun than the Pierce-Arrow or the Dodge roadster that her father and mother used more frequently. A trip to Swedish Haven in the ice-wagon became an adventure, climaxed with an ice cream soda at Frantz's. During the whole summer Ann went to Gibbsville only once, so that the dentist could decide on when to start bracing her teeth. The sojourn in the country was more than half over before her parents had overnight guests, and the guests were not new faces, but they brought boxes of Page & Shaw's chocolate bonbons, Huyler's peppermints, watermelons, picture books, cap pistols, and bats and balls, racquets and balls, and dolls that Ann no longer wanted, and that Joby was beginning to do without. The grownup guests and their gifts, and the trips to Swedish Haven were welcome interruptions of the life on the farm, but they were not more than interruptions; they were not part of the life. Ann's father and mother would go off to play golf at the new club, even, sometimes, on Sundays. On other days her father would have to go to Gibbsville for the day, and on days when there was no golf her mother would be occupied with those household duties that kept her busy: ordering the meals, planning the marketing, seeing about the new curtains, looking for her work-basket, taking a bath, lying down for a few minutes' rest, telephoning somebody, talking to the rug salesman, spending the day with the dressmaker, writing a letter, having a glass of ginger ale. One or the other of the things her mother was always having to do, half of them requiring her speaking to Marian, speaking to Harry, speaking to Margaret, speaking to the farmer.

"Margaret, you have it soft," Ann heard Marian saying to Joby's nurse.

"What if I do?" said Margaret. "I got the responsibility."

But even the responsibility was more than shared by Ann. Margaret would take her Father Lasance's Prayer Book and her beads and her copy of the Catholic *Standard & Times* and sit in the shade of an apple tree, gently fanning herself with a palm fan (compliments: Frantz's Confectionery and Ice Cream Parlor, Swedish Haven, Pa.), and sipping elegantly from the tall glass of spiced iced tea. She never read her prayer book or her *Standard & Times* for more than five minutes at a stretch; it was too hard to concentrate in the heat; the boy was out of your sight before you knew it; there were always so many distracting things going on on a farm. And there was this tendency to doze off. Margaret could not swim, a fact of which Ann was aware, although Margaret claimed the ability when being hired for the job. She had been hired to be a child's nurse in Gibbsville, in a house on North Frederick Street, and swimming had not seemed likely to be an accomplishment she would have to prove, therefore nothing to stand in the way of a good job. Shortly after their arrival at the farm Margaret had a talk with Ann, in which she disclosed to Ann that she was not as good a swimmer as she had once been, and anyway was more accustomed to the ocean than to fresh water. Ann therefore was to be Margaret's helper when Joby was anywhere near the dam.

"Don't worry, Margaret. Joby can swim," said Ann.

"But I can't!" said Margaret, before the truth could be stopped. "I mean, I can't swim in that dam."

"Oh, pidge-podge," said Ann. "You can't swim at all. If you fell in the dam you'd drownd."

The bribe that Margaret had been considering was now forgotten. Instead Ann was in the powerful position of being able to threaten to tell her mother on Margaret, and whenever Margaret began to lose patience with Ann, Ann would say: "*Swim, Margaret. Swim.*" It nullified Margaret as a restriction on Ann's freedom. But Ann in her capacity of third parent was no less conscientious for her secret knowledge. It was just as well. Joby needed someone.

Rose White McHenry did not share Edith's opinion of Martha's Vineyard and the long-nosed residents of West Chop. Far from sharing it; she did not even know of it, and since the White family house on Edgartown had passed on to Rose through inheritance, Edgartown was where Rose and Arthur passed their summers.

Edith tried to resist the McHenrys' annual invitation to spend a week at Edgartown. In other years she might have been successful, since the McHenrys—Rose and Arthur, not Mildred and Arthur— had not visited the Chapins in Ventnor.

"Can't we get out of going to Martha's Vineyard?" said Edith. "We can tell them we're so busy with the farm."

"They've been here, they can see we're not really as busy as all that," said Joe.

"Rose didn't visit us in Ventnor last summer. Not that I was heartbroken," said Edith. "We visited them, but she didn't repay the visit."

"Well, next year we won't go to Edgartown, but this year we almost have to. In fact, we have to."

"Will you please tell me why?"

"Politeness—but it also suits my purpose."

"What purpose?"

"Well, I have to be in Philadelphia next week and again in two weeks. I can arrange our plans so that I can see my man on the way to Edgartown and on the way home, and in between we can visit Rose and Arthur. What's the difference, Edith? You can go bathing and sailing, you don't have to see those Boston people."

"No, of course not. Just every night at dinner, old men asking me what class you were, and what relation are you to the Something-Something Chapins."

"Wrong college, wrong Chapins. Oh, I've gone through it oftener than you have, don't forget. Once more, this one summer?"

"I'm not going to let you forget that promise."

Edith dutifully spent the week on the Vineyard. On the return trip they stopped in Philadelphia. They went to their hotel room and while Edith was taking her bath, Joe telephoned the man with whom he had an appointment. When she came out of the bathroom Joe was sitting on the bed.

"Let's go home on the 4:35," he said.

"What's the matter?"

"Price broke our appointment. He has to be in Fort Penn all day tomorrow. His secretary said she sent me a telegram, but I didn't get any telegram. I'm going home."

"Well, I'm not," said Edith. "I have a great deal of shopping to do tomorrow. There's a sale at Wanamaker's and this will be my last chance to get a lot of things done for the fall. I want to get two new chairs, and order some carpet, and I'm simply not going to make another trip."

"Well, would you mind if I went home on the 4:35?"

"Frankly, I wouldn't mind at all," said Edith. "You insisted on our going to Rose's and I had a perfectly miserable time, and now you want to change *my* plans when I could at least get something done."

"All right, Edith, all *right*," said Joe. "I'll take the 4:35 and you can come home tomorrow. Will you take the 4:35 tomorrow? I'll meet you at Swedish Haven."

"Yes, I'll be on the 4:35," said Edith.

"Tell me which suitcase you'll need and I'll take the others home with me," said Joe.

Philadelphia was so much a part of the Gibbsville middle- and upper-class life that when Gibbsvillians saw each other on Chestnut Street, they bowed and smiled, but it was not an occasion for the gladsome encounter that would have taken place on Fifth Avenue, New York. At four o'clock Joe departed for the Reading Terminal, leaving Edith alone and annoyed at what she considered his selfish lack of consideration, whimsically impulsive behavior, failure to appreciate her efforts at the Vineyard, and preference of the children's company over one more day with her. He had not even stopped to consider that this was the first time in her life that she was left alone in a hotel overnight. Indeed, she was alone in the room for a quarter of an hour before she realized it herself. There was still some time for shopping, not for the major purchases she would make in the morning, but the stores would be open for another hour and she decided to waste no more of it within unfamiliar walls. She closed her door behind her, walked to the elevator, bowing to the white-haired woman at the floor clerk's desk, and in two minutes she was on Walnut Street and making her way to Chestnut.

Edith was an inch or so taller than the run of women, tanned by the sun and in dress so uninspired that she could have been one of the owners of Philadelphia, up from Cape May for the day. She had a good figure that was neither remarkably feminine nor startingly slender. She wore a varnished blue straw hat with a wide black band, and her dress, which was open at the throat, was of navy-blue linen with a white leather belt, and she had on black silk stockings and white buckskin shoes with perforated black strapping across the vamp. Her only jewelry, besides her wedding and engagement rings, was a plain gold circle at the bottom of the V of her throat. She dressed like a Member, belonging exactly to her class, with a Yale husband in the background, tennis and swimming for exercise, Protestantism for her religion, extravagance nowhere in her character, and discontent never far from her contemplation.

She walked slowly, pausing to look at gloves, at shoes, at pianos, at precious stones, at the displays for the August fur sales. Suddenly, inexplicably, she burst into tears. She quickly took out her handkerchief and acted the part of a woman with a cinder in her eye, but turning, she retraced her steps toward the hotel, and the crying somewhere stopped.

It was a hateful experience, like a cowardly blow by an unseen adversary, and it was inadequate to say she was tired. She knew it to be more than that, and she knew it to be related to Joe, but to Joe only as partially a reason. She knew she would make Joe suffer for his part, which was not only his conduct this afternoon, but his docile refusal to let her guide his life, his effortless and natural ease with people and with the children, and his orgiastic fidelity to her, which sometimes was as though he had created her for his pleasure and his needs.

For the immediate moment she wanted to bathe her eyes and remove herself from the presence of all other human beings. She walked briskly up the steps of the hotel and stood at the bank of elevators.

"After you, Mrs. Chapin."

A man in a Palm Beach suit and a black four-in-hand tie moved aside, bowing, and making way for her. He was a Gibbsville man, but she was not capable of recognizing him now.

"Thank you," she said.

He entered the elevator after her. "Lloyd Williams, from Collieryville," he said.

"Yes, I know," she said, and to the elevator man: "Twelfth floor, please."

"Twelve, please," said Lloyd Williams. "Both on the same floor. Been to the seashore? I haven't run into Joe lately."

"Yes, yes we have," said Edith. "Have you?"

"I went down to Atlantic City earlier in the summer, but I only stayed a week. I'm not much for the sun."

"It's been quite warm," said Edith.

"You spend your summers in Chelsea," said Williams.

"Ventnor is where we always went until this year. Now we have a farm quite near Gibbsville. But we've been visiting the Arthur Mc-Henrys."

"Oh, sure. Arthur. Cape Cod."

"Practically," said Edith. "A place called Martha's Vineyard, not far from Cape Cod. Well, our floor."

"After you, ma'am," said Williams. The floor clerk nodded to them and they nodded in return. Williams walked with Edith to her door and held out his hand. After a second's hesitation she handed him her key and as he was turning it in the lock he said: "Tell Joe I have a bottle of prewar rye if he'd care for a little something before dinner. I'm down in 12-20."

"Oh, I'm afraid he's going to be very disappointed. He went back on the 4:35, but thank you. I'll tell him. Good-bye, Mr. Williams. Nice to've seen you."

"Thank you, Mrs. Chapin. It's been a great pleasure." He could see inside her room, and he added: "You oughta turn on the electric fan and get the air circulating."

"Thank you, I will," she said.

She entered, closed the door, and quickly took off her hat and dress and washed her face. Then she removed her shoes and picked up the Bible, the only portable reading matter in the room. Then she remembered Williams' advice and she put down the Bible and turned the switch for the electric fan. The blades began rotating and soon there was a hum and now she began waiting, waiting and wondering what excuse Lloyd Williams would invent for his call.

In some minutes, fifteen or so, there was a knock on her door. "Who is it?"

"The bellboy, ma'am."

"I didn't ring for you."

"I know, ma'am, but the party in 12-20 sent you something."

"Just a moment." She put on her kimono and opened the door. The bellboy placed on the desk a tray on which were a full glass, a half-empty bottle of ginger ale, and a small bowl of ice.

"Compliments of the party in 12-20, it's paid for and I'm to give you this." He handed her an envelope and left the room.

246

She took a sip of the ginger ale and discovered that it was strongly laced with whiskey. She opened the envelope.

Don't think me fresh but as one coal-cracker to another
I trust you will enjoy this cooling libation.

L.W.

It was crude, but it was not so crude as any telephone call would have been, and what was more—and she well knew it and knew that he knew she knew it—the next move was up to her. She could send the drink back, but that would involve recalling the bellboy and informing him of the rebuking gesture. She could write Williams a note for delivery in the morning. But what she knew, as well as though there were open wires connecting their rooms, was that she was going to telephone him her thanks, and that they would see each other alone.

She rang his room.

He answered, and she did not identify herself. "Thank you for the ginger ale highball," she said. "I'm afraid it was just what I needed."

"I oughtn'ta say this to a lady, but I thought you seemed tired."

"Exhausted."

"I was just gonna order some dinner. How about if you let me order you some dinner. They'll serve it to you in your room, and you won't have to go out or anything."

"Oh, I'm not that exhausted. We spent the night on a hot stuffy train, and I must say Philadelphia . . ."

"They're frying eggs right out there on Broad Street," he said. "You don't want me to order your dinner for you, then? But could you stand another drop of rye?"

"I don't really drink, you know. One is all I ever take, and never as strong as this one."

"Well, how about putting a little more stren'th in it?"

"Did you mean come to my room? Don't you think the management would frown on that?"

"They don't frown on regular customers, and you're a regular customer and I'm a regular customer. And don't forget, I'm a politician. I could frown on *them*, and they wouldn't like that a bit."

"All right," she said.

She put on her dress and shoes again and in a couple of minutes he tapped on her door and entered bearing the whiskey bottle unhidden by his coat. She watched him as without a word he carefully placed the bottle on the tray and still without a word stood in the

247

center of the room, a step or two away from where she was standing. Then he moved toward her and embraced her. He held her until she stopped struggling and kissed him, then he let her go.

"You took a lot for granted," she said.

"I had to," he said. "If we'd of sat here and made polite conversation maybe we'd of been too polite and never said anything to one another."

"I don't think we've said anything," said Edith.

"We said more than some people it takes a lifetime to say. A man and a woman want to go to bed with one another."

"It isn't that easy, it isn't that simple."

"I say it is. I got a hard on for you when we were in the elevator."

"Don't talk like that," she said.

"You don't get that kind of a hard on if the other person doesn't feel the same way."

"I wasn't even thinking about you. I don't even know what we talked about in the elevator. The seashore."

"That kind of a conversation is automatic. Feeling is what counted there. Weren't you feeling?"

"No."

"Yes you were, you were feeling something. I know you were, and you can deny it under oath, but you were feeling."

"Well, I was feeling something, but it had nothing to do with you."

"For another man?"

"For myself," she said.

"You're wasting your life and your youth because you think it's proper to appear cold. Were you ever with another man besides your husband?"

"No."

"I thought not. The whole sum total of human experience you think you've had with one man. Only you don't think so, do you?"

"I suppose not," she said.

"A passionate woman, up to now with only the one man. Did you ever stop to think that with a different man you're a different woman, not the same woman that's always going to bed with Joe Chapin? I got nothing against Joe Chapin, but he's not me. I'm me, and another man is still another man. I want you to have all the experience you want, with me now, but later with other men. You ought to have a lot of men."

"This is—let's sit down, please."

"I talk as well on my feet, but you sit down."

"I'm going to," she said, and did so.

"I've been studying you for years, I don't know how long. I used to wonder about you."

"You couldn't have, you've hardly ever seen me," she said.

"You hardly ever see anybody, do you? I mean really see them. Am I right? Don't you go through life with your eyes half closed?"

She nodded. "Very likely," she said.

"Not me. I'm interested in everybody but in women especially."

She made a faint smile. "Then it isn't just me," she said.

"No, not just you, but you for a long time, and especially you. My peculiar desires for you and awakening your curiosity, not that it lies dormant for long. You have curiosity, you have the qualities of a great mistress."

"Is this to tell me that I am going to become *your* mistress?"

"Not quite. This may be our only time together. Now I'll stop talking for a minute and you can get over your shock."

He straddled the desk chair, where he could study her. The silence began and they were both determined not to break it. In formally measured time it was not more than five minutes, but it was long enough for her excitement to turn in cycles, from curiosity at the top to curiosity again, with fear of consequences just before curiosity came around again.

"Why not?" she said.

"Yes, why not?" he said.

She stood up. "I'm going in there and undress."

"I'd like to undress you."

"No," she said.

She took a long time undressing, and when she came out of the bathroom she was in her kimono. She lay on the bed and he parted the kimono, and a calm came over her that separated her mind from her body while he indulged his curiosity that was active, as her curiosity was all wondering what he would do. Then after many minutes she demanded him wholly and grasped him to herself with no thought of his readiness or convenience, and in the end it was she who took possession.

"I thought so," he said, when they were quiet.

"You thought so," she said in exquisite weariness. "What did you think so? Some more of your theories?"

"Sure," he said. "Many men. Many." He laughed.

"That strikes your sense of humor?"

"Doesn't it yours? Many men, but only two."

"And *only* two is right," she said. "And only two there will be. You're not married, are you?"

"No," he said.

"I'm glad," she said. "I don't think you were meant to be a husband. Do you talk? Will you be likely to discuss this with your cronies, whoever they are?"

"I'd like to, but the men I know, there's nobody that could appreciate this. My conquest was in the elevator. In the bed was secondary. My conquest was—let's call it a superior intelligence than most men have. Most men from my world, they wouldn't even permit themselves to entertain any carnal thoughts about you. I went way beyond that. I knew you'd be—receptive. No, dear lady, there'll be no gossip or scandal."

"Thank you. I believe you. And I'm very grateful."

"For the no-scandal or for the love-making?"

"For the love-making. I quarreled with my husband. Now I'll go back to him without carrying over any resentment and he'll think I'm a dear and gentle wife."

"And you will be, won't you?"

"Yes, I suppose I will."

"Where if it hadn't been for me, you and me, that is, you could have easily pestered him for days."

"Have you got a mistress?"

"Yes, although I wouldn't call her that. A woman I go to bed with."

"I'm not going to ask who she is. Is she intelligent?"

"In her own way, but not the way you are, or I am."

"Will she know that you made love to me, or anyone?"

"I never promised her anything, therefore she isn't looking for trouble. Promise things, fidelity, for instance, and you've made a contract. But if you don't make contracts people don't get sore at you."

"Let's you and I make a contract, though."

"What?"

"This is the only time for us, we must never do this again," said Edith.

"Now you're making a contract, and I just told you . . . If we made that contract and we did go to bed again, you'd be sore at me. Not at yourself so much, but at me. Let's see what the future holds in store for us."

"Well, then, let's not *try* to see each other again," she said. "I'd like to know that there was one man, once, who proved to me that all men are not the same."

"That's a very good—uh—point. All men *are* different, and every woman is different with every man. Now that you've found that out through me, I amend what I said earlier. You won't have to go to bed with many men. You know that they're all different."

"Are all women different?"

"Oh, are they!"

"You must go now," she said.

"Yes. What are you going to do?"

"Take a bath and go to sleep."

"You'll wake up," he said. "Maybe one or two o'clock in the morning. You don't want to telephone me. Operators listen in when they have nothing to do."

"I'll leave the door unlocked."

"How long do you think you'll sleep?" he said.

"I have no idea," she said.

"I'll come in after midnight. If you're awake, I'll stay. If you're asleep, I won't waken you."

He left her. At one o'clock he opened her door, but there was no mistaking the deep breathing for simulated sleep. He quickly and quietly closed the door and retired to his own room.

They made no effort to see each other when she returned to the farm. There was only one person who detected any difference in her, and that was Joby. Edith became attentive, sympathetic, maternal with him. He did not understand it, he was suspicious of it, there was no explanation for it, and he did not like it. More than ever he turned to Ann, and so it was always, for the remainder of that summer and for the rest of their lives.

It would not have been remarkable for Edith and Lloyd Williams to live a full year without ever actually seeing each other. Lloyd Williams lived in Collieryville, a mining town three or four miles from 10 North Frederick, but separated from the Chapins' home and their life by the accepted differences of money and social prestige; the miners' poolroom, and the Gibbsville Club; sickening poverty, and four live-in servants for a family of four; The Second Thursdays, and the chicken-and-waffle suppers of the English Lutheran Church. Joe Chapin and Lloyd Williams were courthouse-corridor friends and fellow Republicans, but Joe was a Company man and Lloyd Williams was a Union man, who was a Republican because to be anything else in Lantenengo County was futile and foolish. Edith could not have told within two years the day of her first meeting with Lloyd Williams; nor within three the number of times she had spoken to him. She was acquainted with him in the sense that she was acquainted with members of the Gibbsville Police Department, the driver for the Adams Express Company, the tipstaff in the Number 3 Courtroom, a dentist who was not her dentist, and any of the dozens of men whom she knew principally for their respectable occupations and to whom social introduction was not required. But now, after the affair in Philadelphia, she seemed to be encountering Williams with greater frequency. She thought it might be that she was understandably more aware of his existence; but it was more than that. What she was unaware of was that Lloyd Williams was politicking and making himself ubiquitous.

Their first encounter alarmed her. It occurred in Swedish Haven. She saw him, he saw her, and raised his hat and said, "Good afternoon, Mrs. Chapin. Is this your boy?"

"This is my son Joby," she said. "On our way to Frantz's."

"For an ice cream soda, I'll bet," said Williams.

"No, a comb," said the boy.

"A comb?" said Williams.

"An ice cream comb," said Edith. "We call it a comb."

"Well, enjoy yourself, boy. Give my regards to Joe," said Williams, and passed on.

"Why has he got such a red face?" said Joby.

"Because some people have that kind of complexion," said Edith.

"Why has he got that kind of a complexion?"

"Because the sun doesn't tan them, it just gives them red faces."

"Where does he live?"

"He lives in Collieryville."

"Then what is he doing here?"

"I have no idea, I'm sure," said Edith. "But *we're* here, and *we* don't live here."

"I hate him," said Joby.

"I've told you not to say that about people. *Why* do you hate Mr. Williams?"

"He's dirty," said Joby.

"No he isn't" said Edith. "His clothes are wrinkled because of the hot weather, but he's not dirty."

"He *is* dirty, Mother, and you don't like him either but you're just pretending."

252

"If you want me to buy you an ice cream cone stop talking about Mr. Williams," said Edith.

She saw Williams again a few days later, and this time he was riding in a Ford phaeton with a man in a farmer's straw hat and overalls. She was driving the Dodge roadster on her way from golf at the new country club. The road was narrow and both cars had to slow down. As they passed, proceeding in opposite directions, she bowed her thanks to the farmer and then recognized Williams, who tipped his hat.

The next day she was in her room and she chanced to look in the barnyard and there she saw the farmer, Peter Kemp, their own farmer, in conversation with Williams. He was going too far.

She hurried downstairs and out to the barnyard. He turned when the farmer turned. "Good afternoon, Mrs. Chapin," he said.

"Good afternoon, Mr. Williams."

"I hope it's all right if I try to convince Peter to vote for me?"

"Why yes, if he wants to. Would you care to come over to the porch and have some iced tea?"

"Well, I guess I've finished my oration to Peter, eh, Peter?"

"I guess yes," said the farmer.

"Whenever you're ready," said Edith.

"I'll go with you," said Williams.

They walked in silence to the porch and Edith told Marian to bring the iced tea, and when Marian departed Edith spoke: "Why are you spending so much time in this neighborhood?"

"Getting votes."

"Is that the only reason?"

"I'm all over the county getting votes. Most of these farmers vote Democratic and their votes aren't numerous, but that's no reason why I shouldn't try to change their minds," he said. "I'm not here to annoy you."

"I don't know what I could do if you were, but I'd have to do *something*," she said.

"I went back to your room, but you were asleep. I didn't bother you then, and I don't intend to bother you now, so stop worrying."

"I admit I was worrying."

"Admit it? You didn't have to admit it to me."

"Just as long as you understand that what happened in Philadelphia—I'm not sorry it happened, but it ended there."

"Let's see what the future has in store for us," said Williams.

"You said that once before," said Edith. "*Joby!*" She saw the boy hiding behind a walnut tree, too far away to have overheard anything, but able to see his mother and her guest. "Come here, Joby," she called, in a less commanding tone. But the boy ran.

"He's a quick one," said Williams.

"Quicker than you think," she said. "Well, I'm relieved that you're keeping your end of the bargain."

"I'm a little angry that you'd think I wouldn't, but it's understandable. Joe in town?"

"For the day," said Edith.

"You want me to go," said Williams.

"Yes," she said.

He picked up his hat. "I'll make you a small bet. I bet you'll try to get in touch with me first."

"Oh, I've wanted to, but it's out of the question. If we don't see each other for a long enough time, I won't even want to. I think I could forget you."

"No doubt you could, but be careful. If you do forget me, there might be another fellow that wouldn't be as discreet as I am. You made a big step, Edith, and you're lucky it was with me."

"I'm convinced of that," she said. "Good-bye."

After supper—in the country they went back to calling it supper because all of the farmers and farm people called it supper—Joby came to say good night to his father, who was sitting on the porch.

"Well, did you have a very busy day, Joby?" said Joe.

"A man was here," said the boy. He did not look at his mother, who was sitting on the swing.

"A man was here? Oh, Mr. Williams. Yes, Mother told me."

"Mother gave him lemonade."

"Iced tea, dear," said Edith. "Now run off to bed and don't try to stretch out your saying good night."

"Father, what did he want?"

"Oh, now, Joby, I can see through you. You're stalling your car and holding up traffic. Off to bed. Give me a kiss."

The boy kissed his father.

"Hey, there, you're forgetting Mother," said Joe.

The boy went to the swing and presented his cheek. "I'll be up to tuck you in," she said.

"Ann can tuck me in," said the boy.

And those were some of the occurrences and conversations in the Chapin family in the year 1920. . . .

Joe kept saying he did not want a fortieth birthday party. He said he did not like parties—a palpable untruth—and particularly a birthday party for himself, and most particularly and especially a large party in honor of his reaching age forty, an age which he said a man should hold as secret as a woman held all of hers. But his protests were not strong enough to stand up against the insistence of Edith and Arthur McHenry.

At first there were going to be forty guests, but the invitation list grew larger and the party plans more elaborate, until Arthur said that with so many people they ought to hire an orchestra, and with an orchestra there would be dancing, and with dancing there ought to be a good-sized orchestra. The original small dinner became a dinner dance at the Lantenengo Country Club. Invitations went out to more than three hundred persons, all adults past college age, which did not cost the college set a party, since they would not be home. On the 29th of January they would be having their mid-years.

"All right," said Joe. "But one thing I do insist on. I would like it understood that I wash my hands of the whole problem of invitations. I don't want to *see* the list, or be asked a thing about it. If you forget to invite somebody's Aunt Millie, I want to be able to say I had nothing to do with it."

There were numerous Aunt Millies, because of, and in spite of Arthur's and Edith's triple checking of the list. There were the inevitable few of whom Arthur or Edith would say: "We'll send him an invitation, but he'll have sense enough not to come." (In that category was Lloyd Williams, who did not, however, have sense enough not to come.) The problem of seating the dinner guests was solved, not entirely successfully, with Arthur's scheme: a card was written for each acceptance, and all the gentlemen's cards were placed in one pile, and the ladies in another. Each pile was shuffled, then a third pile was created by Arthur's placing a gentleman's card at the bottom, then Edith would place a lady's card on top of that, then a gentleman's, until they ran out of ladies (who were in the minority). There were sixteen gentlemen left over, but since dinner was to be served to fifteen round tables of twenty persons each, the surplus gentlemen were easily distributed. The invitations were on flip-over cards with only the Chapins' name, engraved, the date, and "Small Dance" written by hand, so that many of the guests were not aware that it was a birthday celebration. The entire facilities and staff of the club were taken over for the party, and two special policemen from a detective agency were hired to keep out the uninvited, a precaution ironically required by the fact that liquor would be served in violation of the national and club rules. The club as a club could not sanction the serving of liquor, and the policemen were employed to see that no outsider saw it being served. There were too many members of the judiciary and the district attorney's staff present to place the party in danger of a surprise raid, even by the most zealous Federal agents. Fewer than half of the ladies accepted the Orange Blossoms that were passed before dinner, but not more than ten of the men refused a drink in the locker room and the smoking room. Gibbsville men were drinking men, and a few of them had proven it by the time the guests were seated. Wine was not served.

The absence of wine from the table controlled the other nuisance which Joe had asked them to dispense with; there were no toasts. In their place there were a few words from Arthur McHenry, who tapped his water glass for attention, and when he got it, said: "Ladies and gentlemen, some of you, but not all of you, may know that this is the fortieth birthday of our host, Joe Chapin. (Applause.) He has threatened to shoot me or anyone else who makes a speech, but I think we can all safely rise and sing, 'He's a Jolly Good Fellow!' "

The song was sung, the tables were rapped and hands were clapped, and the orchestra swung into the lovely measures of "Say It with Music," a new fox trot. The practice of cutting in was already firmly established at the Lantenengo Country Club, but at the conclusion of the first number Bobby Short, the orchestra leader, made the following announcement: "Ladies and gentlemen, I have been requested to announce that there will be no cut-ins. No cut-ins, ladies and gentlemen. Thank you." Some of the older guests had no idea what he was talking about, but they were of an age that upheld the custom of the dance program, with its small tasseled pencil and its unwritten sadness for the plain girl and the gawky young man. The Chapin dance had a little of the old, a little of the new. Joe danced with his wife, with his partner's wife Rose, with Josephine Laubach, Peg Slattery, and Alice Rodeweaver, a cousin of Edith's; and with Jane Weeks, Alec's second wife, and Betty Harrison, Dave's wife, who had come from New York for the party; and Betty Donaldson, who had come down from Scranton.

Edith danced with Joe; with Arthur McHenry, Henry Laubach, Mike Slattery, Alec Weeks, her brother Carter, and Paul Donaldson.

She sat out her dance with Dave Harrison, who had lost a leg in an airplane accident in France.

The dancing ended at the reasonable hour of one o'clock and nearly all of the guests stayed to the end. It was close to two-thirty when the Chapins, the McHenrys, the Weekses, the Harrisons and the Donaldsons sat down to scrambled eggs in the smoking room. The Donaldsons were staying with the Chapins, the Weekses with the McHenrys; and the Harrisons were staying at the hotel because of Dave's leg and the hotel elevator. All agreed that it had been a splendid party, over and above such misfortunes as a lady's lost earring, the early departure of several of the elderly, a man who had lost the keys to his car, another man who had upchucked before quite making the bathroom, Billy English's being called away in the middle of dinner, the orchestra's not playing enough waltzes for the older crowd, one whole table's being served a full course behind the others because it was out of sight in an *L*, one lady's insistence on being at the party when she should have been on her way to the delivery room, and in addition to the misfortunes that were discussed at the supper party there were a few others like the lady who lay moaning and taking aspirin in the upstairs rest room, and the stout lady who committed a loud fart over the singing of "Jolly Good Fellow," and the waiter who had not buttoned his fly, and the small incident of Jane Weeks and her dinner partner in which Jane said: "Are you by any chance a customer of my husband's firm?"

"No," said the man.

"Then take your hand off my leg."

Back at 10 North Frederick the Chapins made sure that the Donaldsons had everything, knew where everything was, didn't want a glass of milk—and retired to their own room.

"Thank you, Edith," said Joe. "It was a grand party."

"Yes, I think it was. I'm glad you enjoyed it."

He was lying with his hands clasped at the back of his neck. "It had a nice friendly atmosphere. Not too pushy friendly, but almost a family feeling. It wasn't so much me. It was Gibbsville. My father was right. This is a good town, and I'm glad I didn't decide to live in New York or Philadelphia. I wouldn't like to feel out of it, the way I would in a big city, and I wouldn't like to do what Paul does, spends more and more of his time in New York. If you're going to be a New Yorker, be a New Yorker. If you're going to be a Scranton man, be one. I wonder what he's saying about us, right this minute. Probably saying I'm a stick-in-the-mud."

"No, Paul couldn't say it. He's still half-stuck in Scranton. Dave might say it, or Alec. But you don't care what they say. You don't really care what anybody says."

"Well, now that I'm forty, I am a stick-in-the-mud for good, and I'm not the least sorry. Not in the least."

"All those people tonight, that ought to make you feel anything but sorry." She entered the bed and turned out the light.

"Forty," said Joe.

"I'm sure it doesn't feel very different."

"No, not unless I look at my friends, Alec and Dave, fellows I don't see all the time, and ask myself whether I've changed as much as they have. In appearance, that is."

"I can answer that. You haven't. Dave has been through a lot of pain and suffering. And Alec's appearance can be blamed on other things."

"Very handsome fellow, though."

"If you like his kind of looks. I happen not to believe that an American should try to look so much like an Englishman."

"It's not English, Edith. It's a certain kind of New York-swell look. Of course he does get everything in London, right down to his collar buttons. And he went to Oxford, remember."

"He rubs me the wrong way."

"Not while he was dancing with you, I hope . . . I couldn't resist that. Well, pretty soon that will be all over for all of us, Alec and me and all of us."

"Yes, all of us."

"I'm ten years away from fifty, and ten years ago I was a young man of thirty. It's easier for me to imagine myself fifty than to remember how I was at thirty. I wonder how long I'll live."

"Till you're eighty, at least."

"Do you think so? My mother and father and my grandparents were all in their seventies or about that when they died."

"At least eighty," said Edith. "You may live to be a hundred. You've never had a serious illness, you do everything in moderation and they say that's the secret."

"Not for everybody," said Joe. "Think of the old drunks in this town, a lot of them in their seventies. But it isn't just living to an old age that I've been thinking about. Crocodiles and turtles, look at them. And there's always some man in Turkey that's just celebrated his one hundred and thirtieth birthday."

"I think they have a different calendar," said Edith. "What would you like to do, or be?"

"I would like to be President of the United States," said Joe.

"You would?"

"I honestly would," said Joe.

"Is that a new thought?"

"Not entirely new. At least I didn't just think of it tonight."

"Do you think you could be elected?"

"Not in 1924. I've never been elected to anything, at least not president of anything. If I ever plan to realize my ambition I'll have to get started soon. I think Mr. Harding is about fifty-seven now, and he was fifty when he was elected to the Senate."

"He looks younger than fifty-seven."

"A very handsome man, even in knickers," said Joe.

"Yes, he looks like a Roman senator," said Edith.

"Well, I don't look like a Roman senator, I'm sure of that, but neither do most of the senators. And I have some qualifications and some I can acquire. I'm more than thirty-five, I'm a native-born citizen. White. Protestant. Republican, and never even a Bull Mooser. I'm blessed with enough of this world's goods without being a Wall Street millionaire. Married to a fine woman, father of two children. Attorney-at-law. Never connected with any scandal. And a grandfather who was lieutenant governor of one of the largest states and ancestors who fought in the Revolutionary War. The one thing against me is my own war record, but people are inclined to forget things like that, and anyway, it would take me ten years to get established in politics. By that time my war record won't seem quite so important, unless my opponent happens to be a war hero. But I wouldn't run against a war hero. Have you ever heard such boasting?"

"It isn't boasting. It's what I've always wanted you to do. Not President. I never thought of that. But I've always thought you should do more in public affairs. And why not aim for the top?"

"It's an insane idea, positively insane, and yet it could happen. If I go about it the right way, build slowly and carefully, it could happen."

On this night, the early morning after his fortieth birthday, she made all her efforts to please him and found that he was also pleasing her, and pleasing her more than Lloyd Williams had pleased her, because this man was her own.

In the months that followed they had many conversations over strategy and tactics. The little bits were considered carefully in their relation to the grand strategy. An invitation to buy tickets for a church supper no longer received a perfunctory small check. Edith would send the check, but she would send with it a brief note to the effect that she and her husband were delighted to help such a worthy cause. Worthy causes, from the Boy Scouts of America to the Society for the Prevention of Cruelty to Animals, were equally delighted to print the Chapin name high on their published lists of contributors. Joe shrewdly by-passed the Merchants Association, a group of men who were forever identified in Mr. Lewis's Babbitt. "They want to use *me*, but I'm out to use *them*," Joe remarked, and regretfully declined invitations to speak at their meetings and at the luncheons of the Rotary, Kiwanis, and Lions.

They did not go in too deeply. "I don't want to do anything that looks like politics," said Joe. "I want people to get to know that I'm alive, but at least for the time being I'm not going to enter into activities that will make people put two-and-two together. That's why these charities are good. We've always given to charity, but until now, it hasn't been getting in the paper."

Among non-charitable organizations there existed a timidity about asking Joe or his wife for support. The people of the town, and the people in the circulation area of the Gibbsville newspapers, were becoming familiar with the name, so that as a name it was beginning to mean something more than nothing. But Joe Chapin held no office and had a successful business in the law, and consequently did not have to yield to polite pressure when a free speaker was needed for a high school commencement or the dedication of a drinking font. He continued to lend his name and give his money to such projects as a public swimming pool, public tennis courts, the public library, the Mission (a recreation center for poor children, having no connection with denominational religion, and conducted by young ladies who in larger cities would have been the Junior League), the Children's Home (an orphanage), the Junior Baseball League, the Gibbsville professional football team, the Gibbsville Historical Society, the Committee for the Maintenance and Preservation of Historical Monuments, the Y.M.C.A., the Y.W.C.A., the Y.M.H.A., and the Y.W.-H.A. A large number of the worthy causes had to do with children, and Joe's contributions and interest needed no explanation. And in some instances the worthy causes had been supported by two or three generations of Chapins and Stokeses. But now the Chapin name was being used, and the happy circumstance that the name stood high on alphabetical lists made for an increasing public awareness of it.

In less than two years there was scarcely an adult (who was not an illiterate) who did not at least know the name Joseph B. Chapin, and know it in a favorable association. There were poor people in the mill section who had never seen Joe Chapin, but that too was going to be taken care of in its proper time. And the campaign to acquaint Gibbsville citizens with the name was accomplished without a single conference with Mike Slattery. It was all done from 10 North Frederick or from Joe's office.

Then one evening in '24 Mike Slattery, reading his Gibbsville *Standard*, said as though to no one: "Well, now, will you listen to this."

"What?" said Peg Slattery.

"In the paper. Joe Chapin. According to this he presented an American flag, a silk American flag, to the Joseph B. Chapin Grammar School."

"He's always giving to this or that," said Peg. "The both of them are."

"Oh, no. Oh, no, my girl. This is different. This isn't one of those five-dollar donations to St. Isaac's Hebrew Sodality."

"Why is this so different, giving a flag to a school?" said Peg.

"This time he went there himself. He presented the flag. He—made—the presentation." He laid the paper on his lap and gazed up at the ceiling, running his upper teeth over his lip. Peg recognized the signs that her husband made when he was planning an important move, and kept quiet.

"Mr. Joe Chapin and I are about ready to have a private talk," he said. "He is a much smarter man than I gave him credit for."

"She's in it somewhere," said Peg.

"You're right she is. She may be at the bottom of it," said Mike. "That's neither here nor there at this time. Now what I do, I make the first move. I could wait for him to come to me, but if I make the first move and offer him something, he'll be flattered and he'll be one of my men. If I wait for him to come to me, he may come to me with plans of his own and I may have to turn him down, and I don't want to do that."

"He may turn down what you offer."

"That won't matter. I'll still be making the offer before he can come to me."

"Don't leave her out of your thinking."

"Oh, you may be sure I won't," said Mike. "They have been doing this together, and I wasn't very smart not to notice it before. The day after tomorrow I'll see him. I don't want him to get away from me. I wish there was some way I could find out all the charities and stuff he's been contributing to. But there isn't time!"

"Then why don't you take for granted that he's contributed to everything? Talk to him and meanwhile you can get someone at your office to examine the back numbers of the *Standard*."

"I'll do that," said Mike. "We don't want this fledgling to learn to fly without us."

"No."

"And I'll talk to him day after tomorrow and find out how high he wants to fly."

It was easy for Mike to obtain an appointment to see Joe. "But I'd rather we met at the Gibbsville Club, Joe. I have a feeling Arthur wouldn't like us to talk politics in your office."

"Your feeling is correct, Mike," said Joe. "I'll meet you there after lunch. I'm having lunch there."

"Great! The more casual the better. I'll eat at the round table and then you and I can have our meeting accidentally-on-purpose."

At about 1:45 the next afternoon Henry Laubach said he would have to get back to his office, and Joe said he wanted to have a look at the New York papers. With Henry safely out of the club Mike joined Joe.

"Joe, I'll be blunt," said Mike. "The time has come for me to talk of many things, and they all concern you. I could fill you up with a lot of high-sounding phrases about the good of the party, and good citizenship, but we wouldn't have been friends so long if you didn't trust me, and you trust me because I've always been pretty darn frank with you. Am I right?"

"I think so, Mike."

"Joe, if you say no to what I'm going to ask you, I'll accept no for your answer. If you say maybe, I'll accept maybe. If you say *yes*, I'll be overjoyed. Is that fair?"

"Seems fair."

"All right. The question: will you run for Judge of Common Pleas?"

Joe paused, then said, "No."

Mike nodded. "You have your reasons and I respect them. I won't even ask you what they are. You're the first man I've asked, and the only favor I ask of you now is, in fairness to all concerned, please keep it to yourself that I asked you. I have two other men in mind, but I wanted to ask you first. Well, that's all, Joe. Thanks for your time. Highest regards to Edith."

Mike knew when to leave, and he left. That evening he said to Peg: "Talked to Joe Chapin. I offered him a judgeship, but he wants something bigger."

"He wants to fly higher," said Peg.

"That's right, he wants to fly higher. I wonder how high he thinks he can fly."

At approximately the same moment, at 10 North Frederick Street, Joe was saying to Edith: "He offered me a judgeship and he was very nice about it when I turned him down."

"What else can he offer you?"

"Assemblyman, state senator."

"I know Mike is the state senator. Who is our assemblyman?" said Edith.

"A fellow named Harvey Goodright."

"You're not going to take that?"

"No," said Joe. "I could have been a judge, ten years. And I could resign. But I've decided something that I haven't had a chance to tell you."

"Which is?"

"No matter what Mike offers me, I'm going to refuse. All the way up to and including the governorship. He's not going to offer me the governorship, but if he did, I'd say no. Do you know what I'm going to do?"

"What?"

"I'm going to start doing all over the state what we've been doing just in this section. I don't want to have to go to meetings of the state legislature, and run for minor offices every two or four or six years, and I don't want to be buried in the courthouse. I'm going to start getting to know people all over the state, and getting myself known. That's going to take longer than two or three years, the way I want to do it, but it's going to be worth it in the long run. Look at Gifford Pinchot and his trees. I'm going to make friends all over the state. If I could arrange to be appointed to some Federal office, that would help too, but I'll have to find out what's exactly right. I'm what is usually spoken of as a deserving party man, and I've never asked for anything in return. There might be something."

"Federal? Would that mean living in Washington?"

"It wouldn't mean closing this house, if that's what you're worrying about."

"That's good."

"But I hope you won't *mind* living in Washington," said Joe, smiling.

"At the right address," said Edith.

A fortnight later, at 10 North Frederick Street.

"Did you see tonight's paper?" said Edith.

"I haven't had a chance to," said Joe. "Something interesting?"

"You'll think so. I think so," said Edith. "On the third page, the article about City Council."

Joe read the article to himself, then aloud quoted a passage from it: " 'The regular party organization is proud of the ticket submitted to the voters of Gibbsville,' said Senator Slattery. 'It is additional proof that the organization has answered the charge of party insurgents that we are afraid of new blood. The ticket contains the names of four outstanding citizens who are making their first entrance into the local political arena. *In next year's mayoralty campaign there will be further proof of the progressive policy of the regular organization when I hope to persuade Joseph B. Chapin, the well-known attorney, philanthropist and one of Gibbsville's first citizens, to run for Mayor of his native city.*' And so forth and so on."

"Did you know anything about that?" said Edith.

"I most certainly did not," said Joe. "I wonder why he did it."

"Isn't that what they mean by smoking you out?"

"Yes, but he knows I'm not going to like it," said Joe.

"Tell him so," said Edith.

"I will, but first I want to think about what I'm going to say. I'll go upstairs and lie in the tub for a while."

He soaked for a quarter of an hour, toweled himself, and telephoned Mike Slattery.

"Mike, I imagine you were expecting this call. This is Joe Chapin."

"Good evening, Joe. You mean the article in tonight's *Standard?*"

"I mean the article in tonight's *Standard*," said Joe.

"I trust you were pleased with it," said Mike.

"Pleased with it? Why should I be? Mike, that's taking liberties that I haven't given you permission to take. I'm not in politics, except for serving on the county committee. You must have realized that when I turned down the Common Pleas job."

"I thought you'd be pleased, Joe. I wouldn't do anything to offend you, you know that. You're too good a friend and too valuable a man in the party. All I did was think out loud, dream out loud, you might say."

"Then you must have been smoking opium, Mike. You haven't the slightest reason to think I'd run for mayor or anything else. I refused the judgeship, and that's a high honor, higher than mayor, in my estimation."

264

"Well, I'm very sorry, Joe. I guess I could get Bob Hooker to print a retraction, although that's going to make me look like a slob."

"Never mind the retraction. I could get Bob Hooker to retract it myself. We'll let the matter die down of its own accord. But in future, before you nominate me for public office, I hope you'll consult me first. And I'd appreciate it if you would call Arthur and tell *him* the story is out of whole cloth. I haven't heard from him, but he's going to be just as amazed as I was."

"I'll do that as soon as we hang up," said Mike. "But there's one promise I won't make, Joe."

"What's that?"

"I'm not going to give up trying to persuade you to run for office. We need you."

"That's very nice, but *persuade* me, don't do it by way of announcing it in the *Standard*."

"No hard feelings, Joe?"

"Well, they'll probably soften up."

They said their good-byes.

Edith, who had been listening to Joe, nodded. "Very good," she said.

"It *is* good. Do you know why? Because now I'll be able to do something I've wanted to do and didn't know how. I'm going to Washington and see about a Federal appointment." He lit a cigarette. "Does What's Her Name, the society editor—"

"Lydia Faunce Brown," said Edith.

"Does she still call you for news?"

"About once a week."

"Regularly?"

"Quite regularly. Tomorrow or next day it's time for her next call. Why?"

"When she calls, tell her quite casually that Mr. and Mrs. Joseph B. Chapin expect to spend a few days next week in Philadelphia. Shopping. Business."

"Philadelphia?" said Edith.

"Well, it's on the way to Washington, but we don't have to tell her everything," said Joe. "If Mike can use the *Standard*, so can I."

"Joe, you're very clever," said Edith.

"Well, don't say it with such surprise. There are hidden resources in me that even you don't know about, Edith."

"Then it's all right for me to be surprised."

"Touché," said Joe.

Joe deliberately made no appointment with the U. S. Senator from Pennsylvania. "You go have a look at the cherry blossoms," he told Edith. "I'm going to beard the lion in his den."

"It's the wrong time for the cherry blossoms."

"I hope it's not the wrong time for the Senator."

He went to the Senator's office and was told that the Senator was not seeing anyone without an appointment. The secretary, an intelligent-looking woman of middle age, was immediately aware that the caller was not a pest or a time-waster, but a handsome gentleman in well-cut clothes. "Would you take in my card?"

"I'd be glad to, but I can't hold out any hope that the Senator will see you, sir."

He handed her his card:

Mr. Joseph Benjamin Chapin
Gibbsville, Pennsylvania

She looked at it and quickly looked up at him. "Oh, Mr. Chapin. The Lantenengo County Committee, is that right?"

"Thank you, yes," said Joe.

She stepped into the Senator's office, and came back in less than a minute.

"The Senator would like very much to see you for five minutes," she said.

The man behind the large desk was white-haired but with a comparatively unlined face. He rose to shake hands with Joe. "Mr. Chapin, this is a long-delayed pleasure."

"Thank you, Senator. I'll try not to take up too much of your time."

"Well, I'd like nothing better than to have a nice leisurely chat with you, but I'm going to be needed on the floor very shortly. How are things in the coal regions?"

"Well, the strike hasn't helped us any."

"No. A mess. That union has gotten out of hand. But of course don't quote me," he said with a smile. "Do you see much of my old friend Billy English?"

"Oh, yes. Our family doctor, and a close friend of ours."

"Billy was a fraternity brother of mine at Lafayette. I believe you're a Princeton man?"

"Oh, no, sir. The *higher* seat of learning, in New Haven."

"Forgive me, forgive me. Now you have the advantage, what can I do to make amends?"

"I'm looking for a job," said Joe.

"Well, those words have a familiar ring, but I have a feeling that Chapin of McHenry & Chapin doesn't want to be appointed postmaster of—whatever the smallest town in Lantenengo is."

"No, the time may come, but not now. The kind of job I have in mind would be on some Federal commission that would preferably keep me in our own Commonwealth."

"I see," said the Senator. "A man in your circumstances usually wants to be made ambassador—London, Paris, or Rome. I'm glad to hear that you're not anxious to supplant the incumbents in those posts."

"They're quite safe, Senator."

"Good. Have you got any one commission in mind, or a specific job?"

"No, sir," said Joe.

"Well, there are some commissions, like Interstate Commerce, that are tough jobs. Then there are others like Battle Monuments that are more or less honorary. The pay varies, too."

"The pay isn't an important factor."

"Then I imagine what you have in mind *is* more of an honorary type."

"But not just sitting with my hands folded."

"Of course not," said the Senator. "You want to serve the country, and our state, in some worthwhile capacity as a Federal appointee. Is that about it?"

"I think that's well put, sir," said Joe.

"Well, I have all sorts of charts and tables of appointive offices, most of them filled, but vacancies do occur, and there may be one or two right now. How long are you going to be in Washington?"

"I'd planned to go back tomorrow."

"It would take me a week or so to see what there is, so would you like me to write you a letter some time next week or the week after, telling you what there is, and then we can get together again? Does that suit you?"

"Very much, Senator. Suits me to a T."

"Good," said the Senator. He rose, held out his hand. "Mrs. Chapin. She was a Laubach, if I'm not mistaken?"

Joe smiled. "A Stokes, but the Laubachs are also two of our best friends."

"Oh, dear. Two mistakes out of two tries. I ought to watch my step or I'll be out of politics."

"Not if I can help it," said Joe.

"What a gracious reply! *Thank* you, Mr. Chapin. This *has* been a pleasure."

Joe, a smiling man, left a smiling man. But Joseph B. Chapin had made his first serious political mistake.

"Joe? Mike Slattery. I'd like to have a word with you. I can come right over if you're free."

In a few minutes Mike appeared in Joe's office. He closed the door and placed his fedora on top of a case of law books.

"Joe, you know enough about mining to know what a pillar-robber is, don't you?"

"Yes, of course," said Joe.

"What is it?"

"A man who pulls out timbers and the coal falls down for lack of support."

"Correct. It's a dangerous job, highly paid."

"All right, Mike. What's on your mind?" said Joe.

"Do you have to go all the way to Washington, D. C., to be a pillar-robber?"

"Who do you think you're talking to, Mike?"

"I'm talking to a man with political ambitions. I'm talking to a man that goes behind my back to *further* his own political ambitions. I'm talking to a man that I could help, and that I offered to help. I'm talking to a man that goes out of his way to weaken the support of an organization that I built up. I'm talking to a man that pretends to be aloof from dirty politics, but that doesn't seem to need any lessons from me. Now what have you got to say?"

"I say you can get the hell out of my office," said Joe.

"I'm gone before you can say Inland Waterways Commission, Mr. Machiavelli."

He picked up his hat and was gone.

And thus ended Joe Chapin's chance of a Federal appointment, even to the postmastership of the smallest village in Lantenengo County.

"It probably was a mistake," said Edith.

"Yes," said Joe. "But the Senator never brought up Mike's name."

"But neither did you."

"I never intended to."

"Well, Mike is jealous of his power and he'd like people to think nothing can be done without his say-so."

"Yes, and with good reason," said Joe.

"Are you going to give up?"

"Oh, no. You ought to know me better than that. I made a mistake, but I may have learned something from it. So far, except for my mistake, we've been successful. Look, Edith. We thought up the idea of appearing more actively in community affairs, and what happened? Mike Slattery offered me a judgeship that most lawyers would give their eye teeth for. I didn't have to say a word to him. He came to me. Well, I repeat, I can do the same kind of thing all over the state and perhaps somebody bigger than Mike Slattery will come to me the way Mike did. In any event, I'll do the state-wide thing and see what happens."

"You could give away a million dollars and it wouldn't be noticed in a state as big as Pennsylvania."

"I'm not going to give away a million dollars. I wouldn't like that, and neither would you. No, the charity scheme is too expensive for state-wide purposes. But for instance, the County Bar Association has been wanting me to serve on this or that committee and I've always turned them down because—I was selfish or lazy. But it would be the easiest thing in the world for me to get on a county committee, then state, and state would give me the opportunity to go everywhere and meet hundreds of lawyers and politicians. And they're often the same. Very few of the important politicians that aren't lawyers."

"I'm glad you're not giving up," said Edith. "This new scheme is going to mean a lot of traveling."

"It is, but you won't have to go. I *will* ask you to go to some of the conventions, where the lawyers take their wives, but the usual run of meetings are stag. And not stag parties, either. If they were, more men would take an interest."

Joe attended the next meeting of the County Bar Association, which was held in Odd Fellows Hall. Those present were the principal officers of the Association and fewer than twenty-five per cent of the eligible members; old men, with time on their hands, and young men hoping to rub elbows with the powerful, and the mediocrities of all ages who had time on their hands and wanted to rub elbows with the powerful. It was the first of several such meetings which Joe attended, never explaining his presence, and he was the least surprised man in the room when he found himself appointed to several more or less imposing committees. And he graciously consented when he was asked if he would accept appointments as a delegate to the regional and state conventions. It was easy: some of the lawyers could not afford the trips, even with travel and hotel bills paid, and those who could well afford the expense could not afford the time. Joe had forgotten about the delegate appointments. It was much simpler and less committing to get appointed delegate than to hold actual office in the Bar Association, and suited his purpose more neatly.

For two whole years he went to meetings and conferences and conventions. Joe was a man who could smoke a big cigar and tell a dirty story without quite becoming one of the boys. And his brothers-at-the-bar did not want him to become one of the boys. In his well-cut clothes, day or evening, and with his figure and his—as more than one man said—snotty good looks, he *graced* the meetings, added tone to the profession, made many of its members secretly proud. At the state conventions men as well as women asked who he was, out of mere curiosity caused by his physical appearance. Moreover—and this was something Joe could not have anticipated—each man, each woman, thought he was discovering Joe Chapin, "of McHenry & Chapin, one of the best firms in Gibbsville, Lantenengo County." Before the two years were up, many men had wondered aloud why Joe Chapin was not in politics. The ready answer, distressingly enough, was that he did not need the money.

Joe and Edith had counted on his getting to know lawyers and politicians. As an almost inevitable consequence of his presence at professional get-togethers, the Chapins were being invited to social functions in widespread sections of the Commonwealth. They could not accept all invitations, but there were some that they did not feel they should refuse. It is a large state, a rich state that has had money for a long time, and within its boundaries there are many large and comfortable homes, with many forms of social activity, from symphony orchestras to cock-fights, from Quaker weddings to bear hunts. It was no surprise—and no great treat—when they were invited to spend a week-end with the Governor at his private lodge in the mountains. The men played poker, which Joe had not played since Yale days, and the women played bridge, at which Edith did not excel. They were looked over at a country home in Sewickley, and at a farm in Lehigh County; and Joe played golf in at least a third of the state's sixty-seven counties. He bought a Buick phaeton, a sporty enough car, but safely a middle-class Buick. Professional politicians went in for the Daniels and the Cunningham, the Packard and the Locomobile, the Peerless and the Cadillac, and Joe had the Pierce-Arrow in the garage, but he left it there during his campaigning. No use flaunting the trappings of wealth when the Buick got you there just the same.

Edith was well satisfied with the way things were going. She subscribed to a clipping bureau, which provided some record of Joe's activities and a measure of their success. She was pleased when Joe was referred to as the prominent, or distinguished, or well-known Gibbsville attorney, but she had no objection when he was also referred to as a leading figure in Republican political circles, particularly since he did not have, and did not attempt to have, official connection with the party other than his membership on the county committee. Joe had no organization as such, but he was unquestionably building up a personal following. It was a long, long way from present accomplishment to ultimate goal, but except for the one *faux pas* with the Senator, Joe was proceeding steadily. He made no major move without consulting her, and she was taking a proper pride in his progress when she had a terrifying visit from an old friend.

It was the summer of 1927 and, as usual, the Chapins were living on the farm. Joe was away on one of his golfing trips, but Ann, on vacation from Miss Holton's, and Joby, on holiday from Gibbsville Country Day, were keeping their mother company in their father's absence. Ann had reached the stage at which she was the first to answer every ring of the telephone, and on one hot afternoon in late July she came back to the porch with the flat announcement that the call was for Mother.

"Do you know who it is?" said Edith, rising.

"They didn't say. A female voice," said Ann.

Edith took the call in the living room. "Hello?"

"Edith, this is Barbara Danworth. Do you remember me?"

"Who? I'm sorry," said Edith.

"Barbara Danworth. Miss Hannah Payne's School?"

"Barbara *Dan*worth. Yes, why, hello, Barbara. Where are you?"

"Not very far from you. I'm telephoning from a garage in Swedish Haven. I'd like very much to see you."

"Well, of course," said Edith. "Do you know how to get here?"

"The garage man said it isn't hard to find. I have a friend with me, an English girl, and if it's okay with you we'll be over in about half an hour."

Barbara Danworth. Someone who had gone on living, and getting older, in spite of Edith's memory of her, which was of a girl of fourteen at Miss Hannah Payne's School; a passionate and passionately devoted little thing who must now be thirty-nine. And she called herself Barbara Danworth, which could but did not necessarily mean that she had not married.

Barbara and her friend arrived in a red roadster of a foreign make that Edith could not identify. The top was down and the two women were wind- and sunburned. In the face of the woman at the wheel there were enough of Barbara Danworth's features to be recognizable, but when she got out of the car she was a stocky woman in a rumpled seersucker dress, with a man's wristwatch and a beret and saddle-strap shoes. Her companion, the English girl, was thin and handsome, rather sharp-nosed, and wearing a tennis dress and blue espadrilles and a crowded bangle bracelet. She too was wearing a beret, which she removed as soon as the car stopped so that she could ruffle and smooth her long blond hair. She was aged somewhere between twenty-five and thirty.

Edith shook hands with Barbara, who said: "This is Veronica Plaisted."

"How do you do," said Edith.

"Hajja do," said Miss Plaisted. They did not shake hands. The girl immediately began searching the landscape with a level, turning glance that seemed to take in everything without being affected by anything.

"We're on our way to Murray Bay," said Barbara.

"It's a song, d'you see? 'We're on our way, to Murray Bay'?" said Miss Plaisted.

"We just landed a week ago and we went to pay our respects to the family on the Eastern Shore, and now we're going to look in on some cousins of Veronica's."

"Canadians. Do you know any Canadians, Mrs. Chapin?"

"No, I don't think so," said Edith.

"Nor I. I've no idea what they'll be like," said Miss Plaisted. "I say, could I wash?"

"I was just going to show you," said Edith. "Then would you like a cup of tea?"

"I'd rather have a gin and something, if you've no objection. *And* if you have the gin."

"Gin and soda?" said Edith.

"Gin and almost anything, barring Co-cah Co-lah," said Miss Plaisted.

"Gin and soda, then. I'll take you upstairs," said Edith.

"Please don't. I'll find my way. I adore to be nosy in other people's houses."

"Barbara?" said Edith.

"I went at the garage," said Barbara heartily.

Miss Plaisted went exploring and Edith and Barbara looked at each other with great frankness. "A long time," said Barbara. "A long time ago."

"I've often thought of you," said Edith.

"And I you," said Barbara. "How do you like married life?"

"What a strange question, after eighteen years of it," said Edith.

"Is it so strange?" said Barbara. "I didn't think you *would* marry. I was surprised when you did."

"And very happily," said Edith. "Two children. A girl sixteen and a boy twelve."

"How old is your husband?"

"Joe is forty-five," said Edith.

"Where is he now?"

"Right now he's at Montrose, Montrose, P A, playing golf. We've become golfers," said Edith. "Tell me about you."

"About me? Well, you have eyes," said Barbara.

Edith nodded slowly.

"I got married when I was nineteen," said Barbara. "I'm afraid the poor fellow had a bad time, but then so did I. It was an ideal arrangement from the point of view of both families, but I couldn't stick it, and he was cheated. We tried to make a go of it for almost two years, and then *I* went to his father and told him the truth."

"You did?"

"We had a very quiet divorce. Since then I've lived most of the time abroad. My family are just as well pleased to have me keep out of sight. When I paid my call last week I had to put Veronica in a hotel. In Europe they take us for granted. They don't *like* us, but at least they don't *stare* the way they do in the States."

"I suppose they do," said Edith.

"I was hoping I could get a look at your husband, but after I called you I wondered. Some married couples tell each other everything under the sun. Did you?"

"No," said Edith.

"Then it would have been all right if he'd been here?"

"Oh, yes," said Edith.

"How about other men?" said Barbara.

"Other men?" said Edith.

"Whether you realize it or not, you've answered my question. Does your husband know?"

"Know what, Barbara?"

"That you've had affairs with other men?"

"But I haven't had affairs with other men," said Edith.

"Have it your own way," said Barbara. "It must be still going on, but I don't blame you for being protective. You have no reason to trust me."

"Do *you* tell everything under the sun?" said Edith.

"You mean does Veronica know about you and me? She guessed it."

"Did you help her to guess?" said Edith.

"She guessed, and I admitted it."

"Don't you think you could have just as easily *not* admitted it?"

"And lied to her? I've never lied to her, in four years."

"What would you do if she lied to you?"

"She has, and I've kicked her out, but she always comes back. Not only for the money, either. I think she'll always come back to me."

"Aren't you ever worried about her going off with some man?"

Barbara laughed merrily. "That one? Men are her competition. She might leave me, but it wouldn't be for a man."

"I guess I'm very ignorant. We don't see much of that sort of thing here."

"Now don't be haughty, Edith. Don't be a one hundred per cent American. Remember, you started me, 'way back at Hannah Payne's School, and you'd never been anywhere but Gibbsville, Pennsylvania."

Edith made no reply.

"But don't worry. I'm sure if it hadn't been you, it would have been someone else. I wonder what's happening to Ronnie?"

"I'll go see," said Edith.

"Let me, I'll call her," said Barbara. She did so, and there was no answer, and Edith heard Barbara's heavy footsteps on the stairway and in the upstairs rooms. "No sign of her," she said, when she came back.

"She may have gone for a walk," said Edith.

"Then let's us go for a walk."

They left the porch and headed for the dam, and long before they reached the dam they saw Miss Plaisted standing on the breast of the dam, her arm about Ann's shoulders, and intently listening to what Ann had to say.

The two women stopped. "I *see*," said Barbara. "Is that your kid?"

"Yes, it is my kid," said Edith. "I want you to take your friend and go away from here as fast as possible. Don't make a fuss, but I want you to leave here this instant."

274

"You bet I will," said Barbara. *"Ronnie!"*

Miss Plaisted, startled, turned away from Ann, hastily withdrawing her arm. "Yes, Bobbie?"

"I'm ready," said Barbara.

"Com-ming," Miss Plaisted called. She smiled at the girl and they shook hands, and Miss Plaisted left her. She once again searched the landscape, never looking in the direction of Edith and Barbara.

"Make any explanation you like," said Edith. "But I don't want to have to speak to her. Good-bye, Barbara."

"Good-bye, Edith. I'll give her hell, you be sure of that."

On an impulse Edith kissed Barbara, then hurried away.

Barbara and her friend went directly to the car, and from a living-room window Edith watched them as the car made the circle at the end of the driveway. Barbara, she could see, was talking angrily to her friend, who was calmly smoothing down her blond hair and putting on her beret. When the car left the Chapins' lane Edith went upstairs and got into her bathing suit and joined her daughter at the dam.

"Is it cold?" said Edith.

"Not so very," said Ann.

"How did you like Miss Plaisted?" said Edith.

"Was that her name? She just said Ronnie. *I'm Ronnie* is how she introduced herself. She was English, wasn't she?"

"I believe so. A friend of a girl I went to school with."

"At Hannah Payne's?"

"Yes," said Edith.

"Oh, I didn't like her or dislike her. Did they go?"

"Yes. Too bad you couldn't meet my friend, but they were in a hurry," said Edith.

"What was your friend's name?"

"Barbara Danworth. I haven't seen her since I was your age."

"Miss Whatever-Her-Name-Was Ronnie wanted to go for a stroll, but I told her there were snakes and she said she wasn't afraid of snakes but I said *I* was. I'll bet she never saw one of the big rattlers, and she'd never heard of copperheads."

"What else did you talk about?" said Edith.

"Nothing. She asked me how old I was, and when I told her she said I looked older. That was all. She said she had a great friend in Italy my age. I didn't care whether she had a friend in Italy." Ann was abruptly silent.

"What are you thinking? Something else she said?"

"Oh, I didn't like her."

275

"You didn't? Why?"

"Something else she said," said Ann.

"What? Tell me. They've gone, and I'm quite sure they'll never be back."

"It's none of her business."

"What isn't?"

"Oh, she said to me, 'You know you have glorious fronts.' Do you know what fronts are? Here." The girl dived and swam under and above the water, and Edith knew that she was doing it to put an end to conversation.

The irony of the unrealized threat was as frightening a part of it as any of the facts, and Edith felt punishment—or a strong enough threat of it to be the same—of a Divinely ironic nature. If the Deity wanted to mete out an elaborate and belated punishment, that was the way He would do it. She came back from her swim without the absolution she had hoped the cold water would give her, and she was glad that Joe was miles away from her, removed from the panicky confession she might have made if he had been near. It was not so much a fear of the severity of his judgment; he was tolerant enough of all aberrations, since he had been affected (so he complacently believed) by none of them. But an outburst of revelation was something she had avoided all her life, simply because utter frankness was not in her nature. *Why* it was not in her nature was not a secret she kept from herself: she gave only what she had to give, to get more in return. A revelation of her old relationship with Barbara would have been greater than any admission she could have got in return, for Joe had long ago admitted that in prep school he and other boys had watched each other masturbate. She had not matched his rather mild confession with any admission of her own (and he had accepted her claim of total purity). Now, at this late date, to have to admit the totality of her schoolgirl affair and the year's time it lasted, would have been to give Joe some kind of advantage that she had resisted giving him all her life. He was a man, her husband, who would hold it over her even now, and she would be compelled to relinquish some of that ownership of him that she needed for her soul. But most dangerous of all— if anything had happened to Ann. If through that ugly irony anything had happened to Ann, Joe's revenge on Edith would have been as calculated and as thorough as his love for the child was complete and instinctive. In the recent years of his going after the prize he wanted, he had, without knowing it, gained new respect from Edith. The travel, the conversations with new acquaintances, the maintenance of

276

an attitude, all were chores or partook of the nature of chores. They were demanding, making demands on his patience, his good nature, and on his strength. But he made himself perform the tasks because he had an objective. If his objective were the punishment of his wife, he could call upon the same kind of reserves; the persistence and even the physical resources that would enable him to achieve her painful destruction. She was thankful (without quite being grateful) that Joe was away in Montrose and safe from her desperate candor. She would be all right again in the morning, she knew, but she also knew she was in for a bad night. And insanely, crazily inconsistently, she realized she was wishing she could talk to Lloyd Williams. There was no one else she wanted to turn to, but Edith of the good sense had the good sense not to turn to him.

After the children were in bed and the house was quiet for the night and she was alone with herself, she wondered whether she might not be getting a little afraid of Joe. If that were so, Joe was in danger. She had always been suspicious and mistrustful of the world, but she never had been afraid of anyone before. She had always been able to despise people without being afraid of them.

At the corner of Christiana and Main, Barbara's red Fiat was halted by the traffic light.

Peg Slattery, crossing Christiana Street, said to her seventeen-year-old daughter Margaret: "Look at those freaks."

"The younger one is pretty," said Margaret.

In Veronica Plaisted's characteristic, evenly semi-circular search of the pedestrians' faces, the one face that stopped her, for perhaps two seconds, was the face of Margaret Slattery, the embodiment of innocence.

The traffic light changed, the red Fiat moved on.

It must not be inferred that during the two years of Joe Chapin's travels about the state, he and Mike Slattery were, in Mike's phrase, on the outs with each other. Within a few weeks of his being shown the door out of Joe's office Mike was collecting money for the party. He saw Joe at the Gibbsville Club and went to him.

"Joe, can I put you down for the same as last year?" said Mike.

"Why, yes, Mike."

"Maybe a little more?" said Mike.

"No more, but no less," said Joe.

Although the two men were momentarily alone, the conversation was conducted almost as though others were present.

"Thank you, Joe. I'm glad there's no hard feelings."

"None whatever," said Joe.

"Once in a while it's good for a couple of friends to fly off the handle. It clears the atmosphere, instead of letting the thing fester. Thank you for the contribution, and if you want to know something, I had you down for it. It's a kind of a compliment. Only a small man would withhold his contribution, and you're not that."

"Thank you, Mike."

"And I'm not soft-soaping you."

"Of course you are, but I don't mind it," said Joe.

Although Mike Slattery was quick and shrewd, and, oftener than not, accurate in his judgments of men, there were some subtleties that escaped him. He was ready and willing to admit the differences between himself and Joe Chapin. He did not pretend to be a society man, a blueblood, an aristocrat—any of the things he would call Joe Chapin. In their judgments of Mike, many men made the mistake of forgetting that Mike wanted power, and not the badges of power. Men wasted valuable time in wondering about what Mike wanted because they thought he must want what they themselves wanted. For example, Mike made many more trips throughout the state than Joe Chapin made, but Mike's trips were furtive, stealthy excursions, with their purpose achieved in offices and hotel rooms and private residences, and no mention whatever in the newspapers. His driver, Ed Markovich, wore a felt hat and a business suit on their trips. Mike owned a succession of automobiles—Packards, Studebakers, Cadillacs —but he never owned the typical politician's limousine. He always bought sedans, and they were always black. Unless he wanted to take a nap on a long ride, Mike would ride on the front seat with Ed so they would look like two businessmen, not chauffeur and employer. (And Ed might conveniently be mistaken for the owner.) The hotel rooms often were taken under Ed's name rather than Mike's, and telephone calls almost always were made by Mr. Markovich. It was Mike's theory that the job of state senator was one that gave a man standing, got him a title, but was not a job that many people wanted. He believed that after a man had served in the lower house of Legislature, he went home and tried to get nomination for Congress. If he was content to stay in the State Assembly he probably was lazy or actually or potentially a thief. And since Mike was the man who usually put the fellow in the Assembly, the fellow had the good sense

278

or the gratitude not to go after the only job Mike wanted. It was no disgrace to be a senator and continue to be one for one term after another. But Mike's power was not, of course, limited to his legislative vote. His power was a personal attribute: first of all, his word could be relied on, except when there was a policy switch for tactical purposes, and such switches did not come under the head of the doublecross. In the second place, Mike was persuasive with a gift for making the object of his conversational attentions feel important, and accompanying the gift was a certain sincerity; Mike liked to talk to people. Thirdly, he was humorous and sociable and he created the illusion of sentimentality, although in fact there was room in his heart only for his family and his Church. In the fourth place, he was clean; he shaved every day, he bathed every day, his linen was clean, his shoes were polished; and his speech was clean and unprofane. His virility was never in question, but his record with women was spotless, and he had never taken a drink in his entire life. But he laughed at dirty stories and he had a bartender's knowledge of and willingness to serve liquor. Fifth, he played the piano, and could carry a tune in his true tenor. Sixth, he had a good memory for faces and names and figures, and what he did not remember he knew how to find out. And the memory was not limited to people and things that were pleasant to remember. And, finally, it was almost impossible to deceive him about men's motives. He was a practicing skeptic, although a patient one, who would listen while a man lied and wait until the man was ready with the truth.

Mike had a working understanding of the mind of Joe Chapin, and where he failed of complete understanding was in the inability to sense that Joe was just as vindictive as *he* was. No matter how long they lived, no matter how closely they might work together or what gestures of friendship they might make, the fact, which Mike missed, was that Joe was incapable of pardoning Mike's impertinence in the scene after Joe's fruitless trip to Washington.

Peg had warned him. "Don't take your eye off Joe Chapin," she said. "You treated him as if you were bawling out a Hunky ward-captain, and nobody ever treated him that way before, that I'll guarantee you. I'll bet those nostrils were quivering. In olden days he would have hit you with a riding whip."

He had worried along those lines himself, but he would not admit as much to Peg. When the meeting at the club came to pass so nicely, he was sure Peg was unduly alarmed. But he followed her advice: he kept his eye on Joe Chapin.

Mike's friends all over the state informed him of Joe's appearances, and Mike did not deceive himself that Joe had developed an overwhelming passion for golf or the legal profession. But Joe's refusal of the judgeship and his haughty behavior in the Gibbsville mayoralty matter, and the fact that Joe had sought an appointive job from Washington—all made Mike believe that Joe would not seek the mandate of the people. Joe was up to something, of that there could be no doubt; but whatever it was, he must have learned that if it was political, he would finally have to come to Mike. In the meantime, Mike got reports as to the dates and places on Joe's itineraries, against the day they might be useful. He could, he knew, have asked Joe point-blank, or more adroitly questioned him as to the meaning of the trips. But he would no more have expected a forthright answer from Joe than he would from Mr. Coolidge, who was refusing to say what he really meant when he said he did not *choose* to run. If you went back far enough, Joe was a New England Yankee too, and probably could be just as stubborn and uncommunicative as the President. Mike wished he knew what Joe wanted if only because he wished he knew what his own answer would be. There would be almost as much pleasure to be had in granting Joe a big favor as in turning him down.

Gibbsville Country Day was in the tradition of the private school that prepared the sons of gentlemen for preparatory school. It was possible to stay at G.C.D. from the fifth grade through senior high-school year, but almost no boy did so. In Buffalo there was Nichols; in Pittsburgh, Shady Side; in Wilmington, Tower Hill; in New York, Buckley and Allen-Stevenson. In Gibbsville the well-born boy went to Miss Holton's until it was time to go to G.C.D., remaining there until it was time to acquire the polish and the label of Andover, Hotchkiss, Lawrenceville, The Hill, Mercersburg—among Gibbsville parents, the most popular of the noted prep schools. Gibbsville alone could not have supported a G.C.D., but it attracted the sons of the quality from the nearby mining and farming towns, and it struggled along year after year, with the annual deficits made up by private subscription by men who believed in the private-school idea. Scholastically, G.C.D. was sometimes a little better and never any worse than the public grammar and high schools. It did not field a representative football team (which was in its favor with the mothers) but it had a baseball team that played, and was always beaten by, Gibbsville High and the high schools of the nearby towns. Once or twice in a decade G.C.D. would beat G.H.S. in a dual track meet, and there were always some good tennis players at G.C.D., but the boys were aware that in most team sports they were outmanned by the public schools. The students of G.C.D. were known to the public-school boys and girls as Willie-Boys and Sissies, and the only support they got was from their sisters and cousins at Miss Holton's; but it probably did no harm to have G.C.D. take its beatings from G.H.S., and it probably did no harm when a G.C.D. boy gave a G.H.S. boy a bloody nose. It balanced things to have the rich reminded that they were outnumbered and to have the poor reminded that a rich boy could also use his fists.

The original G.C.D. building was a converted mansion at 16th and Christiana, once the home of the Rutter family, of the Rutter Brewery. When Jacob Rutter built his house he bought a block of land, with a stand of trees, and he had what amounted to a private park within the borough limits of Gibbsville. The Rutter line died out with Jacob and for more than a year the house was not occupied, until the gentlemen who were organizing Gibbsville Academy, predecessor of G.C.D., bought the property. Half of the block was promptly sold for middle-class home sites, leaving adequate grounds for the school.

Joby Chapin was in one of the last classes to start at the Rutter house, just before the school removed to the new plant farther out on West Christiana Street. The school made real estate money on the move to the new plant, which had all modern facilities, and there was even some talk about making G.C.D. a boarding school, but the objections were too numerous and the enthusiasm too slight. Classes always got smaller after the first high-school year, when the boys were usually sent to the established prep schools. By the time a boy reached senior high-school year his class was so depleted that he was practically being tutored, which would have meant an expensive education if the teachers had been better paid.

The trustees of Gibbsville Country Day would have liked an Oxon. or a Cantab. for headmaster of the school, a pipe-smoker with a blazer and with cricket in his conversation. But Fred M. Koenig had his defenders. Frederick Miller Koenig, as his name eventually appeared in the *Daybook*, the school annual, had gone to Kutztown Normal for two years, taught for two years for money to pay his college bills, graduated cum laude and Phi Beta Kappa from Lafayette, which was an acceptable college; taken his M.A. at Princeton, which gave him a Big Three label; and had been a lieutenant in the Service of Supply in France (which gave him an army record and some European travel). He was teaching English and French at Gibbsville High when he received the call from Gibbsville Country Day, a call to which he responded with dignified alacrity. He was a Reading boy, who had met his bride-to-be at Normal, and since his bride-to-be was the daughter of the third largest grocery store in Gibbsville, the post at Gibbsville High had always been on his mind and in the mind of his father-in-law. The Country Day job meant $200 above the high-school pay, but more desirable than that was the quick prestige.

Fred Koenig's strongest supporter on the G.C.D. board was Joe Chapin, who had originally been in favor of a Rhodes Scholar, any Rhodes Scholar. But when none was to be had, Joe suggested they look into Koenig's record, Koenig having been suggested to Joe by his father-in-law, F. W. Huntzinger, a McHenry & Chapin client and one of the most respectable Lutherans in Lantenengo County. Koenig always remembered that Joe Chapin had been his sponsor, and when Koenig took over at G.C.D., Joby was marked for special consideration. Indeed, for *special* special consideration, for as Joe Chapin's son, Joby was automatically special, without Joe's intercession in Koenig's behalf.

Koenig was always so careful not to show any favoritism that he became self-conscious about it. He would pass Joby in one of the halls, and say "Good morning, Chapin," so stiffly that a duller boy than Joby would have sensed the self-consciousness. And Joby was not a dull boy. He had long since learned the relative positions of the citizens of Gibbsville: there were people like Harry and Marian Jackson, who worked for the family but were not afraid of you. There were people like Uncle Arthur and Aunt Rose McHenry, who gave you presents, but did not care much about you one way or the other. You stood up when they came in the room. There was Uncle Cartie Stokes, to whom Harry and Marian were respectful, but to whom your father was not respectful. There was Peter Kemp, the farmer, who worked all the time and worked for your father and mother but to whom your father and mother were respectful, not in the same way that Harry and Marian were respectful to Uncle Cartie, but still in a different way from the way your father and mother were polite to Harry and Marian. There were the people in the Main Street stores: if they did not know your name, they treated you like just another kid: if they knew your name they called you Mister Chapin, although you were only twelve or thirteen years old. There were men and women, usually older than your father and mother, who liked all children. And there were people like Mr. Koenig, who was known to be fair, but whose treatment of you was cold and almost rude while at the same time he was a little afraid you would think he was cold or rude. In a boys' school the reputation for fairness is a master's greatest asset, greater than a reputation for efficiency ("he knows his subject") or for jolly good fellowship or even for athletic prowess. Among the boys at G.C.D., Mr. Koenig was said to be strict but fair, but Joby did not agree. Mr. Koenig was strict but the fairness was doubtful.

When Joby was called to the principal's office for a lecture, Mr. Koenig would tell the boy about what a fine family the Chapin family were, what high hopes they had for him, what ability he had if it was only directed in the proper channels—and end up without meting out the punishment Joby had been expecting. For certain infractions of the rules a boy could expect to be kept in during recess or after school, but for the same infractions Joby would get a lecture. And Joby knew it, and so did his schoolmates.

Then in 1927-28, the school year, when a more serious offense was committed, Joby was overpunished, for the word had reached Koenig that he was being overlenient with Joby.

"Take your hands out of your pocket," said Mr. Koenig. "What's this I hear about you smoking a cigarette in the toilet?"

"I don't know, sir."

"You *don't know?* What kind of talk is that, you don't know?"

"I don't know what you heard, sir," said Joby.

"Oh, you want to be fresh," said Mr. Koenig. "You think because we've been lenient out of consideration for your parents, you think you're lord and master around here. Well, you're not, Chapin. You're not. Where did you buy the cigarettes?"

"I didn't buy them, I took them from my father's box."

"What would he say if he knew you were stealing cigarettes out of his private box?"

"I don't know," said Joby.

"Well, I think I do. He'd say you were a thief as well as a smoker."

"No he wouldn't. He wouldn't call me a thief."

"Isn't that what you are?" said Mr. Koenig.

". . . I don't know."

"You stole them. Isn't that what a thief does?"

"Yes."

"Yes *sir.* You're not here to receive a medal. You're here to be punished, and don't forget that. When you speak to the masters and the principal you say *sir*, you're no better than any other boy in this school and don't think for one minute that your father wants you treated any differently, because he doesn't. Your father is a fine man and one of the leading citizens of this town, and he doesn't expect any privileges for you, young man. Well?"

"Sir?"

"Well, what have you got to say for yourself?"

"I don't know, sir."

"Are you guilty, or are you not guilty? You know that much, don't you?"

"Yes, sir."

"Well, then, what are you? Guilty, or not guilty?"

"I didn't know that's what you were asking me, sir."

"What do you think I've had you in my office for? To talk about baseball?"

"No, sir."

"Then answer my question."

"*Which* question, sir? Gosh, you ask me a thousand questions, and I don't know which I'm supposed to answer."

"There's only one question. Are you guilty of smoking cigarettes in the toilet and endangering the property, the lives and property of this school?"

"I smoked. You know that, sir. I was caught."

"And I suppose if you hadn't been caught, you'd go right on smoking every day, I don't know how many times a day. Is that about the size of it?"

"I don't know, sir."

"You don't know. You—don't—know."

"*Go ahead and punish me!*"

"Just a minute, there. Just a minute. I'll punish you, don't worry about that. But don't you start giving orders around here, young Mister Chapin. I'll punish you, and you're not going to wish you hurried me. *Tried* to hurry me. You might have received the ordinary punishment for smoking, but we can't tolerate students giving orders and disrespect or we'd have a bedlam, not a school. Once we let the students give the orders around here we might as well close up shop. We won't have a school, we'll have a bedlam, that's what we'll have. All right, since you're so anxious to be punished, you can start now, as of this minute. You are suspended for one week."

"Suspended?"

"For one week. One week from tomorrow you may return to school and resume your classes."

"You mean I'm not to come to school at all?"

"I mean exactly that. An enforced vacation. And when you return you may make up the lost work, if possible. Go put your things in your locker and then leave the school and go home. I will see to it that your parents know, in case you have the mistaken idea that you are going to spend the rest of the afternoon at the moving-picture show."

"I'll flunk if I miss a week."

"You should have thought of that when you were endangering the lives and property of this school, and giving me disrespectful answers when I tried to question you. That's all, you may go."

The severity of the punishment removed the active suspicion among the other boys that Joby was a suck, their word for a teacher's pet who was liable to be an informer. But the disgrace did not have the compensating effect of making him a hero. There were too many boys in the school who did not like Joby anyway, who were glad to see Chapin get what was coming to him. No boy had ever been formally expelled from Gibbsville Country Day, although a few had abruptly transferred to boarding school. Joby's suspension therefore ranked historically among the major punishments and had the effect of convincing parents as well as students that Frederick Miller Koenig was a man of character, who had the courage to stand up against the prestige of the Chapin-Stokes clan. The unfairness of the punishment also had a curious effect on Koenig himself. He knew, without going so far as admitting it, that the punishment had been disproportionately severe and that he had acted not so much on principle as on pique at the boy's manner. It taught Koenig a lesson in self-control, but of course the person who paid for the lesson was a boy just entering his teens, and in the transcript of Joby's school record there was no credit for instructing a headmaster. It was a situation calling for a variant of the medical joke that the operation was a success but the patient died.

The episode of the suspension had the effect of opening an undeclared war between Joby and authority. It was not in Edith to question the established order and she accepted the Koenig verdict without inquiring into the justice of it. In the inevitable meeting between parents and son, behind the closed doors of Joe's den, Joby told the truth, but his account of the interview with Koenig was not phonographic and only contributed confusion. He could not remem-

285

ber exactly what Mr. Koenig had said or what he had said in reply, and Edith lost patience when the boy said: "Mother, you're just as bad as he is."

"How dare you!" said Edith.

"Look here, don't you speak that way to your mother," said Joe.

"I don't care," said the boy.

"You're going to have to be punished at home, too, I can see that," said Edith.

"I don't care! Just leave me alone," said the boy and ran out of the room.

"Really!" said Edith. "Now don't you go and be sympathetic with him. If you do, Joe, he'll never learn to obey."

"Oh, I won't," said Joe. "After all, I was the one that picked Koenig."

"I wasn't thinking of school, I was thinking of his rudeness to me. He should be getting a good spanking, he's not too old for that."

"Well, don't look at me. I'm not going to do it. If you want to, go ahead."

"You know perfectly well I won't. He's too strong. And you're too weak. Too soft with them, both of them."

"Oh, cut it out, Edith."

"All right, I'll cut it out, I won't say a word, I'll leave everything in your hands."

"You've said that before," said Joe. "Always when we have some small crisis over something that happened at school. I'm the one who was too soft with them. When everything's going well I don't hear any of these renunciations of authority, but when something happens, it's because I've been too soft with them. Maybe if I *weren't* so soft with them we wouldn't have these long periods where they seem to behave themselves."

"Seem to. You don't know everything that happens."

"Well, why don't you tell me?"

"Because you're at your office, or somewhere in the western part of the state, playing golf with your politicians."

"If I'm neglecting the children I'd like to know about it."

"Well, today's an example," said Edith. "It just happened that you were here and not in Pittsburgh when Joby was sent home from school."

"That's never happened before," said Joe.

"Not suspension, no. But other things. It isn't the first time he's been punished, or Ann either, for that matter."

"Let's confine this to Joby," said Joe.

"Suit yourself. Ann has been caught smoking too, but you weren't here to hear about that."

"I was here when I got home, and you could have told me then," said Joe.

"When it's something about Ann you don't like to listen," said Edith.

"She's sixteen," said Joe. "If what I hear is true, we're very fortunate that our daughter's worst crime is smoking. I'd be more worried about her drinking this bootleg liquor."

"Would you?"

"Yes. Are you implying that she does drink?"

"I'm not implying anything."

"Then let's get back to Joby. How do you propose to punish him? Cut off his allowance?"

"Yes, or reduce it. Cut it in two. But something else, something to do with smoking."

"Make the punishment fit the crime, the punishment fit the crime."

"If we don't, when he goes to boarding school they won't just suspend him. They'll send him home for good."

"I know," said Joe.

They agreed on cutting Joby's allowance, but they never did find an appropriate punishment for smoking, and Joby was back in school in a week's time.

While he did not return a school hero, he had become a school celebrity. "Hey, Joby, got a cigarette?" the boys would say. He had the ephemeral nickname Lucky, after the cigarette brand. He was invited to join other boys in a smoke and he accepted the invitation if it did not mean smoking on school property. By degrees he became identified with the rebellious element, who were also the physically unattractive: the pimply, the fat, the bespectacled. There was a boy who was a source of supply for obscene versions of comic-strip characters; another boy who often got into bed with a house-maid; another boy who prowled the woods looking for embracing lovers; another boy who frequently carried a loaded .25 automatic; another boy who always had money provided by a middle-aged gardener. The last-mentioned boy said that the other boys could make fifty cents any time they wanted to, and it would not hurt but kind of tickle. But a boy who had once taken up the offer said that

287

that was not all the gardener wanted, and the offer was closed when the gardener was sent to prison, where he hanged himself, and the boy sent to a distant boarding school where there were other boys who had known generous gardeners. The departure of the gardener and the boy was a fortunate accident for Joby, whose allowance had been cut to half of the fifty cents he might have earned from the gardener. On a quarter a week he was even more in debt than usual to Ann, Marian, his Uncle Cartie, and his cronies. For the remainder of his stay at Gibbsville Country Day, Joby was in debt, he was a member of a "crowd," he stayed out of discovered trouble, and he made passing or better grades in all studies. He was coolly polite to Mr. Koenig (who, to be sure, was more than happy to be able to report a total regeneration to the boy's parents), he forced himself to acquit himself adequately in the classroom, he did nothing that would jeopardize his chances of going to boarding school, where there would be a new life and new people, and where it would be fun. So far, in his thirteen years, he had not had much fun.

It was Joe Chapin's custom to make all important announcements at the dinner table, provided they were not unpleasant announcements that might upset the digestion of the food. The custom made for interesting and amiable dinner conversation, as well as being the only time of day when the entire family were sure to be together.

On an evening in the spring of 1928 he smoothed out his napkin on his lap and said: "This is Station JBC Senior about to broadcast."

They looked at him expectantly.

"I wish to make an important announcement to my millions of listeners at this table."

Some laughter by Ann and Joby.

"First, bad news," said Joe.

"Oh," said Ann, with an exaggerated groan.

"The bad news, however, will be quickly followed by the good, so if Miss Chapin, of Gibbsville, Pennsylvania, will please remove her chin from her soup, let us proceed with the announcement."

"Chin removed. Matter of fact, wasn't *in* the soup," said Ann.

"Almost, though. It certainly dropped when I said I had bad news," said Joe. "Well, the bad news, not really bad, is that Mother and I have talked to each other about the whole family going abroad this summer."

288

"Us too?" said Joby.

"The whole family. Mr. and Mrs. Joseph B. Chapin, Miss Ann Chapin, and Mr. Joseph B. Chapin, Junior. No dogs, cats or other livestock."

"But we're not going. That's the bad news," said Ann.

"You are correct, Miss Ann Chapin. You are interrupting, but you are correct. The reason we are not going this summer is that I am going to have to go to the Republican National Convention, which is always in the summer, and there would be no point in my going to Kansas City in the middle of our trip abroad. So, this is the good part of the announcement—we are going abroad next year."

"All of us?" said Joby.

"The whole kit and kaboodle. Now the reason why I'm making the announcement a year ahead of time is because I would like this whole family, myself included, to brush up on our French. And secondly, I think it might be fun if we all studied up on England and France and Italy and learned something about the interesting places we're going to visit. *I've* never been to Europe, *Mother's* never been to Europe—"

"Mother's never been to Chicago, Illinois," said Edith.

"I've never been to Pittsburgh," said Ann.

"I've never been to Boston, and you have," said Joby.

"Only once when I was little," said Ann.

"Well, the Swiss Family Chapinson will start their traveling next year," said Joe.

"Burn my clothes! Wait till I tell the bunch," said Ann.

"What was that expression?" said Joe.

"Oh, it's just an expression," said Ann.

"It's a very expressive expression," said Joe. "Where did that come from?"

"Oh, it's nothing."

"But where did you get it?" Joe persisted.

"It's an expression they use in the South."

"When did you visit the South? I don't seem to remember your taking any Southern trips lately," said Joe.

"There's a new girl at school, they just moved to town. She doesn't mean anything by it."

"No, and I'm sure you don't, but it isn't ladylike," said Joe. "I don't think the French would like to hear a young American girl say *Fumez mes robes,* or whatever the French is. In fact I'm sure the French have no such expression."

"Oh—from what I hear, the French have worse than that," said Ann.

"*Je suis très désolé*," said Joe. "My daughter is too sophisticated. *Elle est très blasée*."

"You better go back to Yale and take your French over again," said Ann.

"*Je suis très désolé, elle est très blasée*. Woe is me," said Joe.

"I can understand the last part," said Ann.

"Yes, and I can understand 'burn ma clothes,' honey," said Joe.

"It's just an expression, Father," said Ann.

They smiled.

There are the luxuries that the rich can afford, and there are the simplicities that the rich can afford if they are the kind of rich who are sure of themselves. The unsure rich buy the luxuries that the sure-of-themselves can do without. When Joe Chapin bought a Dodge for use on the farm he bought a sturdy, inexpensive, hard-riding, economical, clean-lined car. It was what he needed, and it was not a Marmon or a Mercer—or a Ford. It was a car with a tricky gear shift, different from the standard shift and the Buick shift. And because Joe Chapin had bought a Dodge, a lot of people bought Dodges who had the money to buy Lincolns. If it was good enough for Joe Chapin . . . He still had the Dodge in 1928, when he and Edith made a kind of "Dodge" decision.

The decision concerned a school for Ann, who had been at Miss Holton's for thirteen years and was eager to go to boarding school. There were the obvious schools—Foxcroft, St. Timothy's, Farmington, Westover, Shipley, Madeira's, Irwin's. There was some discussion over sending her to live with the Alec Weekses while she attended Spence or Miss Chapin's. Edith's old school, Miss Hannah Payne's, had ceased to exist, and if Miss Chapin's or Spence meant Ann's living with the Weekses, those schools were ruled out by Edith, and Ann promptly gave up the idea of a couple of winters in New York City. "We could talk for years and never get anywhere," said Joe. "Ann, you say you don't want to go to college. Well, your mother and I think you ought to, but we're not going to insist on it, and if we don't insist on it, you won't go. So when we consider a school, we needn't bother about its record as a college preparatory school. A finishing school is what we're looking for. I think it ought to be in the country, but near one of the larger cities. But does it have to be one of the more fashionable schools, so called? There are some good schools that we haven't got down on this list. Do you know a school I always liked? Oak Hill. I don't know much about it, but on the other hand, I don't know a single thing against it. It's Episcopal, and about halfway between Philadelphia and New York. Near Princeton, as a matter of fact. It isn't a Foxcroft or a Westover, but as long as I can remember, back when I was at New Haven, and even when I was at The Hill, I've known girls from the nicest families that went to Oak Hill. Shall we look into it, or is your heart set on one of the others?"

"I don't know, I might like Oak Hill better," said Ann. "I don't really care where I go, just so I go. Thirteen years at Miss Holton's . . ."

They went by motor to have a look at Oak Hill, and on the way home Joe, who was sitting with Harry, asked Ann how she liked the place.

"I think it's swell," she said. "I liked Miss Ringwald and the girls I met seemed nice. I thought it was swell. I'd like to go there."

"Miss Ringwald said you could take the college preparatory in case you should change your mind."

"I won't. Father, if I went to college I'd be twenty-three by the time I got out. Twenty-*three!* Fan ma brow."

"If you changed your mind, you could be out of college at twenty-two. Don't forget your Miss Holton's credits," said Edith.

"But the college boards, Mother. And anyway, twenty-*two* is almost as bad as twenty-*three*, although not quite. I don't think I'm the studious type, if you know what I mean, and *you* didn't go to college, Mother. It's all right for a man, a man has to. But not a girl. Joby can go, he can collect all the laurels. He's bright."

Oak Hill it was, and a timely choice, for shortly after her acceptance of Oak Hill and Oak Hill's acceptance of Ann, the incident of the butcher's delivery truck occurred.

"You talk to her," said Edith. "I can't get anything out of her."

Ann was sent to her father's den.

"Ann, what really happened? I'm your father, and I think you know I love you and will back you to the hilt, but we must know what happened."

"Father, do I have to go over all that again? I've told you, I've told Mother. I've told you both twice."

"I would like to hear it again in full detail," said Joe.

"He stopped. The boy, Tommy, or young man. He asked us if we wanted to go for a ride and we said all right. I know it was wrong, but we got in the truck and drove down country and we got stuck in the mud."

"And there you sat?"

"And there we sat."

"And he made no effort to get the car out of the mud?"

"No," said Ann. "At first we didn't know we were stuck."

"You didn't? Why not?"

"Because we just stopped on the side of the road and we smoked some cigarettes and laughed and talked."

"You and Sara Stokes and the driver," said Joe. "No other young man present?"

"No, just the three of us."

"And all this time the young man never made any advances, never got fresh with you?"

Ann looked at him but said nothing, then turned away.

"Is that what I'm to understand?" said Joe.

She remained silent.

"Is it, Ann? It's what you told your mother."

"I know I did," said Ann.

"But it isn't what you want to tell me?"

"I don't want to tell anybody anything," said Ann.

"But unfortunately I have to know."

"Why?"

"Because—so many reasons. I want to protect you, and I will. Be sure of that Ann, no matter what. But I must know what happened."

"Just you?"

"That depends. I can't make any promises till I know."

"Father, nothing *much* happened."

"Well, tell me what did."

"Will Tommy get in trouble?"

"It's to our advantage to see that the whole thing is kept as quiet as possible. Ann, I want you to have confidence in me, and whatever is done, my first concern is for your welfare."

"My welfare. You mean for my own good?"

"Not quite the way that sounds," said Joe. "I'm not going to treat you like a child."

"I'll tell you," said Ann. "We stopped the truck, and then we smoked a cigarette. We all smoked. Then we started to get hungry and Tommy said there was plenty to eat in the truck and we opened up all the packages of meat, but mostly it was steaks and chops and things that we didn't want to eat raw, although he did. He ate some roast beef raw, without any salt or anything. We didn't have any salt. Then finally we found one package with some bologna and some sausage and Sara and I ate that. It made us awfully thirsty and we wanted a drink of water. So he got out and went up the road and came back with a half a coconut shell filled with spring water and we drank that. Then I guess we had some more cigarettes."

"Mm-hmm."

"Then he said who wants to get in the back of the truck with him. And we both said we didn't. Well, then he laughed and joked and kidded Sara and me and finally Sara said, all right, she'd get in back with him, and she did, and I sat in front alone. I could hear them but I couldn't see them. They were necking, and I said if you two didn't stop necking I was going home, and they said to get in back with them, so I did. And he kissed me."

"Forcibly?"

"No. I let him kiss me."

"I see. And then what?"

"Well, then he wanted us to take off our bloomers."

"And did you?"

"Yes, I did."

"And did Sara?"

"No, just me."

"And?" said Joe. "What about him?"

"He opened his trousers."

"He didn't take them off?"

"No, but he opened them all the way. I could see him. Then he wanted to go all the way with me, but I wouldn't let him."

"Did Sara try to stop him?"

"No, she wanted me to."

"Well, *then*, what *did* happen?"

"Well, I put my hand on him and he put his hand on me, and we did that."

"You say 'that.' Did you know what you were doing?"

"Yes. I've done it before with other boys. I won't tell you who, so don't ask me."

"All right. Then what happened?"

"Well, he fell asleep."

"And you and Sara stayed there? How long was he asleep?"

"I don't know, I guess about two hours," said Ann. "We were

going to walk home, but it was too far, and we weren't sure of the roads."

"What did he do when he woke up?"

"He tried to get Sara to go all the way."

"But she wouldn't?"

"No. She said she'd do what I did but no more. So she took off her bloomers and that's what they did. Father, it's not so terrible. Almost every girl we know does that much."

"Why do you say that?"

"Because you looked so sad."

"I am sad, Ann, but at the same time relieved," said Joe. "And that's all you did? I don't mean to condone it, but is that all?"

"On my word of honor," she said.

"He never touched you with his private parts?"

"No. You're worried that I could have a baby?"

"Well, yes, partly. You've heard of venereal disease."

"The claps? No, he never."

"You've given me your word of honor. Is there anything more you want to tell me? That I haven't asked you?"

"Just that I'm sorry it happened, and it wasn't his fault. He didn't force us to go with him, and he didn't even make us do what we did do. Father, I'm not just an innocent little baby."

"No, not if you know about such things as the claps, as you call it. Have you ever gone the limit?"

"No."

"But almost?"

"As much as I did today, no farther."

"Do you realize that you were lucky? I take for granted you know what rape is."

"Yes, I know. But he couldn't have raped one of us with the other there."

"Sara seems to have wanted to encourage him."

"She was excited," said Ann.

"What?"

"Nothing. I'm sorry I said that."

"Well, I heard you. And you were, too, Ann, or you wouldn't have got in the back of the truck. That's the danger. You can't help getting excited, it's in all of us. But it's there for a good reason, so that when you fall in love with the right young man you can share everything with him. You don't cheapen it with a stranger that takes you for a ride in a truck."

294

"I know, I didn't think. What are you going to do about Tommy?"

"If I did what I want to do I'd give him a good beating, but I have to think."

"What are you going to tell Mother?"

"I'm going to have to tell her the truth."

"Please don't, Father? Please? I beg of you."

"How can I not tell her?" said Joe.

"You can lie for me. Please don't tell her. I don't want her to know. If you tell her what happened today, you'll have to tell her it happened before. I couldn't bear it. I'd run away."

"Why?"

"I don't want her to know, I don't want her to know. If you tell her I'll never tell you anything again as long as I live."

"She's your mother, and my wife. I shouldn't have any secrets from my wife."

"But you have. I'm sure you have," said the girl.

"What makes you so sure?"

"Because I've looked at you, Father. You have secrets."

"They can be a burden," said Joe. "And they get heavier."

"You must have been in love with somebody before Mother. Or maybe after. But there's somebody you love besides Mother."

"Of course—you, for instance."

"I didn't ask you to tell me, I just know."

"Yes. She died before your mother and I fell in love," said Joe. "All right. We'll make up some story. The young man tried to kiss you but you wouldn't let him. But what about Sara? What's she going to tell your Cousin Percy and Cousin Sara?"

"She's not afraid of them. She's stubborn. She bosses them around as if they were slaves. If they ask her too many questions she'll walk out of the room."

"Do you admire that?" said Joe.

"No, but look at Cousin Percy and Cousin Sara. So old and decrepit—"

"He happens to be two years older than I am, that's all."

"Well, they look older and act older. They're afraid of her shadow. Honestly they are, Father."

He took a cigarette from the silver box his ushers had given him. "Do you inhale?"

"Yes," she said. "Could I have one?"

"No," he said. "There's been quite enough maturity in this house for one day. I wonder what you'll be like with your children."

"Like you, I hope."

He suddenly broke, put his head on his hands and wept. "Go now, please get out," he said.

She took away his cigarette and crushed it on the tray. She touched the back of his head. "Good-bye, dear," she said, and went out. . . .

In a little while Edith came in and sat down.

"I suppose you got nothing out of her," said Edith.

"She said there was nothing, and I believe her," said Joe. "You know the expression they use nowadays—he tried to make passes."

"And failed? That's what we want to believe. I'd like to know more about the young man, I don't know a thing about him. I wouldn't know him if I saw him, and the girls don't know his last name."

"Well, what can we do, Edith? Call the meat market and ask them for Tommy's last name? We can't, and anyway, they're probably closed."

"You're a lawyer, find out from the police. They must know him, have some record of him."

"They'd know him, but that would be showing our hand. I say let's drop it."

"I say let's not drop it till we find out what kind of a person he is," said Edith. "There's one man that knows every man, woman, and child in this town."

"Who?"

"Mike Slattery," said Edith.

"He's also one of the last people I'd like to take into our confidence."

"He has four daughters," said Edith.

Joe was silent. "What would I say to him? How much do we want to tell him?"

"It's going to be all over school tomorrow, tell him you want to know what kind of a person this Tommy is. Has he any record with the police? Is he a poolroom boy? Just tell him the girls—he picked up the girls and they went for a ride with him."

"I've always been glad that Mike Slattery didn't have a thing on me."

"What would he have on you, really? What could he say that he could use against you? His daughters aren't grown up yet, and things could happen to them."

"All right, I'll call him."

He did so.

"Yes, Joe, what can I do for you?" said Mike.

"Mike, you have four daughters, and I'm talking to you as the father of one."

"Certainly, Joe."

"This afternoon my daughter Ann, and her cousin Sara Stokes, allowed themselves to be picked up by the young man who drives the truck for the Regal Meat Market. They went for a ride and got stuck in the mud, down country, and they didn't get home till just before dinner."

"I see."

"I've questioned my daughter very thoroughly, and so has her mother, and we're both convinced there was nothing wrong, aside from playing truant. But Edith and I don't know a thing about the young man, other than the fact that his name is Tommy. Do you know him, by any chance?"

"Yes. His name is Willis, Tommy Willis, they call him," said Mike. "I don't know very much about him, Joe. He seems like, oh, any number of young fellows that have that kind of a job. He isn't a Gibbsville boy. He comes from Taqua, originally, but he's been living in town three, four years. He boards at Mrs. Rafferty's, in the Fifth Ward. He must be pretty well behaved or Fran Rafferty wouldn't let him stay. He's a voter, he belongs to one of the hose companies—Perseverance, I guess. Yes, Perseverance, because I've seen him as tiller-man on the hook-and-ladder."

"Is he married?"

"Not that I know of, Joe. He may have a wife in Taqua, but he must be separated if he has. She doesn't live with him here."

"Do you know if he's ever been in any trouble with the police?"

"I don't think so, but I could easily find out. I'll call you back. Are you home?"

"Yes, thank you very much, Mike."

Mike Slattery telephoned in half an hour.

"I have more on young Willis. He's had two summonses for speeding out Market Street, and he *is* married but separated from his wife. She had him up for non-support about a year ago, and he was ordered to pay her fifty a month. That's a lot of money, being's he only gets a hundred a month."

"Has he any children?"

"No children," said Mike.

"Separated from his wife, and has to pay her half his salary. That explains why he picked up two young girls."

"That's what I thought too," said Mike.

"I think the sooner this town gets rid of him, the better for our daughters."

"I'd go easy there, Joe. I know you could have him fired, but you don't want him making a stink. He could make up some very beautiful lies and tell every pool hustler in town, and you know the kind of thing he'd say. I have dealings with a lot of different kinds of people, Joe. If you had him fired he'd have nothing to lose. Why don't you let me handle it for you? A word here or there, in the right place. He can be gotten rid of without it looking like you had anything to do with it. He hasn't fallen behind in his payments to his wife, because there he'd be in contempt and have to go to jail. But he's had two traffic summonses already and he can get in trouble again. Everybody breaks the law driving a car, but this fellow could be a habitual offender, you know. That'd take it out of your hands entirely, because the first two offenses were before this incident today, you see?"

"You're satisfied that that's the best way to do it?" said Joe.

"I think it's the best way."

"Well, then I'll leave it entirely up to you, Mike. All I care about is the reputation of the two girls. You can understand that."

"Joe, I can understand it four times better than you can, and I'm glad if I can be of service to you. That's what old friends are for."

"Thank you."

"My only other advice in this matter, if people say anything to you about it, don't just laugh it off, but don't let on you're too worried, either. If you try to pretend it didn't happen, people will get suspicious, but on the other hand—oh, you know what I mean. Just be casual. It happened. It's over. Girls will be girls. Could have been a lot worse. Handle it that way."

"Machiavellian, Mike."

"Hmm. Where have I heard *that* word before?"

"What?"

"Don't you worry, I'll handle the whole thing. My highest regards to Edith."

"Thank you, Mike."

"A pleasure, sir."

A few weeks later Fran Rafferty told Tommy Willis a man wanted to see him in the parlor.

"What man?" said Tommy Willis.

"Well, I never can remember his name, but he's something in the sheriff's office," said Mrs. Rafferty. "I know him by sight only."

"Tell him I'll be down in a minute," said Tommy Willis. He closed the door of his room and heard fat Mrs. Rafferty slowly descending the stairs. He thereupon opened the window, dropped to the roof of the coal shed and left by the back gate, thereby becoming a fugitive from the justice of the Domestic Relations Court, County of Lantenengo, Commonwealth of Pennsylvania, and Gibbsville saw him no more.

He had unwittingly been instrumental in repairing the still somewhat damaged friendship between Joe Chapin and Mike Slattery. Joe Chapin was properly appreciative of Mike Slattery's machinations, and Mike was enjoying that moment, especially enviable for a politician, of having done a favor for someone who could be kept endlessly in the position of never being able fully to repay it. Politics is trades, trades are the exchange of favors, and if a man owes you a favor so great that he will always want to repay it, but a favor of such unique character that it cannot be repaid in kind, the man who granted the favor assumes the status of dictator as well as benefactor.

Whatever Joe had been doing in his trips around the state, for whatever purpose, Mike was satisfied to let him go, for Joe must have learned his lesson with the Washington experience, and if the trips were adding to Joe's potential political value, they were going to be valuable to Mike. Mike therefore planted the thought, just the grain of a thought, among his own men in the various counties, that Joe not only was making his appearances with Mike's knowledge, but with his consent and even at his suggestion. A man in a distant county would say to Mike: "We had another visit from Joseph B. Chapin the other night. Here for a testimonial dinner for one of our old judges." The man would study Mike for Mike's reaction.

"I know," Mike would say, managing to imply that he knew a lot more that he wasn't saying.

"What the hell's a Lantenengo County lawyer doing this far from home?"

"A lot of people would like to know the answer to that, but I have a whole pocketful of answers for that kind of a question. Only I don't always give away the answers. Sometimes it's better to give away a cigar. Here, have a cigar."

By pretending to know what Joe was up to, and yet being noncommittal, Mike was subtly taking over Joe's private campaign in the event it might be useful, but not assuming any responsibility in the event Joe was getting nowhere. He had some of his politician friends sharply guessing that he, Mike Slattery, had actually sent Joe Chapin on the trips.

Mike was responsible, wholly responsible, for Joe's designation as an alternate delegate to the convention in Kansas City. It was the kind of recognition that keeps a loyal party man happy. Mike was not himself a delegate but he was in attendance at the closed-door conferences, as befitted his standing in a reliably Republican state. Moreover, he was known, wherever he was known at all, to be a devout Roman Catholic, and it did no harm to the Republican party to have a man like Slattery to urge voters to ignore Alfred E. Smith, the inevitable Democratic nominee. As a Republican Catholic, Mike Slattery was worth more to the party than a run-of-the-mill Republican Protestant. The Protestant Republicans could be taken for granted, but the Catholic Republicans were going to be hard to hold as election day got nearer. The convention was a worthwhile excursion for Mike, and he was careful to see that his familiarity with some of the great names of the party was not lost on Joe. He saw to it that Joe met them all, and he saw to it that the important men realized that the good-looking fellow in the white linen suit was a Slattery man. There were so many potbellied men with their pants hanging below their waistlines and their shirts creeping out and their collars soaked with perspiration—that Mike was delighted to make a claim on Joe, who at least looked cool.

Coming back on the train Joe sat up most of the night with Mike.

"It's been a great experience, Mike. And do you know what to me was one of the most interesting things about it?"

"What's that, Joe?"

"Well, it may sound foolish, but I was always under the impression Mr. Hoover was a Democrat."

"You're not the only one had that impression. But my explanation for that was that Woodrow Wilson wanted people to think Mr. Hoover was a Democrat."

"Still, it's interesting, because only eight or ten years ago I'd have all but *sworn* he was a Democrat. The reason it's interesting is how comparatively short a time it takes for a man to become nationally known. I've always been a Republican, as you know, but yesterday we gave the nomination to a man I thought belonged to the opposite side."

"Well, Mr. Hoover was so busy feeding the people in Europe—he kept out of politics."

"It's quite fascinating," said Joe. "This big honor, the biggest in the world, can happen to a man almost overnight. What was Coolidge when he was nominated for the vice-presidency? He'd been governor of Massachusetts and settled the police strike. What was Harding? Well, Harding isn't a good example, because he'd not only been governor of his state but United States senator as well. But look at the other side, the Democrats. Wilson, a governor and a college president. Cox? Nobody. Franklin Roosevelt, the fellow that ran for vice-president, I used to know him slightly. At least I met him at dances when I was in college. A typical New York snob, I always thought."

"And a Democrat. A Roosevelt a Democrat, it's like seeing Abe Cohen the clothier at High Mass."

"What was Roosevelt? Assistant Secretary of the Navy and that was as high as he ever got, but if he'd been elected, God forbid, and What's His Name Cox died, the fellow I used to know could have been President of the United States. It isn't Senator Borah, or Senator Lodge that gets to be President. It's often a fellow that the general public hardly knows at all."

"Some men get elected to the Senate and they have such a good organization that they never have to go home. They can spend half their lifetime in the Senate. I'm not speaking of myself, but the United States Senate, naturally. But it's one thing to get re-elected and re-elected to the United States Senate, and something else again to get the nomination for the presidency. In some ways it's easier to be elected President. You take Dawes. I like Charley personally, but I couldn't see him as presidential timber. He'd make a good President, but not a good candidate, not against Al Smith. Al Smith is an expert at the kind of a campaign Dawes would conduct, and it wouldn't have surprised me if Smith could have beaten Dawes. But Smith won't beat our man. The country's prosperous, and the so-called independent voter, the little difference he makes is going to be even smaller in this election, because the independent voter isn't going to vote for a Catholic. If people have to vote for a Catholic to get a glass of beer, they're going to do without the beer. I look for Hoover to beat Smith so badly that Smith will never recover from it. And speaking as a Catholic, I wish he wouldn't run. I'd vote against him even if I weren't a staunch Republican. Injecting the religious issue isn't going to do any good, and it can do a lot of harm."

"I agree with you," said Joe.

They were tired, but they could not sleep in the hot, dirty train. Every once in a while a half-drunken delegate would stumble into the smoking room. The porter was nowhere to be seen. Joe and Mike were in their shirt sleeves, and Mike could not remember ever having seen Joe without a jacket except on the golf course.

"I wonder what goes on in the mind of a man like Herbert Hoover."

"Tonight?" said Mike. "He's probably sound asleep."

"Do you think so? Knowing that for all practical purposes he's just been elected President of the United States?"

Mike smiled. "He'd be glad to hear that, and so would the National Committee. Yes, I think he's most likely asleep. Don't forget he's a man that's done a lot of traveling. Civil engineer. Lived abroad a great deal, and not always in the lap of luxury."

"I know, but tonight. I know this much, I wouldn't be able to sleep. Here we are going sixty or seventy miles an hour. We can't see out the window in the darkness, but it's easy for me to imagine being in his position, looking out the window and saying to myself, 'I can travel for five days and nights, from coast to coast at a high rate of speed and still be in the country that I'm President of.' Just one man, out of a hundred and twenty million people."

"Would you like to be President, Joe?"

"*What?*"

Mike saw that his question, and perhaps the tone of it, had taken Joe by surprise.

"Me, President? No thank you."

But Mike had seen what he had seen in similar circumstances, when he had asked other men, possum-players, about their political ambitions. If you caught them unprepared, you got your answer. He wanted to ask Joe a great many more questions, but now that he had given the answer to one, Joe would be cautious in his answers to the others.

"Well, I guess we're not going to get much sleep, but I'm going to get off my feet for a few hours," said Mike.

"Take the lower. I'm going to sit up."

"No, I had it coming out, you keep it, thanks."

"Well, if you change your mind," said Joe.

"Good night, or good morning."

Home once more, Mike gave Peg a complete report of his activities at the convention, a report full of the names of men she never had met but on whom she had detailed dossiers. They were not just pictures in the paper to Peg Slattery. "What did Reed have to say? . . . How long were you with Bill Mellon? . . . Did you talk to Mills? . . . Who else besides Fisher? . . ." Her questions helped

Mike to re-create whole scenes, and in the re-creating of them he had a second and better look.

"Did you get along all right with Joe? That was a long time to be with a man, so constantly."

Mike looked at his wife.

"Do you know what that fellow wants?" he said.

Mike and Peg were two people who were often more nearly one person.

"Do I know what that fellow wants?" she said.

"I have trouble saying it, the words have a hard time getting out of my mouth."

"Now it *isn't* what I'm *thinking*," said Peg.

"I'll bet it is, though," said Mike.

"The same thing Al Smith wants?"

Mike smiled. "You can't say it either," he said. "Can you imagine? How do you convince yourself you can be, or ought to be?"

"You marry Edith Stokes."

"Do you think that's why it is?" said Mike. "No, I think he convinced himself. Maybe Edith encouraged him, but you should have heard the way he talked about it. Putting himself in Hoover's place."

"You're sure, eh?"

"Well, sure of what? I'm sure he wants it, but I don't know if he knows he wants it. But now I have the explanation for all these dinners and getting-to-know-the-boys and so forth. Do you remember a fellow ran for vice-president with Cox?"

"I have to think a minute. In 1920? Yes, a cousin of Teddy Roosevelt's. Franklin K. Roosevelt."

"You're thinking of Franklin K. Lane, Secretary of the Interior under Wilson. But that's the fellow. Well, Joe Chapin used to know him. I gather they went to society parties together. Joe didn't like him, but that's neither here nor there. In fact, the fact that he didn't like him—well, Joe didn't think much of him, but all the more reason why he could convince himself he could do as well or better. This particular Roosevelt got to be Assistant Secretary of the Navy. Appointive, of course. Well, you remember when Joe went to Washington that time, to get some appointment. The time he went behind my back."

"Oh, I remember, and I'll bet he does too."

"Can you see it the way I do?" said Mike.

"He thought he could get an appointment without getting tied up with the organization."

"Sure. On his own. No political tie-up. Then get a reputation and maybe run for governor, or United States senator. It all works out."

"Joe is what? Forty-five?"

"Forty-six. We were born the same year, '82."

"Then he still has plenty of time," said Peg.

"He'll need it," said Mike.

Peg laughed heartily.

Joe Chapin was now reaching the point in his life and the position in his activities where it could be said, and was being said, that he was *a* first citizen and, more and more, *the* first citizen of Gibbsville. There would be conversations in which Citizen A would say: "The biggest man in this town is Joe Chapin."

"Joe Chapin?" Citizen B might say.

"Who's bigger? If you mean richer, yes. There's a half a dozen guys that have more dough, but who does more with their dough? Who does more for this town, and doesn't ask anything in return?"

"I wouldn't put Joe Chapin at the top."

"Then who would you put at the top? The Mayor? Some politician? Joe's for good government, but he kept his hands out of politics. Listen, whenever anything's good for the town, not just for Number One, who's the first guy they get to serve on the committees and all that? When you see Joe Chapin connected with something, it's good for Gibbsville, or Lantenengo County, not just for Joe Chapin. That's the way I look at it. And who would you rather have representing Gibbsville? One of those loud-mouths at the Rotary Club? Mike Slattery? Doc English? Henry Laubach?"

"How do you mean represent?" Citizen B might say.

"Represent? By represent I mean I don't mean in politics. I mean if say they had another Sesqui, who would you want to be there representing Gibbsville? You'd want a guy that was honest and did something for the community, and looked the part. Listen, there isn't a thing that's for the good of this town that Joe Chapin is left out of."

"Well, maybe you're right."

"He isn't a crook, he isn't a hypocrite—Joe'll take a drink. Friendly, kind. Does a lot of things for people. I say you'd have a hard time getting anybody to say anything against Joe Chapin and prove it. You take a guy like Lloyd Williams, and he's a whoremaster. Then you take a guy on the order of Henry Laubach, and that son of a bitch, all he cares about is making more money. Henry isn't a *real* son of a bitch, but he's cold. One of those cold fellows. Doc English, he does a lot of good, but don't forget he gets paid for it, and if it came down to that I'd rather have Doc Malloy operate on me. No sir, the biggest all-around man in this town is Joseph B. Chapin."

In the course of an average two-block walk from his office to the bank Joe Chapin would bid the time of day to at least ten persons and usually many more. There would be many *Good morning, Mr. Chapin's* that he would answer with a *Good morning* and a smile but without a name. People liked to speak to him, and when they could engage him in a few minutes' conversation they wanted to be seen talking to him. Merchants liked to have him seen in their stores; the cops liked to wave to him; people would call to him from their cars. He had his suits made in New York, but he patronized Main Street for socks and underwear, which gave him the opportunity to appear in the store, and gave the merchant the benefit of his patronage above the actual money spent. Joe's suits, shoes and hats came from out of town, but almost everything else he bought was bought in town or ordered through town merchants. If he wanted a Lee Dreadnaught-Driver he had it sent through the hardware store; if he was buying a 410 gun for Joby, it was ordered on Main Street; if Edith wanted a black caracul, it was a Main Street transaction.

The feeling generally was that Joe Chapin, except for his set taste in clothes, was the best of Gibbsville. He had achieved his status first by living to the age of forty-seven, having been born in Gibbsville of Gibbsville parents. He had returned to Gibbsville after getting his education. He had married a Gibbsville girl, the daughter of Gibbsville parents and with many Gibbsville relatives. Joe had then gone into partnership with a lifelong Gibbsville friend and native. He made his money in Gibbsville, he spent most of it in Gibbsville. Whenever he went away he "reflected credit" on his home town—and he always came back to it. He had avoided messes, and he had given the people confidence in their town and in themselves: Joe Chapin was not a New Yorker or a Philadelphian or a Chicagoan or a Bostonian, but wherever he went, he would be on equal terms with the best—and he was one hundred per cent Gibbsville. They did not quite love Joe Chapin, but they were proud of him and grateful, and if he had died in 1929 they might have found out that they did love him. But he did not die in 1929.

Joe Chapin was almost the last of the upper-middle-class Gibbsvillians who had not been abroad. He had never been to Europe because in the days preceding the World War he had not been attracted to the Eastern Hemisphere by culture or by sin. Young men in his circumstances sometimes took their brides to Europe on their wedding trip, but during their engagement period Edith had told Joe that the very thought of a great ocean liner gave her *mal de mer*, and in accordance with her wishes, that ended the discussion. After the World War there was a longish period during which Joe mentioned Europe, and especially France, as seldom as possible. France, in the American language, was a word that had a quick association with the word *army*, and both words stayed out of Joe's conversation. But ten years after the Armistice the embarrassment had lessened to the point where Joe could make plans to take his family on a six weeks' trip to England, France, and Italy, and the plans, once postponed on account of the Kansas City convention, reached the passport and sailing-date stage. They would go in a French Line ship, which was "wet," and you could begin to try out your bilingual ability as soon as you went abroad. The Chapins were given the names of the little restaurants that were known all over the United States as truly French and off the tourist-beaten path. Warning letters were written to the three or four Gibbsville expatriates. Morgan, Harjes were alerted through the good offices of Dave Harrison ("We have a man there that can do absolutely anything for you, whether it's good for you or very bad for you," he wrote). The names of reputable physicians were obtained, and Joe and Edith even had serious discussions over the advisability of having the children's appendices excised in advance. They were reassured by the existence of the hospital at Neuilly. They promised themselves to drink no water but Evian and to drink no milk whatever. They would use their oldest, most decrepit luggage until they got to Paris and the establishment of Louis Vuitton. Ann was never to be let out of their sight, particularly in Italy, and most particularly in Firenze. The right kind of letter was being sent to our ambassadors in London, Paris, and Rome; to the purser of the *Ile de France*; to Bob Hooker's not very close friend Larry Hills, of the *Herald Tribune*; and to the managers of White's Club in London and the Travelers in Paris. Monsignor Creedon was arranging for a private audience with His Holiness Pius XI, and for months Joe and Edith took down the names and addresses of Rosa Lewis, Bricktop, Joe Zelli, George of the Ritz, Italian tailors, shoemakers more expensive than Peal, certain clerks at Asprey's, dons at Oxford, car-hire people who were cheaper than Daimler, Louis Bromfield's secretary George Watkins, and Nita Naldi, Erskine Gwynne, Sparrow Robertson, Jimmy Sheean, and Ben Finney. The mention of each name was introduced by the urgent *Be sure and see* . . .

They were to leave Gibbsville two days after Country Day closed for the school year, sailing two days later. On the night that school closed Joe broke his right leg.

Edith and Joby had gone to bed early, having finished all but the final packing, and Ann was at a bon voyage party at the Laubachs'. Arthur and Rose had given Edith and Joe a party the night before Country Day closed, so that that ceremonial of the trip was out of the way. ("A good idea to get that out of the way so you won't be exhausted boarding your ship.") The trunks had gone to New York, and Marian had even put the slip covers over some of the downstairs furniture. The house was not quite abandoned, not quite occupied, and Joe was busying himself with last-minute chores, mostly of a paper-work nature. Although Edith had retired, he had gone twice to their bedroom to ask her questions. On his third visit to the bedroom he found her deep asleep and he closed the door gently and walked softly to the top of the stairs.

In later months he tried to recall exactly what occurred—whether his loose-fitting house slipper caught on the carpet-covering, or he misjudged the turn that he had made literally many thousands of times. In any event, he started falling at the top of the stairs, which were quite steep and had sixteen risers.

He fell all the way to the first floor and lay there. He was unconscious, his fall unheard by his wife or their son or any of the three servants. He was later able to estimate how long he lay there: from about ten minutes past eleven until Ann's return at twenty-five minutes to one.

Ann quickly recovered from her first horror and determined that he was alive. She called her mother, who did not answer, and she went upstairs and shook Edith out of her sleep. Together they went downstairs again, and they noticed what Ann had not noticed earlier: the blood on his trouser-leg. Edith telephoned Billy English, who, as Ann said, took forever to get there. He announced that Joe had a broken leg, compound fracture, and a concussion of the brain. He sent for the ambulance. Nobody remembered to wake Joby.

Ann in her party dress went to the hospital with her mother and Dr. English, who was an extremely careful and slow driver. The Chapin women waited in the superintendent's office for Billy English's first report, which was an hour in coming.

"He has a bad fracture of the leg, that we know, and he must have done a complete somersault falling down the stairs, to account for the concussion. We're lucky, very lucky, he didn't break his neck. That sometimes happens in falls of that kind. I won't try to underestimate his condition. He's badly hurt. However, he's alive and right now he's sleeping. Our danger now is from the concussion and of course shock. I've arranged for a room for you, Edith, and you, Ann, if you'd care to stay. It'll be down the hall from Joe's room. I know you're not going to feel much like sleeping, but the floor nurse will get night-gowns for both of you. Regular hospital nightgowns, but it might be a good idea for you to try to get some rest tonight so that you won't be exhausted tomorrow."

"Has he recovered consciousness?"

"Not completely, Edith, and he won't for several hours, how many I don't know. That depends on several factors. We don't know how long he was lying there, and of course we don't even know what hap-pened, do we? You can have some coffee, if you like, or tea, but I'd suggest you both have a cup of bouillon. I have a room here myself, so I'll be here through the night, and I'll see that you're notified the minute there's any change either way. I don't want to alarm you, but at the same time our dear Joe has had a very close call and I can't honestly tell you ladies that he's entirely out of danger. Joe's more than a patient to me, too, you know."

"Thank you, Billy, we realize that," said Edith. "I've had *some* sleep and I'm quite awake now, but I think we'll follow your sugges-tion."

"Mother, I'm wide awake," said Ann.

"But let's do what Dr. English says. We have to think of tomor-row, and we're not going to be much help if we haven't had any sleep. Will you show us our room, Billy?"

"Come with me," said Dr. English. "Your mother's right, Ann. Tomorrow's when you're going to need your strength."

"I know that, Dr. English. It's just that I know I won't sleep."

"Well, try," said the doctor. "I can give you a tablet that will put you to sleep . . ."

"No, and don't put anything in my bouillon," said the girl.

"That never crossed my mind," said the doctor.

"And you'll apologize to Dr. English for your rudeness."

"I didn't mean it rudely. I'm sorry, Dr. English," said the girl.

"We're all under a strain," said the doctor.

The Chapin women got little sleep. They were kept awake by their concern for Joe, but that was not the only tension that made sleep come hard. They were extra-conscious of each other; it had been a long time since they had slept in the same room. What it came down to was that it had been a long time since they really had been together. Edith was proud of her daughter's exquisite form, and Ann was pleased that her mother had not gone to fat as so many mothers had. But Edith had preached modesty all through Ann's childhood and girlhood, and now the act of undressing in the same room was an intimacy that neither Edith nor Ann was prepared for. They did not appear wholly nude in front of each other; the putting-on of the hospital nightgown was accomplished in the bathroom. But they could not help looking down at each other's gown, where the bosom extended, and lower down where the pubic shadow could be seen under the summer-weight cotton. The intimacy made them strangers, and since neither wanted to talk about what was worrying both of them, they told each other good night, try to get some sleep, and lay listening to each other's breathing and turning in the beds. They were placed in each other's company, but it could not be said that Joe's accident had thrown them together.

However, they had been apart for years. A teacher at Miss Holton's had had to instruct Ann in the frightening mysteries of menstruation, and with that opportunity gone, Edith neither was given nor had contrived a second chance to get on close terms with the matured and maturing girl. And Ann, therefore, was independent of her mother, but with no one of her sex to take her place. The whole world of sex was between Ann on the one side, and, on the other, what she did and did not know. This very night, before her discovery of her father at the foot of the stairs, she had touched a boy, a boy had touched her, with such exciting effect that her capacity to feel put her, in her own mind, a million miles away from a candid relationship with her mother. She was in the stage where what *she* was discovering and experiencing was unique, notwithstanding her complete knowledge of the act which, performed by her parents, had caused her existence. She thought about it little enough, but when she did she thought of her father visiting her mother in total darkness, without visual or tactile enjoyment or prolonged excitement such as she herself had enjoyed, and achieving the ultimate embrace (which she had not yet achieved) in the fashion of all married couples. So far she had not been able, or permitted herself, to imagine her father in the positions of love-making. It was easier for her to imagine her mother making love with an anonymous, featureless figure that was her father, but not Father. She was convinced otherwise, but it was not impossible for her to imagine her mother as a partner in love-making with almost any man; and except for the dirty trick it would have been on her father, she would not have been irreparably shocked if her mother had used her body for pleasure with another man. To Ann a woman's body was designed for two related purposes, pleasure and child-bearing, and her mother as a woman was no different from any other woman. As the wife of Father, however, she owed him complete fidelity, and there was nothing to indicate that she had betrayed that trust. She knew that when *she* got married she was not going to fool around.

The mother and daughter were not visited until seven-thirty o'clock in the morning, when a nurse brought them coffee, toast, and soft-boiled eggs. Edith telephoned Marian to have Harry bring some day clothes and she then spoke to Joby. To her annoyance and relief Marian had already told the boy the bare facts of Joe's accident.

"Why didn't you tell me about Father?"

"Because you were asleep and there was nothing you could do, now don't be upset, Joby, don't be upset."

"Can I come over with Harry?"

"Yes, of course, although you'll only be able to see Father for a minute. He's still asleep."

"Are we going to Europe?"

"Oh, dear," said Edith. "No, we'll have to cancel all that. A broken leg takes months to heal."

"Will Father have to carry a cane?"

"At least. In the beginning, crutches."

"Is he going to have to stay in the hospital?"

"I imagine so, quite a while."

"All summer?"

"Possibly."

"Then he won't be able to play golf, either," said the boy.

"Oh, no. Now I must stop talking, unless there's something important you want to ask me."

"Is Father going to *die*?"

"No, no, no, Joby. You mustn't think that," said Edith.

"Well, the paper called up and asked if it was true Father had concussion of the brain."

"How do you know that?"

"Because I answered, they thought I was you on the phone."

"Well if they call up again, don't tell them anything. Tell them to get in touch with Uncle Arthur McHenry, if they want any information."

"A boy that was on Gibbsville High football team, he got concussion of the brain and he died. I remember."

310

"There are different kinds. Now I must hang up, and you get ready to come with Harry."

There was gloom on Main Street and in the Lantenengo Street homes with the report of Joe's accident, and in the barber shops and the Gibbsville Club and the Elks Home and on the Market Street one-man trolleys and in cigar stores and soda fountains and at bus stops and in the forty-five speakeasies of Gibbsville, wherever men and women gathered by the half dozen. There was no one to say, "It served him right," and there were many who said, "It's a goddam shame." Bob Hooker ran a daily bulletin, a one-column box on Page One, on Joe's condition, and when it was announced, after the third day, that Joe was "off the critical list but unable to receive visitors" Gibbsville accepted Joe as among the ailing, who would be a long while "on the mend."

Joe was allowed to go home, to the farm, in the second week in August, almost exactly two months after entering the hospital. A bone man from Philadelphia was called in for an opinion when the leg was slow in healing, and in return for his $1,000 fee he provided the information that Joe was forty-seven years old and that he approved the treatment Joe was getting under Dr. English.

"Otherwise, I don't see what good he did," said Arthur to Edith. "It's nice to know that Billy's a good doctor, but we knew that all along. Of course I'm not particularly enthusiastic over Philadelphia specialists."

"Forty-seven," said Edith. "Your bones don't knit as quickly. I just hope the right leg won't be shorter than the other."

"Billy says it won't be," said Arthur. "What I don't like—it seems to me Joe himself is still low in spirit."

"Billy says that's the result of the shock and the concussion."

"And it may be, but I don't like it. He'll say to me, 'I'll be back in harness after Labor Day,' and then he'll wonder aloud whether he'll be ready for the November term."

"Of court?"

"Yes. November's always very heavy because we lawyers ask for postponements in the September term. But one good thing, one consolation. He's achieved one ambition."

"Which?"

"Just sitting here and lying in the hospital, Joe's made enough money in the stock market so he can give you and each of the children pretty close to a million dollars. Joe's a very rich man. So am I, I might add. At least we don't have to worry about money. Edith, I wonder if it might not be a good idea for you and Joe to go abroad this winter."

"Let's not talk about that again till he's all recovered."

"But think about it. Take some of that money and go to the Riviera and have a real rest. Joe's been working hard and scooting about the countryside as though he were running for office. Why don't you start inculcating the idea of a real vacation? The children will be going away to school in the fall."

"He likes scooting about the countryside."

"It'll be quite some time before he's able to do it again, and you might as well get him away from temptation. If not Europe, Florida. It doesn't have to be Palm Beach. There are other places. Or California. Sit in the sun and see some new people and get his mind away from work. In less than three years we'll be fifty, Joe and I. "

Joe called to them. "Hey, you two."

He was in the living room, which had been converted into a downstairs bedroom. The main house on the farm was always cool, what with the shade of the walnut trees and the two brooks that passed in front of and at the side of the house. A hospital bed was set up in the living room and Joe was able to escape most of the August heat.

They went inside and Edith washed Joe's face.

"What dire deeds of derring-do were you plotting?"

"Arthur was doing all the plotting. He thinks we ought to go abroad next winter."

"That's odd. I think *Arthur* ought to go abroad next winter."

"Well, then somebody in this firm is going abroad next winter," said Arthur.

"Not necessarily. Arthur could be just as stubborn about it as I plan to be. Result: neither goes."

"Result: we'll both collapse. It was just an idea I had, and Edith doesn't take kindly to it."

"Well, I certainly don't. I don't expect to win the Harvard game with a sixty-five-yard dropkick, but I'll be well enough to let you have a vacation. You're entitled to a good one, and I'm going to insist you get it."

"It isn't only the office, Joe. You're going around as though you were a traveling salesman."

"Oh, well, that's fun, that comes under the heading of relaxation."

"Relaxation? Joe, I've seen you come home from one of those relaxations. Last winter. I remember one time you'd been to Erie, I think it was. Yes, Erie. I don't remember what that trip was for. In fact, I seldom do know. You used to tell me, but in the past year or so you just announce that you're off for Lancaster, or Altoona, and away you go. Sometimes it's an overnight Pullman, other times a long drive, a long exhausting motor trip. Say, hadn't you just come back from one when you tried to take the steps all at once?"

"I don't remember," said Joe.

"Yes, you had. We had our party for you, and the next day you went to Whitemarsh for the Lawyers Club tournament. And the next day was when you cracked your leg."

"It might have been, but don't try to see cause and effect there, Arthur," said Joe.

"Why not? If I can show you that the relaxing trips, as you call them, are taking too much out of you, I'll be doing you a favor. Joe, I was just telling Edith, we're getting close to the fifty mark, and whether we like it or not, we're slowing up. If Billy English were to tell you that the reason—"

"I beg your pardon, Arthur. I know what you're going to say. I don't think Billy English is going to tell you that I broke my leg because I was tired. But even if he did, I'm doing something I like to do, and if I get tired while doing it—at least I'm getting tired at a pastime I enjoy. Fellows we know are out risking their necks fox-hunting, down around Philadelphia. And others are chasing women instead of foxes, and others are ruining their guts on bootleg hootch."

"I know all that, but you seem to me to be tiring yourself out for thirty pieces of silver."

"What?"

"Those little cups and cocktail shakers you pick up at golf tournaments, those cigarette boxes they give you for making a speech."

"Thirty pieces of silver has another connotation that I'm sure Joe doesn't like any more than I do, Arthur," said Edith.

"It was unfortunate. However, to thine own self be true, and you can be a traitor to yourself, you know."

Joe moved in his wheelchair. "Ah, I'm glad you said that. I'm doing the exact opposite. If I didn't make those trips, I wouldn't be true to myself." He turned to Edith. "Shall I tell him?"

"I think you're going to, so why ask me?"

Joe lit a cigarette. "Arthur, in a way I am a traveling salesman. I'm peddling a commodity called Joe Chapin."

"I see."

"The trips have often been exhausting, but they've had a purpose, and not just the thirty pieces of silver."

"I'm glad to hear it," said Arthur.

"Until this minute Edith has been the only other person to know what's been behind the trips. Oh, I imagine there have been some guesses, but that's all they've been. Guesses."

"Go ahead."

"Unconfirmed guesses. The fact of the matter is, I'm running for office."

Arthur looked at Edith and laughed, but she did not smile. "I'm laughing because I was just saying to Edith, you appeared to be running for office."

"Well, you were right. I'm running for lieutenant governor."

Arthur rubbed his chin and stroked his nose with his thumb and forefinger. "It all becomes clear, once you clarify it," he said. "An ambassador of good will, like Lindbergh. Mending fences before they've been broken."

"You might say," said Joe.

"Then I take it you're planning to run next year? That's the next time we vote on lieutenant governor."

"I hope to," said Joe.

"Am I to keep this a secret?"

"Oh, yes indeed. I'm waiting for the psychological moment."

"To announce it to Mike Slattery and the others?"

"Yes."

"How will you know the psychological moment has come?"

"Well, to some extent I'm relying on instinct. When I'm satisfied that I have enough friends in all the counties of the state, then I'll make my position known. You know, Arthur, I've made at least one appearance in every county in the state, and in some counties, like Allegheny and Lackawanna, Dauphin, Philadelphia, Berks, I've made as many as ten appearances."

"Good God, there are seventy-six counties in the Commonwealth. You *have* been busy."

"You're damn right I have."

"Haven't the professionals been suspicious?"

"Suspicious, but careful. They've had nothing to go on. I've made no political speeches except for a few last year in support of Mr. Hoover."

"Thereby declaring yourself against Al Smith, and you did declare yourself all right."

"Well, I'm a Republican. That's no secret, and I meant every word I said against Al Smith. The audacity. Tammany Hall."

"Well, we've had some rotten eggs in our own basket. However, that's neither here nor there. Water under the bridge, they say. I'm more interested in your campaign. You think you'll have enough of a following to be able to convince the Slatterys and people like that that you're the man?"

"That's what I'm counting on."

"But for all you know, they've picked their candidate for next year."

"If they think I'm strong enough, they'll change their minds."

"True."

"I notice you haven't expressed any approval or disapproval," said Joe.

"You've always known how I feel about politics, but you'll always know how I feel about you."

"Arthur, that's all I wanted to know."

"I'll back you with every word I can speak and every dollar I can rake up."

"Yes, I always believed that," said Joe.

"And I think I can guess why you want the job."

"I'll tell you if you're right."

"You want to be as good as your grandfather," said Arthur.

"Yes," said Joe. He looked at Edith, who returned his look expressionlessly. He said no more.

"Well, you are, in my opinion, without going to the bother of a political campaign, but I don't write the history books and I guess that's what you have in mind. As a matter of fact, Joe, now that I've had a moment to think it over, it's a praiseworthy ambition. We've had some judges in our family, and I've often thought I'd like to go down in the books as a judge. But never enough to go into politics. However, your ambition, your pride, is stronger than mine, and I always knew that. They couldn't hope to find a better man. But first—before you start mending fences, mend that leg. I must be going."

When he had gone Edith said: "I was afraid—"

Joe nodded. "I was going to tell him everything. I could tell that. But I feel much better now that I've told him that much. It isn't that we can't trust Arthur, but I think it might *shock* him to know what I really have in mind."

"Oh, he was shocked anyway," said Edith. "He doesn't like it."

"And that's the proof that he's a real friend. He'll support me in spite of his true feelings about politics."

"What else could he do?" said Edith.

The visits of Dr. English were becoming as much *punctilio* as *medico*. There was little he could do to hasten Nature, and his thrice-weekly calls at 10 North Frederick were scheduled to coincide with the serving of a cup of tea.

"I brought my chauffeur with me, I hope it's all right," he announced one afternoon. He was followed into the den by his son Julian.

"Hello, Julian, how nice of you to drop in," said Joe.

"Hello, Mr. Chapin. I'm sorry you had such tough luck, but you're in capable hands. At least that's what my father tells me."

"Really, Julian. I don't talk that way," said the doctor.

"Would you like a Scotch and soda?" said Joe.

"He would not," said the doctor. "He very kindly offered to be my chauffeur, just for this afternoon, but he knew what that entailed. No chauffeur of mine drinks."

Julian and his father rose as Edith came in. "Oh, it's Julian," she said. "How are you?"

"Fine, thank you, Mrs. Chapin. Sorry to be so healthy with Mr. Chapin laid up."

"Would you like a Scotch or something?"

"That problem's just been settled, thanks," said Julian.

"How's Caroline?" said Joe.

"Great," said Julian English. "She's been wanting to come and see you, but your physician discourages visitors. Did you know that?"

"Not Caroline," said Joe. "Billy, don't you know a pretty girl is the best tonic in the world?"

"Well, while we're on that subject, you have one in this house. Ann," said Julian. "If Caroline ever acts up, I'll wait around for Ann to grow up. She's a knockout. What is she now, eighteen?"

"Yes, a little young for you, Julian," said Edith.

"More's the pity, and say, speaking of the Chapin younger generation, I guess you're all getting ready to retire on Joby's earnings."

"Joby's earnings?" said Joe. "I can't even get him to caddy for me."

"Caddy for you? In two more years he'll be making records," said Julian.

"What kind of records? The hundred-yard dash?" said Joe. "He scoots out of the house fast enough to break that record today, but I have no idea where he's in such a hurry to get to."

"Seriously, am I the first to tell you you have a damn near genius in your family?"

316

"You must be," said Joe. "What at, may I ask?"

"At the eighty-eight. The piano," said Julian.

"Why I've never heard him play anything but popular jazz, what we used to call ragtime."

"Oh, Mr. Chapin, come on," said Julian. "That boy could sit in with any dance orchestra—well, almost any dance orchestra. He plays better piano right now than anyone else in Gibbsville."

"No, I don't think he plays anything but that jazz stuff," said Joe.

"But that's exactly what I'm talking about, Mr. Chapin. I'll tell you where he goes when he leaves here. He goes to Michael's Music Shop and listens to Victrola records, and all he has to do is hear a record played once and he can duplicate Roy Bargy, Arthur Schutt, Carmichael. Have you ever heard him play 'In a Mist'?"

"Is that the name of a tune?" said Joe.

"If you have to ask that question, I'm sorry. You don't know about Joby. You must have heard him play 'Rhapsody in Blue,' by George Gershwin. He's been playing that for at least two years."

"Yes, I rather like that one," said Joe. "Is that the one . . ." He hummed the four notes of the great theme.

"That's the one. 'Rhapsody in Blue,' by George Gershwin."

"But it's only jazz, Julian. He never plays anything worthwhile."

"Worthwhile! I've heard about prophets without honor, et cetera. But this is almost fantastic, your not knowing about Joby. The sad part is, I don't think you'll appreciate him even after my outburst."

"And it is an outburst," said the doctor.

"And I don't apologize for it. I hear you're sending him to St. Paul's, which is an all-right school for ordinary boys. But Joby ought to be going to some place like Juilliard or Curtis."

"I've never heard of either one of them," said Edith.

"I've heard of Curtis, so I guess the other's a music school too," said Joe. "But I think we'll go on with our plans to send him to St. Paul's. I'm certainly not going to encourage him to play that jazz stuff."

"No, I don't imagine you will," said Julian, in tones of such disgust that his father rose.

"I won't bother to take your temperature or your blood pressure now, Joe," said the doctor. "I'm sure my own's gone up to the danger level."

"Well, I'm sorry, Mr. Chapin, and Mrs. Chapin. The fact of the matter is, Joby's what I wish I'd been. He's a great jazz piano player, whether you like it or not."

"Well, frankly, Julian, I don't," said Joe. "But it's always nice to know we have *some* talent in the family. I'll try to appreciate it."

"I won't," said Edith. "I'm free to admit."

"No. You have a Steinway, and it isn't even in tune," said Julian.

With that remark there was no further effort to simulate cordiality, and the doctor and his son left.

"And that's what Caroline Walker has to put up with every day," said Edith.

"He makes it very difficult to defend him," said Joe.

"Not many people try any more. And those that do, they're like you, fond of his father."

"No, not altogether that, Edith. He has that certain indefinable thing called charm. And the whole thing started over his well-intentioned overpraise of Joby's piano-playing. His motive was all right, but his enthusiasm and impatience got the better of him. Impatience, that's what it is."

"Oh, rot. It's common, ordinary bad manners by an ungrateful spoiled brat. Caroline can be glad they have no children. That's going to make it easier when the time comes."

A conversation at the Gibbsville Club on an afternoon in 1930:

ARTHUR MC HENRY: Billy, is there anything organically wrong with Joe?

DR. ENGLISH: No, why?

MC HENRY: Are you sure? You can tell me.

ENGLISH: And I would. He's on his feet. Walks almost normally. What do you think is wrong?

MC HENRY: He's never come back since his accident. I don't mean to the office, of course. I mean—well, he has no pep.

ENGLISH: Has anybody any pep these days? You told me yourself Joe lost the better part of two million dollars.

MC HENRY: Hell, Billy, we're all in that together.

ENGLISH: Yes, but some of us are taking it harder than others. We haven't all got your disdain for money.

MC HENRY: Disdain, my ass. But it's gone and there's nothing we can do about it. We're lucky to have anything left.

ENGLISH: Those that *have* anything left. I wanted to retire this year, go abroad, but I'm going to have to stay in harness the rest of my life. I'll be extremely fortunate if I don't end up as an old quack, treating gonorrhea, examining men for lodge insurance. I wish I had Joe's money.

MC HENRY: I'll bet he'd give it to you if you could make him his old self.

ENGLISH: Arthur, damn it all, Joe's nearly fifty. By the normal optimistic life expectancy his life is two-thirds lived. That's the optimistic outlook. Well, at the two-thirds mark he has had a serious accident, and aside from the things that we know that happened, there are *millions* of things about the body that haven't been discovered. Millions. *I* don't know what's the matter with Joe. Something, yes, of course. When I go there to dinner I see it, as a friend as well as a doctor. It's almost as though he'd been dropped, like a magnet, and demagnetized. Not as bad as that, but—

MC HENRY: Sometimes it *is* as bad as that.

ENGLISH: Well, all right. Maybe it's Edith. Maybe it's a personal matter too delicate for him to discuss, even with you. When men begin to lose certain powers—and you know perfectly well what I'm talking about—they sometimes seem to age overnight. And to all intents and purposes that's what they do. But of course I can't bring that up with Joe until he asks me about it, and even if he should, I'd probably send him to a G.U. man or a psychiatrist, and Joe wouldn't go to a psychiatrist. I know that in advance, and I can't say I blame him. Don't worry so much about him. A bad fall shakes you up, and the older you are, the longer it takes to recover from it. You must have noticed that elderly people seem to go on forever until one thing happens—they get a fall. And invariably that's the beginning of the end. It shakes up their insides, disarranges everything, including the unknown, undiscovered elements I spoke of. An elderly person almost never recovers from a fall. Well, Joe's not an elderly person, but he's forty-eight. There's a lot of good sound medical advice in that old saying, watch your step.

MC HENRY: I suppose so.

ENGLISH: We've got him walking again and he may just be taking a long time making a complete recovery. Although I don't look for a complete recovery, frankly. If he tried to run to catch a train, or if he tripped stepping off a curbstone—no good. It'll be another year at least before I give him permission to drive a car. No more horseback riding, at least for several years, and I'd just as soon he forgot about it for good. As to his spirit, if you really want to know what I think, I think one trouble is he misses his daughter, Ann.

MC HENRY: You know, Billy, I think so too.

ENGLISH: Oh, I'm pretty sure of it, pretty sure. But he's going to have to get used to that. I never had a daughter. Wish I had. But I can readily understand how a father could get so attached to one. Why, the way I've got attached to Caroline, and to her all I am is an old ogre that's stingy with Julian.

MC HENRY: Oh, I don't think that's how Caroline feels.

ENGLISH: Spare me your consolation, Mr. McHenry. I'm much wiser than you think. But I'm sure we're right about Joe. He misses Ann. But we can't very well go to a friend of ours and tell him to take his daughter out of boarding school.

MC HENRY: No.

ENGLISH: You and your father always seemed to hit it off very nicely, but that isn't usually the case. It's usually father and daughter that get along well, and Joe and Ann do, only more so. However, when you have an attractive, sweet creature like Ann, you're going to lose her eventually, so this may turn out to be a blessing in disguise.

MC HENRY: Let's hope so. Let's hope *some* good will come of it.

It was the custom among the younger set of Gibbsville to form a group for a swim, a picnic supper, and a visit en masse to one of the amusement parks to dance to the music of the name bands. A band would be booked so that in five successive nights it was never more than seventy-five miles from Gibbsville. After the World War all of the famous bands were booked into the coal regions—Earl Fuller, Fletcher Henderson, Red Nichols, Jean Goldkette, Garber-Davis, Lopez and Whiteman, the Great White Fleet, Waring, Ted Weems, the Scranton Sirens, Art Hand, the Original Dixieland, Ted Lewis, Paul Specht, Ellington, among the readily recognizable names, and others, on their way up, like Charley Frehofer's, which had made a couple of recordings that placed the band among the promising. It was the summer of "Sweet and Lovely," which Frehofer had recorded, and anyone who had an interest and an ear could tell that the unbilled piano soloist had technique, imagination, taste, and heart. The style anticipated Duchin but was a fuller, two-handed discourse, and Joby Chapin brought the record home and played it over and over again on his portable.

"This fellow's good," said Joby.

"What's his name?" said Ann.

"I've written to find out but I haven't got an answer yet."

"He *is* good."

"I'll play his solo again. The last chorus is all band, all out for Swedish Haven. Everybody. But I can't get enough of that piano. Listen."

Ann heard the record so many times that when a party was being

320

organized to hear Frehofer, she mentioned the fact to her brother.

"No use my asking if I can go. They won't let me. But will you try to find out the name of the piano-player?"

"All right," said Ann.

At the dance pavilion Ann moved up to the stand and at the end of a set she asked a saxophone-player to tell her the name of the pianist.

"Hey, Charley, what's your name?" the saxophone-player called.

"I'll bite. What's my name?"

"No kidding, Society Girl wants to know."

The piano-player came to the edge of the stand and leaned down. "Why do you want to know my name? Have you got a subpeeny?"

"First I want to know if you made the record of 'Sweet and Lovely.'"

"I plead guilty," he said. "Did it meet with your approval?"

"Yes, but I'm not asking for myself. My brother is an excellent pianist. He's only fifteen, but he's terribly good, really he is, and he thinks your playing is superb, really."

"Well, good for him."

"Well, what's your *name*, so I can *tell* him?"

"Charley Bongiorno."

"How do you spell that?"

"I'll write it down for you. Sure you don't want my telephone number? Do you live around here?"

"Yes, I live around here. I hope you don't think I came here to spend the summer."

"Here's the name. I hope you can read my writing. How about a drink?"

"Are you inviting us, or what?"

"Inviting you. I have a pint," said Bongiorno.

"Okay," said Ann. "We'll meet you at intermission. We'll be standing to the right of the exit."

"Don't fail me."

The music resumed and Ann's partner said, "I like that—I don't think."

"Oh, don't be a stuffed shirt. You haven't got anything to drink, and I'd love one."

"Well, I'm not going to drink any of that fellow's liquor."

"Well, isn't *that* just too bad."

"What's the matter with you, anyway? Picking up a bum out of an orchestra."

"He didn't seem like a bum. He had nice manners and as far as being a bum, I'll bet he makes more money than you'll make when you're thirty."

"I won't be making it that way, you can be sure."

"I'll say you won't. You can't play 'Chopsticks.' "

"Let's go out in the car."

"No."

"Is that final?"

"It's as final as—the Declaration of Independence."

"Then excuse *me*. Go home with someone else. Your God damn piano player, for all I care."

"Good night, chopsticks," she said. He walked away from her and she had to wait fifteen minutes before Bongiorno met her.

"Where's your boy friend?"

"I'm sure I haven't the faintest idea."

"Is he sore on account of me?"

"Yes, but don't let that worry you."

"Okay, let's get a couple bottles of ginger ale and go to work on this rat poison. Have you got a car?"

"No, have you?"

"No," he said. "How are you going to get home if your boy friend took a run-out?"

"Oh, I came with a crowd. I'll get home."

They bought ginger ale and seated themselves in the back of an unoccupied Buick.

"Straight with a chaser, or a highball?"

"Highball, please."

He made highballs in paper cups and they drank them quickly. "Another?"

"No thanks," she said. "But you go ahead."

"Not right away, thanks."

"Don't thank me," she said.

"I only need one or two at intermission. It keeps me going through intermission, otherwise I'd get tired. I don't get tired as long as I'm playing, but when I stop I do. Where you from? And what's your name? I told you my name, but I was too stupid to ask you yours."

"Ann Chapin. I'm from Gibbsville."

"Yeah, I played Gibbsville last winter, I mean the winter before last, not last winter. This is summer but it's still last winter as far as I'm concerned. We got different suits and we're working outdoors, but the only difference is the temperature. Otherwise it's always the same. But I remember Gibbsville. That's where you live, hey?"

"All my life. Born there."

"I was born in Jersey City, N.J. We just call it Jersey, but people think we mean the whole state when we say Jersey."

"Are you married?"

"Married? Not in this business. Are you?"

"Lord, no. Will you have a cigarette?"

"Thanks. I got a match. I wouldn't get married if I was in this business. I seen too much of it."

"Where'd you learn to play the piano?"

"Where'd I learn to play the piano? From the sisters. You know, the nuns? I'm Catholic. I went to Catholic parochial school and my old lady, my mother, she insisted on I take piano lessons and beat my ears if I din practice an hour a day. But she din have to beat my ears because after at first, you know, I liked it. Then I began making a dollar out of it, oh, then I was Vincent Lopez or somebody. Any piano-player she ever heard of, I was better. Well, she's right I'm better than Vincent Lopez, I'll say that much. 'Nola.' Jesus, if you only *knew* how that offended me. What's the use of playing a piano if you can't play it bettern that? And it's just as much trouble to play bad as good, the way he plays. He moves his fingers as fast as anybody, and he hits the key all right. But Jesus. Your kid brother's good, hey? Who does he like?"

"You."

"Who else? Besides me."

"I'm not very good on their names."

"Well, if he knew I was good on 'Sweet and Lovely' he's got some sense, I know that much. He ain't a 'Nola' man if he liked what I did with my solo. He couldn't be, that I'll guarantee you. I love good piano. If it wasn't for piano I coulda been a dead gangster by now. I knew a couple friends of mine that I grew up with, they end up on the Jersey Meadows and it coulda been me. You come from a well-to-do family, Ann?"

"Yes."

"What would they say if they knew you were out here having a drink with me?"

"I dread to think."

"Well, you oughtna be here, either. I'm glad you are, but some guys with bands, they'd have half your clothes off by this time."

"I was taking a chance, wasn't I? But I did."

"Why, I wonder?"

"Who can tell?"

"Well, to show you how much I respect you, I ain't even gonna ask you for a kiss. And you're pretty, too." He looked at her face and her bosom. "Yeah, you're pretty all right. There's nothing wrong with you, baby. But now I get started thinking that way we better amscray. It-hay the oad-ray. Ann Chapin. I never heard that name before, Chapin. What nationality is that?"

"American. I don't know. English, I guess."

"Chopin, he was really a Polack, you know. He wasn't French. Polack. But you're Chapin. Ann, I know a lot of Annas, but no Ann. I knew an Irish girl named Anna, called herself Ann to put on the dog, but you were always Ann, right?"

"Uh-huh."

"My old lady used to tell me, don't say uh-huh, it ain't polite. But it sounds all right. You want another drink, Ann? Highball out of warm ginger ale?"

"No thanks. Let me see your hands."

"Three over an octave," he said.

She took one of his hands, and impulsively put it to her cheek.

"Now you *want* me to kiss you, don't you?" he said.

"If you want to."

"If I want to? Do you know what, Ann? I love you."

"I believe you."

"Do you love me?"

"I think I do, a little," she said.

"Ann?"

"What?"

"Are you a virgin?"

"Yes," she said.

"Then let's go back."

"All right, Charley," she said. "But kiss me first."

"Not too much of a kiss, though. I ain't responsible."

Two days later, in his hotel room, she ceased to be a virgin, and within a month she was pregnant. In September they were married in a small town in the northern part of the state, near the New York line. An incurious justice of the peace performed the ceremony and there was no vigilant newspaper space-writer to report the event to the Gibbsville papers. The new Mr. and Mrs. Charles V. Bongiorno drove the Chapin Buick to 10 North Frederick Street, and the process of nullifying the marriage was begun immediately. The abortion was performed in a private hospital near Media, Pennsylvania, and once again Mike Slattery was called upon for his unique services, which in this instance required the destruction of an official record of the Commonwealth of Pennsylvania. But "Sweet and Lovely" became what is known in the musical trade as a standard, and indestructible, and with the power in just the first four notes to torture Ann Chapin for as long as she might live.

It had not been a good year for Joe Chapin. His trudging recovery from his accident had prevented his making any effort to try for the lieutenant governor nomination in the spring; and Ann's disastrous romance had taken away some of the strength he had been able to gain during a lazy summer on the farm. Arthur had helped him to accept philosophically the financial defeat of his plan for Edith and the children: it was quite true that "we were all in that together." Everybody wanted to talk about his losses, but no one wanted to listen. The potential listener either had his own losses, or if he had not been seriously affected by the market's behavior, he felt declassé and even a bit of a chump not to have had a million or so on paper. Joe had not yet reached the age at which his own conversation, his half of a conversation, dominated his relationships with other people. He therefore did not inflict the story of his losses on his friends, and by the time most of them were finished with their own woeful accounting, his own losses were made to appear lighter.

And so, for 1930, Joe Chapin had missed out on an opportunity to further his political ambition; he had lost the money that would have realized his financial ambition; and he had been a full partner in the decisions that introduced tragedy into the life of the one human being he loved without reservation, without limit.

What Joe could not know was that after the first hatred of her parents, of the abortionist and his nurse, of Mike Slattery and Billy English and even Arthur McHenry—Ann began to feel pity for her father. The man who had given her understanding and support and secrecy during the Tommy Willis escapade was the same man who had grieved and been shocked and destructive in the Charley Bongiorno episode. As she watched him about the house, moving now with deliberate care where a few years earlier he had been quick and graceful, she was learning what happens to people, even to people whose love you can count on. This saddened man, whom she had once looked upon in what she was afraid was death, had banished her lover and ordered her to an operating table in a house that was disguised as a family home and once had been one. Her father was kind and solicitous when she came home. "We're not going to talk about it, Ann," he said. "Let's consider it as—let's try to think of it as something that didn't happen to us." To talk about it at length, with him, was exactly what she had wanted to do, but she knew he must be feeling guilty of disloyalty to her. He became awkward with her; he was overpolite and overcasual, where always in the past he had been casual and polite and sure. When she kissed him good night he would lay his fingers on her arm, where in the other days he had always given her a loving squeeze. He was not treating her as though she had become fragile, although the things he had been responsible for had made demands on her toughness. Well, maybe not toughness. Strength.

She was around the house as a secret invalid, a girl who belonged back in boarding school, a full-fledged woman, a graduate of emotional torture, an only daughter, the equal of her parents, the sister of her not-much-younger brother, a person who was suddenly allowed to have a cocktail and a cigarette because to forbid her to have a cocktail and a cigarette after her recent ordeal would have been as silly as trying to force her to play with dolls in order to make her a girl again. The ambiguities of her position in the family were in evidence from one minute to another.

"Ann dear," said her mother. "We thought you could wait awhile before going back to school. I'll write and tell them you've been ill, but will be going back for the second fall term."

"But I'm not going back, Mother," she said calmly.

"You're not?"

"Oh, that would be ridiculous. A married woman living with a bunch of schoolgirls? Of course not."

"She's right, Edith," said Joe.

"But you haven't finished any school. You really ought to go somewhere and finish."

"I went to that hospital, that's finishing enough for me. Don't let's talk about it, or I'll go away. Mother—and you too, Father—I'm liable to go away anyhow. I'll keep my word. I won't see Charley. But that isn't saying I won't go away. And if I go, I'm not going to ask you if I can go. I'll just go. I have three hundred dollars in the bank—"

"I will put a thousand in the bank for you tomorrow," said Joe. "If you can't stand it here, tell us, but don't think of us as using money as a hold over you. If a thousand isn't enough, I'll make it two. But we want you here because we love you, and maybe we can help you. If we can, we'll try."

"We ought to have some excuse for your not going back to school. Everybody knows you have another year," said Edith.

"A lot of girls quit school at nineteen," said Ann. "Say I'm thinking of taking a secretarial course in New York. And I am, as a matter of fact."

"People will believe that, Edith."

"All right, just so we agree on a story. That's what I'll tell them at Oak Hill, too," said Edith.

The people who knew the truth of her relationship with Charley Bongiorno—Dr. English, Uncle Arthur McHenry, Mr. Slattery, the abortionist, the nurse—had all been of her parents' choosing. She realized one day that except for her mother and father, there was no one whom she had told by choice. And although the weeks were passing, the need to confide was not. It was not only a question of telling her *side* of it; it was a matter of telling the whole story. And there was only one person in the world for that.

She said to her mother one morning: "Can Harry drive me to the club today?"

"Why of course. I won't need him, and your father's been at the office for hours. Are you going to play golf?"

"No. Just have lunch."

"Alone?"

"There's always somebody there."

Ann sat on the front seat of the Cadillac sedan.

"The club?"

"Philadelphia. I have a lot to tell you."

"Do you mean that, Philadelphia?"

"Depends on how long it takes. Don't drive fast."

She made him promise not to interrupt until she told him she was finished. They were not far from Philadelphia when she said, "And that's all."

He turned the car to the side of the road and stopped. He bowed his head and wept. He kept his hands in his lap and then he put his hands on the steering wheel and rested his head on them and wept more wholly. At last he spoke as he took out a handkerchief.

"I knew there was something," he said. "They did a great job of camouflaging, but I knew you were in some kind of trouble. Where's your husband now?"

"I'm keeping my promise. I don't know."

"Do you want me to find him for you?"

"No," she said. "They'll make trouble for him."

"Trouble? *Trouble*? What do you want to do? That's all I want to know."

"Oh—whatever I am doing. Whatever that is. Just going on living and not shooting myself."

"Don't say that! Jesus Christ, girl!" This time he cried out and the weeping began again, but now it was not wordless; it was full of mutterings and incoherent sentences, and she put his head on her shoulder and patted his face. But it always stops, and his weeping stopped with a deep sigh.

"Harry. Dear sweet Harry," she said.

He smiled. "Dear sweet Harry, with a whole head full of salty tears and nothing else."

"That's why you're sweet and dear."

"I brung along me pipe and tobacco. I think I'll have a smoke," he said. The operation of filling and lighting his pipe, the something to do, brought him back from his misery.

"Marian and I have over fourteen thousand dollars saved up, not including six thousand dollars in Liberty Bonds. You ought to go away."

"I may."

"We'll give you the money. Don't take it off of them."

"I don't know," she said. "If I go I might as well let them pay for it."

"No, that'll let them salve their conscience. That's letting them off too cheap. It isn't money either one of them sweated over. All it is is writing a check. It's time they realized writing a check doesn't make up for things. I'd rather you took our money, good hard work and long years behind it."

"They wouldn't like that if I did."

"Oh, I'm giving notice anyway, whether you take the money or don't. I wouldn't live in the same house with them any more."

"If you leave, I'll leave."

"All right, that's what I want you to do."

"No, Harry. I'm going to stay. At least for a while."

"Why?"

"Oh—it's my home, and they're my parents. I think there's been enough harm done for one family, without my adding to it. If I leave, what good will that do anybody? Now I pity them. They're beginning to realize they did something awful and they're not sure what they ought to do to make up for it. And I'm just as well off there as I would be any place else. Maybe better."

"There's one thing you mustn't let them do. You mustn't let them make you think you made a mistake. Never let them do that. You made no mistake, girl. They made the mistake. Ah, what a mistake they made, and it'll plague them."

Before she could reply they heard the short whirl of a police siren and immediately there was a face under a Stetson at the left door of the car.

"Having trouble?" said the highway patrolman.

"Well, not your kind of trouble," said Harry.

"Are you the owner of this car?"

"I work for the owner."

"Me see your owner's registration and your driver's license."

Harry handed them to him. The cop held onto them while he questioned Harry. "Do you think this is a safe place to park, right on a main highway?"

"Well, I don't know."

"Do you always stop on a main highway when you want to have a chat with your girl friend? I've been watching you for ten minutes."

"We been here ten minutes?"

"More than ten minutes. I've been *watching* you for ten minutes."

"And we didn't break any law."

"No, but if you want to park why don't you get off the main highway? Who're you, young lady? The maid?"

"She's the maid."

"Pretty soft for you. Go on, why don't you roll?"

"All right," said Harry.

The cop mounted his motorcycle and moved up to the door again. "Give him the air, baby. He's too old for you." He laughed, looked behind him, and deliberately backfired the machine and roared away.

The fresh cop changed the trip home into a cheerful journey.

Edith Chapin often wished that the family physician had not been so early in life and so permanently a man who was also a family friend. It was not so much that she felt embarrassment through the presence and the touch of Billy English; she had long ago accepted Billy in his impersonal, professional role; there was nothing more for him to see or to know. Except that there *was* more to know, that she never could let him know. She had no confidant as, for example, Ann had Harry Jackson as confidant. She had no woman friend to whom she would entrust a secret that was more her own than the more or less routine intimacies that she could tell another woman as another woman would confide in her. There were, so to speak, body secrets, functional secrets that finally were not secrets at all. They had, for instance, nothing to do with desire. She would not even go so far as to tell Josephine Laubach or Rose McHenry that she considered a man handsome. She seldom told any of the secrets of her mind, whether or not they were related to the actions or needs of her body. Even with Joe she had assumed and maintained an identity that went only as far as she wanted to go—and seemed to be as much as he wanted. They could revel in extremes of passionate experiment, but in the morning, after they had slept, they managed to make no reference, by word or by look, to the departure from conventional husband-and-wife that had occurred in the night. They would speak of each other as "my husband," "my wife," in such terms as to make the appellation seem to be a form of approval and applause, but at the same time a warning to the listener not to inquire into the sub-surface relationship.

During the long convalescence Joe had not been in bed with her, and there was enough of drama and alarm about the accident to render them both impotent during the early stages. But when Joe went back to wanting her actively, the nature of his injury kept them apart. He had been warned of the serious consequences of a re-fracture, and when he was walking again and wanted to stay with her, she was still so fearful of his breaking his leg again that she could not want him. He would kiss her and touch her but the effect on her was no more exciting than a warm bath, and after his first attempts to force entrance into her, which were sufficient for him but inadequate for her, she would let him kiss her good night and no more. If he put a hand on her breast she would lift it away. "Wait till you're all well again," she would say.

"But I am all well," he would say.

"Not till I hear it from Billy English," she would say.

But Billy English neglected to volunteer the advice that they could resume their full marital relationship. (Joe was his friend, but not his whole practice.) And in just such matters Edith was unable to speak frankly with Billy. She could not say to him: "I want to sleep with somebody." There was no one in the world to whom she could say that, although that was the truth: the truth was not only that she wanted to sleep with Joe; she wanted to be slept with, and it didn't have to be with Joe.

Lloyd Williams was getting to be somebody in the county, no longer the nobody of the affair of ten years ago. He was getting to be so much of a somebody that he could, almost, safely boast about it if she slept with him again. She knew that as a nobody he had been astute enough to realize that to boast about the single night in Philadelphia would have been dangerous to his career; might even have been dangerous to his life. Ten years ago Joe might conceivably have shot him, Arthur McHenry would have beaten him, her own brother Carter might have defended her honor. And any or all of them would have hurt him professionally in the ways at their command, from political preferment to bank credit. Now if she were to use him and he were to brag about it, now that he was the district attorney and on his way up, he could blab it in any saloon in the county and be believed and remain unharmed. And now she would have another woman to contend with, for Williams had married Lottie, and Edith was one of the women who had always looked right through Lottie without seeing her.

Among her friends and acquaintances in Gibbsville there were women who had looked at her with expressions of bold curiosity. There were women who Edith was sure had had other men, and there were the others who had not had other women but were wondering whether she might not be the first. Sometimes she would be at the club, sitting on the terrace, and she would turn to discover a woman staring at her with such open, relaxed inquisitiveness that the woman was caught off guard, revealing more of herself than had ever been actively suspected of Edith. And Edith would smile politely, for the woman was always someone she knew, and say to herself: "Wouldn't you like to know?" The truth was that Edith had a great deal of contempt for members of her own sex. They could not lead the life of idleness without playing bridge or getting into some kind of trouble, spending too much money or incurring imaginary ailments, taking to the bottle or pretending to be unaware of their husband's whores.

Ann's elopement was a frightening experience for Edith, and she was thankful that her own circumspection had kept her from being in the midst of some kind of extra-marital affair to match her daughter's rashly romantic impulse. An affair of her own would not have made her tolerant of Ann's, but she would not have been secure in her position of stern but kindly parent. Besides being a frightening experience it was an alarming one, alarming because of the detail of Ann's pregnancy; for Edith, who had not been bothered much by the candles on her birthday cakes (everyone in Gibbsville knew how old everyone else was), now realized that for a few months Ann had carried in her belly the first Chapin grandchild. Edith was forty-four, but it was not the number of years that mattered so much as the status of grandmother. As a mother only, a woman indulging in misconduct can have romantically forgivable excuses, but the same behavior in a grandmother becomes foolishness that is hard to forgive, even by other foolish grandmothers. For the moment, and possibly for the last time, Edith had been granted a respite. And for the moment she was not sure what she wanted to do with it. But she was having the respite.

A new and distinct kind of impoverished aristocracy was in the making during 1930 and 1931. Its members were those men, and their families, who had made money in the stock market or through the general prosperity of the country in the latter half of the Twenties. They were quick aristocrats in the sense that their standing was based on recent dollars, but they were also quick to copy the spending habits (not yet the thrifty habits) of those families that had had money for more generations than could be measured by the new-rich in years. Moreover, the rich of the latter Twenties had so easily accustomed themselves to the tokens of wealth and, when possible, the company of older money that they also learned how to spend with the same free gallantry, if not quite the grace, that had been acquired by the old-rich through several generations. And when the stock-market ticker refused to answer their prayers they continued to spend and speculate until they had nothing left but their vote. With some misgiving, but hopefully, they gave or loaned their vote to the newer Mr. Roosevelt.

Joe Chapin had not been sufficiently impoverished to impel him to cast his vote for a Democrat, and the lasting impression made by the 1932 Democratic candidate as a Harvard undergraduate gave Joe Chapin a special reason for remaining a Republican. It was not feasible or desirable for Joe Chapin to stump the county and the state and tell the voters he had not liked Franklin D. Roosevelt at New York debutante parties. In the national mood of that moment such talk would have been paid for gladly by the Democratic National Committee. But Joe expressed himself at the Gibbsville Club and elsewhere, and since a lost cause makes aristocrats rather more attractive, and since Joe Chapin was already well thought of, his support of Mr. Hoover hurt him personally not at all; and actually was of some value in later years when he claimed the distinction of uninterrupted party conformism. He never had to make that hackneyed, apologetic admission that he had "voted for him in '32, but once was enough."

Arthur McHenry confessed that right up to the very last minute, even as he entered the voting booth, he had not decided not to vote for the Democrat. "But then I thought of who my friends are, and I voted right," he said. There was enough of Arthur's and Joe's kind of thinking to carry the state for Mr. Hoover, but there were not enough of them in the country as a whole, and Mike Slattery and a thousand men like him took a hard look at the figures and knew they had their work cut out for them. In Mike's case the test would be in '34, when the voters would elect a governor and a United States senator. "Give him enough rope and he'll hang himself," said Peg Slattery, of the new President.

"Ah, now, but will he?" said Mike. "You won't listen to him on the radio, but you ought to, Peg. Know your opposition is one of the first rules of this nefarious profession of mine. Know your opposition, and take stock of what you've got to buck up against it with. Three things licked Hoover. The Depression, the fellow they elected, and Hoover himself. Say a few Hail Marys we'll develop a spellbinder by 1936, nationally."

"Put up Graham McNamee," said Peg.

"A funny remark, but closer to the truth than you realize. Say another few Hail Marys he stays out of the governor and senator campaign in '34. Which he won't, of that you may be sure. He wants Pennsylvania. He has to have Pennsylvania if he wants to win again."

"Win again, Mike? He's hardly in the White House."

"It'll take dynamite to get him out. Do you think that fellow's going to be satisfied with the one term? The campaign he ran? The wanting to show his fifth cousins? He'll run in '36 and he's going to make a fight for this state the likes of which you never saw. We haven't put in a Democrat for governor since 1890, and if it wasn't for somebody named Gill that ran on the Prohibition ticket we'd have won then, but that was 1890. This'll be 1934 and there won't be enough Prohibitionists to cut any ice one way or the other. We're not going to be running against the fellow that gets the Democratic nomination, either for governor or senator. We're going to be running against the fellow they just elected President. He'll see to that."

At 10 North Frederick Street there was another conversation of a political nature.

"Well, our friend had his parade," said Joe.

"Our friend? What parade?"

"You know our friend, the friend of the common people. The Harvard snob."

"Oh, of course," said Edith. "He had a parade?"

"Didn't you know about the parade? The N.I.R.A. parade, the Blue Eagle. What fools these mortals be. Every day I pick up the paper and it's getting so that if there isn't some new socialistic scheme, I'm surprised. Arthur thinks the N.I.R.A. may be unconstitutional, even though he's rather sympathetic toward some of our friend's wild schemes. I don't know whether it's unconstitutional or not. I haven't examined it that carefully, but I'm damned sure it's dictatorial."

"Well, if it's dictatorial isn't it unconstitutional?"

"That will have to be decided in court and it'll take some time."

"When does he get out?"

"When the people get some sense and vote him out, in 1936."

"How old will you be then? Let me think," said Edith.

"In 1936 I'll be fifty-four."

"And in 1934 is when—"

"Yes. Is when we go to the polls to elect a new governor. And lieutenant governor."

"You're going to run, aren't you? You still plan to?" said Edith.

"As fast as my legs can carry me," said Joe. "A rather appropriate remark, considering the shape of my legs, or one of them. Feeling the way I do about our friend, I *have* to run. It isn't only the honor any more. It's something I feel inside me, a matter of conscience, not to be too high-sounding about it, but that's what it is. Anything I can do to shorten his stay in the White House or to make it unpleasant, I'm duty bound to do. I'll campaign, I'll spend as much money as I can afford without endangering your financial security. I'll run as fast as my legs can carry me. And that's appropriate, too. You know our friend is worse off than I am, much worse. I can walk. He can't."

"Yes, you told me that," said Edith.

"I'm struck by the points of similarity between us. First, the kind of background he had, not too much unlike mine, although he's trying to destroy people like us. Second, this isn't a point of similarity, but I did know him slightly and couldn't stand him, and the

334

point of similarity is that he didn't like me either. Third, remember when I told you how he'd run for vice-president without any political experience?"

"Yes, I remember."

"And then there's the similarity of handicaps. Mine isn't serious, but his is. He contracted infantile paralysis, and I broke my leg. I think it's fascinating. I could probably think of a better word than fascinating, but fascinating will do."

"And of course Arthur thinks you look a little like him."

"Arthur also used to think I looked like Woodrow Wilson. Arthur would like me to be a Democrat so that he could be one too."

"Not really," said Edith.

"No, not really, but it does irritate me," said Joe. "Oh, he told me a rather amusing thing that happened at The Second Thursdays. Last week it was unanimously agreed to stop drinking the customary toast to the President of the United States."

"Well, I should hope so," said Edith.

Joe smiled. "They couldn't wait till next winter. Henry Laubach polled the members and they all agreed."

"Didn't he call you?" said Edith.

"He didn't have to. Arthur said he felt sure he could speak for me, and he was right," said Joe. "It's interesting, you know. Woodrow Wilson wasn't the most popular man with the Second Thursdays, but they kept on drinking the toast."

"We were at war," said Edith.

"Yes, so we were. Well, I'd have felt like a damned hypocrite toasting Roosevelt, and now we won't have to."

"In 1936 you'll be fifty-four," said Edith.

"What made you come back to that?"

"Thinking ahead," said Edith. "Suppose you were elected lieutenant governor next year. Does the lieutenant governor get to be so widely known that they'll consider him for President?"

"Frankly, no," said Joe. "It would be an accident, politically. But I'm afraid 1936 isn't the year I'll try for. Nineteen-forty's the year now."

"In 1940, you'll be fifty-eight," said Edith.

"Yes. Still in my fifties."

"Your late fifties, though," said Edith.

He smiled. "Well, I hope by that time our friend will be forgotten and I won't have to campaign so hard. Is that what you were wondering about?"

335

"No, just getting the dates arranged in my mind," said Edith.

"I've decided not to spend much time thinking about the presidency. Our friend is a good man to oppose, and if I run for lieutenant governor, I'll start right out opposing Roosevelt and everything he stands for. I'm not going to bother my head about the other candidate for lieutenant governor. I'm going to campaign against their top man, because they're going to try to make the short-sighted voters believe that Roosevelt is thinking of them night and day, every step of the way. Preposterous, of course, but that's what they'll try to argue. And I'll bang away at Roosevelt, Roosevelt, Roosevelt in every speech I make."

"Are you sure that's the best idea?"

"Because it might hurt me? Edith, if I campaign against Roosevelt and lose, at least I'll have campaigned against Roosevelt, not against whoever the Democrats put up for lieutenant governor. And even if I lose the election, it can still be a successful campaign as far as I personally am concerned. There are some fellows at the club that say we have nothing to worry about. Just sit tight and let him ruin himself. I don't agree with that. In the first place, he's going to have to be ousted, kicked out. If we just let him hang himself, he's going to take his own good time doing it. In the second place, I'm not going to pass up a glorious opportunity to say what I think about him, and simultaneously prove that I can be a good campaigner, a fighter. I've never had that opportunity because I didn't want to take it and waste it on a campaign for Common Pleas. When Mike offered me that job, Judge of Common Pleas, he and I both knew that all I had to do was say yes, and go get measured for my robe. I wouldn't have had to make any speeches. I could have gone to Atlantic City for the whole campaign. But if I want to be elected to anything next year, anything at all, I'll have to campaign. All Republicans will, because we're out to beat Roosevelt. It will be a great pleasure."

"Especially if you win."

"Especially if we win," said Joe. "Well, first I must convince Mike Slattery that he must convince that State Committee that I'm the logical man for lieutenant governor. Logic. There is no such thing as a logical man for that job. But I suppose if logic had anything to do with it, I could be called the logical man on account of Grandfather Chapin."

"What is there against you?"

"Against me? Well, first the State Committee has to decide on the governor, and not always, but usually, they allow him to have some say in picking his running mate. I don't think Gifford Pinchot would want me as his running mate, for instance, but Gifford Pinchot won't be nominated again. Then there are other considerations. I'm not a breaker boy, I've never pretended to be poor, and if having some money worries a voter I don't see how he can vote for our friend. Our friend has a family place up the Hudson that—oh, well, you know. I've never believed that having money hurt a candidate. Mr. Hoover is a *very* rich man, *very*."

"But he was defeated."

"Before that he won," said Joe. "What is there against me? Well, I'll find out."

Joe met Mike Slattery by appointment at the Bellevue-Stratford in Philadelphia. If they were seen together, what more natural than two Gibbsville friends running across each other in the city? If they were not seen together, so much the better for Joe's first plan, which was to have an uninterrupted discussion in which he could sound out Mike. Mike came to Joe's room, where lunch was served, and when the waiter was dismissed, the two men smiled at each other.

"Mike, I think my best strategy with you is to be completely frank with you," said Joe.

"Well, I wouldn't know about the strategy, Joe. But at least it'll be a change from the way fellows usually approach me. Naturally you didn't lure me to your room and give me a fine big lobster just for a change from Bookbinder's."

"For a long time I've been working at building up my contacts, as some people call them, and when I had my accident I was just getting ready to have this talk with you. But it's taken me a long time to get on my feet again, you might say, but now that I am on my feet, both feet, I'll put my cards on the table."

"Right," said Mike.

"Next year we're going to have the two big state contests. For governor, and for United States senator."

Mike nodded, but said nothing.

"I don't want either of them."

"You don't want either job, is that it?"

"Yes."

"I'm only making you say these things so there'll be no misunderstandings. Some men who are somewhat less experienced might think we've already picked our candidates. But we haven't."

"I see," said Joe. "Well, as I say, I don't want either job, I don't want either nomination."

"But now that you've told me what you don't want, you're going to tell me what you *do?*"

"Yes," said Joe. "I want the nomination for lieutenant governor."

Mike leaned forward and took a tiny sip of his ice water. "Who knows that you want it?"

"Edith knows. Until now, no one else. Arthur has a pretty good idea. But that's all."

Mike whistled softly an unrecognizable tune, unrecognizable to Joe because it was the Stabat Mater. He uncrossed and recrossed his legs. "I'm not going to waste both our time by asking you a lot of questions that you've thought out the answers to. I'm sure they're the right answers and good ones. You know you want the nomination, you have your reasons, going back, I suppose, to your grandfather. You're pretty well convinced that your contacts will support you?"

"Yes and no. I've spoken to no one about what I want but I modestly believe that I could count on a great deal of support from my contacts, which by the way are in every county in the state. I've used my Bar Association connections to make a great many after-dinner speeches. It usually worked out that I'd go to some Bar Association function, then get invited back for something like the League of Women Voters, and various Republican organizations, and Boy Scout dinners—all sorts of things. I've never talked politics, or at any rate not the kind of politics we mean when we say we talked politics. I wasn't actually running for anything, but I was, and I admit it, running in a sort of popularity contest, personal variety."

Mike took another sip of ice water. "I haven't heard much talk about lieutenant governor so far. To that extent you have nobody to compete with. However, there may be several fellows have their eye on the job and are waiting to see which way the blanket turns. You know how these things work. If we nominate a governor from this part of the state, you haven't a chance. But if he's from west of the Nesquehela, that'll be in your favor. Speaking personally, and going only that far, I'd like to see you get the nomination, and not only as a friend. Joe, I'll tell you this much. I've known for some time about your building up contacts, and I know you made an excellent impression. That doesn't surprise me in the least. But you also know how it is in practical politics. Personal considerations, and attractive personality—they often mean less than nothing. And I'm a practical politician. I'm not a statesman. I'm a successful, fairly respectable ward-heeler. And if the rest of our fellows want somebody else, I'll see it their way. If on the other hand, they have nobody ticketed, I'll fight for you."

"That's what I hoped you would say."

"Now. Practical politics. Are you going to ask friends to help with the finances? Henry Laubach? Arthur? People like that?"

"Not for the nomination. I'm willing to do that myself."

"Are you sure you want to do that, Joe? Sometimes, in fact, usually, it's a better idea to have a lot of people putting up moderate sums than one or two people putting up the whole war chest."

"I'll take all the help I can get after I get the nomination, but whatever I have to spend before the nomination I'll do myself."

"It may be a considerable sum."

"I know."

"You may spend a considerable sum and not get the nomination."

"That's why I don't want my friends to give me financial support till I know they're going to get a run for their money."

"Now by a considerable sum, Joe, I mean a considerable sum. You may find yourself spending money, your own money, where another fellow that wants the nomination won't be spending anything because he's an organization regular. Remember, you're new at this, and it can be an expensive education."

Joe reached in his pocket and took out a long envelope and laid it in front of Mike. "You want me to look at this?" said Mike.

Joe nodded.

Mike emptied the envelope on the table. "I think I see twenty thousand dollars."

Joe nodded again.

"Do you want me to put this in my pocket?" said Mike.

Joe nodded again.

Mike smiled. "Joe, don't worry about a dictograph being hidden somewhere. If there's one here, which I doubt, we've said enough already."

"I haven't said anything in any way incriminating," said Joe.

"Have it your own way," said Mike. He got up and went out into the hall and beckoned to Joe to follow him.

"There's no dictograph out here, we can be sure of that," said Mike. "Don't be too suspicious, Joe. Money changes hands all the time. Now as to this money, I'll see that it gets where it'll do the most good. And I'll time it right. I'll wait till our fellows begin asking about money before they see a cent of this. Is that satisfactory to you?"

"Perfectly."

"Fine, now let's go back and have another cup of coffee and forget political intrigue."

Joe laughed. "Mike, you're a wonder."

"Oh, well," said Mike, not entirely displeased. "At least you didn't call me a smart Irishman."

"Only because I forgot to."

"I like it when people forget that," said Mike. "You'll be hearing from me in about a month, not before. If it's a big fat no, that'll end it for good. But if it isn't a no, just a perhaps, will you want me to continue trying?"

"As long as there's a good chance," said Joe.

"I'll almost guarantee you that much. As to this—" he tapped his coat pocket—"you understand you've kissed that good-bye."

"I understand," said Joe.

In about a month Mike telephoned Joe: "I'm a day or so late," he said. "But I just wanted you to know. I told you if there was a big fat no, that'd end it. Well, there hasn't been a big fat no or a little thin one, but I was right. A couple of other fellows think they'd like the same thing you'd like."

"Are they important?"

"Oh, more or less, but they can be dealt with. I'll call you again in three or four weeks."

Edith tried to persuade Joe to exact more detailed reports from Mike, but Joe argued against it. "The less we know of Mike's maneuverings at this stage of the game, the better off we are."

The next call from Mike was a week later than he had said he would be. "Do you remember what you handed me in Philadelphia?"

"Of course," said Joe.

"How many times would you be willing to multiply it? In other words, is your limit twice that? Two and a half times it? Or five times? What is your outside limit?"

"I'd have to know a lot more than I do know before answering that question," said Joe.

"I understand. Well, do you want to run into me at the club in about an hour or so?"

"I'll be there," said Joe.

Mike was reading his New York *Herald Tribune* in a back corner of the reading room. "Why, hello, there, Joe. As the Indians say, long time no see."

"May I join you for a minute or two?" said Joe.

"Well, we've made it casual," said Mike. "Have a seat. The fellows want to know this: how much is Chapin willing to spend on the campaign as a whole, and take his chances on the nomination?"

"I could spend a hell of a lot and never get anywhere."

"Exactly," said Mike. "But that's what they want to know, and they want me to find out. They won't make a single promise, not a single one. The twenty thousand, that's in the war chest. You're credited with it, but it had no strings attached to it."

"I fully realize that."

"They argue this way, Joe. Whatever you contribute, you're going to be taken care of somehow, proportionately to what you give. But they want to know are you going to hold out money in order to get a handshake deal on the particular job you want. If that's the case, they won't do business. You see, voting being what it is, they're not going to shake hands on lieutenant governor if you don't qualify for the ticket. You have to make a strong ticket, and you personally may not make it strong because of where you come from, or your background, or any number of things. That's only right, Joe. That's the way it works in politics. But what they *will* guarantee you is that they'll take care of you, although it may not be lieutenant governor."

"But that's the job I picked. What else is there?"

"Governor, and United States senator. And you won't get either one of those. A million dollars wouldn't get you senator. Now I don't say you're not going to get lieutenant governor but we're not going to—I say we, I mean they—they're not going to promise you something they may not be able to deliver."

Joe thought a moment. "I'll tell you what I'll do. I'll go five times as much as I have gone. In plain language, up to a hundred thousand, but with the understanding that that will also be my campaign contribution if and when I get the nomination. In other words, a hundred thousand between now and the primaries, but after that nothing. If my friends want to contribute, all right, but no more from me. If I don't get the nomination, no more contributions for twenty years."

"Oh, they're not going to like that last part. Do you really want me to tell them that? It sounds as though you were trying to give the orders."

"Not the orders. The money," said Joe. "And don't forget, Mike, I didn't say it was my final contribution for twenty years if I *do* get the nomination. I only said that if I don't get the nomination, I'll stop contributions for twenty years. It's like a life membership in a club. I usually give about five thousand a year to the organization. And to tell you the truth, I have been giving it for so long that I could argue that I shouldn't spend anything *like* a hundred thousand to get the nomination I want."

"What you gave in the past was the contribution of a regular party man. A lot of fellows in your circumstances give that much and more without wanting anything in return. And, Joe, I hate to bring this up, but there's that matter upstate, the thing I took care of with that justice of the peace."

"I always knew that would be brought up sooner or later."

A laudatory page-one piece in Bob Hooker's newspaper—two-column measure, 12-point Ionic on a 14 slug—was so skillfully done that many citizens actually asked Joe Chapin if he approved of Bob Hooker's article. Since Joe had read the piece as soon as it came out of the typewriter, and had reread it in galley proof, the question was not hard to answer. But among the older friends of the Chapin family a publicly active participation in politics was still regarded as a relinquishing of one's privacy. Mr. Taft was said to be a gentleman, Teddy was a gentleman, Woodrow Wilson was probably a gentleman, Gifford Pinchot was a gentleman but a strange one, and there had been other gentlemen who ran for political office, but as a rule, as a good, sound general rule, it was better to stay out of politics when politics meant running for office. It was all very well to be a strong supporter of the party, and to accept, say, a Cabinet office, but it was not all very well to ask people to vote for you. What was to be gained? On the evening that Bob Hooker's Call to Arms was sounded there were, therefore, quite a few older people on Lantenengo Street and South Main who characterized the editorial and its author as "fresh." They agreed that the party, as Bob Hooker said, needed a man like Joseph B. Chapin, but they were sorry that Bob Hooker had taken it upon himself to specify not a man *like* Joe Chapin—but Joe Chapin!

The telephone at 10 North Frederick began ringing at about six-thirty, and the first calls were politely indignant. But after Edith had told various friends that Joe had seen the editorial, was flattered by it, and felt that if that was where his duty lay . . . On the following day Joe's statement was published. It was a nice combination of modesty and forthrightness.

"I was highly complimented to read the editorial which urged me to campaign for the high office once held by my grandfather and namesake, Joseph B. Chapin. I have always believed that the office should seek the man rather than the reverse. At the same time, I believe that good citizens of whatever party affiliation are becoming increasingly aware of the danger to the American way of life which is now threatening us in the national capital; and it is my conviction that no man or woman can shirk the performance of any task, great or small, which may contribute to the restoration of the fundamental principles on which this country was founded and which have made it great. If it should fall to my lot to be chosen to fight for those principles in a campaign for high office in our beloved Commonwealth, I shall accept the charge and carry our message to the people of Pennsylvania. If this be done, if the people are acquainted with the conditions which are leading us down the road to state socialism, the issue can never be in doubt. Suffice it to say that as an American and as a Republican I shall campaign to the best of my ability."

In several homes on Lantenengo and South Main and West Christiana, the head of the house was moved to say: "Good for Joe Chapin!"

In Collieryville, in the home of the district attorney, Lloyd Williams, that public servant exclaimed: "Oh, dear."

"What?" said Lottie Williams.

"Oh, dear. Dear me."

"*What?*" said his wife. "What are you oh-dearing about?"

"Oh, I don't like to see a thing like this happen to a nice fellow like Joe Chapin."

"What's happening?"

He tossed her the newspaper. "Read it."

Lottie was a slow reader of items longer than four lines, and when she finished Joe's statement she looked at her husband inquiringly. "What are you worrying about? It's an honor, isn't it?"

"It's an honor if you call letting Mike Slattery make a horse's ass out of you an honor."

"Oh," said Lottie. "You mean he's not going to get elected?"

"That's some consolation," said Williams.

"That he won't get elected?"

"That he won't get nominated. At least he won't be making a

343

horse's twat out of himself all over the state," said Williams. "He's an honest son of a bitch that hated Roosevelt and let himself get sucked in." He slapped the newspaper with the back of his fingers. "From here I'd be inclined to say that that statement cost Chapin about twenty-five thousand bucks."

"Really?"

"For openers. That damn Mike Slattery's a real bastard to do this to Joe Chapin. I don't know, God damn it, I'm all for taking it away from the rich and giving it to the rich politician but there's such a thing as common decency. Well—maybe that's asking too much in politics. But he could have done it to Henry Laubach. Or could he? No. Not that cold fish. He's too smart. Not too smart. Too unfeeling. He wouldn't know how to hate Roosevelt the way Joe Chapin does."

"I don't follow you. You ask yourself a question and then you answer it and then you contradict it."

"Don't pay no attention to me."

"How can I help it when you talk like you were delirious? I hope he gets a good kick in the ass."

"Joe Chapin? Why?"

"Oh, him I don't care about one way or another. But her."

"What about her?"

"Who does she think she is, looking straight through a person as if I was nothing? You talk about Henry Laubach. There's the cold fish, that Edith Stokes."

"No."

"You bet she is."

"No, I screwed her years ago," said Williams.

"Yeah, that was when I was the Queen of England. I don't think she has a good screw in her, if you want to know what I think."

"She has two children," said Williams.

"That's just getting pregnant. You know darn well what I mean."

"Well, you never can tell," said Williams. "She may be just right for Joe."

"Then I don't think much of him. I wouldn't vote for him, on account of her. She's high-hat enough so's it is."

"I'll bet you a good dinner you won't get a chance to vote for him."

"Well, if I did, I wouldn't," said Lottie.

He was off by himself again. "If I had some common decency about me I'd go and have a talk with him. But would I? He wants it, or else it wouldn't get this far. It's none of my business if he wants to throw away twenty-five thousand bucks. He has it."

"Over a million, I hear," said Lottie.

"And I've got myself to look out for. He isn't what you call a real friend of mine. I never went to his house."

"Fat chance of that," said Lottie. "I'll bet you never even saw their house. When were you ever on North Frederick Street? I lived over in that part of town for a couple years. I went to school to William Street. Fourth and fifth grade. Maybe it was fifth and sixth. I know I went to fifth at William Street. Fifth I remember. I think I remember fifth because twice five. I was ten years old. But part of the time I was either in fourth or sixth. I know I was ten when I was in fifth. That I do remember. But I'm not sure if I was there when I was *nine*, or *eleven*. I can't make sure whether I had my tenth birthday when I was in fifth or when I was in fourth. I'da still been ten if I had it when I was in fourth because school starts the Tuesday after Labor Day, in September. The Catholics used to start the Friday before Labor Day, or the Friday after. Before. That's right. Before. They always started earlier than we did. They never used to start the same day. And they used to get days off, holy days, but we got Institute Week. We always got off Institute Week and boy were they sore! But then they'd have some day like Holy Mother, or something, and they'd get the day off and we'd have to go. Let's see now, we got the week off for Institute Week. That was five days. The whole week. But they got all those religious days off, must have been five at least. Oh, more than that. And we used to argue. Would you rather have the whole week for Teachers' Institute, or have it a day at a time, here and there, scattered. Which'd you rather have?"

"Oh, I don't know," said Williams.

"I think I'd rather have Institute Week. It was more on the order of a real vacation. But they gave us plenty of home work. *Oh*, that *home* work. I guess you didn't mind it because you liked to read, but I always wanted to be out playing baseball or games like that. There for a while I was a real tomboy. I hated being a girl. Well, I got over that all right. Do you want anything out of the kitchen?"

"What is there?"

"Well, I'll get you a snort, as far as that goes. Do you feel like a snort? I got some of that rye you brought home the night before last. Do you want a ball?"

"All right, give me a ball."

"We did have plenty of ginger ale unless we drank it all the night before last. I think we still have some. If we don't do you want just a straight?"

"Either way," said Williams.

"I think there's a whole bottle left, though. You brought home six bottles and I think we only used up the five. I'll go see."

"That's a good idea," said Williams.

"I could go and take a look instead of stand here and talk about it," said Lottie.

"Well, if you don't, I will."

"All right, don't get excited. I'll bet two pins that Edith Chapin wouldn't go out in the kitchen and wait on her husband. Not her. *She* has a *butler*."

"I'll get you a butler."

"Yeah, so you could have a French maid."

"Are you gonna get the drink or will I get it?"

"Keep your shirt on, Attorney. I'm getting there, slow but sure."

Williams telephoned Mike Slattery the next morning. The two men were not friends, chiefly because it was traditional in Lantenengo County for the Welshmen and the Irishmen not to be friends. But they managed to maintain cordial relations.

"What could the district attorney be wanting at this hour of the day?" said Slattery. "Let me quick examine my conscience."

"That's your trouble. When you examine your conscience it's God damn quick. Spend a little time at it one of those days."

"All right, now we've exchanged pleasantries, let's get down to business," said Mike Slattery.

"That's all right with me, Mike," said Lloyd Williams. "Like everybody else, I've been reading the newspapers."

"And?"

"Did Joe Chapin ever fight a duel?"

"Did Joe Chapin ever fight a duel? Now you're asking me that for some sly purpose. I don't know if Joe Chapin ever fought a duel. What's your sly purpose?"

"Well, if he did, I just looked it up, and according to Article Twelve, Section Three of the Constitution of this great state, any man that ever fought a duel, or even challenged another lad to fight a duel, is prohibited from holding an office of honor or profit in this great state."

"You're driving at something and I don't know what it is."

346

"You don't? I'm not too sly for you this morning?"

"I confess you are."

"Well, maybe you can get a couple guys to swear that Joe Chapin once fought a duel, and then when the time comes to give him the gate, all you gotta say is he's unconstitutional."

There was a long silence at Mike Slattery's end of the telephone connection.

Williams broke the silence: "Are you still there?"

"I'm still here," said Mike Slattery. "Let me ask you a question, Lloyd."

"Go right ahead."

"Is that your joke for today? Are you getting your laughs all over the courthouse with that one?"

"No, I thought I'd try it on you first," said Williams.

"Well, you've tried it, and I didn't laugh a bit. I didn't even smile. I'm not smiling now. If you know what's good for you—and I never saw the day you didn't—you'll lay off that kind of witticism. If you have your eye on Congress or Common Pleas judge, don't repeat that little joke or any like it."

"Well, I didn't think it'd go over so big."

"Then why did you go to all this trouble?" said Mike Slattery.

"Because if I was only born yesterday I could still see what you're going to do to Chapin, and you could have picked somebody else."

"I can hardly believe my own ears. Are you the new self-appointed guardian angel for Joe Chapin?"

"No."

"Then I'll give you some free advice. Keep your nose out of where it doesn't belong. You just go right on serving the people as the able district attorney for the County of Lantenengo, and have a good time doing it, because it could be your last opportunity to serve them. You may find yourself retiring to private practice at the end of your term, and that isn't what you want."

"No, but God damn it, I'll sleep better tonight for what I've been telling you this morning."

"Oh, I slept all right *last* night, Lloyd. I'll bet I sleep better than you most nights. And I'll sleep all right tonight because I showed you where you might be making the biggest mistake of your life. You made your little protest, now keep your big mouth shut." Slattery hung up without another word to Lloyd Williams, but he immediately telephoned an assistant district attorney in Williams' office.

"Jameson speaking," said the assistant.

"Ralph, is your boss anywhere near you?"

"No. Who is this?"

"Mike Slattery."

"He's in his own office and the door's closed."

"I want to hear anything and everything he has to say about Joe Chapin, even the slightest little wisecrack. Check with me promptly. That's all."

But the precaution was unnecessary. Lloyd Williams had made his only protest, and it was the only one of its kind.

The regular party organization would be announcing its ticket in the spring, and with few exceptions the announced ticket had become, in the fall, the elected candidates. Party members were allowed to vote for the regular or the independent candidates for the nominations, but the regular organization had had a comfortably consistent record against independents. Even in 1934, with the Democrats in power in Washington and rising in the state, a Republican seeking office wanted the support of the regular organization. Moreover, Joe Chapin was by habit a regular organization man, and he had uncompromisingly aligned himself with the regulars. His nomination therefore depended entirely on his being announced on the organization ticket. In the months preceding the announcement of the organization ticket he repeatedly declared that the independents were merely New Dealers in disguise, and several times he implied that they ought to be read out of the party. It was not subtle politics, but it was Joe Chapin's, and no one stopped him.

Joe had accepted Mike's invitation to "put yourself in my hands" and he obeyed Mike's command to "do nothing without consulting me." Mike was his personal envoy at the higher councils of the organization, and was therefore presumed also to be speaking for the organization leaders when he told Joe to be careful about accepting requests to speak at dinners and rallies. As a consequence Joe's speaking engagements were fewer than he had expected them to be. "It was all right before, but that was small stuff. Now you're out to get the nomination, and that's big stuff. And the wrong speech at the wrong place could hurt everybody, the party *and* you," said Mike.

"I'd like to know a little more about what's going on."

"There's no secret about it, goodness knows," said Mike. "We've got men all over the state finding out who'll make up the strongest ticket. We don't want to win for governor and lose for United States senator. We want a clean sweep. My man for lieutenant governor is Joseph B. Chapin, but aside from you, I keep an open mind. I could tell you who I'd like to see senator, but who I like and who gets on the ticket are two separate matters. I give advice, they listen to it, and if they think I'm right, they adopt it. But they don't always adopt it. Many's the time I came from Pittsburgh, tired and weary and wishing I'da been a schoolteacher or a doctor. Those were the times when my advice was thrown right out the window of the Duquesne Club, and I wished I'd gone out with it. But it's nice to win. Oh, it's nice to win. Then you forget the disappointments as though they never happened. And it's a team job, Joe. The Penrose days are gone forever. That's why you're lucky to be going along with the organization."

Early in February of 1934 Mike showed Joe Chapin a clipping from a Pittsburgh newspaper, a story in a political column. "This is the first sign of any trouble, and in case you didn't see it, I show it to you for what it's worth."

The column quoted a local politician, an organization man whose name was new to Joe. "In the eastern part of the state they are giving early support to Joseph B. Chapin (for lieutenant governor). Chapin, a lawyer, has had no previous political experience, according to William J. Murdock, who went on to say that the presence of an 'unknown' on the organization ticket could do irreparable harm to the party as a whole, particularly in a year which is expected to see close contests deciding the outcome in November."

"Well, he never heard of me, and I never heard of him," said Joe.

"I know him. He's pretty well thought of out that way."

"Do you think I ought to meet him and have a talk with him?"

"I thought of that, but I don't think you'd get along very well. He only wants men that came up from ward-heeler."

"Like our friend in the White House?"

"Well, our friend did have some experience. Murdock will do as he's told when the time comes. He'll deliver a whole congressional district," said Mike.

"Mike, you sound as though you like this fellow."

"He's very useful, Joe, and that's what counts, not my likes or dislikes."

Edith received Joe's account of the conversation calmly. "As Mike Slattery told you, this man Murdock will do as he's told. I don't see that he's anyone to worry about."

"He isn't if he's only stating his own opinion. Or if he's the only one that has that opinion of me. I'll start worrying when I hear that there are more like him."

He was not long waiting. "Did you see the Philadelphia *Sun* today?" Mike said, over the telephone.

"I missed it this morning."

"It isn't good, Joe. Have you got it at the office?"

"I think Arthur has a copy. I'll get his."

The Philadelphia *Sun* employed a political columnist who was a sarcastic delight to everyone except his victim of the moment. He wrote: "My Old Lady and I are going to have to pass up the hospitality of Lantenengo County which we have enjoyed in the past at the hands of jovial Mike Slattery and his Peg. Our reason is that Mike is trying to convince The Powers That Be that Joe Chapin ought to get the nomination for lieutenant governor. I don't know what is happening to friend Mike unless it be that he is getting in sassiety up Lantenengo way. Joe Chapin may be Joe Chapin in Gibbsville, the county seat of Lantenengo, but the only time I met him he was so forbidding of mien, so condescending in his attitude toward plain folks, that it is stretching the imagination to picture him allowing Mike to call him anything but M' Lord. Lord Chapin is so lofty in manner that we are amazed that lieutenant governor is noble enough for him. If we had a Viceroy in this here Commonwealth, we could understand how he might 'stand for election,' as they say in jolly England. Not having a title of that nature, we suppose lieutenant governor has to do. But it must be frightfully boring, doncha know?

"Seriously, we are not at such a loss for prospective candidates that we can afford to try out an amateur who has only one thing to recommend him, that being a grandfather who likewise served a term as lieutenant governor. If we are selecting candidates on that basis, can't we find a Republican who is a collateral descendant of George Washington? Furthermore, if Mr. Slattery is seriously proposing that the second place on the state ticket be handed on a silver platter to a rank amateur, who never has held public office in the fifty-two years of his life, it could be that Mr. Slattery is 'losing his touch.' If so, it is fortunate we are discovering it before the harm is done."

Joe Chapin called Mike Slattery back. "Mike, I don't remember ever meeting that fellow."

"That isn't the part that worries me."

"What does?" said Joe Chapin.

"His sources."

"His what?"

"His news sources. All newspaper fellows have news sources. And this fellow has the best. He's the mouthpiece for The Powers That Be that he mentions. In other words, he knows something I don't know, because I haven't been let in on it."

"About me?"

"Well, yes. I'm going to be out of town for a few days, beginning tomorrow. I'll be in touch with you when I get back."

"Shall I go along with you?"

"Oh, no. Thanks for offering to, but I have to do this job myself."

Mike went home that evening and did not wait for dinner to be finished before his chat with Peg. "I suppose you saw today's *Sun*."

"Oh, sure."

"They've started to give it to Joe."

"They gave it to you a little, too."

"Oh, that did me no harm. I knew it was coming. I heard about it last week. They asked me if I'd mind and I said of course not. Philadelphia papers can do me a little good, but they can't do me any harm. Quite the opposite. I probably made a few friends through that article."

"Well, Joe Chapin didn't."

"That's different. He was ridiculed where he's vulnerable. I was made to look like a loyal pal. I wish Joe'd quit before they really start to work on him."

"Why? He knew what he was getting into."

"Oh, no he didn't. They never know. He was upset, I could tell over the phone. Nothing he said, just his manner, the tone of his voice. What have we got for dinner?"

"Roast lamb," said Peg. "With mint sauce."

Mike nodded. "I wish you were friends with Edith."

"Well, I'm not, so you can rule out that consideration."

"How's Michelle's cold?"

"She was over this afternoon. It's gone," said Peg. "She and Howard are thinking of getting a Plymouth."

"It's a good little car, a Plymouth. 'Don't buy a big car,' I told Howard. Ed likes a Plymouth better than a Chevy. What worries me is if they give him the works too soon. He's going to get it, that's as sure as the Lord's above, but we want it to look good. We don't want him or anybody else to think we took his money and gave him a seat in the bleachers. That's a lot of *money*, Peg. A *lot* of money. He'll get something out of it. They can dream up some kind of a commission to be chairman of, if necessary—"

"That's if we don't lose the election," said Peg.

"I must ask you not to voice that thought," said Mike. "Or we could put him farther down the ticket, but he wouldn't go for that, and he shouldn't. Not with that money to his credit. I wanted to have a talk with him myself, but they decided against it. They decided they were going to make it look like, uh, spontaneous combustion. One of them said spontaneous protest. When Murdock let go his blast a while ago, that was to see how Joe'd take it. Well, he took it like Joe Chapin. He wanted to convert Murdock, and thought he could. Just like today, he wanted to go away with me tomorrow and talk to them, but I got out of that fast."

"Well, what's next?"

"Oh, I don't know. Probably have him to a meeting and ask him if he'll withdraw gracefully and take something else. If he squawks, then he'll get nothing, nothing. That'll make it easier for all concerned. If he listens to reason, they may be able to satisfy his ego. We'll see."

Two weeks passed, then Mike was instructed to bring Joe to a meeting. It was being held in a building on North Broad Street, Philadelphia, in an office that had no name but only a room number on the door. A girl sat reading a magazine at a desk in the outer office, and she nodded in greeting to Mike and Joe, who proceeded to a larger room which was furnished like a board-meeting room. There were eight men present, one of them the former senator whom Joe had interviewed in Washington. There were numerous paper items and ash trays and water carafes on the table, and it was apparent from the ash trays that the meeting had been in progress for a considerable time. The men remained seated.

"Gentlemen, this is my friend Joe Chapin. Joe, I think you know almost everybody here."

"I think so," said Joe.

The well-tailored man who seemed to be chairman spoke up before there could be any further delays for the exchange of courtesies. "Mr. Chapin, if you'll have a seat?" He indicated a chair facing his own and halfway around the table.

"Thank you."

"Mike, if you'd like to sit next to Mr. Chapin," said the chairman. "I think we're ready to begin. Mr. Chapin, the party is genuinely and deeply appreciative of your assistance in all matters, and by no means the least of them, of course, your very generous monetary assistance, which I can assure you was needed and timely, and we wish there were many, many more Republicans like you. I will say to you here, and not for repetition—nothing said here is to be repeated, please—that in this room we are all realists. We don't kid ourselves, we don't kid each other. We try to be polite, but sometimes we even fall short of that. But as I say, we are realists, all of us, and the plain, stark, unvarnished truth is that I don't exaggerate when I tell you that the party is in for the toughest battle in its history, not even excepting the days of Woodrow Wilson, which I'm sure you remember. Wilson was elected President of the United States, but his party didn't carry Pennsylvania. We haven't had a Democrat for governor since I believe 1890. Pattison. And even he was an accident, due to splitting of the ticket by a group that called themselves the Prohibition party. If we had had those Prohibition party votes, which rightfully belonged to us, we'd have beaten Mr. Pattison, but he won because something like 16,000 voters defected. And defected is the word.

"Now then, you may wonder why I dwell on something that happened nearly fifty years ago. I do so, because—again, I remind you, we are realists here—I do so because this is going to be a close election, closer than you'll get any of us to admit in public. I have here the latest figures on Relief. Or, as the British more honestly call it, the Dole. They are startling, but you are probably familiar with them yourself. What they represent to us, and to the party, is potential Pattisons. *We could lose this election*, Mr. Chapin. The people have their beer again, but the President is also giving them cash. Some people will tell you that we are being taxed out of existence, but though I happen personally not to believe that, I do subscribe to the theory that our *party* is being taxed out of existence by the very money we pay in taxes. It isn't a pretty thought, but I believe it's a true one.

"Now then, I mean it literally when I tell you that we cannot afford to lose a single vote. Votes that we used to be able to count on are now being taken away from us by the President and his dole. We can't hope to compete with the Federal government in handing out money, notwithstanding a few contributions like yours. All we can hope for, Mr. Chapin, is to hold on to every vote we've ever had in the past, and possibly, just possibly, attract a few voters who can look past the cash the President offers, and see which direction he is taking us. In order to attract any voters and to hold on to those we've had, we must put up the strongest ticket the party can supply.

"Mr. Chapin, the party needs you and men of your caliber. But this year we can't afford to gamble on a man who is not a proven vote-getter. I'm afraid it's as coldly simple as that, and knowing you to be a man of principle as well as a loyal Republican, I, speaking for myself and for the other men at this table, am going to ask you to withdraw as a potential candidate for lieutenant governor.

"I am not going to ask you to give us your answer here and now. You can let us know through our friend Mike Slattery in, say, a week from now. We meet here nearly every day, and Mike can let us know when you've made your decision. In the meantime perhaps you might like to say a few words to this meeting. The floor is yours."

Joe got up from his chair, which, since the chairman had remained seated, led the other men to believe he was about to make a speech. They frowned slightly, but they looked at him and settled back in their chairs. Then he looked at each man individually, slowly making the circle of the table and at last coming to Mike. He then faced the chairman and said: "Gentlemen, I withdraw."

He then quickly walked out of the room, leaving them with their astonishment.

He went to a cheap hotel and registered as Joseph B. Champion, City. "Do you have any luggage, Mr. Champion?"

"No, I'll pay in advance. Three days."

"Be twelve dollars in advance. The boy'll show you your room. Boy, front."

He followed the bellboy into the elevator, which the boy operated, and down the hall to an inside room. "Will that be all, sir?"

"Not quite," said Joe. "I want you to get me two bottles of Johnny Walker Black Label Scotch."

"I can't leave the building till my relief gets here, but I can get you a bottle of other Scotch, eight dollars a bottle."

"All right, bring that."

"It's good Scotch, but it just ain't Johnny Walker Black. I keep a bottle for late at night and people come in and want Scotch, I always have a bottle or two."

"Well, if you have two, bring both. Here's twenty dollars."

"Meaning I keep the change?"

"If you have two bottles of good Scotch, yes."

"I'll be right back."

He was back in five minutes with two bottles, one different from the other, but both Scotch. "I brought you some ice, in case you wanted ice."

354

"Thank you."

"Anything else, sir?"

"Not a thing, thank you."

For two days Joe stayed drunk in the dismal room. On the third day the telephone rang and he answered it. "I'm afraid we're going to have to ask you for your room, Mr. Champion. Your three days are up today."

"Thank you for telling me."

He had the boy bring him shaving supplies. He took a bath, dressed and went to the Union League and had some eggs and coffee and a few drinks, and then he took the 4:35 for Gibbsville.

The 4:35 was a train that got the well-to-do home in time for dinner and the less well-off home late for supper. The Gibbsville station was only three blocks from 10 North Frederick Street, and Joe Chapin always walked.

Edith was reading the *Standard* when he appeared in the den. She looked up at him, then looked back at her newspaper.

"I've been quietly getting drunk," he said.

"Do you want me to hold dinner, or do you want to talk now?"

"Are you hungry? If not, let's wait."

"I'm not very hungry," she said. She rang for Mary and told her there would be an hour's delay. During this time Joe made himself a Scotch-and-soda, then sat in his favorite leather chair.

"Mike Slattery's been trying to get you. He called a couple of times today. Yesterday. The day before."

"A touching concern. What did you tell him?"

"Well, I only spoke to him once, the day before yesterday. I told him you were expected home that evening. After that I had Mary or Marian take the calls. He left word to have you call him when you got home."

"I went to a hotel and got drunk."

"Were you alone?"

"Yes. Oh, did I have a woman with me? No. I never thought of it, to tell you the truth."

"Or you would have," said Edith.

"No, I don't think so, Edith," said Joe. "The way I was feeling, I wanted to be alone, not even with myself. That's why I got drunk. The tender ministrations of a whore were the last thing I wanted."

"No, the tender ministrations of your wife. You apparently never thought we might be worried about you here. I did telephone the

Bellevue, but of course you weren't registered. I thought of calling the police, to check the hospitals in case your leg was hurt again, but then I decided you'd be identified if you got in an accident."

"It was very inconsiderate of me."

"Very," said Edith.

"It was wanting to be alone. I remember one time you were cross with me, oh, long ago. We'd been to the Vineyard, and we were going to spend the night at the Bellevue. I think I had an appointment to meet somebody, and whoever it was broke it, and I wanted to go home. But you had some shopping to do, so you stayed in Philadelphia and I came home. Do you remember that?"

"I remember it very well."

"Well, you wanted to be by yourself that time, and this time I wanted to be by *myself*."

"Yes, but you knew where I was. For three days I haven't known where you were or who you were with. I still don't know, but I suppose you're going to tell me."

"Yes."

"If you want to," she added.

"There's nothing to hide, Edith. Nothing to be ashamed of except my lack of consideration for you, and my own real, deep, congenital stupidity. It's a hell of a come-down at my age to suddenly realize that all your life, at least all your mature life, you've been hoping for something that you had no more right to hope for than . . . Like picking an apple off a bowl of fruit. Or a paper off a newsstand. Drop a few pennies on the pile of newspapers, and walk away with the paper you want. That's really how simple I thought it would be, if I ever thought at all. At fifty-two I still went on thinking that because I wanted something, I could get it. I deceived myself so completely that I even deceived you. My ambition, I can't even put it into words, it's so absurd. Only three days ago I was still thinking that . . . Oh, what a fool! It's cost me a hundred thousand dollars, but that isn't punishment enough for being so stupid. It's no punishment at all, really, because I won't miss it. Dave Harrison has the word for people like me. A chump. Well, all this isn't telling you anything. I'll tell you exactly what happened. Mike Slattery and I, as you know, took the eight-thirty-five, and after we got to Philadelphia we went to an office building on North Broad Street. . . ."

He told Edith every detail that he could recall. At the end she said: "Is that all you said?"

"That was all. I think they expected me to make a stirring appeal to their I don't-know-what. I'm sure they expected me to make a little speech. But long before that I was ready to go. I knew it was all over. What else was there to say? Eight important men, nine with Mike Slattery, were watching me to see how I was going to react to being told that I was a useless chump. Well, what *is* there to say? I couldn't graciously tell them, 'Gentlemen, I know I'm a chump.' They knew that better than I did. They'd known it for a long time. What do you do after you've been given the coup de grâce? I've never seen it, but I suppose you shudder a little and die."

She looked at him before speaking. "You haven't lost."

"I haven't lost? Edith, what do you mean I haven't lost? I've wasted dear knows how many years, how many miles of travel, a hundred thousand dollars—and my conceit."

"Those things, yes. But you still haven't lost an election."

"Small comfort, that. I never lost the Harvard game, either. But I never played. Never made the team. Never sat on the bench."

"They'll offer you something, if only because you gave them all that money. Aren't you going to accept?"

"No."

"What *are* you going to do, Joe, with the rest of your life?"

"I've been wondering. First, I'll try to get back my self-respect without the conceit. I'll try to get over my embarrassment. I wasn't embarrassed at the time, but since then I can't *tell* you the embarrassment I've felt, thinking of myself sitting there facing those men while they stared at me and told me I was a useless chump. They were being courteous to a hundred thousand dollars. Mother's money, incidentally. Not even money I earned myself. Not even money a Chapin earned. Money a Hofman earned. What am I going to do? I'm going to live at 10 North Frederick Street, go to my office, spend the summers on the farm—and yes, I know one thing I want to do. I want to be a better father to my children. I'm a useless chump to the world, but my children love me. And you love me, don't you?"

"Yes."

"Or do you?" said Joe.

"Of course," said Edith. "Do you love me?"

"You have every right to ask that." He got up and kissed her forehead.

"I'm not much," he said. "But what there is is yours, Edith.

Never once anybody else's. Just think, Edith, no more trips to Tioga County, no more golf tournaments at Bedford Springs. I'm almost happy."

"Joe, you're not. It's too soon to say that."

"I know it," he said. "The fellow that did all the talking in Philadelphia, he kept saying, 'We don't kid ourselves, Mr. Chapin. In this room we don't kid ourselves.' My trouble, one of my troubles, is that I kid myself. I'm one of the little princes of Gibbsville, Pennsylvania, and I wanted to be President of—"

"Don't hurt yourself, Joe. Nobody knows that that's what you wanted, and the only way that that could hurt you is if people did know. And they don't. And they never will."

He moved to his desk. "Any interesting mail?"

"Letters from the children. Oh, some invitations. Two wedding invitations. Mostly ads and bills. Are you going to telephone Mike Slattery?"

"Why?"

"Well, I think you ought to, in the morning."

"Why?"

"I don't know the first thing about politics, but I think I know Mike Slattery. If you let him think you're angry or cross, he'll get angry and cross right back, and if you don't want people to know about what happened in Philadelphia, it's better to have Mike on your side."

"Yes. I agree."

"And he may be worried about himself. That article in the Philadelphia paper wasn't very kind to him, either. I think you ought to at least pretend that you and he are just the same as you always were. Friends. Not like Arthur or Henry. But the kind of friends you and Mike have always been. He likes you, Joe, and there's no point in antagonizing him."

"Oh, I'll call him. I would anyway, to see what he wants. I'll do it now." He telephoned Mike Slattery.

"Mike, this is the people's choice," said Joe.

"Joe, I'm glad to hear you taking it that way. Really and honestly glad. They didn't know what to think when you left that suddenly, and they asked me. I said, 'Gentlemen, class tells. Class tells,' I said. I said what was there for you to do? Prolong it into a session that would be painful for all concerned, or make your announcement and leave before anybody had a chance to get embarrassed. I just want to know first and foremost, you're not sore at me, I hope?"

"No, I think you probably did the best you could," said Joe.

"What I wanted to hear you say. I'm on my way to Washington tomorrow, but let's have lunch when I get back."

"Any time at all," said Joe, hanging up.

"Well, that's that," he said to Edith.

In the Slattery living room Mike said to Peg: "I don't know. He made it too easy for me."

"Don't look for trouble, Mike. You said yourself, class tells. I don't know about the class, but he was raised a gentleman."

"Uh-huh. And he'll never trust me again as long as he's alive to draw breath."

"Well, why should he? And what do you care?"

"I care because now that he's completely out of politics I can like him again," said Mike.

"The way I look at it, twice you came to his rescue to get the daughter out of trouble. The first time wasn't anything, the time she had her little whatever-it-was with the truck driver. But that second time was worth a hundred thousand dollars."

"Well, thanks for reminding me. I guess it was."

"A hundred thousand dollars, a lot of money even if you say it quick. But not much to what they would have spent. If you could get that thought across to him maybe he wouldn't take it so hard, not getting on the ticket."

"I don't think he minds the money so much, but it's a good idea to remind him of what he would have spent. And I never even asked him for carfare to give that marriage record the tear-up."

A brief telephone call from Mike Slattery to Bob Hooker disposed finally of any further local publicity regarding Joe Chapin. At Mike's suggestion Joe issued a single statement concerning his candidacy, which ran in the *Standard* and in some other newspapers in the county, but nowhere else in the state. "Upon the advice of my physician, who informs me that the rigors of a strenuous statewide campaign could lead to serious complications of the recent accident to my leg, I have asked the members of the State Republican Committee to withdraw my name from consideration in shaping up the ticket for the coming elections. In doing so, I have assured the Committee that I shall continue to lend my wholehearted support to all Republican candidates in the forthcoming campaign, short of public appearances involving extensive travel. I wish to thank my friends, who have so loyally rallied to my support, for their good wishes and offers of assistance. I know that they, like me, will now direct their energies toward the only satisfactory conclusion of the campaign; a sweeping Republican victory in November!"

Joe saw Billy English at the club the day after the announcement appeared. "Joe, I'm sorry to learn you have a new doctor."

"A new doctor? Oh, the statement."

"As a matter of fact, I've always warned you that the leg could give you trouble, so I didn't mind. Is that why you withdrew, or did a little taste of politics turn your stomach?"

"Well, between you and me, a little of both. My leg and my stomach were involved. But I'm not going to admit that to people."

"For people who don't need it in their business, the best publicity is no publicity. The biggest men I've ever known have stayed out of the newspapers as much as possible. When Julian died I developed such a hatred for notoriety that I told Bob Hooker I never wanted my name in his paper again. Well, I knew that couldn't be. The hospital, and the Medical Society, they come in for a certain amount of publicity, and my name gets printed in those connections. But articles about me or my family, even squibs on the society page, I don't want them. You wouldn't have liked it after a while, Joe. I saw one article in one of the Philadelphia papers, I guess you saw it too. I wanted to horsewhip the fellow that wrote it, and I was thinking about it last night after I read your statement. You're well out of the whole thing. I'm all for helping the party, but I'll do it with money, as long as I can afford it, and whatever my opinion is worth to the people I come in contact with. There's Arthur."

"Where?"

"Isn't that Arthur at the bar?"

"No, Arthur's still in the dining room. I don't know who that is. A guest, I imagine."

"Oh. I thought it was Arthur, but on second look I can see it isn't. Well, glad you haven't changed doctors, Joe. Wouldn't like to have to change lawyers."

Some men at the club commented on Joe's withdrawal from politics, and others ignored it. Partly on Mike's advice, and partly on Arthur's, Joe was making himself visible at all of his usual places—the club, the courthouse, Main Street, the country club—for the first few days after the statement. In a little while, probably as little as a week, people would accept him as a non-candidate, and in only a little more time they would forget he had ever been considered a possibility. After that Joe and Edith were to visit the Dave Harrisons at their new house in a place called Hobe Sound, Florida. They had not at first intended to accept the Harrisons' invitation, but as Edith said, "This would be a very good time to remind Gibbsville, and Pennsylvania, that one of your best friends is a Morgan partner. It won't do any harm, just in case there's any talk about your not getting the nomination."

The Harrisons had the Alec Weekses and the Paul Donaldsons from Scranton as their other guests with the Chapins. The men fished and played golf and drank large quantities of whiskey and nursed their grudge against their friend in the White House. The women swam and played bridge and went to Palm Beach to shop or to the nearby St. Onge's for Kodak film. Hobe Sound was less than an hour's drive from Palm Beach, and was only just becoming known. It was a resort that was in effect a private club, and the theme of it was the new simplicity: houses that could be run with staffs of a minimum of servants; multimillionaires driving inconspicuous Plymouths instead of Rolls-Royces; a place where the powerful could relax unobserved by the trippers from West Palm Beach, and yet could tie up their Diesel yachts. A visitor could be made a member of the Jupiter Island Club for ten dollars, but he could then find himself in a dollar-a-point bridge game every afternoon and night. The man in the old Groton School blazer might be a Morgan partner, and the man in the shredded khaki pants might be the brains of the motor car industry.

Dave Harrison and Alec Weeks went fishing one day and left the Pennsylvanians, Chapin and Donaldson, to play golf. But the rain fell heavily and the Pennsylvanians decided to do some rainy-day drinking together while the women visited the shops of Worth Avenue.

"Joe, I understand they gave you a real royal screwing a month or so ago."

"I guess you could call it that."

"Well, what would you call it?"

"Oh, a real royal screwing," said Joe.

"Is what I heard true? A hundred and fifty thousand smackers?"

"No, not that much, but it was a large sum. But I see their point."

"I wish you'd talked to me," said Paul Donaldson from Scranton.

"What would you have done?"

"I'll tell you what I'd have done. I'd have got together about a half a dozen fellows and said, 'It's Joe Chapin or else.'"

"Well, thanks, Paul. But I think it worked out all right. I'm here in Hobe Sound with my friends, instead of dragging my tail around Pennsylvania."

"Balls to that, Joe. If you thought enough of it to give them a wad of money, you wanted the job. Lieutenant governor is what you were after, that right?"

"Yep."

"Well, I don't know if it's any consolation to you, but according to my sources of information, we're going to have to take a little punishment in the fall."

"So I gather. Oh, hell, Paul. Water under the bridge."

"Does that finish you with politics for good?"

"I'm inclined to think so."

"But you're going to keep on living in Gibbsville."

"Christ, yes."

"Is your leg all right again?"

"Well, I took forty dollars away from you yesterday, and twenty the day before."

"The way we go around that golf course, Dave could play," said Donaldson. "What are your plans? I know of a few things in New York that might interest you."

"Law business?"

"No, not exactly. Investment trusts. This is the bottom, this is the time to get in. There's going to be a war in Europe."

"How do you know that?"

"That fellow with the Charlie Chaplin mustache. You won't read about it in Bob Hooker's rag, but that crazy bastard is going to take over the whole Continent of Europe before he gets his ass in a sling. And we're going to get rich."

"Oh, come on, Paul."

"Well, how long since you talked to anybody that really knows what's going on over there?"

"I haven't."

"I have. You ask Dave. He'll be cagey, but just ask him if I don't get some pretty good information."

"I don't doubt that, but this Hitler, he's a God damn freak."

"Well, if you're not interested in money, what are you interested in? You don't want to just vegetate in Gibbsville the rest of your life. Have you got a girl friend?"

"Nope."

"You ought to come to New York with me some time and I'll fix you up with a little group I know. They aren't hookers. Most of them are getting alimony from some poor sucker, and all they want is somebody to take them to El Morocco so they can doll up. A couple of them even live with their husbands, but the husbands don't give a damn either. They've got girls of their own. I saw one of them in Palm Beach the other day. In fact I almost went down there this afternoon and got myself a good piece of tail. They aren't kids, but who wants kids? The only trouble I ever got into was those young kids that think all they have to do is holler and you'll shell out. No, these dames I'm talking about, they're all in their thirties or more, but there isn't a thing they don't know, and you don't have to go to Paris. New York is overrun with the most perverted, fanciest, good-looking dames in the history of the world. And all they want out of you is take them out to a good dinner and a show and a night club."

"How do you get time to make all your millions?"

"Listen," said Paul. "I'm downtown by ten o'clock, just after the bell rings. A good piece of tail and a good seven hours' sleep, and I think more clearly than if I was some guy that tossed and turned wishing he had what I had. A lot of our friends go to a gym. I get in bed with a woman and I sleep better. I'm a great believer in sleep. Not ten hours, not twelve hours. Six or seven or eight hours of sound sleep."

"How do you get away with it?"

"You mean Betty?"

"Yes."

"That's just it, my boy. If I came home looking debauched. But I don't. I don't drink too much. I drank more in the time we've been here than I ever do in New York."

"But doesn't Betty wonder what you do at night?"

"She's in Scranton, most of the time. She knows I'm not going to stay in the hotel and have dinner in my room every night. She knows I go out."

"I know, but when you're gone all night."

"No calls between midnight and eight-thirty."

"And you've never been caught."

"Never been caught. Why should I be? Listen, boy, I don't want you to think I get laid every night. I don't. But every time I go to New York, yes. You know man is naturally polygamous, Joe. You know that. A stallion always has as many as forty or fifty mares. I've got a girl in Boston and one in Chicago and two or three in Philadelphia. And if Betty weren't along on this trip I'd be kept busy in Palm Beach."

"Paul, you amaze me."

"Yes, I imagine I do. The one big trouble with living in a small town, the best people haven't got the facilities for high-class adultery. Automobiles. Country roads. Sneaking off to camps in the woods. In New York nobody gives a damn. And I don't live there. I'm home every week-end, unless I'm out on Long Island or up in Connecticut. I'm a visitor. So my wife doesn't have to run across the dames I go to bed with. Not that they'd ever run across each other anyway. These dames are not exactly the Bryn Mawr type, but they're a damned sight better looking because they haven't got a worry in the world except looking their best after six o'clock."

"What would Betty do if she did find out?"

"Betty is very careful *not* to find out."

"Oh, then she knows."

"No, she doesn't know. But she doesn't try to know. And I don't want her to know. Listen, boy, I'm not a damn fool. I believe in our marriage. You don't think I'd ever marry one of these dames? I wouldn't leave Betty for anything. And don't forget, it's often harder to keep a marriage going than it is to break it up."

Joe looked at him and said nothing.

"You're too much of a gentleman to ask me what's on your mind," said Paul. "Yes, Betty and I sleep together. If I had to give up the other women, I would, if it meant breaking up with Betty."

"Well, you have a daughter coming out next year."

"Oh, not only that, Joe."

"I must say you make it all sound like the only way to live."

"Not for everybody. But for me."

"No, I think you're a fucking hypocrite. And that's a good use of both words."

"Well, and I think guys like you are the real hypocrites. You want it, but you're afraid to go after it."

"It isn't always a question of being afraid. But I don't think you'd understand what I believe. It'd sound too sanctimonious."

"I'll bet it would."

"Oh, but I'll say it anyway. There's such a thing as respect. Giving up those other dames because you respect the woman you're married to."

"You think I don't respect Betty?"

"I know damn well those dames don't think you do, and that's what matters, whether Betty ever knows about it or not."

"You *are* a little Lord Fauntleroy. Tell me the truth, Joe. Did you ever stay with anybody but Edith?"

"Yes. But not since we've been married."

"You know, you're almost due for some middle-aged wild oats, and then we'll see who's the hypocrite."

"Oh, I'm probably a hypocrite, too, but in different ways. I don't think I could ever have an affair with a woman and then try to kid myself that I was having it because I liked to get eight hours' sleep. I don't say that I'm better than you are, but I believe my imperfections are less harmful than your imperfections."

"Let's go up to the pool and have a look at the girls in their bathing suits."

"They won't be there. It's raining."

"So it is. Well, let's tie one on. I was thinking of asking you to go to Palm Beach, but you're too damn sanctimonious."

"And I'm a very sound sleeper."

Paul Donaldson from Scranton held his glass at arm's length and stared at it. "You know, I don't know but what you may be right. But I won't admit it. If I had to do over again there isn't a single piece of tail I'd want to give up. So I guess I consider myself a happy man. God knows I don't consider *you* a happy man. You go ahead and consider me a fucking hypocrite, but I consider you a miserable, unhappy bastard. You never got anything out of life and, boy, you wouldn't know how to start now."

"But that's assuming I'd *want* to start now," said Joe.

Ann was one of a thousand, and many more than a thousand, girls of good family who were living in New York, working in New York, getting from their jobs some sense of belonging to something besides the Junior League and the country club, which were the community in which they would have lived back home in Dayton, in Charlotte, in Kansas City, in Gibbsville. Each girl thought she was living according to her own plan, but there were so many like her that a pattern had developed. They would go to New York, stay at one of the women's residential hotels until the search for a job, any respectable job, was successfully ended. "I thought I'd go to secretarial school and do some modeling." The job found, the next move was to find an apartment with a girl of similar background and tastes and not much more and not much less money at her disposal. Sometimes the apartment would start with three girls instead of two, but a three-girl arrangement almost never worked out. In the first year or two the girl would be invited to dinner at the homes of Mother's and Dad's New York friends, and then the Friends of the Family would forget all about the girl from Dayton and Charlotte and Kansas City and Gibbsville, and she would begin to make her own life with office friends and friends of office friends and young men who had grown up in Kansas City or Gibbsville, attended Choate and Williams, had jobs in New York and, usually, considerably less money to spend than the girls. The Kansas City girl and the Choate-Williams boy might become fond of each other, fond enough to go to bed together, but there was little talk of love. The boy was not really interesting, not as interesting as The Boss. The girl was not really desirable to the boy, who was busy using Squadron A as the first step toward the Racquet Club and with an eye on the richer and just as pretty girls on the North Shore of Long Island. The boy would practice economies by buying his suits at Broadstreet's or Roger Kent while still going to Brooks for the right shirt. He also would economize by taking the Kansas City girl to the Italian restaurant on Bleecker Street, so that he could swing a dinner at "21" for a girl he had met through the Squadron. The boy would learn the language of his type: "I went to a place called Choate," he would say to the sister of a Grottie. "I come from a place you probably never heard of—Indianapolis."

The outlander boy and the outlander girl stayed away from their Bohemian fellow-townsmen who lived in the less expensive sections of Greenwich Village. "Carol? Yes, I saw her last fall, at the theatre. Yes, she still keeps up with her painting. At least she was then. I think she was going to marry a Jap, but it fell through."

Ann's first job was found for her. "I'll find a job for her, Joe," said Alec Weeks. "It probably won't be anything very interesting or exciting, but it'll give her something to do and pay her a small salary." The job, paying twenty-five dollars a week, was in the library of the firm of Stackhouse, Robbins, Naismith, Cooley & Brill, the successor to Wardlaw, Wardlaw, Somerfield, Cooley & Van Eps. The lawyers at Stackhouse et al. liked to look things up themselves, but when only a certain book or two were needed they would telephone their library, give the titles of the books, and Ann would carry them to the lawyers making the requests. Her other duties consisted of seeing to it that the yellow paper and sharpened pencils were on the refectory tables, and that the lights were turned off after the lawyers left the library, and that no cigarettes were left burning in the glass ash trays or on the shelves of the stacks. She also saw to it that the room temperature was kept fairly uniform and that there were extra packages of Zymole Trokies for Mr. Meade, the firm's librarian, an elderly gentleman who had once done a-year-and-a-day in Atlanta but preferred not to talk about it.

Ann grew weary of the subway trips between her apartment and Cedar Street, and the unstimulating work, and Mr. Meade's throat-clearing and spitting. She heard about, and took, a job in a bookstore on Madison Avenue, where she could walk to work and have her opinion sought and make five dollars a week more than Stackhouse, Robbins, Naismith, Cooley & Brill had been paying her. It was 1935 and she was twenty-four years old.

The girl who lived with her in the East 64th Street walkup was from Buffalo, New York, and always said "Buffalo, New York." Her background was the same as Ann's, in that her father was a lawyer, quietly rich, and a class behind Joe Chapin's at New Haven. She was likewise an only daughter and a non-college girl who had gone to Farmington and an American school in Florence, Italy. The apartment arrangement was more or less inevitable after they compared backgrounds over many cups of coffee in the Barbizon drug store, where they both were living during their early New York days. They might also have taken the apartment together without the common backgrounds, since they had liked each other from the beginning. They never were introduced. They introduced themselves in the drug store, and after they began sharing the apartment one of them would occasionally say to the other, "I don't believe we've met."

Kate Drummond was a cool, self-sufficient beauty, whose hair was black and whose skin was creamy. She was half an inch shorter than Ann, who was five feet, five inches tall, but Kate, with her slender nose and narrow shoulders, seemed taller than Ann. She was one of the girls who had made good her announcement to do some model-ing, but the work bored her and exhausted her and she took her name off the lists, even before giving up the room in the Barbizon. It was not until they had lived in the apartment for a month that Ann re-alized that she really knew nothing about Kate, nothing that could not have been guessed by any observant person.

Ann had not known, for instance, that Kate did not have a job. She had known about the modeling work, and assumed that that was what she did in the daytime. But after they began living together, Kate remarked that she was looking for an easy, but entertaining and not confining job. She would get up and have a morning cup of coffee with Ann, wash the breakfast dishes, make the beds, and "putter" until it was time to go out for lunch. She kept the household accounts, sent out the laundry, bought the magazines, the phonograph records, the gin and vermouth, and ordered the food for their evening meal.

Ann's protests that all the work was being done by Kate were answered by Kate's insistence that it all gave her something to do. And then they had their first confidential conversation.

They had had their cocktails and lamb chops and ice cream, and they were having their cigarettes and coffee. "Tonight I insist on doing the dishes," said Ann.

"All right."

"Why, Kate? No argument?"

"No. There may be an argument, but not about that. Ann, have you ever wondered why I never seem to go out with men?"

"Yes, but I thought you probably had a beau in Buffalo."

"I have a beau, but not in Buffalo. And he's not a beau. I have a lover, or I'm his mistress, as you prefer. He doesn't keep me, and I certainly don't keep him. But there is a man that I'm having an affair with, and I've got to tell you about it because I took the apartment with you under false pretenses. I wasn't completely frank with you."

"Well, you didn't ask me anything like that, either."

"No, but there's more to it than that. This man is married and I'm in love with him, which is why I haven't taken a job. He comes here in the afternoon."

"Oh," said Ann.

"We very seldom have any nights together, but he's been here—at least once a week. I know *you're* not a virgin, without your ever coming out and saying so. But if you consider it messy to have me meet my—lover—here, I'll stop until you can find another girl to share the apartment. Or, if you feel very strongly about it, I'll give you my half of next month's rent and leave right away."

Ann took a deep drag of her cigarette. "So you knew I wasn't a virgin," she said. She smiled.

"Right away," said Kate. "I wouldn't have liked you if you'd had that lingering virgin look."

"Well, *I'll* tell *you* something that will make you and your lover look very inexperienced." She then told Kate the story of her marriage to Charley Bongiorno, all of it. As she finished, she looked at Kate and saw that there were tears in her eyes. Kate got up and put her arms around Ann, who now wept for the first time in years.

"What I meant when I said I knew you weren't a virgin, I put it

368

badly. What I meant was I could tell you'd been in love. It left a mark on you, Ann, but it isn't a scar. It's beautiful."

"Oh, dear. I'm all right."

"You started to tell it flippantly, didn't you? But halfway through I almost wanted you to stop, because I knew the ending. I could guess."

"Well, I'm glad you let me finish. I feel better, I really do. And I guess you know the answer to your question about moving out."

"I think I knew anyway," said Kate. "Do you want to have men here, I mean spending the night? Is there anyone you would like to have spend the night?"

"No, but I won't say there never will be."

"The best way is for us to be completely honest about it. And if you bring somebody home and I'm still up, you come in first and I'll go to my room. We ought to avoid seeing the other's gentleman friend as much as possible. My activities are pretty much restricted to the afternoon, but you go out in the evening and you may want to finish the evening with breakfast, here. We'll make up some house rules."

"Well, I was wondering about that, because I have somebody that I've liked well enough to spend several nights at his apartment. But we can't always go there because he lets a suburban friend sleep on the davenport."

Kate smiled.

"What's the big smile for?" said Ann.

"When you really come down to it, isn't this what we left Gibbs-ville and Buffalo for?"

"Well, partly," said Ann.

In her first year in New York, Ann had slept with four, and possibly five—she was not sure—men. She had not slept twice with the same man, or even gone out with a man after she had slept with him. In every case, she had deliberately taken more to drink than mere party spirit required, and one morning she awoke in a man's apartment, nude, and in the single large bed, with no idea of the man's name or what he looked like. She found enough letters and bills in his desk, addressed to the same person, to convince her that that was the name of her departed lover. She searched for a picture that might recall what he looked like, and on a sudden inspiration she looked up the name in a college yearbook in his bookshelf. His name was there, and a distinct photograph, but she remembered nothing about him. Her dress, her hat, her underclothes, her stockings, and her shoes were scattered in various parts of the apartment. She looked up the man's name in the telephone book and from it learned where she was. She found her handbag with more than forty dollars in it, and she remembered having cashed a check for fifty dollars before going to a cocktail party the day before. She now knew the man's name and age and college and home town and parents' names and fraternity and college record and nickname and apartment address. But she did not know his height. Then on another inspiration, she tried on his dinner jacket and made a guess that he was fairly tall. But she could not be sure she would know him if she saw him again, and when she began to realize that at least he was not a thief, that he had gone to a good school and college—she also began to realize that she had been lucky not to have spent the night with a gangster or some such. There was evidence that they had had an affair, but the details of her behavior, and of his, were known to him alone. But how much or how long they would be his alone depended entirely on his personal code and discretion, and she had no reason to have confidence in their existence. And she would have to wait out the possibility of a pregnancy.

She did not become pregnant, and in thanksgiving, she discontinued the practice of casual promiscuity. To make it worse, although making it better, he telephoned her at the Barbizon.

"Ann, I'm sorry I was such a bastard that night. Are you all right?"

"Yes, I'm all right."

"In other words, not pregnant? You told me you got pregnant easily."

"No, I'm okay, thanks."

"Would you like to have dinner Friday night?"

"I'm afraid not."

"Would you *ever* like to have dinner, or go out with me?"

"Don't you think it'd be better if we didn't? You're nice to call, but I think we'd better not."

"I meant to write you from Toronto, but I didn't have your address."

"Well, thank you for calling."

"I like you, Ann. It isn't just—you know. I've thought about you all the time I was in Canada. But I understand."

She kept seeing young men who looked like the fast receding likeness of the college yearbook, and then one night, she did see him and knew it was he. He was dining with a girl. He saw her; he bowed; she bowed; and he was forever out of her life.

370

After that, there were dates for dinner and the theatre with young lawyers and friends of young lawyers; and one young lawyer whom she liked well enough to spend several nights at his apartment. The young lawyer's suburban friend was an actual person. But Ann sometimes suspected that he did not stay in town every time the young lawyer said he was staying in town. It was a give-and-take relationship between Ann and the lawyer, who was a Harvard College, Harvard Law man named Howard Rundel. He was a conventional-looking young man, unsmilingly handsome and recently taking to wearing spectacles. He dressed well; in the manner, but tailor-made, and always wore a starched collar. He was self-centered and impatiently snobbish, but he had a surprising streak of sensuality that was the last thing Ann suspected in her office contacts with him. She knew he was using her, but to the same degree she was using him. And she also knew that part of his long-term plan was to go back to Chicago after three years with Stackhouse, Robbins, and marry into the family of a girl he was engaged to, and to whom he represented the ultimate in Atlantic Seaboard suavity. Sometimes Ann would look at him and imagine his small face half hidden behind the wedding Ascot, but he could excite her in many ways, and he had been successful with an astonishing number of women of all ages. He was not a gentleman, but she admitted to herself that she would have a hard time telling anyone just why she thought so. No single thing was wrong, but the total effect was of incompleteness. Her father would know; but she was not likely ever to ask him.

"Do you mind if Yale spends the night next Saturday?" said Ann.
"Isn't Yale a little young for you?" said Kate.
"It's my brother."
"Oh, Joby. I want to meet Joby," said Kate.
"I hope I haven't given him too much of a build-up," said Ann. "Are you sure you won't mind? It won't become a habit, because I have a feeling he won't be there much longer. He's a sophomore, but barely. He says he's taking a private course in Afro-American music at a place called the Famous Door. And extra work at the Onyx Club. It's all he cares about."
"Jazz."
"Jazz. And I don't know one orchestra from another, except Guy Lombardo. But I hope you like Joby, so don't mention Guy Lombardo or he'll bare his fangs, show his unsocial side."
Joby turned up in a Chesterfield and a tan hat with a stitched

brim and a gabardine jacket and flannel slacks. To that extent he was indistinguishable from the great mass of Yale-Harvard-Princeton undergraduates of the period. He was introduced to Kate Drummond, and he continued to conform to the undergraduate pattern by uttering the polite greetings, and then seating himself, still in his Chesterfield and fingering his hat, in the most comfortable chair in the room.

"Where's your bag?" said Ann.

"No bag," he said. "All I'll need is a razor and a toothbrush. You must have a razor you shave your legs with."

"You're so sophisticated, and so vulgar," said Ann.

"And so wrong," added Kate.

"All right, I'll *buy* a razor. Kate'll let me borrow her toothbrush, I'm sure."

"Sure, you can borrow it. That's not saying *I'll* use it again."

He laughed for the first time. "Kate, if you weren't such an ugly old hag I could go for you."

"Joby!" said Ann.

"I might. I really might. Why don't you ditch the guy you're going out with and go out with me instead? You must have thirty or forty dollars I can spend on you. By the way, Anna Banana?"

"I'm prepared. Ten dollars," said Ann.

"Always ten dollars. Couldn't you make it twenty, just once?"

"No, and if it's getting monotonous I'll make it five."

"Well, I have to go," said Kate.

"Isn't he picking you up? I'd like to have a look at the guy that's getting the benefit of all this," said Joby. "Is he old, is he young? Blind? Paresis? Fag? Why won't he show himself?"

"I'm not sure who he is," said Kate. "I'm going to a dinner party."

"But you're going alone," said Joby. "Still, that doesn't say you'll be coming home alone, and I guess that's what counts. I'll look in on you when I get home."

"No you won't," said Ann.

"What are the sleeping arrangements, by the way?" said Joby.

"You can have my room, and I'm going in with Kate."

"Oh, let's do something original," said Joby. "*I'll* go in with Kate."

"Do you think that would be so original?" said Kate.

"Well now if I answered that truthfully—are you sure you don't have an old razor lying around somewhere, Kate?"

"All my men grow beards," said Kate. "Good night, my prince."

"*Sweet* prince," said Joby.

"On your feet," said Ann.

He got up and bowed to Kate, who left smiling and regal.

"How old is she?" said Joby.

"Twenty-four."

"She seems older. At least she seems older than you."

"Oh, but I'm a very young twenty-four," said Ann.

"Are you going out, too?" said Joby.

"I'm going out to dinner and the polo matches."

"The polo matches? What's that a new name for?" said Joby. "I've heard of riding academies."

"A polo match is where three men on horses play against three other men on horses."

"Are you serious?" said Joby.

"Haven't you ever heard of Squadron A?"

"Oh, yes. And who are you going out with?"

"A lawyer named Howard Rundel. He'll be here in a few minutes."

"That means I don't get any dinner here, eh?" said Joby.

"That's what it means."

"Is it all right if I fix myself something?" said Joby.

"There's a steak, but I'm saving that for tomorrow. Help yourself to anything else," said Ann. "How are things at Yale?"

"Oh, I guess I'm flunking out," said Joby.

"That'll be a nice Christmas present for Father," said Ann.

"It's a damned sight better than hanging around for another year and not making Wolf's Head."

"How do you *know* you're not going to make Wolf's Head?"

"Oh, come on," said Joby.

"Father's had an awfully tough time the last few years, and we haven't been much help. Me. And that political thing. And his leg."

"Go ahead, say it. And me and St. Paul's School. And getting ready to flunk out of dear old Yale."

"Well, I didn't have to say it. You did."

"But it was on the tip of your tongue. All right, I haven't been what every father wants his son to be. But don't forget, Ann. I haven't been what *I* want to be."

"A piano-player in a jazz band."

"I never wanted to be that, and what's so bad about that? You married one."

"I knew the minute I said it," said Ann. "What are you planning to do after you've so carefully flunked out?"

"I'm going abroad. I'm going to live in Paris for a couple of years. I play good enough piano to get by. I can get a job on a boat for my passage, and jump ship at one of the French ports, and then play for my room and board."

"Something you overlook. The French have some kind of labor laws against foreigners. You won't be able to get a job because they won't give you a work permit."

"Well, there goes that brilliant idea. Christ, I don't know what I'll do. Go home and marry Miss Laubach."

"You make it sound so easy."

"It could be arranged," said Joby.

"Have you got a girl?"

"Several," said Joby.

"Tonight, for instance."

"Well, tonight it depends. There's a staff musician at NBC, a trombone player, and if he decides to put on a package, I have a girl. If he stays sober, no girl. I won't know till half past eleven."

"Is this one married?"

"Not *quite*," said Joby. "There's one guy she can't find to serve papers on to get a divorce, and the trombone player is going to be next, but meanwhile she isn't quite *sure* of the trombone player, so there am I."

"At half past eleven," said Ann.

"How's Madam?" said Joby.

"Don't you know. Don't you write to her? I'm sure she writes you."

"Oh, she's got a letter that she writes every couple of weeks. 'Joby dear—love, Mother.' You could fill in what she writes in between. She'd love to give me hell, but she knows I'm wise to her."

"*Wise* to her? What ever are you talking about?"

"Wouldn't she love to give me hell?" said Joby.

"Yes, but doesn't she?"

"No, she doesn't. She's very careful not to. She'd give me hell if she thought she could get away with it. But as I just told you, she knows I'm wise to her."

"Well, explain that to poor simple-minded me. Wise to her."

"All of a sudden cat's got my tongue."

"All of a sudden you're not wise to anyone."

"Have it your way. But you notice Father gives me hell, wherever and whenever and for whatever. He bawls me out and cuts off my allowance and so forth. He has nothing to fear."

"Mother most likely feels that one of them giving you hell is enough. She wants things to be peaceful."

"Now there you're cooking. If there's one thing she wants it's peace."

"My lawyer gentleman," said Ann, at the sound of the doorbell. She pushed the clicker button and in a minute Rundel was at her door.

"This is my brother, Joby Chapin. Joby, Howard Rundel."

"Nice to see you," said Howard.

"I'm all ready," said Ann. "See you at breakfast, any time after ten. Good night, wee one."

"Good night, Anna Banana. Good night, Mr. Rundel."

"Nice to see you," said Howard.

They went out, but Ann was back immediately. "I didn't give you a key. Here."

"Did you say he went to Harvard, or did I guess it?"

"Good night, sophomore," said Ann.

"Porcellian? Or not *quite*," said Joby.

"You little sonofabitch," said Ann, but she laughed when she said it, and not in the Wisterian tradition.

It is foolish to say a man's life is over while there is life in him that will respond to new life, whether the new life is in the form of a drug out of the live earth, or new love exchanged. In his recent confidences to Arthur McHenry, Joe had repeatedly been returning to his lament that his life was over. Arthur was too sincere and too shrewd to offer routine reassurances as his responses to the lament. As far as possible he had always been truthful with Joe, and Arthur had long ago discovered that the conventional polite responses exasperated his friend and automatically put an end to conversation. "It's true, you've had three knockout punches," said Arthur, in one of their evening chats at 10 North Frederick Street.

"Which three?" said Joe.

"The obvious ones. The leg. Ann's troubles, and the nomination."

"There's another one. Not a knockout punch, but a sort of sneak rabbit punch."

"What was that?"

"Getting to be fifty."

"Oh, well I think that's horseshit," said Arthur. "We're both almost fifty-three, but I'm making my plans to live at least another twenty years."

"You are?"

"I am. I'm planning on another twenty years. I've taken care of the contingencies and emergencies. But my attitude toward the future is that I'll take another twenty years of it. According to my estimate, we can make our fiftieth reunion and have a year to spare."

"*You're* planning to go to a *reunion?*"

"To our fiftieth, you're damn right I am. Not any other, but if I'm around I'll be at our fiftieth."

"It's still a long way off, and I think I'll wait till 1953 before I send my check to the reunion committee."

"Oh, *well*, if you're talking about *checks*," said Arthur.

"From the way you talk, you ought to have your bag packed and train reservations," said Joe.

"Yes, and from the way you talk we'll both be lucky to last out the week," said Arthur.

"We will be," said Joe.

"Oh, cut it out, Joe."

"Your rosy optimism is very pretty on the surface, but underneath you're kidding yourself. I've stopped kidding myself. We are fifty-three, just about, and we're liable to keel over any day. I've had moments the past few years when quite frankly I wouldn't have minded. I'm not in quite as much of a funk as I was, but I don't know what there is left. I'd like to see Ann happily married to a nice guy. Joby—I don't worry too much about my son. But girls need somebody to take care of them."

"What about Edith?"

"Well, what *about* Edith? Does she need anyone? If I were to kick the bucket tomorrow, would Edith be any the worse off? I don't think so. But I wish Ann would find somebody."

"She will," said Arthur.

"Maybe that first guy would have been all right."

"Better not say that to Edith."

"I won't," said Joe. "But I'll say it to you. How do I know that what we did was the right thing? The answer is, I don't know. And never will, and therefore there'll always be a doubt in my mind. You can be sure of one thing. The next time I won't interfere. If she loves the man, I'll be all for it."

"That's good. I'm glad to hear it. I don't know, there's something about Ann, I've always told you."

"Yes," said Joe. "Joby's about to get himself fired out of college, and I suppose that's at least partly my fault for sending him there when he didn't want to go. But boys are supposed to have tougher hides."

"How tough is your hide?"

"Well, you answer that. Pretty tough, I'd say."

"I guess so."

"I went through life without my hide getting put to the test, then everything seemed to come at once. That's why I may appear to be thin-skinned now. Or, I may just be naturally thin-skinned. You had your toughest break when you were much younger, don't forget that. And you had Rose to help you."

"True."

"I'm sorry I said that, Arthur. It implies that Edith didn't help me. She did, and you and I both know she did. I can't blame Edith."

"No, of course not. Well, home for me."

"Yes, we're not supposed to need so much sleep when we get older, but I don't find that to be true. See you in the morning."

"See you in the morning."

The two friends had many such conversations, which Rose McHenry was wise enough to encourage and Edith wise enough not to interfere with.

Joe went to New York early in '36, as much to see Ann as to transact business that could have been discussed over the telephone. He had not yet timed a visit to New York that made it possible for him to meet Kate Drummond, but on his visit the meeting took place.

"Father, how long are you going to be in town?" said Ann.

"Tonight and tomorrow night," said Joe. "Why?"

"Would you think me a perfect beast if I had dinner with you tomorrow night instead of tonight? They're taking inventory at the shop."

"Well, I think you're a perfect beast, but there's nothing I can do about it. Kate, are you free?"

"I am, Mr. Chapin."

"We can have dinner at '21' and I understand you can get theatre tickets through them at the last minute."

"Lovely, that would be lovely," said Kate.

In the taxi he opened the conversation with the safe subject of her father. "How is Father Drummond? Did you know that was his nickname in college?"

"Yes, but I never knew why," said Kate.

"Oh, you didn't? Well, it was because a lot of fellows thought he looked like a priest. I must say he didn't behave like one, but he certainly had the look of innocence. Which I suppose he still has. I haven't seen him in twenty-five years."

"He refers to you as Duke."

"Duke. Yes, luckily that was confined to Yale, it never got back to Gibbsville, P. A. I'm awfully pleased that you and Ann became friends."

"Imagine how pleased I must be. I think Ann's the most attractive girl I've ever known."

"Well, she tells me you're the most attractive girl *she's* ever known. And I agree with both of you. I'd like to pump you a little bit about Ann."

"Well, you can try."

"Oh, nothing awkward, Kate. I love Ann—well, I guess Father Drummond thinks he loves you the same way. And I'm sure he does. You and Ann have become so close, does she confide in you?"

"I know about her marriage," said Kate.

"Thank you. You saved me a lot of devious questioning," said Joe. "Knowing about it, you no doubt have some preconceived ideas about me, and Mrs. Chapin."

"Yes," said Kate.

"Well, when you become a parent you'll justify a lot of selfish acts on the ground that you were acting in your child's best interests."

"I hope not, but probably."

"In recent years, I've questioned my own actions at the time of Ann's marriage, but that doesn't make things right today, *and* in my own defense, we can't be sure that the marriage would have worked out well."

"No, but I don't have to tell you, Mr. Chapin, you didn't give it much of a chance."

"No chance at all," said Joe.

"Go on. Please go on."

"Shall I? If you're sure we haven't reached an impasse."

"As long as you don't try to change my mind."

"I don't think I'd have a chance, and I'm not at all sure I want to change it. I told you, I'm slowly coming around to your way of thinking."

"Slowly."

"Not really so slowly. Well, to continue, whatever damage I've done—"

"Don't you take all the blame, Mr. Chapin. At least half the blame belongs to Mrs. Chapin."

"But she's not here to state her case. So, whatever damage, whoever's responsible, it goes without saying that I want Ann to be happy. And that's where I'm going to pump you. Is she?"

"Ann is too loving to be happy without somebody to love," said Kate. "Does that answer your question, Mr. Chapin? The one you didn't ask me? No, Ann isn't in love with anyone, not a bit. She has beaux, but she's not in love."

"I see. I'm sorry to hear it. Every time I come to New York, or she comes home, I keep hoping it will have happened."

"And get her off your conscience."

"Get her off my conscience, but don't forget, I'd have wanted her to be happy even though she hadn't been on my conscience."

"That's a good point, and it puts me in my place. I'm sorry I've been captious."

"Think of your being able to produce a word like captious, out of thin air."

"It *was* out of thin air, too. I don't think I've ever used it before."

They got a table upstairs in the restaurant, and their conversation progressed past nine o'clock before Joe looked at his watch and said: "Kate, I've robbed you of the theatre. You name the show, and I'll send you two tickets any time, next week, any time."

"I'd have spoken up if I'd really wanted to go."

"Do you mean it, because I know I'm enjoying *myself*," said Joe.

They stayed in the restaurant through the post-dinner lull and into and beyond the after-theatre activity. Twice people spoke to Joe, and three times people spoke to Kate, but the people who knew Joe did not know Kate, and the people who knew Kate did not know Joe—and Joe and Kate knew that the others were wondering about them. "I've been thinking back, and do you know, this is the first time I've ever dined out alone with a lady other than Ann's mother."

"The first time?"

"In all the years we've been married," said Joe.

"The way some of those people looked at you, and didn't come over to say hello, I'd have thought you were an old hand at it."

"They were so astonished to see me out with a pretty girl. Not just a pretty girl. A handsome young woman. You're not just a

379

pretty girl. But your friends didn't seem at all surprised to see you out with an elderly old hand."

"They obviously didn't think you were so elderly, and anyway, I do have dinner with friends of my father's, older men."

"Are they all friends of your father's?"

"No, they're not."

"I shouldn't have pried."

"Pride? What has pride got to do with it?"

"I meant pried, p-r-i-e-d. Pried into your affairs."

"Oh, the past of pry. I'd only tell you what I felt like telling you, no more."

"They're slapping the check. When a waiter slaps a check I always know he wants me to pay up and go. He also reduces his tip. What would you say to a night club? Have you any special favorite?"

"Yes, but I don't have to get up at the crack of dawn, and you probably do."

"I'm not going to retire to my quarters at the Yale Club as long as you'll stay up."

They went to Larue, an institution which provided society-bounce music and always at least one or two familiar faces to any customer who had gone to Yale, Harvard, or Princeton in the preceding thirty years. The same Joseph C. Smith of F. Scott Fitzgerald's Plaza Hotel. The men who had been patrons of Dan Moriarty's speakeasy. The women and girls of the fashionable New York day schools and boarding schools from Foxcroft to Milton.

At Larue—sometimes called Larue's—sometimes called Larry's Bar & Grill—Joe and Kate saw four of the mystified patrons of "21." "They're wondering," said Kate.

"Yep, they're wondering. This is fun."

"Our fun is as the strength of ten because our hearts are pure," said Kate. "Are you going to ask me to dance?"

"Well—of course I am," said Joe.

They got up and danced two choruses of "They Can't Take That Away From Me" and then Joe steered her to the edge of the floor and back to the banquette.

"That's the first time I've danced since I broke my leg."

"You should have told me."

"No. Because it was the first time I've felt like dancing, so I did."

"You don't always follow those impulses," said Kate.

"No, I don't, but how did you know?"

380

"Not from what Ann has told me directly, but from what I've put together, and what I've observed tonight."

"Good God, Kate, what you've observed tonight? You've been observing a man having the time of his life. Do I seem stuffy even when I'm enjoying myself?"

"Reserved," said Kate.

"Yes," said Joe.

They stayed for an hour and then took a taxi to the girls' apartment. "I'm taking Ann out tomorrow night," he said. "Will you join us?"

"I'm terribly sorry, but I can't."

He told the driver to wait, and walked with her to the downstairs door. "You want to kiss me, don't you, Mr. Chapin?"

"Not and seem an old fool," said Joe. "At my age a kiss has other implications, Kate. At least, the way I want to kiss you."

"Yes. Well, I can't imply any promises, or promise any implications, or whatever I'm trying to say. Ann's upstairs, and I'm not ready, and I have a lot to think about, an awful lot to think about."

"Well, think about it, Kate, because I'll be back to find out what you've thought."

"I know you will. Oh, I know that."

"I'm 'way past where I ever thought I'd be again, and if it isn't you, it'll never be anybody. Good night, dear Kate."

"Good night," she said, and went inside.

Joe got in the taxi. "Yale Club, please."

"Fifty Vanderbilt. Fiff-ty Vandabilt Avenya. You know I was thinkin' if the City of New York wunda save the taxpayers about two million dollars a year, what they oughta do is . . ."

In a month Joe went to New York again when he knew Ann would be in Bermuda. He telephoned Kate from Gibbsville so that she would be free, and he appeared at the apartment at seven o'clock in the evening. "Let's have an evening before we get down to cases," he said. "This time I *have* the theatre tickets."

They again dined at "21" and were at the theatre in time, but as they were getting up to go out for a smoke after the first act Kate said: "Let's take our things and not come back."

She asked him to take her to the apartment, and they rode in silence after she said: "What was the use? I wasn't paying any attention to the play. I didn't eat my dinner."

At the apartment she said: "Will you fix me a weak Scotch and soda and I'll be back in a minute."

She returned and lit a cigarette and took up her drink, then put it down again. She sat in a corner of the sofa and began making circles with the ember of her cigarette in the cloisonné ash tray on the end table.

"I've done a lot of thinking. A lot. But I couldn't do it all alone. I had to have you to help me," she said.

"Yes," he said.

"I couldn't live with Ann any more. I'd have to find another apartment."

"Yes, that's true."

"And you know what else, too. That's where we'd always have to see each other. We couldn't go out together any more. Your wife and Ann and Joby would know right away, and my family'd find out too." She took a quick look at him and then looked away. "I'm by nature a faithful person. That means that it wouldn't be long before I didn't even see anyone else. I'd really be alone except for when you could come to New York. And how often would that be? Once a month at the most. But I've taken the first step."

"You have?"

"I've broken off with the man that I've been having an affair with. I *am* by nature a faithful person. I had to stop seeing him the day after you and I went out together. And please don't say I shouldn't have. It was my decision."

"That's what I *was* going to say," said Joe.

"Marriage would be out of the question for you and me, even if you asked me, which hasn't entered into the discussion. But I'm not in a hurry to get married. Nobody's come along that made me want to be married to him for the rest of my life, and when I get married that's what I want it to be. And so—that's how it is with me. I've said just about everything, not much for a month of thinking, but I guess I'm a plodding thinker. In any case, that's my side of it, and I thought I ought to tell you. Oh—and needless to say—I wouldn't be saying any of this if I didn't *want* to be your mistress."

He sat with his elbows on his knees and his finger tips at his temples, and for a long time he did not speak. At last he spoke and softly: "This is something that I could easily have lived all my life for. I'll tell you now, Kate, that I love you as I've never loved anyone else. As surely, and deeply, and completely, and happily—never like this, never anyone. When it happens, you know. You're sure.

And the millions of men it never happens to, and the millions of women. But it happened to me.

"And now I'll tell you what I was going to tell you, and why I wanted to have an evening together.

"Everything you've told me, I knew. Except, of course, your breaking off with the other gentleman. But I realized two weeks ago, three weeks ago, maybe four—I knew you'd have to take another apartment, and all the rest of it. Seeing me every month or two. Hiding from people. Never going out. Kate, my dearest Kate—what do you think I was going to tell you?"

"You have to tell me," said Kate.

"Two things. I *was* going to ask you to marry me, although I know better than you do the objections to that. And since I knew what you'd say—I was going to tell you to stop thinking and to stop worrying. *You* can't be my mistress. You alone in an apartment, waiting till I came to New York, and then hiding from people while I was in New York? Would I let you do that?"

"No, I don't think you would. But I'm willing."

"I said to you the night we went out, when I was saying good night to you, I told you I was past the point with you where I ever thought I'd be with anyone again. Well, that was only my way of saying that I was already in love with you. But now that I've actually told you I love you, I can add something. I can add that I always will love you, and that I'll always feel that you loved me."

"And I do," said Kate. "I wasn't going to say it. But I do."

"Will you marry me?"

"No," said Kate.

"Why?"

"Because my marrying you would be just as bad as your making me your mistress. It would do almost the very same things to your life. Cutting you off from your friends. You'd be embarrassed when you saw my father. You'd worry about what Ann was thinking. You'd be conscious of the difference in age between you and my friends. Even now, on account of Ann, I can't quite make myself call you Joe."

He smiled. "I noticed that."

"I was afraid you had."

"Then it's settled, and I'm not unhappy, Kate. I can't tell you how un-unhappy I am. The fact that you love me and that I love you. I want you to let me give you a wonderful present. I don't know what. But something exquisite and extravagant. Will you let me?"

"Yes."

"A ruby. Would you like a ruby?"

"Yes."

He stood up. "Now I think I'll leave you," he said.

"No," she said. "You're not going to leave me tonight."

"I'm not?"

"I want you to remember all your life that I meant it when I said I love you. You'll have to leave me tomorrow, but tonight I want you to stay, just as though I were your mistress or married to you. We'll make love and sleep together, and we'll always have it."

In the morning when she awoke he was leaning on his elbow, smiling down at her. "It's morning, Kate," he said. "Good morning, my love."

"Good morning, Joe," she said. "What time of morning?"

"About twenty of eight," he said.

"Naked as the day we were born. Isn't it nice?"

"Yes."

She reached out and folded up the traveling clock on the night table. "Turning off time," she said. "Let's ignore it."

"All right," he said.

"I want you," she said.

"You're going to have me," he said.

"Not just right away, very sensually, darling. Very sensually and nicely. And sleepily. Are you wide awake?"

"Yes."

"Isn't it wonderful? I'm not. But I know what's going on, sweet. Oh, do I ever?"

That day they had lunch together at one of the hotels where they were not likely to encounter anyone who had seen them the night before. At the coffee Joe said: "I know the moment you leave me the sadness will begin. But I've been putting it off, and I haven't really been thinking all day."

"No, neither have I."

"Kate! In a few minutes—do you realize? It'll all be over?"

"Yes, I realize. But we've got to stick to it."

"That's why it's going to be so sad, because right now I feel as though my full life had just begun."

"Don't think of it as beginning or ending. Think of last night as a separate part of your life. That's what I'm going to do. You know, that song that Grace Moore sings, 'One Night of Love.'"

"Tonight I'll be in Gibbsville, going from the station to my house. And I'll know every face I see, and the houses I've passed a thousand times. I know which sidewalks are brick and which ones are concrete. Everything the same as when I left there yesterday morning. But I won't be the same. Practically nobody in the town will know I've been away, and won't know I've come back to what? To nothing. To everything that's away from you, Kate. To nothing. To death. To the end of life. To death. To life away from you."

"Oh, Joe, I know. Please."

"Then I'm coming back tomorrow, Kate."

"No, please. Everything we said last night is true, all the things we thought out."

"They've stopped being true, Kate."

"No, they haven't. They're *worse* true. More true and worse true."

"No, you're wrong."

"I won't be here. I'm going away."

"Where?"

"I won't tell you, but I'm going. And I won't tell Ann where I'm going. It's the only solution."

"Wait till tomorrow, Kate. I'll have my talk with my wife when I get home tonight."

"By that time I'll be gone. I mean it, Joe. I'll be far away."

"You'd really go away, Kate?"

"I'm going. Please believe me. Please impress it on your mind. I'm going, and I don't know when I'll be back. So don't say anything to your wife, don't do anything that will make your life different."

"That's already happened."

"But I mean your life in Gibbsville. Your home, your law practice. Joe, you decided everything that I decided, we decided the same things, and then I weakened because I love you. But everything we said was true. And I take that back. I didn't weaken. I wanted you, and I love you, but everything else is wrong for us. So don't say anything to your wife, because if you do you won't change a thing. You'll only make things worse for us and for goodness knows how many other people. Please see that. Do you love me?"

"Oh, Kate."

"And I love you. I love you just as much as though we were both going to be killed today. Love me that way, Joe. As far as love is concerned, it'll never change. But the other things won't change either."

"Waiter, will you bring me the bill, please?" said Joe.

"My dearest," said Kate.

"You're right," said Joe. "But you don't have to go away, Kate."

385

"Yes, I'm going."

"But don't go because you want to run away from me. I give you my word of honor, I'll stay away, I'll stay out of your life."

"I want to go away."

"Yes, I'm beginning to see that, too. Yes, I guess you have to go." He looked at the check and put down a fifty-dollar bill. "You may keep the change."

"Twelve-forty, gentleman. This is a fifty, gentleman. Keep the change?"

"I want to make somebody happy," said Joe.

"Merci, m'sieur, and much happiness to you, sir, and mademoiselle. Thank you."

The waiter stood away from the table. "The waiter now thinks that the middle-aged gentleman has persuaded the beautiful young lady—well, we know what he thinks," said Joe.

"The unhappy young lady thinks that the middle-aged gentleman will be with her till the day she dies, in her heart."

"The unhappy middle-aged gentleman loves you, Kate, and is grateful to you for being all that you are. I have a soul now, and I never believed in it before. But I wouldn't have missed it for the world. I want you to go home now, and start packing, and I know you'll cry when you get home, but Jesus, we'll always have this, won't we?"

She suddenly kissed him and walked away from him fast, much faster than he could have walked even if he had tried to pursue her.

It was late evening in the den at 10 North Frederick Street and Edith sat looking at her husband while he spoke of this and that in New York.

"Did you get a chance to stop in at Lord & Taylor's?" said Edith.

"No, I'm sorry I didn't."

"Oh?"

"I'm sorry, but a lot of things went wrong. I didn't get downtown till this afternoon."

"Downtown?" said Edith.

"Yes. Wall Street. Where did you think I meant?"

"I didn't know whether downtown meant downtown from the Seventies or the Sixties or what."

"Downtown in New York always means the financial district. Wall Street. Broad Street. Cedar. So forth."

"Well, since I hate New York I never have learned much about it. How did you come home? By way of Philadelphia?"

"No. Reading. I was downtown, more convenient to go over to Jersey City."

"Did you see Dave?"

"For a few minutes. And Alec. I got everything done that I wanted to do, but I'm sorry about Lord & Taylor's."

"Where did you spend the night?"

"Yale Club. I might as well get something out of my membership."

"No, Joe. You registered at the Yale Club, but that isn't where you spent the night."

"Oh, didn't I? I thought I did."

"Well, you didn't."

"Well, if you're so positive, I guess I stayed at the Harvard Club by mistake," said Joe.

"I'd believe you if you told me you were with Alec Weeks. He's always been that kind. Is that where you were?"

"I saw Alec this afternoon."

"Were you with him last night?"

"Don't you think you ought to swear me before asking a lot of these questions? I declare, I feel as though I were on the stand. What's got into you?"

"Were you with Alec last night?"

"Now look here, Edith, let's have a little common politeness. Have I ever said to you, 'Edith, what did you do while I was in Philadelphia, while I was in New York?' Have I?"

"No, you haven't. You've been so smugly complacent about me that you were never even curious."

"I don't call it smugly complacent. I call it trusting you. You're right if that's what you mean. I have trusted you, and do."

"It would be unthinkable that I might sleep with another man."

"Why, yes, I guess it would. Yes, I'd say that."

"Why?"

"Why? Because you're not that sort of person. Because our marriage has been a happy one."

"What sort of person am I? How long is it since you gave any thought to me as a person. Not as your wife, but as a person."

"The sort of person you are? Well, I think the answer to that is in how long we've been married, with never the slightest suspicion on your part or certainly on mine."

"Don't be so gracious. I'm suspicious of you right this very minute, but the reason you haven't been suspicious of me is that I happen not to be pretty or flashy or cheap. But you've had good reason to know that I'm not a cold woman, and wouldn't it take some of the wind out of your sails to hear that someone else knows that?"

"Are you trying to tell me that you're having an affair with another man?"

"What if I were?"

"Are you? Or have you?"

"Yes, damn you, I have."

Joe lit a cigarette before asking another question. "Since we've been married, of course?"

"Yes."

"Recently?"

"I don't think I'll answer that."

"Just as of course you won't tell me who the man was."

"Of course I won't."

"But you'll let me guess."

"You'll try to guess, I suppose for the rest of your life, but I'll never tell you."

"Is it someone I know?"

She hesitated. "I've decided I'll answer that just to infuriate you. Yes, it's someone you know."

"Well, you don't like Arthur, so it wasn't Arthur. And he'd be the only one that would infuriate me."

"No, I don't think so. If you ever knew, you'd be infuriated."

"A friend of mine rules out Harry Jackson."

"Oh, it wasn't a servant," said Edith.

"I didn't think so. You're too much of a snob for that. Well, I suppose I'll spend the rest of my life studying how you and Henry Laubach look at each other, and the rest of our men friends."

"If you'd studied me a little more carefully it might not have happened."

"I wonder if you'll answer this question. Have you discontinued it?"

"I think I've indicated that I have."

"Well, have you?"

"It is not going on now."

"Well, will you answer this? Would you resume it?"

"I've thought of it," said Edith.

"Your best opportunity, of course, was after I broke my leg. Was there just one man, or have there been others?"

"One."

"Yes, a woman can probably get away with one, but when two

people have been married as long as we have, they know each other too well for the woman to be promiscuous. And men gossip. They brag about their conquests, which is not only ungentlemanly, but I've always thought unsound."

"Women know that."

"And that's what keeps so many of you from being promiscuous?"

"No more questions. Let me ask a few. Did you spend the night with Alec?"

"No."

"But you didn't stay at the Yale Club."

"Edith, you've been so astute, suppose you arrive at your own answer to that one." He picked up the telephone and asked for Long Distance, and then gave the Butterfield 8 number of Ann's and Kate's apartment.

"Why are you calling Ann?" said Edith. "You're surely not going to tell *her.*"

Joe smiled at her. "Keep ringing," he told the operator.

"You might as well hang up," said Edith, suddenly, triumphantly. "Ann's in Bermuda."

"So she is," said Joe, and hung up.

"Why should you tell Ann? I know why. You wanted to make her feel better about her elopement. You wanted to make her feel superior."

"No, I didn't, Edith," said Joe. He stood up. "You're going to hate me because you told me, but I'd like to tell you something. There'll be no reprisals. Whether we like it or not, we're both getting old, and I'm going to bed. Good night, Edith."

PART TWO

The biographer has certain rights and duties and among them is the right, which is also a duty, to say that at such-and-such a point the biographee's life left one phase and entered another. It is not the same as saying that a change occurred overnight, for there are few occurrences—if there are any—that bring about radical and quick change in the lives of human beings. Change is almost always fluid; rapidly fluid, or slowly fluid; but even major events in a human life do not make the overnight personality changes that they are too often said to make. Marriage, parenthood, the successful culmination of an enterprise, a severe punishment, a dreadful accident resulting in blindness, a frightening escape from danger, an exhilarating emotional experience, the unexpected report of a five-inch gun, a sudden view of something loathsome, the realization of a great major chord, an abrupt alteration in a human relationship—they all take time, to be absorbed by the soul, no matter how infinitesimally brief a time they took in occurring or in being experienced. Only death itself causes that overnight change, but then of course there is no morning.

If it is foolish to say a man's life is over while there is life in him that will respond to new life (whether the new life is in the form of a drug out of the live earth, or new love exchanged)—it is just as foolish to deny that in a man's life a time comes when he does not respond, because he is unwilling, or unable. It is that time, that point, which now has been reached in the chronicle of Joe Chapin. And what does the biographer gain by saying more than that Joe Chapin went on living for those extra years? When Joe Chapin had begun to cease to feel—unable and unwilling to respond to new life—the story became not Joe Chapin's but the stories of other people, and with Joe's part in the stories one of diminishing importance. Their stories, to be sure, are just as important as Joe's story, but they are other stories, not Joe's, and this is his.

Well, then, what was Joe's life during the final, unresponding years?

It was night after night of the warming companionship of Arthur McHenry in the den at 10 North Frederick Street. From there Joe watched the Anschluss and the carryings-on in Washington and never

393

told the story of Kate Drummond. The new highway was by-passing Gibbsville, and the two friends could not decide whether it meant that Gibbsville was becoming important, or passé. A large bakery was going up on South Frederick Street, and Joe's opposition to the change in zoning ordinances was disregarded. A Gibbsville High School boy became runner-up in the national junior singles championship, and neither Joe nor Arthur knew the boy's parents. A man at the Lantenengo Country Club told Joe that a fellow named Chapin, who never played golf, underwrote the expenditures of the greens committee (which was not completely true). The young Pennsylvania Law Review fellow was doing splendidly at McHenry & Chapin. The new slag roof on 10 North Frederick had cost Joe not quite one-third as much as the entire dwelling had cost his grandfather. Arthur was sure he had seen the last of the Chapin Pierce-Arrows—without tires, the windshield smashed, the top crumpled—just sitting in a ravine near Collieryville. Harry Jackson had an operation for hernia, successful. Billy English had a prostatectomy. Joby Chapin had informed his family and friends that he preferred to be called Joe or Chape.

The two friends hardly ever discussed professional matters at 10 North Frederick. In the office they called each other by their first names, but each referred to the other as Mr. Chapin, Mr. McHenry, and the relationship was conducted on such politely businesslike terms that the long silences and the informality of 10 North Frederick could not have been suspected by acquaintances who had not witnessed them. The Chapins and the McHenrys did not go out much any more. There were the Second Thursdays and some smaller and some larger dinner parties, and the two annual Assemblies; but they stayed away from the regular dances at the country club and the Gibbsville Club, and they would appear at cocktail parties only when the parties were in honor of a friend or a friend's guest or had something to do with a coming wedding.

The meetings in the den at 10 North Frederick were a fixed custom, without ever quite losing spontaneity. Each night before leaving his house Arthur would say to Rose: "Going over to see Joe," just as he had said it to her sister and predecessor Mildred. And Joe would say to Edith: "I think Arthur's going to drop in this evening." There were just enough breaks in the strings of meetings to keep them irregular. There were no meetings on Friday or Saturday or Sunday evenings, although Arthur sometimes dropped in on Sunday afternoons.

As the years went by, and beginning rather soon after Joe's hotel luncheon with Kate Drummond, the silences often were longer, and whiskey became more a part of the meetings. The bottle of Scotch, the glasses, the ice, the water carafe, the soda for Arthur would be placed on a large silver tray on an old mahogany taboret, the last act before Mary retired for the evening. Arthur continued to drink Scotch and soda, but Joe, after the last lunch with Kate, stopped putting ice in his drinks and the proportion of water to whiskey became closer to even. The quiet drinking never increased to the point where Arthur, saying good night, could have called his friend drunk, but he could not help noticing that every night there was a fresh, new bottle, and without asking, Arthur had no way of knowing how long Joe would sit in the den, smoking a pipe, humming old songs, sipping watered whiskey and reviewing his life.

The habit of politeness, the early discipline in good behavior, were upon him, and Joe made Edith the beneficiary of the boyhood training and the mature execution. He had no cross words with her, no recriminations, no proud confessions. He gave her no cause for disturbance other than his more orderly repetition of her own father's devotion to whiskey. At midnight, at one-thirty, at two, he would come to their room and undress by the light of a heavily frosted small bulb, hanging up his suit, putting the trees in his shoes, disposing of the linen, and quietly lowering himself into his bed. "Good night, Joe," she would say.

"Good night, Edith," he would say.

They would exchange their good nights as though taking pains not to disturb anyone in the sleeping house, as if to let a baby lie in his slumber. Then soon Joe's long inspiration and expiration would begin, and then the snoring, and then the talking, and she would listen for a telling word or name, but the only sensible sentence she ever heard was, "We know what the waiter thinks."

As a younger man Joe had always used Harry Jackson as a social chauffeur as distinguished from a chauffeur who drove him in his professional rounds. Joe always walked to and from the office of McHenry & Chapin, and the distances between offices and banks in the business district were too short to require a car. Following the leg fracture, during the first months back in the office, Joe had used Harry on trips to the courthouse, the hill being too steep for a man with a bad leg. It was, indeed, too steep for many lawyers with cardiac and vascular imperfections, and the incidence of damage worsened by the courthouse hill was high but virtually unrecognized. When the leg got better, Joe restored Harry to his previous household status,

395

but Arthur had taken over as much of the courthouse work as he could, and Joe was in effect the downtown, or office, partner.

He thus became an even more familiar figure on Main Street, and to be seen so often helped to create the illusion that he was as active as ever. Gibbsville consequently was not immediately aware that Joe was slowing down. He was cutting out more and more of his community-charitable endeavors, but the reduction was easily attributable to his cessation of all but nominal political activity. His quick two Martini cocktails before lunch at the Gibbsville Club were so quick that they often were not noticed at all, and his way of drinking them was as neat as the small-figured neckties he always wore, his well-boned English shoes, his narrow-sleeved double-breasted suits. He would stand at the bar and he would not touch his glass until he was ready to drink, then he would take one sip, consuming half the cocktail, another sip for the other half. He would nod to the barman, and another two-sip cocktail would be on its way. Then he would go to his reserved table or to the common table and eat his lunch. There was no standing with glass in hand, no glass at the table. Sometimes, but not every day, and in the beginning never on two successive days, he would go to the club before going home for dinner; on the non-club days he would drop in at the John Gibb Hotel bar. His afternoon visits to the club and the hotel bars were moved up from six o'clock to five-thirty and to five, the changes in schedule taking place over a period of three years. The extension of the hours was followed by an understanding with both barmen that the Martinis were to be served as doubles, without being so ordered. In about five years Joe was having two double Martinis before lunch and four double Martinis before going home to dinner, and a single Martini with Edith before going in to dinner.

The changes were not lost on Arthur, but he withheld comment. For Uncle Arthur knew something that Joe Chapin did not tell him. And he had known it almost from the beginning of its existence: he knew of Joe's hopeless love for Kate Drummond.

Arthur's meeting with Ann took place at her request in New York, when three or four months had passed from the time of the last meeting of Kate Drummond and Joe Chapin. The meeting took place because Ann had a conversation with Kate.

"Where did you ever get this ruby? Isn't it something new?"

"An unknown admirer," said Kate.

"Well, unknown maybe, but rich. Boy!" said Ann. "Someone you met in California, no doubt."

"No doubt," said Kate.

"The way you say it, there is some doubt," said Ann. "You know, Kate, I have to admit that when you suddenly upped and took off for Santa Barbara, I though it was because you were unhappy in New York. But I guess this shows you weren't, whether you got the ruby from California, or here."

"I never wear the ruby."

"Or at least I've never seen it before."

"It's something to look at and touch. If I wear it, I'll be asked questions."

"Believe me, if I owned it, I'd wear it and to hell with the questions."

"Well, then I might as well tell you, I've left it to you. In my will. I'd give it to you, but I can't while the person's still alive."

Ann thought a moment. "That's a strange statement. It sounds as though you expected him to die."

"I don't, but I wouldn't ever want him to know I gave you the ring. If he saw it on . . ."

"Somebody that's likely to see it on me? I don't know anybody that I see that's likely to give you a ruby, do I? It is somebody older. Who do I know older?"

"Don't guess any more, Ann. It's no good. But I've left it to you, so consider it mine only temporarily. And change the subject."

A few days later Ann said to Kate: "Kate, did my father give you the ruby?"

Kate nodded her head.

"I thought so. I'm glad."

"How did you guess?" ·

"Well, it wasn't too clever of me. I knew you were protecting somebody, somebody older, somebody fairly well-to-do, somebody that sees me. And I always knew that night you went out together, when I couldn't go . . . Kate, did you have an affair with my father?"

"Yes."

"Well, I love him too. But it's over?"

"It's been over. It never really was. It was one night and that was all."

"How sweet you were. My father at last! Oh, rubies aren't good enough for you, Kate. To have someone lovely and young and beautiful. You don't know, Kate. You don't know. And you fell in love with him?"

"Yes."

"Yes, he'd take off the armor with you. He wears armor." Ann smiled. "Where did he hang it? In this apartment, I hope."

Kate nodded.

"I'd love to be able to talk to him, but that's impossible."

"Yes, everything's impossible."

"I can see how that would be. You've made up your minds? Yes, of course you have. It couldn't be any other way with my poor, dear stuffed-shirt father."

"A stuffed shirt didn't give me the ruby."

"No, you're damn right. I'll always look at you differently now, Kate. I hope it doesn't make you self-conscious, because I'm full of admiration. And I'm obligated to you. A lot of things I want to ask you, but—"

"Don't," said Kate.

"I won't," said Ann.

She called Arthur McHenry. They met at a restaurant and she said: "Uncle Arthur, what do you consider the holiest thing you know?"

"The holiest thing I know? Give me a moment."

"In other words, what would you swear on that would make it the most solemn promise you ever made?"

"Ann, if I gave my word to you."

"Good enough, as long as you appreciate the seriousness of it." She then told him about her father and Kate Drummond. "He'll never tell you, I know that," she said.

"He tells me a lot, and he's had a lot of chances to tell me that, but he hasn't. But it explains some things."

"What things? Is he in trouble?"

"It's a kind of trouble you or I can't do anything about. You might call it stopping the clock. It can't be done."

"Yes, and he not only wants to stop it. He wants to turn it back," said Ann. "Well, another secret of the Chapin family for you. God knows you have a full share of them."

A year later, in an elaborately chatty letter to her father, Ann wrote:

> And my nice Kate Drummond has announced her engagement to a man from Santa Barbara, California, whom I have yet to meet but she has asked me to be her matron of honor and I have accepted with alacrity. Wedding in Buffalo, Oct. 20th. Stuart also to be an

usher. *Kate's fiancé was also '27 Princeton although they were not close friends, but since Stuart is a Buffalo native and Jack Rupert, Kate's fiancé, is having most of his ushers from the east, it is a logical choice.*

Arthur would often—in the beginning—try to present Joe with an opportunity to talk about Kate Drummond. Soon, though, he realized that Joe would not speak of Kate, short of the direct questions that Arthur could not ask. Arthur began to realize too, that it would be futile to try to separate his friend from the bottle. Nor was he sure that a separation was desirable. The pious attitude would have been to talk to Joe, reason with him, preach to him. But Arthur's piety was his own kind of piety. His friend was now in his late fifties, he had spent his life in a manner that did harm to the fewest possible people, and—according to Arthur's view—life had not given much to Joe Chapin. Even if he could have summoned the impertinence to ask Joe to stop drinking, Arthur believed he ought to have something to offer Joe as a substitute. Joe had his booze; what was there to offer to take its place? There was, Arthur concluded, nothing. So far, in the late Nineteen Thirties, the early Nineteen Forties, Joe had not made a fool of himself, and whatever he might be doing to his heart and liver, so far there had been no cause for alarm. No dramatic collapse, no signs that could not be merely the signs of getting to be close to sixty. By the time of the Pearl Harbor attack, Joe Chapin had become known as a steady drinker, but not a drunk. He continued as a senior partner in McHenry & Chapin, offered no resistance when another Law Review young man was taken on, yielded gracefully to Arthur's considerate maneuvers that relieved him of the firm's important work. Arthur saw to it that Joe took longer vacations; the entire summer, two months in the winter, a week or two in the spring, a week or so in the fall. If anyone had pointed out to Arthur that he was protecting Joe, he would have denied it, but that was not to say that Arthur did not believe his best friend had an incurable disease called weariness. If a friend has an incurable disease, you do what you can to make his last years comfortable, and Arthur did what he could: he respected his friend's reticence, he allowed his friend to administer alcohol, precisely as though Joe secretly had diabetes and gave himself insulin.

At fifty-nine a man's indignation at an insult to his country's honor is likely to be controlled by the knowledge that there is nothing much he can do about it. It soon became apparent also that Joe's *protest was not going to be carried to the front by his son, who was drafted and released because of the inner-ear trouble which no one had known about. Ann's husband, Stuart Musgrove, accompanied his Ivy League friends to Quonset and Naval Aviation in the Pacific, and Ann spent much more time at 10 North Frederick, which gave Joe Chapin pleasure, but not all pleasure, for it was inevitable that Ann should begin to confide again in her father, and she confessed that if it had not been for the war she would now have been divorced from Musgrove. She could bring herself to say no more—even to Joe—than that she and Musgrove were incompatible, that incompatibility had led him to other women and her to other men.*

"Well, after the war you can try again," said Joe.

"Not with Stuart," said Ann.

"Oh, as bad as that?"

"Well, maybe I'll try. Yes, I'll try. But maybe he won't want to. I keep hoping he'll get a girl somewhere and want to marry her." And so it was, and Musgrove did ask Ann to get a divorce, and she got it. But he did not marry another girl. Instead he begged Ann to try again with him, and she did, on his leave. She left him in the middle of the night in a Washington hotel, and waited in the Union Station for the first of the trains that would take her back to 10 North Frederick Street.

That was in 1944.

"What really was the trouble, Ann?" said Joe. "I have a considerable knowledge of such things, and you can tell me."

"No, I couldn't tell you. It's a sexual matter and nothing will change it."

"I see," said Joe. "Well, at least you didn't marry him again, and we have you home, the old place. You know it's approaching its hundredth anniversary, this dear old shack. Gloomy old barn, but I love it. Don't you?"

"Yes, I guess so. I always seem to come back to it," said Ann.

"Don't worry, you'll have a place of your own. You'll meet somebody that you can love, then you can bring your grandchildren here."

"You mean your grandchildren."

"Of course I mean my grandchildren. Your children, my grandchildren. But you might bring your grandchildren here too. If Joby, or Joe, as he wants to be called, if he gets married and lives here, although I can't say I expect to live to see the day when that happens. Joe is going to want to live in some God damn foreign country and shake the dust of Gibbsville from his heels, if I know Joe."

400

"Most likely," said Ann.

"I'll live out my life here, and then your mother will, but after she's gone I'll bet you and Joby sell the place. Well, why shouldn't you? It's too expensive to run, and people aren't coming along to take the place of the Marians and Harrys. Still, I'm glad you had a Marian and a Harry. You'll be able to tell your grandchildren what it was like to have servants, decent, capable, self-respecting people. I understand there's a new kind of servant called a baby-sitter. Fifty cents an hour, use of the radio, eat everything they can out of the icebox, rationed or not. Young man at the office, inclined to think of us as candidates for the guillotine. But I happened to hear him complaining about these baby-sitters, how they steal his cigarettes and go home with half a pound of his butter, besides getting paid fifty, seventy-five cents an hour. But he didn't see any inconsistency, looking down his nose at us for having servants, at the same time complaining about the quality of the servant he has to have. I wanted to say to him, 'Frank, you've got the kind of servant you deserve. Just ask Marian and Harry to work for you, for any amount of money.' They'd laugh him to scorn, because Harry's more of a gentleman than Frank is, in every way except that Frank is a member of the bar, and Harry is a butler, if that difference means anything any more. Which I doubt. I guess the truth of the matter is that people like us treated servants better than we did our own children. But Frank wouldn't know that." He smiled, and she returned his smile. "After you're sixty you're expected to say these things, but I never had any difficulty saying them when I was fifty. Or thirty. I haven't changed my mind much since I was thirty."

"Why should you, if you were right then?"

"If I was right," said Joe. "Some things don't change, but all people do. And that isn't as inconsistent as it sounds. I haven't changed my mind much since I was thirty. By my mind, when I speak of my mind, I mean the things I believed in then. I still believe in them. But of course I've changed, you need only to look at me. You've changed. We all do. There was a nice girl that used to be a friend of yours, Kate Drummond."

"Well now, she hasn't changed."

"How do you mean she hasn't changed? I'd like to hear about that."

"She looks the same as when we had our apartment, just the same."

"Beautiful, smart, lovely," said Joe. "Yes?"

"And still in love with the same man."

"Her husband," said Joe.

"No, Kate was in love with someone else, and still is, whoever it is. But she's happy with her husband. I suppose that's inconsistent, too."

"Well, of course life is full of inconsistencies, Ann. I'd like to think that your friend Kate can be happy and still continue to love the other man. Very fond of Kate. Never got to know her very well, but she was quite a remarkable girl."

"I just love her," said Ann.

"Yes, you were great friends. Well, you must be tired."

"And you want to read. All right, you dear man, my lovely father." She kissed him and hurried out of the room, hurrying—although she could not know it—from their last good talk together.

Between Joe and Edith there came into being a relationship that never quite reached hostility, but with each day onward from her angry admission the relationship moved away from love. The practice of love had gone out of their life together; they continued to live in the same house, eat their meals together, expose themselves to the intimacies of living together; and Edith could count on Joe to pay the bills, to be the husband "for show." Mr. and Mrs. Joseph Benjamin Chapin took pleasure in this, Mr. and Mrs. Joseph Benjamin Chapin regretted that, Mr. and Mrs. Joseph Benjamin Chapin requested this, Mr. and Mrs. Joseph Benjamin Chapin were among those . . . There was nothing, certainly, in the public prints or in the public view that could be inferred to be proof or hint of a change in their relationship. They were getting older, like a lot of people their age, and unlike a good many people their age, they behaved toward each other with the same precise politeness that they had observed all their lives.

Edith's angry admission had, of course, been provoked by the sudden first suspicion that she no longer owned Joe, a doubt that never had given her the slightest reason for being in all the years of their marriage. The admission, she first feared, was a tactical error, but almost immediately she corrected herself: it had not been an error; it had been a lucky accident, for simultaneously, in the same scene, she and Joe had overtly put an end to pretense and deception. It was not one partner to the marriage who had done the disrupting thing; it was both. "I charge you—and I have done the same." There was no lingering doubt between them; no miserable humility on the part of the guilty one; no waiting for a reprisal; no miserable humility on the part of the offended one; no waiting for the opportunity to strike back. Realizing all this, Edith at first referred to the situation, in her mind, as a clean break. But when she had time for more reflection she saw that it was not a clean break at all, but something in its way better. It was a new relationship, brand-new, with a man she had lived with most of her life and whom she had secretly, secretly despised. She had despised him because he, the catch of the town, had taken in marriage her, the plainjane, the notquite. In her mind she had condemned him because for so many years he had come back to her body, and hers alone, for the satisfaction and renewal of his passions. She remained convinced that until the affair of the woman he was protecting, he had known only one woman, and that herself. And she had other reasons for her secret scorn of him; he was too polite, too considerate, too easily defeated, and not very lucky or very unfortunate. But then she had found him out and had boasted of her own infidelity, and as the relationship was undergoing one sort of change for the worse, it was also undergoing another sort of change for the better. She saw him as someone who had more to him than he had ever revealed. She could not like him in the new relationship, but she accorded him a sort of retroactive respect, and some of it carried over into the new relationship.

It was thus not difficult to maintain outward appearances of felicity, even though she found a new reason for the old contempt. She was, inevitably, the first and for a long time the only person to notice Joe's drinking. The matter of quantity became apparent on their household liquor bills, then on the chits Joe signed at the Gibbsville Club. She looked for, and always found, the progressive signs that indicated the effect on his body. "The Mister is off his feed," Marian would say. "I try to give him all his favorites." And Edith would lie Joe out of it by pretending to believe he was eating bigger lunches at the club. She herself cleaned up after his first hemorrhage and vomiting, and she obeyed him when, in reply to her soft suggestion, he forbade her to call Billy English, but Billy English went to her.

"Edith, Joe is drinking too much," said Billy English. "We'd better do something about it."

"I wish you'd talk to him—or have you?" said Edith.

"No, I haven't, and I consider myself remiss, the way I found out. I, his friend, I didn't notice it. Do you know who noticed it?"

"Is it noticeable?"

"It is to an eye doctor. He went to Ferguson to see about new glasses, and Ferguson wouldn't give him new glasses. He told Joe straight from the shoulder, he told him it was liquor that made him think he needed glasses. Central retinal degeneration. Trouble seeing things straight on, and I should have noticed, because a couple of people have commented to me, asked me if Joe was worried about something or working too hard. He looked right through them. Edith, I want you tell him to come in and see me at my office."

"I'd like to, but how can I do that?"

"I don't know how. You're his wife. Have you taken a good look at your husband lately? I mean that seriously."

"What a question!"

"All right, answer some of these questions: has he had to have his pants let out lately?"

"Well, yes."

"Have you noticed whether his pubic hair is thinning out?"

"No, I haven't noticed that."

"Well, maybe you don't look in that direction any more. Have you noticed the palms of his hands?"

"No."

"Then notice them. They're probably turning pink," said Billy.

"What are you leading up to?"

"You've heard of cirrhosis of the liver. Your father died of it."

"Oh," said Edith.

"Ferguson did a very unusual thing, coming to me, but he knows Joe's a friend as well as a patient, and he knows I've been seeing fewer and fewer patients. But he likes Joe. Now I'll tell you, Edith. If Joe had any timidity or doubt about coming to see me, that's all right. I'll forgive him if he goes to another doctor. But you get him to somebody, and don't take too long about it."

"I'll try," said Edith.

"You'd better more than try. And you watch out for a hemorrhage. If Joe starts vomiting blood, you call me right away."

"Thank you, Billy."

"Don't thank me, thank Ferguson."

"I hardly know Dr. Ferguson," said Edith.

Well, what was the use of having a talk with Joe when a man named Ferguson, whom he hardly knew, had already told him he was drinking too much? And what was the use of talking to a man who obviously was drinking because of an affair with some woman in New York, the misdirected gallantry of protecting a cheap tart?

It was never any great problem for Edith to find a reason to be *failing in admiration for her husband. And in the new relationship—now no longer so new—they avoided as though by agreement discussions that would entail the disclosure of any feeling of concern, one for the other. If, as seemed to be the case, they had condemned themselves to the habit of intimacy without even a friendship, that at least was a way to live that had advantages over living apart; and to disturb the way, to risk losing the advantages through a distasteful scene, was not according to Edith's accepted plan. And besides, Edith told herself, she was according Joe the courtesy of allowing him to live as he wanted to.*

Only once was her philosophical decision subjected to a judgment. Joby, who was teaching code-work at an O.S.S. camp near Washington, came home to Gibbsville "for a steak" one day, and during his visit he encountered Dr. English at the Gibbsville Club. As a result of the encounter he presented himself in his mother's sewing room.

"What's happening to Father?" he said.

"Why, he's at the office."

"No, I don't mean this minute. Or I do mean this minute. Every minute. I think he looks like hell."

"Do you?"

"Well, don't you?" said Joby.

"You get home so seldom, naturally we've both changed. And there'll be changes the next time you come home, I daresay. "

"Look, Mother, I don't know a God damn thing about medicine, but anybody can see that Father's falling apart."

"Really? How do you think you're going to look when you're sixty-two? You're not yet thirty, but you don't look the healthiest."

"Never mind me. How long since Father has seen a doctor, gotten a check-up?"

"Oh, I don't really know."

"A year?"

"Possibly," said Edith.

"Two years?"

"It could even be two. Or three."

Joby stood up. "Will you make him go to a doctor?"

"Why, no, I don't think so."

"He's old enough to take care of himself. Is that the idea?"

"That is exactly the idea."

"And you refuse to make him go see a doctor?"

"Refuse? Joby, it isn't a question of refusing. If I understand you correctly, you're ordering me to tell your father to see a doctor—"

"Yes, I am."

"And I pay no attention to orders from you. It isn't a question of refusing. Do you order people about in this job of yours? Are you really a lieutenant or a captain or something of the sort?"

"God orders you, not me."

"Oh, dear, dear, dear, dear, dear. You must be higher than a captain, to be so close to the Almighty."

"Mother, I don't think I'll ever set foot in this house again."

"Oh, you said the same thing in the very same words at least half a dozen times before, beginning when you were about twelve or thirteen. You always seemed to think that the way to solve your problems was to announce that you were never going to set foot in this house again. But that threat isn't as effective as it may have been when you were a naughty, helpless little boy. We forgive our children a lot because they are children. What if I said you're not welcome here? What if I reminded you that it's time you had a home of your own, and a wife to give orders to as long as her patience held out? I can't abide rudeness, never have, and I've never had to, except from you. We always tried to understand you, and we put up with a great deal because you were—I'm sure these modern child psychologists have some word for it. But we just thought you needed a little more understanding than most children, and we tried to give it to you. But of course we've known for a long time that our efforts were wasted. Well, now you threaten to leave us forever, I for one no longer consider it a threat."

"No, I guess you don't. A woman that would commit murder wouldn't be bothered by any threat I could make."

"I wish you'd pack your things and go, and before you ever come back here you'd better write me and make sure you'll be allowed in this house."

"All right, Mother. But you didn't have to lie to Dr. English."

"Lie? I never even mentioned your name to Dr. English."

"No, and you never mentioned his name to Father, did you? How long is it since he ordered you to have a doctor for Father? Mother, I know what you're doing, and it stinks."

He was gone from the house in less than half an hour, and he never again saw his father alive.

Joe's second hemorrhage occurred at the McHenry & Chapin office, and Dr. George Ingram was called because he was Arthur McHenry's physician and because the Chapins had no family doctor since the complete retirement of Billy English. They took Joe to the hospital.

"Mr. Chapin has had a rupture of an esophageal varix," he told Edith. "Could you tell me about any previous hemorrhage, Mrs. Chapin?"

"Well, I suppose vomiting blood several years ago—would that constitute a hemorrhage, Dr. Ingram?"

"It would indeed. Well, then Dr. English must have warned your husband."

"Dr. English wasn't called."

"Oh? Who was?"

"No one. My husband wouldn't have it."

"But it must have been—well, never mind. The point is, another hemorrhage like this—we know what it's from, Mrs. Chapin. Your husband has cirrhosis of the liver."

"Can you tell that right away?"

Ingram smiled joylessly. "You can make a pretty good guess if you've been watching a man put it away at the club for several years. Dr. English would have had Mr. Chapin on a full diet, proteins, carbohydrates, et cetera."

"Is Mr. Chapin going to die?"

"We're all going to die, Mrs. Chapin."

"But Mr. Chapin is going to die sooner than the rest of us."

"It looks that way. I'm sorry."

"Today?"

Ingram hesitated. "I'd advise you to send for your son and daughter. You've always been known as a woman of great courage, and that's why I've felt free to speak frankly to you."

"Thank you, Dr. Ingram."

Shortly after eight o'clock on an April night in the year 1945, Joe Chapin died, never having come out of the coma that followed the hematemesis. In the Gibbsville Hospital room with him when he died were Edith Chapin, Arthur McHenry, Dr. George Ingram, Sally Orloski, R.N.; Mr. and Mrs. Charles W. Rohrbach and daughter Bertha Rohrbach, of Collieryville. The Rohrbachs were present because Charlie Rohrbach, the popular driver of the Collieryville-Gibbsville bus line, was recovering from an operation for appendicitis which had been performed that morning. At that, Joe Chapin was lucky to get a bed in the overcrowded hospital.

Out in the corridor, which contained two broken lines of beds,

Arthur said to Edith: "Now, you get some rest. I'll take care of everything."

"No, Arthur. I want to do as much as I can. I want to keep busy."

Arthur smiled. "So do I. We'll both have enough to do."

They had enough to do. There is always enough to do while the heart keeps pumping. There is never, never enough time to do it all. Even when to remember is all that one has to do, it is enough, and there is not enough time to remember it all. And one man's life is more than any one person can fully remember, just one man's life, and so we remember what we can, what we are reminded of, what gives us pleasure or sadness to remember. There is here, in the biography of Joe Chapin, nothing that could not have been seen or heard by the people whose lives were touched by Joe Chapin's life. Whatever he thought, whatever he felt has always been expressed to or through someone else, and the reader can judge for himself the truth of what the man told or did not tell. Just as, ten years after Joe Chapin's death, the people who remember him slightly or well have to go by what he said and did and looked like, and only rarely by what he did not say or do. Somewhere, finally, after his death, he was placed in the great past, where only what he is known to have said and done can contradict all that he did not say, did not do. And then, when that time was reached when he was placed in the great past, he went out of the lives of all of the rest of us, who are awaiting our turn.

ABOUT THE AUTHOR

JOHN O'HARA'S first novel was *Appointment in Samarra*, published in 1934 and now available in The Modern Library. Ever since its appearance he has been a major figure on the American literary scene.

Son of a doctor and the eldest of eight children, Mr. O'Hara was born in Pottsville, Pennsylvania, in 1905. After graduation from Niagara Prep School, he worked as a ship steward, railway freight clerk, gas-meter reader, amusement-park guard, soda clerk and press agent. For a time he was secretary to the late Heywood Broun.

O'Hara's career as a reporter was equally varied. He worked first for two Pennsylvania papers and then for three in New York, where he covered everything from sports to religion. He also was on the staff of *Newsweek* and *Time*.

His two recent novels were *A Rage to Live* (1949) and *The Farmers Hotel* (1951). He was the author of the smash-hit musical comedy, *Pal Joey*, for which Lorenz Hart wrote the lyrics and Richard Rodgers the musical score.

His column, "Appointment with O'Hara," is now a regular feature in *Collier's* magazine. In 1954 Random House published *Sweet and Sour*, a series of weekly columns he wrote for the *Trenton Times-Advertiser*. Mr. O'Hara lives in Princeton, New Jersey.